Sometimes You Know

by Melinda Harris

To Maya:

Thanks for sharing your religious experience with me.

Meeting you was mine.

CHAPTER 1 - SYDNEY

I was thirteen when I met Simon for the first time – ten years ago today, to be exact – and I'm currently celebrating my "*fan*-iversary" with a not-so-festive apple in the break room. It's not nearly as tasty as my beloved Chubby Hubby, but much easier on the waistline.

I honestly can't believe it's been ten years. It feels like yesterday.

It was my first concert, and I was determined to look my absolute best that night. But unfortunately, puberty had left me with a head full of frizzy hair, awful skin and loads of insecurity. Plus, my body at the time happened to be crafted by my mother's Southern cooking and a foul she-devil named *Little Debbie*.

And on top of my regrettable appearance, I actually *liked* school at that age, making me a first round pick for "Team Nerd". I could count my friends on one hand back then, with fingers to spare, and boys didn't even give me first glances, let alone a second.

But thanks to one deliciously handsome boy band member, all of that was about to change.

I used my babysitting money to buy a light yellow baby-doll dress that graciously hid my pudgy tummy, and accentuated the only thing I had going for me at the time – a blossoming C-cup. I paired my new dress with my black Doc Martens that I begged for and finally received for my thirteenth birthday, and I topped everything off with my Grammy's silver locket, hoping between the locket and the Docs I'd have all the luck I needed for the evening.

I wasn't allowed to do much of anything at that age outside of school, but my mom's sister Dana has always loved breaking the rules. She lived in Atlanta at the time and arranged to take and me and my friend Maggie for the weekend so we could go to Simon's concert. My aunt scored the tickets from a friend who worked at the venue downtown and wanted to surprise me. Boy bands weren't her thing, but she agreed to suffer through it because she knew it would make me happy.

Did I mention she's my *favorite* aunt?

Dana brought her friend Suzette along to ease the suffering, but you can imagine their disappointment when they found out no alcohol would be served, since the members of the group were all underage. My aunt still likes to give me a hard time about that one, even though Suzette was smart enough to pack a flask.

Maggie and I, on the other hand, were ecstatic! I still remember the feeling when we first entered the arena. The seats were as good as my aunt had promised – front row, center. Simon was sure to see me. He would see me, we would fall in love and he would whisk me away to a secluded island on some fabulous private jet he was sure to have and we would live happily ever after.

Because like most thirteen year old girls, I of course had the details of my fantasies down to home décor and bridesmaids dresses back then. No lie.

There was an opening act before the object of my desire took the stage, and the thousands of pre-teen girls in the crowd were going wild. Personally, I don't even remember who the opening act was because I was too busy smiling, thinking about finally having the chance to be up close and personal with my sure-to-be future husband. And at around half past eight, the guys finally took the stage.

There are three other members of the boy band quartet, known as The London Boys, but my heart has always belonged to only one. Simon Young.

The minute he walked on stage, I couldn't take my eyes off of him. Simon was seventeen years old at the time, already a little over six feet tall, with dark blonde hair that hung charmingly in his soft brown eyes. His killer smile was heart-stopping, and if the smile didn't do the job, the rest of him surely would. Sitting that close to the stage, I could see every line of every lean muscle rippling underneath his tight black t-shirt. I could see every bead of sweat forming on his forehead and running down his high cheekbones and perfectly chiseled jaw. He was beautiful, flawless and I remember wondering if I would ever find another man who could possibly compare.

And unfortunately, the search continues.

About a half hour into the concert, I started getting nervous. He wouldn't look at me, and he had to see me for my ridiculous, champagne-and-caviar-filled fantasy to work. Another half hour goes by, and I still couldn't get him to even look my way, and at that point, my head hurt from trying to will the act with my brain.

It was a few minutes later when, for the first time since the guys graced the stage, Maggie leaned over to say something to me. For the most part, we had been smiling silly smiles at each other and screaming periodically, but this time she was grabbing at my arm, desperately trying to get my attention. I reluctantly peeled my eyes away from Simon and glanced at her.

"What's up?!" I yelled, hoping she could read lips. I knew there was no way she could have heard me over the music and the crowd.

"James is bringing someone on stage!" she screamed, pointing excitedly to our left.

I looked to where she was pointing, and noticed another member of the group, Jameson Waters, was in fact bringing a girl – who was bawling her sweet eyes out – onto the stage with him. With an arm draped around her shoulder, he leaned in and whispered something into her ear. The girl wiped at her eyes with a huge smile, and Jameson leaned down and gave her a kiss on the cheek, causing nearly every concert goer in attendance to melt into a huge pile of swooning goo.

As the current song started winding down, two more members of the group, Robert Griffiths and Oliver Sutton, started searching and finding fans to bring on stage. The first thing I thought of was how these girls had won the freaking fangirl lottery! Then my eyes went back to Simon.

I recognized the beginning of my favorite song – *Just You and Me* – about to be played, and my pulse started racing. I never let him leave my sight as his eyes roamed the crowd, and finally, for the first time all night, our eyes met briefly. I felt my entire face light up like a kid on Christmas morning, and I just knew everything was about to fall into place. But then two very pretty girls several seats down on my left started waving furiously trying to get his attention. And it worked.

Simon walked to the corner of the stage and gracefully down the steps toward the girls. Maggie rubbed my right arm soothingly and I hung my head, trying to hold back my tears. I knew I would regret missing the opportunity to see his beautiful face that close, but I couldn't bear to see him make the choice he was about to make. I felt the tears threatening to fall, when all of a sudden, Maggie grabbed my hand and squeezed it so hard I yelped. When I turned to look at her, she was staring straight ahead.

"Ouch! What's the matter?" I asked, trying to pry my hand out of hers, but she wouldn't budge.

As a matter of fact, her body was rigid and her face was ghostly pale. I followed her line of sight thinking I may see Freddy Krueger or something, but instead a pair of shining brown eyes met mine. Simon was standing behind a metal barricade, less than ten feet in front of me holding out his hand.

I wish I could say I smiled, took his hand, jumped the barricade with the skill of an Olympic pole vaulter and followed him onto the stage. But unfortunately, I cannot.

I stared at him for what felt like hours, eyes-wide, mouth open and panting. Sweat started pooling in my armpits, soaking through my denim shirt, and my legs were shaking so badly, my teeth were chattering. I was a total mess.

But instead of moving on and choosing someone else who was a little less of a teenage freak show, Simon smiled at me and extended his hand further in my direction.

"Join me?" he asked, in what had to be the sexiest voice God ever created.

Thankfully, his words seemed to be exactly what I needed to regain my ability to function like a semi-normal human being. I reached for his hand and I'll never forget Simon's smile, all pearly white teeth and dazzling, as one of the security guards opened a part of the barricade so I could squeeze through and take the stage with the man of my dreams.

The next thing I know, I'm standing on stage being serenaded by Simon Young. And for those three and a half minutes, I wasn't an overweight, over-acned, pre-teen from the small town of Delia, Georgia. I wasn't the same girl who the week before had gotten the news that her beloved Grammy was dying of cancer. And I wasn't the same girl who spent every waking moment of her pre-teen years obsessing over a guy who was completely unattainable because she knew that no one living in *Planet Reality* would ever date her.

At that moment, for the first time ever, I felt larger than life as Simon stared into my wide, blue eyes. But in what felt like a nanosecond, the song was over. Simon bowed graciously to me, then raised my hand to his lips and placed a soft kiss on my knuckles.

"Thank you, angel. It was an honor," he said, in his charming British accent, and then I was swept away by one of the security guards and ushered back to my seat.

"Oh my God! No way!" Maggie was obviously freaking out by the time I made it back to her. She was tugging on my arm and jumping up and down, and I started jumping right along with her.

When I looked over at my aunt, she waved her camera at me letting me know she got some pictures. I smiled at her, excited, knowing I would cherish those pictures until the end of time. Then I turned back to the stage and watched until the concert finally came to a close.

The London Boys took their final bows after a second encore, and the arena lights were sobering as they came on, like waking up from a dream.

I remember standing there, staring at the stage for several minutes after the concert was over. Unfortunately, Simon never took another glance in my direction, and of course there was no whisking away on private jets or marriage proposals as I had hoped. But in the end, out of all of the girls at the concert that night, Simon chose me and that's all that mattered. I wasn't naïve enough, even then, to think it was because he thought I was the prettiest or the worthiest. I knew it was probably because of my proximity to the stage or because he felt sorry for me. But the bottom line was...

He. Chose. Me.

My luck had finally changed. The planets had aligned. And I left that concert with more confidence than should be allowed for one person. From that day forward, I promised myself I wouldn't let anything bring me down. Nothing would stand in my way. And I stood by that promise.

I joined the track team shortly after the concert and a year later – after dying my brown hair blond, losing thirty pounds and most all of my unfortunate acne – I finally gave into my mom's dream of me being a beauty queen. I won nearly every pageant I entered, and by the time I started my junior year in high school, I was the reigning Miss Teen Magnolia County and had more boys knocking on my door than I knew what to do with.

I even channeled some of my newly found strength to get through the death of my sweet Grammy a little over a year after my night with Simon. It was one of the hardest things I've ever had to do, but at least I had a chance to say goodbye, and for that I am very grateful. She told me she would always be with me, encouraging me, making me stronger, and it took some time and a little personal growth, but I eventually started to believe it. She, more than anyone, would have been so proud of me and my accomplishments, and believe it or not, everything was jump started by those three beautiful minutes with Simon.

Even now, ten years later, as I sit in my office break room, with my long-time guilty pleasure streaming through my ear buds, I shudder at the thought of never having that moment with him. What would have become of me? That short, seemingly insignificant moment changed me forever, essentially shaping me into who I am today, and it's all because of Simon Young.

I'm nibbling on my apple, still deep in thought, when my co-worker and friend, Lacey, bursts into the break room swinging a magazine in my face, nearly giving me a heart attack.

"Okay, so I know you've seen this, but humor me. I'm trying." She tosses the open magazine on the table in front of me, and I glare at her as I pull out my ear buds and try to dislodge the piece of apple she just caused me to choke on.

"What?" she shrugs, waiting for my coughing fit to pass.

I wipe the tears from my eyes, and look down at what she's given me. I put my hand over my mouth when I see the face of my teenage affections on the page. It's not the best picture, since he seems upset, probably trying to hide from the cameras. But in a simple gray t-shirt, jeans and a Dodgers cap, he's as gorgeous as ever, and still makes me weak, even after all of these years.

I look back up at Lacey, and the frustration on her usually very poised face is amusing.

"Read the headline," she says through gritted teeth as she points at the words across the page.

I look back down and read the words that I already read four days ago online.

"Yes. I see it, my dear. So?" I smile and risk another bite of my apple. Lacey trying to present *me* with new gossip about Simon is kind of adorable.

"He left her," Lacey speaks slowly, as if the added emphasis will trigger something for me. "Which means he's single," she adds, and her face is practically glowing now with frustration.

"Lacey," I sigh, "it's no big deal. He's had lots of girlfriends and lots of break-ups. He's a total playboy."

"Maybe he just hasn't found the right girl yet."

"Like Simon Young is interested in finding the *right* girl," I scoff, but I have to wonder where this strange conversation is coming from. "Are you saying you think the right girl is *me*?"

The question is ridiculous, I know. But the expression on Lacey's face forced me to ask.

"Maybe," she says with too innocent of a shrug. *What in the world is going on?*

I know something is up, but I'm too tired today to drag it out of her. "I'm pretty sure *settling down* isn't even in Simon Young's vocabulary, Lace, and even if it was, I doubt I'm the girl of his dreams."

"Why not?"

"Why so?"

Lacey puts a hand on her tiny hip and narrows her green eyes at me, obviously not appreciating my insecure quip. "Excuse me? Who are you, and what have you done to my Sydney?"

She actually has a point. What in the world *has* happened to me?

For the most part, I've lived a pretty charmed life; especially "post Simon experience". I'll admit that I quickly grew accustomed to getting my way on looks alone, which I try not to abuse, but it comes in handy from time to time. Sue me.

However, when I started my new job a little less than a year ago, I hoped it was my chance to finally prove myself, to be something other than a pretty face. That's been a little harder than expected.

Honestly, all I've ever really wanted to do is get the hell out of Delia. My tiny hometown feels like a noose around my neck getting tighter and tighter every minute I spend there. I've always wanted more. I've always wanted bigger and better, but unfortunately, I keep finding myself back at my parents' house with my tail between my legs, right after I screw up yet another attempt to escape. My latest attempt is a job at the Atlanta office of a well-respected Manhattan based public relations firm. I'm lucky enough to have friends in high places these days, like my friend Sam's super star boyfriend who got me this job, and my best friend, Liz, who is currently letting me stay in the condo she owns in the city so I can be closer to work.

I've been working my butt off, trying to make an impression, but it's becoming glaringly obvious that as a college dropout with nothing on her resume but "beauty queen", I may never be accepted as anything other than a pretty, blonde, cubicle-dwelling assistant in the corporate world. I'll most likely end up back in my shitty little hometown once again. I'll marry some redneck who will inevitably treat me like the uneducated bimbo everyone thinks I am. And the next thing I know, I'll be old and gray with wrinkles, saggy boobs and a pathetic room full of trophies and tiaras that I sit and cry in every night as I reminisce about the "good ole days".

Okay, so obviously I'm becoming a bitter hag. *Whatever.*

I've thought about going back to school and finishing my nursing degree, but sometimes I wonder what's the point? College was just more proof that no one takes me seriously. I'm your stereotypical, blue-eyed, (fake) blonde with a body and chest that some women pay thousands for. I'm not being conceited. I'm just pointing out facts. I've worked hard to look the way I do. Other than the hair color, it didn't cost me a dime.

And trust me; I know all of that will fade. I've already been told so on more than one occasion, and sometimes in a not-so polite manner. But the facts are that most women hate me, and most men want to date me. Even married professors, it seems, which was the reason I left school in the first place. So again I ask, what's the point?

"I'm not the girl of anyone's dreams, at least not long term," I tell Lacey. "So please let me feel sorry for myself in peace?"

"I don't think so." Lacey's sporting that smug smile of hers. "You know me better than that. And besides, I think I have some more news that may help cheer you up a bit."

I check the clock on the wall to see I have about five minutes before I need to get back to my desk. "Well then you better talk fast. I don't have much longer."

Lacey leans in, and her excitement is contagious. I find myself leaning in toward her as well.

"Okay, so this isn't confirmed yet, but I think your big break may be coming soon," she tells me, as my eyes widen in surprise.

"Oh really? Do tell."

"Well, I heard Jasper chatting with Lena about a new client we've recently signed. Jasper told her he thought she should let you take the lead on this one."

"No way!" I squeal, grabbing at Lacey's hands until she reminds me where we are.

"Keep it down, for goodness sake!" she whispers harshly. "I'm not supposed to know this stuff. Remember?"

"Sorry." I apologize but my oversized grin stays firmly in place.

"Anyway, Lena is supposed to meet with them next week to finalize some things. I'm not sure if you'll be at that meeting or not, but I did hear Lena tell Jasper she would think about it."

"*Think about it?*" I huff. "That moody heifer. She'll never let me have a chance at that account, no matter what Jasper says. She hates me."

"She does not hate you," Lacey tries to lie but fails miserably. "Okay, so she may hate you a little, but I think she may give you a chance this time."

"What makes you so sure?"

"For starters, Jasper seemed really adamant when he mentioned it to her, and despite what you think, we both know how she feels about him. I don't think he'll have to try too hard to convince her."

I nod and smile. My boss Lena is head over heels in love with the president of the firm, Jasper White. Everyone knows it, except Jasper it seems.

And regardless of how I feel about Lena, it's a crying shame really, about her and Jasper. I think they'd make a hot couple – not very conventional, since he's as conservative as they come and she's all tattoos, piercings and blue-streaked hair, but I still think they'd be great together. They're both beautiful in their own way – tall and lean and both with dark eyes and hair. Jasper is all soft intellect, while Lena is wild and off sides most of the time, except when she's around Jasper. She typically bows to his every whim, unless she's really firm about something. She even laughs at his extremely non-funny jokes. I mean you can practically see her light up when he enters a room. Normally I would think that's kind of pathetic, but seeing rough-around-the-edges Lena get all mushy like that helps remind me she's human.

"I wish I could talk to Jasper," I confess. "Maybe I could get him to work a little harder at convincing Lena. But I guess since I'm not supposed to know any of this, I can't say anything, which totally sucks."

"Sorry girl." Lacey frowns. "I know I probably shouldn't have told you. I don't want to get your hopes up, but I thought this was worth passing on."

"No, I appreciate you telling me," I assure her." You actually may be better at the gossip stuff than you think."

Lacey smiles at me. "Just helping out a friend. I try and keep most things to myself, but this one was too good to pass up."

"And that is why I love you best," I tease. "We'll just hope and pray Lena grows a heart in the near future."

"I hope that too." Lacey's smile spreads wide across her face. "Because I still haven't told you the best part."

"And what's that?"

"Well," Lacey starts, lowering her voice as she moves a little closer to me. "I happen to know who the new client is, and I think you may be pretty excited about this one."

"Oh really?" I start racking my brain for possibilities, but I'm coming up blank. "What do you know?"

"I know that two tickets were delivered today for an event that Jasper told me Lena will be attending in an effort to get to know the client."

"An event?"

"Mmm hmm."

"Well, are you going to tell me or not?" I ask, getting more and more frustrated by the frequent pauses and that smug smile Lacey keeps pointing in my direction.

"The tickets are for a cruise."

"A cruise?"

"And not just any cruise," Lacey adds, but doesn't say anything further.

I wait a moment, getting impatient again as I watch the last minute of my ridiculously short break pass by. "Ok, I'll bite. What kind of cruise?"

"It's a cruise hosted by...The London Boys."

Ummm...excuse me?

"You're joking, right?" I stutter out as my heart starts to pound in my chest.

"Of course I'm not kidding." Lacey leans in again and puts her hands on my bouncing knees. "It's a five day cruise – Thursday through Monday, Miami to the Bahamas. And did I mention The London Boys will be on the ship?"

Her excitement makes me smile, but my insides are roiling. With all of this excitement about possibly seeing Simon again, I forgot that I'm positively terrified of boats. I feel like my apple may be coming back up at any moment.

"I have to be on that cruise, Lacey," I tell her in a panic. Fears be damned. "Lena has to give me a chance on this one. This is my dream come true in more ways than one."

"I know it is, and Simon's single now. Is this perfect timing or what?"

So that's what the magazine was about? I have to wonder what's up with Lacey and her ideas about any romantic possibilities with me and Simon. Truthfully, the opportunity to be close to him again in any capacity is good enough for me. But God...now all I can think about is seeing him on the beach, shirtless, wet from a dip in the warm Atlantic waters...*wow*.

I look up at the break room clock again and realize I'm now several minutes late getting back from my break. Lena's probably already searching me out.

"Lacey please keep your ears open about this one for me," I beg, as I stand and take my half-eaten apple to the trash. "When is the cruise?"

"Two weeks," she tells me. "And I'll definitely keep you posted, and do anything I can to make this happen for you. Meanwhile, you should try and get on Lena's good side, at least for the time being."

I exhale in a huff as I walk toward the door. "Lena doesn't have a good side."

CHAPTER 2 - SIMON

"I can't believe you still have that thing after all these years." James shakes his head at me, as I twirl the silver locket around in my fingers.

"It's my good luck charm."

"*Good luck*?" James is obviously a skeptic. "We haven't had a hit song in years. We're riding around on yet another pointless tour, spending time away from our families, singing songs that are over a decade old to a bunch of over-aged fans. I think it's about time you find a new good luck charm."

"I said it was *my* good luck charm. Not yours," I smirk. "And those *over-aged fans* are providing your family with a pretty comfortable living, mate. I suggest you start appreciating that and stop all of the damn whining."

"You think I'm in this for the money?" James leans in toward me, anger rolling off him in waves. "I don't give a damn about the money, Si. I do this because I love to perform. I love what we do, who we are, or at least who we used to be." I frown at him, as he leans back in his chair. "We could be great again, but some of us can't seem to get our shit together to make it happen."

"*Some of us*? My name is Simon, arsehole, in case you forgot."

"Un-fucking-believable," James mumbles as he tosses his magazine on the floor and stands to move over to the table with Ollie and Rob.

To hell with him. I don't understand why the pressure's always on me. I'm not the only one on this bus with any talent. Lazy bastards.

I honestly can't believe I still have to endure this torture. For starters, James insists on us traveling by bus to save costs, but that also means more time together. None of us have gotten along in years, and it keeps getting worse. If I wasn't under contractual obligation from the label, I would have told them all to sod off a long time ago.

I take another swig of whiskey as I study the locket. I don't care what James says. It's *my* good luck charm. This locket has been my saving grace more times than I can count.

I remember the sweet little girl who lost it that night all those years ago. We all had plenty of admirers back then, but this girl was different. I remember being drawn to her like a magnet as I scanned the crowd. I remember her beautiful blue eyes, as they looked at me with reverence. That look set the standard. I would do anything for that look. It's what I work for every time we perform, but to this day, I've never experienced anything like what I saw in that sweet angel's eyes.

Breaking me from my reverie, Ollie comes over and plops down in the seat James was previously occupying. I frown at his ratty jeans and faded RUN DMC t-shirt. He looks like he hasn't showered in weeks, and I'm the cock up in the group? Fuck James.

"What the hell did you do to James?" Ollie asks, then grabs my drink and takes a huge gulp.

I quickly snatch it back from him and frown. "Nothing. He's just a grumpy arse."

"That's the truth." Ollie laughs, and settles deeper into the chair. "He just misses the ball and chain and his God awful offspring. Why the fuck anyone would ever want kids is beyond me." Ollie shudders, his mess of white blonde hair falling into his eyes.

I run a hand through my own shaggy mess. "Agreed, my friend."

No kid would want a dad like me. That's for sure.

We sit for a moment in silence, as the bus travels bumpily down the highway. "So," Ollie begins, "what happened between you and your latest victim? You held on to that bag of tricks for a while."

If it were any other girl, I probably would have tried to defend her, but with Tricia, I don't really give a shit.

"Got bored," I admit truthfully. "She was crazy and only in it for the money, and that gets old after a while."

"Yeah, but she was hot." Ollie's cheeky grin makes me smile.

"Don't you ever get tired of *hot*?"

"What the fuck are you talking about?" Ollie asks, looking at me like I've gone mad. "What else is there?"

Ollie leans toward me in his chair. "Hey, you aren't going soft on me are you, Si? I mean, James is married with two ankle-biters, and I'm thinking Rob is probably going to propose to that lame twat he's been dating any time now. Don't tell me you're in search of the happily ever after bullshit, too. Say it isn't so, brother."

"No fucking way," I assure him. "I just need a break, maybe some time to clear my head."

Ollie sits back in his chair, obviously more relaxed now that I'm not rushing to the alter any time soon. "So, just a little action from town to town and no strings? Like old times. I can dig it."

I give him a half smile for his incorrect interpretation, but say nothing further, ready to end this conversation.

"Hey, I think we're stopping for supper in a few. Any suggestions?" Ollie asks.

I look down at the locket in my hand. I hadn't realized I'd been squeezing it so tightly, but the design on the outside has left an imprint in my palm. "I don't care. I'm not really hungry."

Ollie leans in toward me again. "You sure you're okay, Si?"

I look up at him, surprised by the honest concern in his eyes. Typically, Ollie is about as deep as a toddler pool, which leaves me suspicious.

"I'm fine." I finish off my drink and place the empty glass on the table next to me. "Just let me know where you guys decide to eat."

"Will do." Ollie rises and gives me a fist bump. Then he heads back over to Rob and James, once again leaving me alone with my thoughts.

I drop the locket into my lap and scrub my face with my hands, thinking Ollie's idea about going back to the old days – different town, different girl – may be my best bet. Sometimes I think it might be nice to find someone who wants me for more than a meal ticket, but I just can't find it in me to get serious with anyone. I'm starting to think that part of me is permanently broken, which may be for the best.

As I pull the locket up to my chest and rest it above my heart, I think about the picture of the smiling couple inside. I've always assumed they were the girl's grandparents, but I'm not sure. I secretly like to pretend that they're my grandparents – that I actually have someone left in this miserable world that gives a damn about me. At least for a while I still had the guys, but like everything else in my life, I managed to fuck that up too.

Gripping the locket tight against my chest, I feel the familiar urge to jump off this moving bus or maybe take a razor to my wrists or a gun to my head. I still fight these urges constantly, but I don't give in. The locket saves me. The locket always saves me.

Shit. Maybe Ollie's right again. Maybe I *am* getting soft.

All I know is that the locket helps me remember when things were better, and how I used to have it good, if only for a short while. It helps me remember the look in that little girl's eyes, and how that look made me feel important, necessary. I want to feel that way again. I want to be loved again, inspired again. More importantly, I want to feel I deserve it.

CHAPTER 3 - SYDNEY

It's been two days since Lacey told me about our exciting new client, but I still haven't heard a word from Lena. I even tried getting it out of her a few times – dropping hints about possible new business opportunities, or maybe a group that needs a facelift. I tried not to say too much. I don't want to get Lacey in trouble. But it didn't matter anyway. Lena never picked up on any of it, at least not that I could tell.

Now, I'm desperate and about to do something that I probably shouldn't, but I can't miss this opportunity. It's time to bring out the big guns.

"Hi Sam," I say cheerfully when she answers the phone. "How are things going out in sunny California? How's Jake?"

"We're great, Syd! It's so good to hear from you."

I was a pretty upset when Sam left a few months ago, but I know being across the country from the love of her life was killing her. And honestly, her son Jake was so attached to Ethan by then, I think he may have been more excited about the move than Sam. In the end, I was glad she finally decided to go, but that doesn't mean I don't miss her terribly.

"I'm sorry for not calling more," I confess "I've been so busy with work lately. Liz threatened to call the police for a search and rescue if I didn't come visit her soon."

"I miss you girls so much," Sam laughs. "The four of us need to get together again ASAP – Skype, conference call, whatever works. I need another group therapy session to help me survive this L.A. lifestyle."

And by "therapy session", Sam means we'll all sit in our pajamas, talking and laughing for a couple of hours while each downing a pint of Ben and Jerry's.

"Let's talk to Liz and Rose and see if we can make that happen immediately," I recommend. "I miss you guys too."

"Speaking of Liz, how's the condo?" Sam asks. "That was so sweet of her to offer you a place to stay, but I hate that things didn't work out with Rose. She's the best friend and roomie around. I would know."

"Your bestie *is* wonderful," I admit. "And I would have loved to live with her, but she had a good reason for moving back to Delia. I just wish it was under better circumstances."

Rose moved to Atlanta with Sam last year, and I had planned to move in with her when Sam left for California. Unfortunately, Rose had to move back to Delia when her mother and father sprung a divorce on everyone after thirty years of marriage. It turns out Rose's dad was a cheater – multiple times, multiple women – and her mom was devastated. Rose represents the best of us, with her kind heart and unwavering loyalty, so it was no surprise to anyone that she would want to be by her mom's side.

"So true. Poor Rose," Sam agrees. "But luckily *your* bestie has more money than she knows what to do with, so things still worked out in the end."

"Don't they usually?"

"Sometimes, they do." Sam gives me a contented sigh that I envy. "So what else is going on? How do you like the new job?"

"I love it," I answer quickly. "I can't thank Ethan enough for the opportunity. It's been an amazing experience so far."

"He was happy to do it and knew you'd be great at it. So did I."

Her confidence in me makes me teary eyed. I truly have the best friends in the world.

Sam and I catch up for a few more minutes before I finally get to the real reason I'm calling. "Sam, would Ethan happen to be around?"

"Actually, yes. He's here tonight but heading back out to Vancouver in the morning to wrap up some filming. Did you want to speak to him?"

"I just have a question to ask him about the job, if he has time." My pulse starts speeding up as I wait for her reply, but I can't back down now. I haven't wanted something this badly in a long time.

"No problem," she tells me, and I can hear her flip-flops as she starts walking. "Promise to come and visit soon, okay? And see if you can talk Liz and Rose into coming along. I really do miss you guys."

"I promise. You know we would all love to see you, and L.A. has my name written all over it."

Sam giggles. "Yes it does, Syd. You would love it here."

"I love you more."

Goodness, I feel weepy again. *Ugh*. I've been living alone too long, it seems.

"I love you, too, girl. Here's Ethan."

I hear Sam tell him it's me, and I clear my throat as I wait for him to take the line. "Hey, Sydney. How's it going?"

I have to pause a moment before I can answer. Forever a fangirl at heart, I still get a little giddy when I think about the fact that I'm talking to Ethan Grant —former actor, turned hot shot director. And did I mention ridiculously beautiful and as sexy as they come? Yes, he's my dear friend's boyfriend and actually a very down-to-earth guy, but he's also *the* Ethan Grant! I can't help myself!

"Hi Ethan," I squeak, and I know he's smiling on the other end. Lucky for me, he takes my fangirling in stride. "I'm good. How are you?"

"Never been better. What can I help you with?"

"Actually, I kind of have a small favor."

"Anything for you. Just let me know what you need."

Oh *swoon*. Sorry, Sam.

"Well, there's been talk that I may be getting an opportunity to try my hand with a new client. Jasper apparently suggested Lena give me a shot, but she's yet to mention anything to me. I was wondering if maybe you could..." *Oh God.* Am I really about to do this? Yes. Yes I am. "I was wondering if you would maybe talk to Jasper? Put in a good word for me? You know Lena hates me."

"She doesn't hate you," Ethan laughs. "You're impossible to hate, Syd."

Double swoon. Sam, you're one lucky girl.

"Well, I appreciate that, but I think Lena may be an exception," I admit. "I just really want this, Ethan, and I can't tell you how much I would appreciate your help. I can do this job. I know I can."

Jasper was Ethan's rep while he was acting, and I know how much they like and respect each other. I have this job because of Ethan, so I know Jasper will listen to him on this. I just know it.

"Of course you can do it," Ethan tells me. "That's why I suggested to Jasper that you have a go at The London Boys account. I think it's a perfect fit for you, and Sam told me you're a big fan."

Oh. My. God.

"You're the reason Jasper wants to give me a chance?" My voice is shaking. I'm so overwhelmed by his faith in me.

"No, *you're* the reason Jasper wants to give you a chance. I just planted the idea," Ethan confesses, to my complete surprise. "He agreed immediately. Said he would talk to Lena, but I'll tell you what. How about I ask Jasper if I can give Lena a call? I've worked with Lena a few times in the past. Maybe I can help convince her to give you a shot."

"You would do that for me?" *Don't cry, Sydney. Don't cry.*

"Of course. Make me proud, Syd."

"Ethan, you're the best! I promise I won't let you down."

"I know you won't," he tells me, and my smile is so big I can feel my lips start to crack. "Now if you'll excuse me, I need to spend some time with my girl before I leave tomorrow."

That's it, Sam. I officially hate you.

"By all means, and Ethan, thank you so much. I appreciate this more than you know."

Ethan and I say goodbye, and I hang up the phone with a very positive outlook on this whole cruise situation. I've got my game face on now. It's go time.

I move fast after my call with Ethan and Sam so I'm not late meeting Lacey at the mall. I have no money and my credit card debt is mounting, but I desperately need some new clothes if I'm going – no scratch that, *when* I go on the cruise, and I haven't bought a bathing suit in a couple of years, which is borderline blasphemy.

As planned, I meet Lacey in the food court at the mall and our first stop is the swimsuit store a few shops down.

"Who would ever wear something like this?" Lacey asks as we thumb through bikinis. "These are more *string* than *bikini*."

"I would wear them." I smile at Lacey as I add a few possibilities to my pile. "And you could too. Don't tell me you cover that hot bod up with a one piece."

"What's wrong with one-pieces?"

"There's nothing at all wrong with one-pieces." Lacey looks so hurt, I give her a quick, one-armed hug as we continue skimming the racks.

The truth is Lacey is gorgeous. She's petite with smooth, mocha-colored skin, silky dark hair, stunning green eyes and a body that won't quit, but Lacey insists on camouflaging all of that sexiness, if you can believe it. Her hair is pulled back in a tight bun every day. Every. Damn. Day. She wears very little make-up, and her wardrobe consists of ill-fitting slacks, the occasional knee-length skirt and lots and lots of cardigans. I've never seen her in anything over one or two inches when it comes to heels, even when we go out, and her jewelry of choice? Pearls. *Pearls!* Utterly hopeless.

Lacey comes from money, and lots of it. She grew up with silver spoons, private schools and debutant balls, and I've often questioned how she and I could ever be friends. But the more I've gotten to know Lacey, the more I've realized you can't judge a book by its cover.

For example, Lacey's a college dropout like me, but not because of a sleazy professor. Lacey dropped out because her parents forced her into business school at Harvard and she finally decided to take a stand. Lacey happens to be a creative genius. The woman paints, writes, sculpts – an artist to the core. But that career path was unacceptable in her household, so she was basically cut off, although she told me she still speaks with her mom from time to time. She got the job at the firm with Jasper a few years ago, and she's paying her way slowly through art school, living in a small loft in midtown and loving every minute of it.

However, creative genius or not, it seems some habits are tough to break, like her horrible wardrobe and conservative ideals. But I know that hidden underneath those hideous cardigans and her grandmother's pearls is a hell-raiser begging to go for a ride. I've been trying like crazy to bring her out of her shell, and I can see it slowly cracking bit by bit but we're far from raising hell, especially if I can't even get her cute butt in a bikini.

"How about this one?" Lacey asks, as she holds up a suit circa 1955, and I immediately give her a thumbs down. "Sydney, I will admit you have one of the hottest bodies I've ever seen, but don't you want to leave a little to the imagination?"

"Why would I do that?"

"You're impossible."

"You could always join me in my scandalous ventures, you know." I smile and look down at the ten or so suits I have on my arm. "I have plenty here to get us both started. Let's go."

"Fine," Lacey says with a huff. "I'll try a few on to shut you up, but I'm not buying anything," she states, rather stubbornly. "And as for you, I want to make sure you don't embarrass yourself on this cruise by presenting yourself to a new client, looking like a Playboy bunny."

Lacey taps her patent-leather flats at me, and I'm laughing at her again. "If I let you pick out my suits, I'll look like Mother Theresa, and that's just not my style. I'm sure we can compromise."

Lacey crosses her arms and narrows her eyes at me. "Perhaps. Or perhaps you need to find some class."

Burn. Goodness, I'm so proud of her in moments like these.

We head for the dressing room with smiles on our faces, and in the end, we probably each try on about twenty suits. I leave with three that Lacey and I were surprisingly able to agree on. One of the suits is even a once piece, but the deep v-neckline and low back earned my *Seal of Sexiness* approval.

Lacey looked fantastic in every single suit she tried on, but her insecurities got the best of her and she ended up leaving the shop empty handed. I'm a little disappointed, but I won't let this minor set- back get me down. I'll continue to work on jazzing up Lacey's style, but I'm obviously going to have to ease her out of the "Jackie O." look. I mean for God's sake, even today she looks every bit the ex-President's wife in grey slacks, black patent-leather flats, a pink, short-sleeved sweater and those wretched pearls. It may be a cute look if she wasn't *my age*, and if I hadn't just seen her bodacious bod in a string bikini. Take her hair out of that ridiculous bun and she could have posed for the cover of *Maxim* right in that dressing room, no airbrushing required.

Lacey and I stop in a few more shops before heading home, and I do finally talk her into a couple of things a bit outside of her comfort zone. I pick up a few adorable outfits for myself as well, but as soon as I hit the parking lot of my condo complex, the buyer's remorse sets in. I practically bought a whole new wardrobe for the trip. The amount of money I spent is downright shameful.

Plus, I have a hair appointment scheduled for Monday morning, and I even let Lacey talk me into a mani-pedi next Wednesday afternoon. But the expense will be worth it if I can score this opportunity, right?

Hmmm...let's see...finally getting some recognition in the corporate world, AND a second chance to meet the man of my dreams? Why yes. I think it will be worth every damn penny.

CHAPTER 4 - SIMON

I grab my aching head wondering what in the hell that ringing sound is, until I eventually realize it's only my alarm. It takes me a moment to figure out why I would even set an alarm, and then I remember the damn cruise.

This is the third one that we've done, and I'm just not feeling it this year. But unlike James, I do have appreciation for the fans, young and old. We may not be topping the charts or cranking out hits anymore, but we still have loyal fans there to pump us up and always keep us coming back for more.

With that thought in mind, I roll out of my bed and head to the loo. Even wearing nothing, I'm sweating like a pig. There's just not enough air conditioning in Miami to keep you cool in July. It's hot as Hell down here.

As I'm walking, I hear someone say my name from outside my bedroom door. I'm about to respond, when I realize they weren't calling for me. They're talking about me. *Again.*

I don't want to hear this right now, but like a glutton begging for punishment, I move closer to the door and listen in.

"It's been four years, Ollie." James is angry, as usual. "Four years is a long time, long enough for him to come back around and start living his life again."

"Come on, James. Have a heart." I close my eyes as I listen to Ollie try and defend me. "We're all he has left."

I don't deserve Ollie as a friend. I've shit on him, just like I've shit on everyone else, but Ollie never seems to give up on me for some reason.

"I've given him plenty of chances," James snaps. "Our numbers are dwindling. People are getting sick of coming out to see us do the same damn songs over and over again. We need new material. We need a fresh start."

"But he's doing better, I think." Ollie comes to my rescue once again. "Maybe we can wait until after this tour and see how it goes."

"No more waiting," James says, and now I'm curious what we're waiting on exactly. "We're telling him now, before the cruise even. I'm done."

"You think that's a good idea?" Ollie questions. "With the new rep coming on the cruise? All of that tension is probably not going to make a good first impression."

"Doesn't matter."

And now I'm completely lost. *New rep*?

"I already told Jasper's team the plan last week when we met," James continues. "They all know what's going on, so the new rep knows what to expect."

I stand at the door for a moment longer, trying to get my pounding head around what I just heard, but I can't seem to make sense of it. I take a moment to try and decide if I'm pissed about not knowing what's going on, or if I just don't give a fuck.

The latter wins.

I make my way to the bathroom and turn on the shower, but I don't have a chance to get in before Rob comes bursting into the room.

"Just making sure you're up," I hear him say, and it takes everything inside of me not to go punch him dead in the throat.

As usual, he had nothing to say in the conversation I just overheard. He was probably sitting there, bobbing his head politely at everything James said. Pathetic git.

"Did you not hear the water running?" I make sure my tone is dripping in sarcasm, as I poke my head around the bathroom door. "Did you not hear my alarm clock going off? I don't need a babysitter, contrary to what James may think."

"Whatever." Used to my foul attitude, Rob rolls his eyes. "Look, I'm going to order breakfast. You want your usual, or would you like to *eat* rather than *drink* your breakfast for a change?"

Okay, so maybe I deserved that one, but I still decide to call him on it.

"Do you have a problem, Rob?"

We've never been big on holding things in over the years. It's nearly impossible, when you spend as much time together as we do.

"No, mate. Just nervous about the cruise." Rob sighs. "We'll see you out there in a bit."

Rob leaves and heads back out to the suite, but I know he was lying to me. None of us get nervous anymore about performances, especially Rob. I think Rob would have quit us years ago if it wasn't for James.

Rob's the quiet one of the group, and a total pushover. He idolizes James and typically follows his lead. He's a great guy and a good friend, but the hero worship has always gotten on my nerves.

The truth is he's probably pissed at me, like everyone else. Well, fuck him and James too. I don't need anyone dictating my life.

I jump into the shower, and despite the Miami heat, I make sure the water is as hot as I can stand it. It feels good, and I stay in for a while, letting my mind go blank, trying to relax before the mayhem starts tomorrow.

When I'm done, I rummage through my luggage and realize I didn't pack very well. I make a mental note to have our assistant pick me up some shorts for the boat, but for now, I pull on some jeans, a t-shirt and my favorite pair of black Docs. I don't bother with my hair, knowing I'll be a sweaty mess after all of the sound checks and such this afternoon on the boat.

When I walk out of my room into the living area, the other guys don't even look up. I notice all of them are already done with their breakfasts and are involved in various activities around the suite. James is deep into something he's reading at the table. Rob has his guitar and is lightly strumming, while Ollie sits next to him doing the same with his bass. I move toward the table with James in search of some sustenance.

"I had Rob order you pancakes," James tells me, without looking up from whatever he's reading. "But if you choose to drink your breakfast, there's Jack Daniel's in the freezer."

Wow. So it's going to be that kind of morning, yeah?

I reach for the pancakes, and when James finally looks up, I give him a sarcastic smile. "Happy?" I ask, as I pour two small bottles of syrup onto the stack.

"Not quite," James says under his breath and goes back to his papers.

I eat my pancakes in silence for a moment, while James studiously ignores me. "What are you reading?" I ask, breaking our silence.

"I'm looking over the itinerary for the cruise. You know this cruise is nearly half the size of the other two? I'm not sure if we'll even be able to do another one."

"The smaller crowd will be nice." I try and keep things positive. "We'll have a lot more one-on-one time with the fans."

"Of course you'd be concerned about *that*," James sneers. "Well, don't worry. We'll make sure everything is taken care of. You can just go about your business drinking and shagging anything with a heartbeat over the next few days."

Seriously? I don't know what the hell is going on, but I'm thinking it's time I find out.

Pushed to my limit, I stand up so fast from my chair it falls backward behind me. The low music coming from Rob and Ollie stops immediately.

"All right. Someone better start talking and fast." I stretch my arms out in invitation and look around the room. When there's no response, I turn my attention back to James. I place my knuckles down on the table and lean toward him. "No more games. If you have something to say, then say it, and stop with this passive aggressive bullshit!"

James doesn't even flinch at my outburst, which pisses me off even more.

I step back from the table and run a hand through my hair. I'm pacing, trying to control my temper as I watch Ollie stand and lean his bass against the sofa. He moves over toward me and takes a seat at the table with James, then looks around my now trembling body and gives a pointed look at Rob.

"Take a seat, Si," Ollie suggests, but I continue to pace, clenching my fists even tighter. "Take a fucking seat," he says again, and with a curse – or five – I pick up my chair and sit as requested.

Rob sits next to Ollie, and I cross my arms across my chest and look at each of them in turn. We all sit in incredibly uncomfortable silence for a while, waiting for someone to start.

"Si, we need to talk." James is the first to speak, and my anger subsides a little at the anguish in his voice.

"No shit," I snap, but at the same time, I uncross my arms and scoot my chair closer to the table.

I watch as James exchanges a look with the other guys. "Si, I don't know how to tell you this, without you flying off the handle, so I'm just going to be blunt."

I hold my breath, anticipating what's about to come. I have an idea, but I don't want to hear it, not from them.

"Si, we're worried about you, and we think it's about time you get some help." James looks up at me, and I stare back at him impassively. "This conversation is long overdue, and you know it. We tried to help in the beginning. We did everything we could, but..." James runs a frustrated hand over his face. "It's been four years. We kept thinking you'd snap back, but you've only gotten worse."

"So, what? Is this some kind of goddamn intervention?" My voice is quiet, as I strain to keep the bitterness in check.

"You could say that," Rob pipes up, and I turn my glare on him.

"You guys think I have a drinking problem? Is that it?"

Are they kidding me with this? I don't have a problem, and they know it.

"Not for drinking, Simon," James interjects. "We think you should see a psychiatrist or a therapist, someone who can help you through whatever you're going through. I know you saw one a couple of years ago, but it obviously didn't do any good. You're still down, and you're bringing everyone else down with you."

"I just wish there was a way for you to understand why we're doing this, and not get so pissed off about it," Rob adds. "We're your friends, Simon."

"Yeah, we love you, brother. We want you to get better," says Ollie, but when I move my eyes to his, he looks down. That's when I know there's something more they're not telling me, but what could possibly...

I gasp and my eyes go wide. I look around at each of them, landing finally on James. He's always been the "father figure" of the group. Even though we've managed to keep things fairly democratic over the years, James always seems to be the one in charge, making all the final decisions. I never minded in the past, but now that I know it's my livelihood at stake, I wish it was someone besides James in the driver's seat.

"You're tossing me out, aren't you?" As soon as I voice my conclusion, James hangs his head.

"Like I said..." James looks back up at me with empty eyes. "This conversation has been a long time coming."

To hell with this.

Neither Ollie nor Rob will look me in the eyes, so I pound my fists on the table, sending all of James's precious paperwork flying everywhere. I push back in the chair and stand, once again sending it crashing onto the tile floor.

"You can't fucking toss me out!" I scream, pointing at James while pacing in the living area. "You think you can replace me? Is that it?"

I continue to pace – and pace, and pace, and pace – trying to catch my breath. I clutch at my chest, taking short, painful breaths. God, I can barely breathe.

But haven't I wanted a way out of this for a while now? I can't stand being around the guys, seeing their disappointment, knowing I've fucked our friendship beyond all recognition. But this...this is them telling me they're giving up on *me*, not the other way around. They don't want me anymore. And I know I deserve that, but damn it's hard to hear.

"We're not replacing you," Ollie's voice is sad, quiet, and I stop my pacing to look at him. "We just won't be The London Boys anymore."

I stare at them in disbelief. "A new group?" I ask, still grabbing at my chest, not believing my ears. "You're forming a new group?"

Rob and James nod in unison, and Ollie looks down at his lap again. *Holy shit*. They've been planning this. It's obvious a lot of thought has gone into how things are going to work.

My, how easily I'm forgotten.

I start pacing again, and I don't know how many minutes pass. It could be hours for all I know, but eventually Ollie comes over and sits on the sofa. I see him sit, but I don't stop pacing. The only emotion I have left now is anger. I can't believe they're doing this to me. After everything we've been through. They were there for me when Melissa died. They were there when my happiness, my entire life was ripped away from me. If it wasn't for them, I wouldn't have made it through that first year.

I know I haven't been the best friend in return, but am I not entitled to a little grieving? I lost everything. In a flash of light, I went from being on top of the world to the darkest corner of Hell. *Dammit!*

"Si, stop it," Ollie's voice breaks me from my thoughts and from my pacing.

I'm once again shocked at the sincerity in his eyes, but I don't need that right now. This is about to become another "let's pity Simon" party, and I can't take that shit any more. They want to end this? Fine. I'm officially done. No one to nag and pester me anymore, and it's about damn time.

I glare back at James and Rob at the table before moving toward the suite door and slamming it in my wake. I don't know where I'm going, but anywhere is better than here, and I'm in desperate need of a bloody drink.

CHAPTER 5 - SYDNEY

"We're here! We're here!" I squeal with delight, as Lacey and I walk out of the Miami airport to find our shuttle to the hotel.

I still can't believe I actually got the job! I'm yet to figure out how to handle my slight aversion to boats, and the idea of seeing Simon in person again after all of these years is exciting, yet quite horrifying at the same time. But I'm pushing every bit of that aside for this opportunity because I'm finally getting my big break, and I won't let anything stand in my way.

"There it is!" I point an excited finger at the bus in the distance. "Pick up the pace, girl!"

I start walking – well more like slowly jogging – as Lacey hurries to keep up. When we finally make it to the hotel shuttle, the driver takes our over-stuffed suitcases and places them in a compartment on the side. *Thank God.* I sigh in relief, glad to be rid of that load. I packed an embarrassing amount of clothes, but a girl's gotta have options, right?

The only seats left are in the front, so Lacey and I grab them. Lacey opens her purse for her compact to check her face, and I smile to myself wondering if I'm creating a monster. We still need to work on her standard uniform of loose slacks and pearls, but lip-gloss is a small step in the right direction. I watch as she adds a little more gloss and smacks her lips together.

"You could use a little too," she says, giving the gloss to me. "And stop chewing your nails. You're going to ruin your manicure."

I pull my hand from my mouth and stare down at my nails. I hadn't even realized I was biting them.

"I can't believe you're afraid of boats and you're going on a cruise." Lacey smiles at me. "That is serious Simon—I mean *career* dedication."

"You're hilarious."

I put on some gloss using Lacey's compact, and glance at myself in the mirror. I check out my new highlights and cut and think *here goes nothing*, as I remember the instructions I received from Lena when she finally conceded to give me a shot on this account.

"This account is very important to Jasper," she told me. "He has a personal relationship with James and has apparently wanted to work with him for years. I'm not comfortable letting you have full reign, but that seems to be important to Jasper as well, and I have to trust his judgment."

She sure didn't look too happy about trusting Jasper on this one, but my smile was huge, regardless, until she made her final comment.

"But let me tell you one thing. You will do whatever it takes to make these boys happy on this cruise, Sydney. Are we clear? My job and yours are on the line here," she said to me and then emphasized once again, "Whatever. It. Takes."

Despite what some people might think, I'm not an idiot. I caught her meaning – even before receiving the emails she apparently felt she needed to send to drive her point home – but I was a little surprised to find out Lena worked that way. She doesn't seem the type, and I have to wonder if Jasper knows. Past experience would lead me to believe that he probably does know, and that's most likely why I got a shot at this account. Maybe Jasper only sees me as a pretty face too – *Put her on a cruise ship in a bikini. That'll make the boys happy, while Lena handles the real business.*

Either way, I've decided I'm not letting them bring me down. I'm confident I can impress these guys with my ideas and work ethic alone. I know I can.

"You look gorgeous, Syd, as always," Lacey tells me, and I wince at the compliment, as I hand her back her mirror and gloss. "And there's nothing to be nervous about. You're going to be great."

"Thanks, Lace."

"You're so very welcome."

Lacey gives me a huge smile, and I smile back, thankful Jasper agreed to let her come with me on this trip. Jasper suggested Lena send me in with some back up, and I of course requested Lacey. I don't think Jasper was too happy to let her go, but she can be pretty good at persuasion when she wants to be. I'd like to think part of that is my doing as well, but I can't take credit. Poor fashion taste aside, Lacey is smart, confident and a genuinely likable person. That's not something you can teach.

"I know The London Boys are the selling feature, but I'm sure the ship will be beautiful," Lacey says, as we drive down the palm tree-lined streets of Miami. "Maybe we can even fit in a relaxing massage or two. Should be a blast."

"I'm sure it will be. And thanks for having confidence in me, Lacey. It means more than you know."

"You deserve it," she smiles. "So do you think Ethan sealed the deal?"

"Definitely. Lena even said as much," I confirm. "Jasper suggested me for this account but ultimately left it up to Lena. She wasn't going to let me have it until Ethan called. She still didn't seem too happy about it, but she told me she likes and respects Ethan. His recommendation was the main reason she gave me a chance."

Have I mentioned how much I love Ethan Grant? The man is a saint. If I didn't love Sam so much, I'd be secretly planning her murder so I could have a chance at him.

"Well, I'm glad you have such great friends, but you truly do deserve this opportunity, Sydney. You're a natural, you work hard and I think these guys will love you."

"Ok, that's enough of that." I wave her off, feeling the warmth rise in my cheeks.

Lacey bumps my shoulder with hers, and I look over at her with a smile. We fill the remainder of the ride to our hotel with light conversation about sunbathing and cute boy band members in compromising positions. By the time we finally pull into the hotel, I'm ready for a cold shower and an adult beverage. The summers in Georgia can be brutal, but nothing compares to this south Florida heat. I feel like my skin may literally catch fire if I'm out in it too long.

Lacey and I check in and make our way up to our room. We both take turns showering and pretty soon after, we find ourselves famished and ready for some dinner.

"I vote we venture out. South Beach, perhaps?" I suggest. "Maybe we can get some restaurant suggestions from the concierge."

"That sounds good," Lacey agrees. "I've never been to Miami, so I wouldn't mind a little local flare."

I'm finishing my make-up as Lacey walks out of the bathroom in her outfit of choice.

"Please tell me the rest of your wardrobe isn't reflected by that disaster."

"What?" She looks down at her Bermuda shorts, polo shirt and sandals. "It's hot outside, and we're just going to dinner. Were you thinking fine dining? I was hoping for something more casual."

"Okay, Lace, but a collared shirt and knee shorts? How old are you? Fifty?" I get up from my chair and walk over to her. "If the remainder of your suitcase comes from Old-Ladies-R-Us as well, we're shopping after dinner. Where are those cute dresses you bought with me the other day at the mall?"

"A dress?" Lacey asks, confused. "I was going to save that stuff for the cruise."

"We have one night in Miami," I tell her, grabbing her shoulders. "Do you know how many fabulous people hang out in Miami?"

"Oh for the love of all that's holy," she mumbles as she walks over to her suitcase, hopefully in search of something more "Sydney friendly" for dinner.

She pulls out a short, teal blue cotton dress and a pair of flat, white sandals. "How's this?" she asks, holding the ensemble up for my approval.

"The dress is fine, but the shoes are not happening. Heels, my dear. Really high heels."

Lacey rummages in her suitcase once again. "These?" she asks, holding up a pair of sky-high silver heels with an ankle strap. "And I can wear my new necklace with it," she suggests. "The long silver one you picked out last weekend."

"Perfect!" I give her two thumbs up. "And wear your hair down? For me?"

I cross my fingers in front of my chest and wait for her answer.

"Fine," she grumbles. "But you do realize how far I'm stepping out of my comfort zone tonight, right? No pictures or blackmailing, got it?"

"Got it."

Lacey goes to change her clothes as I slip into a hot pink, one-shoulder number with heels to match. I pull my long blonde hair into a messy bun at the base of my neck, and add some funky jewelry my best friend, Liz, bought me for my birthday last year.

Lacey comes out of the bathroom and I fan myself dramatically. "Oh my God! You are smokin' hot, girl!"

She gives me a shy smile. "You don't look so bad yourself."

"I know."

"You're impossible."

"Yes. I know that too," I agree, as I take Lacey's arm in mine. "Now let's get you to the ball, Cinderella."

After chatting with the concierge, we decide on a Cuban restaurant not far from the hotel. He let us know that they don't take reservations, so we may have to wait, but the concierge assured us the food would not disappoint. My mouth is watering already.

When Lacey and I pull up in the cab, we both decide the outside of the restaurant is nothing fancy – cream-colored stucco with Spanish-tiled roofing, and the restaurant name written in swirly lettering on a brown awning above the door. But as we walk inside, we're impressed from the moment we enter. The flooring design is done in small, mosaic tiles in deep reds, oranges and yellows to match the walls. The dining area is set up to look like an outdoor garden with exotic plants, a huge fountain in the middle and soft, twinkling lights strung loosely around. And as we approach the hostess stand and request a table, I notice the beautiful flooring stretches into the dining area casting a warm glow throughout the room. Simply stunning.

The hostess tells us the wait will be well over an hour and suggests we have a drink at the patio bar while we wait. As we make our way in the direction we were given, the ambience and crowd become a little overwhelming. My insecurities about being here and my ability to do this job start trying to take root, but I cut them off quickly. We won't be having any of that. Not now. No way.

"Good grief," I smile over at Lacey, when we finally make it to the patio. "Can you believe this place? The people here are unbelievably pretty."

We both smile as we stand at the bar and scan the crowd. The patio is huge and just as fabulous as the rest of the place. It's dimly lit with nothing but white lights strung through the surrounding trees and the fading sunlight, and also like the rest of the place, it's packed with bodies. There are several tables scattered about, with three or four plush chairs surrounding each, and I notice every seat is taken. Everyone else is either standing around, drinking and chatting, or they're on a small dance floor to the right, dancing to the Latin music pumping through the speakers.

Thankfully, the sun's going down, but it's still really warm out, especially with all of these people crowded around. Eager for a drink to cool me down, I look back over to find Lacey waving down the bartender who notices her immediately.

"What can I get for you, *hermosa*?" the bartender asks, and Lacey grins. I don't blame her. He looks and sounds like a young Antonio Banderas. *Muy caliente.*

"What do you suggest?" Lacey is flirting with the hunk of a bartender, whose nametag says "Ramone".

Ramone smiles suggestively at her. "My mojito will change your life."

"Excellent." She smiles back with a confidence that flushes me with pride. "We'll take two."

Lacey motions my way and Ramone notices me for the first time. He smiles and shakes his head, after undressing me with his eyes. He mutters something in Spanish as he goes to make our drinks, and my Spanish is a little rusty, but I'm able to make out "beautiful", "sex" and I believe "spank", but I could be mistaken.

When Ramone returns with our drinks, I can tell he wants to linger awhile and chat, but the bar is three to four people deep, so with a wink and a promising grin, he returns to his work.

Lacey and I grab our drinks and start to make our way through the crowd. We find a nook against the wall with a small shelf lining the middle, so we sit our drinks down and once again scan the room.

It's not long before I see him.

"No way!" I say a little louder than intended, but the crowd is so large – and the music is so loud – no one even notices.

"What?" Well, no one except Lacey, apparently.

I stare a little longer, making sure my eyes aren't deceiving me, but for some reason, I just know it's him. As ridiculous as it sounds, it's like I can *feel* him.

As I'm studying his perfect profile in a completely unprofessional manner, he lifts his eyes from the leggy blonde in his lap and stares directly at me. I'm suddenly hit with a heat wave that has nothing to do with the Miami weather.

Lacey grabs at my arm, breaking Simon and me from our stare down. "Ummm...Sydney? Is that Simon Young?"

"I can't believe it, but I think it might be."

I move my eyes back over to where he's sitting, and he's concentrating again on the blonde in his lap. As I stare, I start to notice how tight his smile his, and I can see the dark circles under his eyes, even from this distance, but the blonde doesn't seem to mind. Of course she doesn't. The thought makes my stomach turn.

"Oh my God, Syd." Lacey clutches my arm even tighter. "This is no coincidence. You have to go talk to him."

"No way." I quickly turn away from Simon before I'm busted for staring. "I'll save that for the cruise. He's on his own time now. I don't want to bother him."

"Oh, come on!" Lacey pleads. "I'm sure he would appreciate your company one hundred times more than that tramp sprawled across his lap."

I'm about to counter that fact, knowing the girl on his lap would do whatever he asked of her, making her much more appealing than me. But I don't get a chance.

"Sydney," Lacey leans in so I can hear. "Don't look now, but he's staring at you."

"No, he's not."

"Yes he is...and now he's coming over here."

And suddenly I'm thirteen all over again.

My heart starts pounding in my chest and the sweat begins to pool under my arms. How is it possible this man still has this effect on me? Like I'm still some love sick pre-teen? *Ridiculous*!

But when I finally get the courage to look his way, I know exactly why. Simon is still the most beautiful man I've ever seen. His tall, lean frame stalks toward me purposefully, confidently. His light brown eyes are curious, with a hint of seduction, and his jeans and t-shirt hug him perfectly, as if they were tailor made. I stop breathing as I watch a sexy smirk form on his full lips while he drags a hand through his dark blonde hair. He's one of those guys that crowds seem to part automatically for, as if making room for his remarkable male prowess. The lethal combination that is Simon Young quickly has me panting on unstable legs. *Sweet heavens.*

I look over at Lacey to find her smiling at me, surprisingly self-assured, not a drop of sweat on her impeccably powdered forehead. Well, isn't this a changing of the guards? I could really use some of that confidence right about now.

I somehow succeed in getting myself together by the time he makes it within a few feet of us. I pull my shoulders back and hold my chin up, refusing to make a fool of myself in front of him. I've waited too long for an opportunity like this, and I'm a mature adult – even though I may not feel like it at the moment. The most important thing is that my job is on the line and first impressions are everything, so here goes.

"Hi."

Simon flashes me a killer smile, and I extend a shaky hand.

"Hi. I'm Sydney."

Simon takes my hand, swaying a little on his feet. "Hello, Sydney." *Goodness.* My name sounds so sexy with that accent. "It's a pleasure to meet you. I'm Simon."

I feel Lacey pinch my side, but I don't pay her any mind. Honestly, I can't concentrate on anything at the moment except for the perfection standing in front of me.

"I know who you are," I say to Simon; trying to smile, while hyperaware of the fact that my hand is still in his. "It's nice to meet you too."

I'm surprised when disappointment flashes briefly across his face, but he's quick to hop back into his panty-melting smile.

We stare at each other a moment, his hand still wrapped firmly around mine, until I loudly exhale a breath I hadn't realized I was holding. My blunder breaks our trance and causes Simon to release my hand. He laughs nervously and runs a hand through his hair again.

"So, Sydney..." He takes a careful step backward, and I can see he's trying hard not to show his wrecked state. "What brings you to Miami?"

"Well, actually..."

I'm about to tell him the reason that I'm in Miami is in fact *him*, when I glance to my side and find that Lacey is no longer next to me. I do a quick scan of the room, praying she wasn't kidnapped or something while I was lost in Simon's eyes, but I can't see her.

"She's over there, chatting with the bartender," Simon informs me, and I immediately look toward the bar. My eyes find Lacey, and I exhale in relief.

"Speaking of..." Simon starts, and when I turn I see him sway again. He subtly grabs the ledge next to me to steady himself. "How about I buy you a drink?"

I grab my mojito – still half full – and hold it up. "I'm good, and by the looks of it, so are you. Rough night?"

I smile at him, but he doesn't smile back. Instead, I watch as something sinister darkens his brown eyes. His shoulders tense and his fists tighten at his sides. He pulls himself up to his full height, slowly crossing his arms across his chest, and his face is rigid with barely controlled anger. It's pretty intimidating, and I have the sudden urge to run – not walk – away from him.

"You know, I think I've had enough people bossing me around today," he claims, with a nasty sneer. "Last time I checked, I'm a grown man. Therefore, I can eat, drink and fuck whatever and whomever I choose, so how about everyone just back off and let me live my life, yeah?"

Wait a minute. My eyes widen and my mouth drops open. Did I just get scolded by Simon Young? *Seriously*?

My shock turns quickly to anger as he glares at me. I square my shoulders and take a step toward him, refusing to let him intimidate me or stomp on my teenage fantasies in his drunken state.

"I'm not telling you what to do." I calmly cross my arms to match his defensive stance, as I look him dead in the eye. I'm thankful that with these heels, I'm nearly as tall as he is. "It's not hard to tell you've had a few drinks this evening, even without all of the stumbling around. As for me saying you're *good*? That was an observation, not an order, but you can take it however you please. And lastly, I don't know how you usually talk to women, but I'm not the kind of girl that will stand here and take that kind of shit from you or anyone else. Now, if you'll excuse me, I'm going to go enjoy the rest of my night. Why don't you go have a few more drinks and do the same? It's your life, after all."

I take a step back from him and uncross my arms. I decide to leave my drink – disgusted by it now, thanks to Simon's current state. My heart's beating like a race horse's as I turn from his open-mouthed stare and walk toward Lacey at the bar, but fear and a massive amount of guilt set in as soon as I walk away. *Dammit! What happens when he finds out who I am? I'm going to lose this job before I even start!*

And regardless of how he was acting, I shouldn't have said those awful things to him. I was cruel and hateful, and no one deserves that. But as I continue to push through the crowd, I realize I'm angry with myself but mostly upset with Simon. I can't believe what an utter disappointment he turned out to be. I silently pray it's just the booze, unwilling to give up on him just yet, but I know in my heart that's probably not the case. I read the articles. I see the pictures. I don't want to believe it's true, but maybe it is. Maybe Simon Young has turned into a complete ass, with no hope of redemption.

I'm almost at the bar, trying in vain to keep the tears from falling down my cheeks, when I feel a warm hand grab my elbow. I swing around ready to pounce, thinking it's probably some sleezeball trying to hit on me, and I'm in no mood to deal with that right now. But when my tear-filled eyes lock with a fierce set of sparkling brown ones, I have trouble deciding whether to pull away or jump into his arms.

Without a word, Simon pulls me toward him. He takes his free hand and gently wipes the tears from my cheeks with his thumb.

"I made you cry."

His voice is low and troubled, tugging at my heart and giving me every reason I need to run away as fast as I can. This moment has the potential to be the granddad of all the stupid mistakes I've ever made.

But I can't move.

I can barely breathe.

My gaze shifts impulsively from his eyes down to his mouth, and before I can catch my breath or come to my senses, he slides both of his hands behind my neck, and that beautiful mouth is on mine.

I try to push him away, but it's a weak attempt at best. I shove against his chest, but the feel of his warm skin under his thin t-shirt, and the way his sweet-tasting mouth is ravishing mine, has me caving in no time. I close my eyes as Simon glides his tongue along the seam of my lips, and I part them eagerly, allowing him access. I feel the vibration from his quiet moan all the way to my toes, as he moves one arm around my waist and pulls me against his chest so hard, it's like he's trying to pull my entire body inside of his.

And I would go. Without a fight.

Simon's hand grasps the fabric of my dress at the small of my back, as I clench and unclench his t-shirt in my fists. His other fingers are squeezing the base of my neck, pushing my mouth against his, and I feel the last of my control slipping away. Simon ends the kiss with a few soft nibbles on my bottom lip that have me more turned on than the full on kiss we just shared, and we're both breathing heavily as he drops both hands to my waist and rests his forehead on mine. When I finally open my eyes, he watches me closely as I move my hands up and around his neck. I run my fingers through the back of his hair, and watch his eyes grow heavy. He leans down to bury his face in my neck and inhales deeply, as I close my eyes again, blocking out the crowd around us. I know we must look crazy just standing here in a heated embrace, mashed between throngs of people coming and going throughout the room. But I've barely felt them bump against me as they pass. I've barely noticed the loud music or roar of voices surrounding us. I've been completely absorbed by Simon, and it's been everything I ever thought it would be.

I continue pulling my fingers through the back of his hair, and as I'm reveling in the silky texture, he moans quietly again and somehow manages to pull me in even closer. "I'm so sorry," he whispers roughly against my neck, and despite my concern over his seemingly fragile state, my entire body responds to his warm breath on my skin.

I tremble against him, and he squeezes my waist in a soothing gesture. We continue holding each other until Simon looks at me, and I get a brief glimpse into his troubled soul. I know that apology wasn't meant entirely for me, and I want nothing more than to erase the hurt I see in his eyes, but I know I can't. Instead, I simply put a hand on either side of his face.

"You're forgiven," I tell him, as I struggle against the urge to pull his full lips back to mine.

Simon sighs and I reluctantly drop my hands. The look we share then is...I have to grasp his strong arms to steady us both.

Simon stares at me a moment longer, then slowly removes his arms from around my waist. I drop my hands from his arms at the same time, even though I'm far from steady on my feet. We're still only inches apart, but even in this crazy heat, I feel cold away from his touch.

"Sydney..." He leans in toward me, with a surprising grace he didn't have just moments before. "It was so lovely to meet you."

He places a soft kiss on my cheek, and my traitorous body trembles yet again, as I close my eyes and breathe him in. The smell is intoxicating – all cologne and spice and just...*Simon.*

After that, he pulls away and I stare after him dumbfounded, as he turns and walks out of the restaurant.

I'm still staring after him when Lacey walks up to me. She grabs my shoulders and turns me, forcing me to look at her.

"What in the world just happened?"

Lacey looks almost as shocked as I feel. *Almost.*

"I have no idea," I confess. "Absolutely no idea."

CHAPTER 6 - SIMON

Bloody hell! Who was *that*?

Barely holding it together, I walk quickly from the restaurant to find a cab. I rub my face with my hands as I walk, trying to gather my wits.

Who *was* that girl? Or more like, who was that goddess I just encountered and what has she done to me?

I reach the valet and ask that he call me a cab. I pace while I wait, not believing with as much alcohol as I've consumed today, I feel totally sober. An hour ago, I wouldn't have known my own name.

Damn, she was beautiful. It was almost like my body responded to her before I even knew she was there. I was more than satisfied with my conquests for the evening, when I had the urge to look up and there she was.

That soft blond hair and those eyes...*Christ*, I could get lost in the depth of those ocean blue eyes. They were so tempting and almost familiar, but I know I've never met her. I would remember that one.

I stop my pacing and squeeze my eyes shut, as I remember how I basically...*oh God*...how I basically attacked her. *Shit!* I felt awful for being so cruel to her, and even more surprising was how watching her walk away from me felt like some sick form of torture. That kiss was the only way my foggy brain could think to smooth things over and still get the taste of her I was so desperately craving at the same time. I'm such a fucking bastard.

I move a hand to my chest, over my pounding heart. For the second time today, I feel like I can't breathe. Already, I'm aching to touch her again. I want her back in my arms.

Gasping for air, I lean over and put my hands on my knees.

Get it together, Simon!

I take a few deep breaths and right myself. What the hell am I doing? It's just a girl – probably just another in a long line of females that want nothing more than a piece of *Simon Young: London Boy.*

I won't give into her charms, no matter how wonderful she may have been, or how good she may have tasted... *Shit! Shit! Shit!* I need to get her out of my mind, and fast.

"Simon!" a female voice calls, and I turn to see it's the two girls I was chatting with earlier this evening coming toward me.

Katie and Megan? Kristi and Maya? I can't remember, and it doesn't matter anyway. My problem is solved.

"Ladies," I give them my best smile, hoping they don't see through my now broken shell. Some mysterious goddess succeeded in cracking it wide open moments ago, which I thought after all of these years would be near impossible.

"So..." one of the girls starts, "who was that you left us for in there? Please tell me it was your sister or something."

She gives me an obnoxiously flirty giggle, causing me to have to choke back the bile that rises in my throat, but I still manage a smile.

"Not my sister, but no one you need to worry about. Where are you ladies headed?"

I'm aware this may not be the best way to handle my situation, but I need an escape. I need to forget about Sydney and everything she represents and I think these girls are just the ticket.

"We're going dancing," the other girl says. "Want to come?"

I give her a devilish smile, just as my cab pulls up. The valet opens the door for me, and I gesture for the girls to get in first. "After you, ladies."

Once inside, the girls give the driver the name of the club and we're off.

As we drive away, I glance back at the restaurant and an unexpected emptiness washes over me. I already miss the scent of her flowery perfume, the feel of her soft skin under my fingers and the way her body seemed to fit perfectly against mine. In mere minutes, she penetrated my long-standing defenses and now, here I am – stuck between hoping I never see her again and wondering how in the hell I'm going to live without her.

The next morning, I take another long shower, trying to work through what happened yesterday with the guys before I have to face them this morning. Although it still hurts like hell, I know if I chat with James, we can probably work all of this out. I'm just not sure that's what I want.

I love music. I love to perform, and I love the fans. I've spent a large part of my life as a member of this group and leaving would be one of the hardest things I've ever had to do. These guys are my brothers – the only family I have left. But in the sober light of day, I realize that the guys may be better off without me. And I may be better off as well.

Besides, everyone knows the pop scene has never been my calling. We were all forced into what would sell records when we first started, and none of us were prepared to pass up the deal that was being laid in our laps at the time, but it's no secret I prefer a softer, more acoustic style. I've tried to incorporate it over the years, but it always gets pushed back by the label. Maybe this is my chance to finally break free.

And more importantly, even though I'm not ready to admit it out loud, James is right. I'm still struggling, and I love these guys too much to continue bringing them down with me. I'm not sure things will ever get back to the way they used to be. Hell, I don't know what that old me looks like anymore. I'm pretty sure I wouldn't even recognize him at this point.

As I come out of my room, I see James is sitting in the exact spot at the table where I last saw him the day before. He's on his iPad this time, probably Skyping with the wife and kids back home.

"What are you doing up at this hour?" he turns to ask me, as I head toward the kitchen of our suite for some coffee.

"I missed the run throughs yesterday. I thought I'd head over to the boat this morning and get acquainted."

I don't even have to look at James to know his mouth is open, his eyes wide. He may have even stopped breathing. With my back to him, I smile victoriously when he exhales then clears his throat.

"No *hair of the dog* for you this morning then?" James asks, and my smile falls.

I know I've been a prick, but didn't they deliver the final blow yesterday?

"Nope." I keep my face impassive, still too stubborn to let him see me sweat. "I didn't drink that much last night."

That's a lie of course. I was hammered before my encounter with Venus last night, which this morning I've decided was nothing more than a moment of weakness brought on by a beautiful woman. I know I'll never see her again, so no need to dwell.

After I left the restaurant with whatever the hell their names are, I tried to regain my buzz at the club, but the alcohol started to blur the memory of my Venus's face, so I decided to quit. For the first time in a long time, I chose a clear head instead of drinking myself into oblivion, so I could remember our moment together...and at the same time, wish it never happened.

Then I came to my senses and realized I didn't like feeling so unsettled, so I decided to smoke some pot and have a threesome. Worked like a charm.

"No drinking? Really?" I look over at James as I stir my coffee. He's turned in his seat to face my direction. "What happened?"

"Just not into it," I shrug.

"Not that into it?" James repeats. "It's just that you were pretty angry when you left. I thought for sure your face would be on the cover of every tabloid in town this morning."

I take a deep breath, as he's making it extremely tough for me to hold my temper. "Look, I know we need to continue our conversation from yesterday, but I vote we just get through this cruise. We can all have a chat when we return to L.A. next week, yeah?"

James is quiet as he studies me. "Fine," he huffs. "But we do need to discuss this, Simon. It's been going on too long."

"Yes, James. You made that abundantly clear yesterday. I've got it."

James continues to stare at me, and I can feel myself about to snap. I need to get out of here before I make things worse. Luckily for James – and for me – Ollie walks into the living area just in time.

"Si? What's up, brother? Where are the hunnies?"

Leave it to Ollie to make me smile. "Still in my bed, and I would let them sleep it off, before you try and impress them with crepes or eggs benedict."

"That's my man." Ollie rubs his palms together excitedly.

"Don't you feel even the least bit pathetic for taking his hand-me-downs?" James asks, a disgusted look on his face.

"Nope. Not one bit," Ollie assures him, as he plops down across from him at the table. "That's what friends are for. Besides, I would have gone out and gotten my own hunnies last night, but you insisted on working us like dogs yesterday, so I was too tired to do anything by the time we got back." Ollie looks over at me and winks. "I can always count on Si to bring the ladies home, and I'm all rested up now."

I laugh as I drink the last of my coffee. Ollie's trying to play it cool this morning, after what went down yesterday, but he can't fool me. I've known him long enough to notice the worry in his eyes and the slight tension in his smile, but at least he's not bringing it up, and at the moment I love him for that.

"Have fun, mate," I tell Ollie, as I place my mug in the sink and walk toward the door. "See you guys later on."

"Where are you going?" Ollie asks, turning to watch me walk out the door.

I take a quick glance at James, who is back to studying his iPad, ignoring me and obviously still very pissed off.

"I'm going to the ship, since I missed everything yesterday. I'll see you guys in a bit."

I know I should apologize for yesterday, but I just don't have it in me. Not yet. However, I don't want to disappoint the fans. I may be struggling with my commitment to the guys, but I'll never give up on the fans.

"Cool," Ollie says to me, with an overly pleased look on his face. "Want us to have your luggage brought on board later?"

Without thinking, I place my hand in my jeans pocket and check for the locket.

"Sure," I nod, satisfied that the only thing I need is safe and within reach. "I'm all packed up. It's in my room."

"Got it. We'll see you later, Si."

I give the locket a squeeze, give Ollie a wave with my free hand, and then walk out the door.

CHAPTER 7 - SYDNEY

After dancing and clubbing most of the night with Lacey and her new bestie, Ramone, I felt exhausted by the time we made it back to the hotel. But thanks to Simon Young and his unexpected kisses, I knew sleeping would be out of the question.

"Did last night really happen?" Lacey mumbles, as she starts to wake up next to me.

"Yes. Last night did in fact happen."

I'm already up, showered, dressed, packed and ready to go. I'm so anxious about seeing Simon again, I can barely sit still. It's probably my bouncing knee on the bed that woke Lacey up.

Lacey rises up, stretches and yawns. "Are you already dressed?"

"Couldn't sleep."

Lacey shakes her head. "Did we ever decide on how to officially handle your *situation*?"

"I'm clinging to the hope that he won't remember," I lie. "And *he* came on to *me*, so if I act like nothing happened, I think that will be best." Another lie.

Of course I want him to remember. I don't want to act like it never happened, but I know that's my best bet, if I want to keep my job. *Oh God*. What have I done?

"I still can't believe he kissed you." Lacey winks at me and I have to smile.

"He did, and it was wonderful," I admit, failing to hide the dreamy look on my face. "But we have to be professionals about this.

It shouldn't have happened, and I'm sure Simon will agree. I'm not worried."

I plan to talk to him on the ship as soon as I get a chance, try to explain things. I'm certain he'll see it was all just a misunderstanding. No big deal.

Sweet Jesus, I need to stop with the lies. But for some reason, Lacey believes the nonsense I'm spewing at her.

"I think you're right," she tells me. "We're all adults and can handle this accordingly, and I also think there's a good chance last night will be a bit of a blur for him."

"Absolutely." I smile, although the idea of him not remembering me makes my chest ache.

"So, what do you think had him so wrecked last night? The way he held you after that kiss...I was almost in tears just watching from the sidelines."

I have a feeling I know what had him in such turmoil last night, based on the information we got in our meeting with Jameson last week, but I didn't share that bit with Lacey. I feel like saying it out loud makes it true, and I want to do everything I can on this cruise to try and change Jameson's mind. He can't get rid of Simon. He just can't.

"I'm not sure what was wrong with him." I lie to her yet again, as I nervously twist my fingers together. "And we may never know."

"Tell me again what you said to him before he came and grabbed you," Lacey smiles. "I love that part."

I smile too as I take a minute to go back over some of the details regarding our heated conversation, on through the...whatever the heck that was at the end.

"From what you see online, it seems like he parties like that all the time," I say, after I finish up the play-by-play. "I'm sure what happened last night is some kind of nightly ritual – another reason for him to want to wipe it under the rug. No harm, no foul."

This is what I've been telling myself, but I can't deny the connection I felt with him. And as much as I wish he felt the same, I know better.

"Based on what you've told me about him, the partying is commonplace and maybe even the kiss," Lacey points out. "But I thought he was more of the love-em-and-leave-em kind of guy, and the look on his face last night made it seem like leaving you was painful."

"But he did leave," I remind her, and she brushes my comment off with a shrug. "You know, Simon hasn't had an easy life. From what I understand, his father has never been in the picture, and his mother wasn't really either until the guys hit it big in the industry. I've heard that Ollie's parents practically raised him from the time he was twelve or thirteen years old."

"Really?" Lacey frowns. "That's awful."

"I'm sure that left him with some pretty serious trust and abandonment issues," I continue. "But then you add in the accident with Melissa...I would imagine it takes a long time to recover from that, if you even do. Last night, I obviously caught him in a weak moment. He needed comforting, and I'm sure he found it in those girls that chased after him when he left."

I pout, and Lacey smiles.

"Sounds like he has quite a bit of baggage. You up for that?"

"Simon is my *client*," I calmly explain. "His personal life is not my concern."

"Mmmm hmmm." Lacey rolls her eyes. "I kind of hope he does remember you. Maybe he'll want to pick up where you left off."

The discussion I had with Lena before I left briefly flashes through my mind. *Whatever. It. Takes.* It's like she was almost giving me permission to have my moment with Simon, right? *Oh my God! Sydney, what are you thinking?!*

"Whatever." I need to erase that image from my head and fast. "I certainly didn't put up too much of a fight last night. He probably already thinks I'm some super hero slut or something, *if* he even remembers me at all."

Lacey looks over at the clock, then jumps off the bed and heads to the shower. "Well, in about two hours, we're going to find out!"

It seems like it takes years for her to get ready. "Is that what you're wearing today?" I ask and she frowns as she shoves her hair products in her suitcase. "Of course you look gorgeous in anything, but after last night, I hoped I may be seeing a new side of Lacey on this trip."

"Last night we were clubbing in Miami." She gives my outfit a once over. "And today we're on the clock. That calls for more respectable attire."

"Since when do we work in a nunnery?"

"Gee. Thanks, *friend*."

"I'm just saying," I laugh. "I think business on a cruise ship can be done in more suitable, beach-friendly attire."

Lacey looks down at her knee-length skirt, flats, short-sleeved blouse and those god forsaken pearls. "What's wrong with what I have on?"

I sigh, knowing it's no use to try and change her now. Maybe I can get her into something cute for dinner later, after our meeting with the guys. At least she's wearing her hair in a ponytail instead of the usual bun. Baby steps, I guess.

"It's fine. For now," I tell her. "And I promise to keep my wardrobe as respectable as possible for you, Sister Lacey."

Lacey narrows her eyes at me. "I'm comfy," she says, defensively.

"You look fabulous," I assure her, and she gives me a shy smile. "Now go finish up and let's go."

I decided on a short red dress earlier with silver sandals. I kept my hair down this time, although I'm sure it will be up in a ponytail shortly with this crazy heat. I add some bright red lipstick while I wait for Lacey, and then poke nervously around the room, making sure I packed everything.

After I've checked and re-checked, I sit on the bed and wait not-so patiently for Lacey to finish up. I can't seem to get the images of Simon from last night out of my mind. I know my job is on the line, and I should be upset about how I handled myself last night, but as I remember the way his arms felt around me, the way his lips felt on my overheated skin...

"Lacey, for the love of God, let's go!"

CHAPTER 8 - SIMON

By the time I get done going through everything with the crew, there's less than an hour before show time. I rush to take another shower, and I'm grateful when I see the bags of new clothes on my bed from one of our assistants. I pull on a pair of shorts and a shirt and quickly make my way to our pre-show meeting.

"So, are we all set?" James asks, as we sit around the small table in his suite, preparing for everyone's arrival.

"The passengers are going through the safety run throughs now," our tubby manager, Xander, informs us. "They'll be making their way on deck soon for the concert and meet-and-greet. You guys will walk down the side of the ship – where they have the banner – stay there for a bit so everyone can snap some pictures as they finish boarding, and then you'll make your way onto the stages on the lido deck. You'll do the three songs we discussed to get everyone pumped up, then you'll have a little time for pictures and autographs, if you want."

It's a different ship, but mostly the same schedule every year. We all know the ropes by now.

"After the show this afternoon," Xander continues, "you have the meeting with the new PR rep, before dinner, followed by the welcome party. You'll be having dinner with the fans this time around, due to the smaller crowd." James and Xander share a pointed look, and I trade my bored sigh for a yawn. "You'll be introduced at dinner and the party, but after that, the rest of the evening is yours to do as you wish." Xander turns and looks directly at me. "There is the breakfast early tomorrow morning for the contest winners, so let's try not to get too crazy, all right?"

I take a huge gulp of water from my bottle. "It's vodka," I taunt. "Want a sip?"

I hold the bottle out to him and he lifts a chubby hand to stop me. "Whatever, smartass." Xander smiles and runs a hand over his nearly bald head, but there's doubt in his eyes. "It's my job to make sure this cruise goes smoothly. I'm just doing my job."

"And you do it so well."

"Enough," James pipes up, and I can see he's in "work mode", so I decide to back off.

James is all business when it comes to events. He doesn't like fooling around before show time, at least not any more. There was a time when we used to have fun together. Those days are long gone.

"Okay then." Xander claps his hands together, breaking the tension in the room. "Do you guys have any other questions? I'll be hanging in here before the show starts checking my emails, if you need anything."

"I'm going to go check out my suite." Ollie stands and moves toward the door, and I'm glad to see he's cleaned himself up a bit. He's lost the stubble, found some decent clothes and apparently showered. It's about damn time.

"See you later, Ollie," Rob says, keeping his seat next to Xander.

Rob has always been a bit conservative, and today is no different. Like James, his brown hair is trimmed short, unlike Ollie and me who have opted to stick with a shaggier, I-just-don't-give-a-fuck look. And his shorts are pressed, as well as his t-shirt, it appears. What a prick.

Rob will actually be sharing this suite with James. They started giving us single guys our own suites a long time ago. Thank God.

"I'm coming with," I tell Ollie, not wanting to be left alone with these three.

"Be on time," James says to us as we walk out the door, but I know that order is meant more for me than Ollie.

Ollie's suite is right next to mine, and fairly identical in layout. This ship is smaller than the other two cruises we've been on, but the suites are actually much nicer than the ones we've had in the past.

"Crazy posh," Ollie says, and I smile. "The hunnies will love this."

While Ollie looks around, I plop down on the sofa and put my feet up on the table.

"How about a beer?" Ollie suggests, as he raids the refrigerator and comes back with two Stellas.

"Look, Si," Ollie starts, and I cringe, knowing what's coming. "I think we should have a chat about what happened yesterday. I—"

"Don't worry about it," I interrupt. "It's all good."

"*All good*?" Ollie scoffs. "It's not good, mate. It fucking sucks."

"What? You think I'm surprised, Ollie?" I take a long pull from my beer. "Sure, it stings a bit, but it seems you've all been planning this for a while, as you should have been."

"I wanted to say something to you, but..." Ollie's face is twisted with guilt. "You can still talk to James, you know. It's not a final decision."

I purse my lips as my bitterness returns, so I don't lash out. I'm not upset with Ollie. He's always been a good friend, and I know this is killing him. But Ollie's right. This situation undeniably sucks.

"Don't let this happen, Si," Ollie continues. "Talk to James. We can make this work. We just want you to get better."

I keep my gaze straight ahead and give him a slight nod. At the moment, I have no plans to chat with James about staying in the group. I'm too proud and the wound is still too fresh. Plus, I'm still not sure that would be the best course for any of us. But I don't want to let Ollie in on that fact, at least not right now.

"I'll talk to him," I say, keeping it vague. "But I asked him to save it for after the cruise, and I'll ask the same of you. Let's focus on the next few days. We'll figure the rest out when we get home."

"Yeah. All right." Ollie pauses to take another swig from his bottle. "You know, James said the crowd is a lot smaller this year, but I think I actually like this ship better than the others." Ollie looks excited now, and I breathe a sigh of relief for the subject change.

"It'll probably be a lot of the same girls from the past couple years."

"I hope not," Ollie smirks. "I'm hoping there will be a new crop for us to divide and conquer."

"I told you I'm taking a break from that shit for a while," I remind him with a smile.

"It didn't look that way last night," Ollie says and I shrug. He's got me there.

"I was pissed off last night." I try and save face. "I'm better now."

Ollie and I both laugh, which is actually a nice sound. I would really miss this, if I left the group – all of us chumming around, laughing and having a good time. It's rare these days, and deep down, I know that's mostly because of me.

"So what's with the new PR rep?" I ask Ollie, remembering the mention of a meeting with him or her a moment ago in James's suite. "I guess I'm not privy to this information anymore?"

I didn't mean to let that last question slip, but the resentment is leaking out of me like a broken faucet these days.

"I really don't know much either," he confesses, avoiding my snide remark. "James's wife is good friends with the guy that owns the company. They chatted a bit at some boring family cookout or some shit, and the next thing I know, James is signing us up for new representation. Says this company is going to help us freshen up our image, get us back on the charts. You know none of us really digs this bubble gum nonsense anymore. I agree we need to change things up. I'm just not sure yet what the plan is. Guess we'll find out soon."

"Guess so." I love the idea of finally making some changes. It's a shame I probably won't be around long enough to be a part of them. "You know anything about the new rep?"

"Not really," Ollie admits. "It's not the guy that owns the place. I think James mentioned there's someone in the company that specializes in musicians. Heard it's a chick. Hope she's hot."

"*Christ*, Ollie. Keep it in your pants for longer than five minutes, yeah?"

Ollie laughs and we keep up the light banter and each get another beer down before Xander comes looking for us. "It's time!" he calls from behind Ollie's door, and Ollie and I look at each other and smile.

"It's go time!" Ollie says excitedly and the energy in the room is palpable. This is the best part. This is what I love, what we all love.

The excitement before a show is indescribable. Confidence oozes out of all of us as we make our way to the side of the ship where we'll make our first appearance. As we get closer to the spot, we start to hear all of the screams and shouts from the fans. I can feel the anticipation rippling through me, as we all look at each other, smiling like idiots.

"The MC is going to introduce you on stage in ten, so toss out a few smiles and waves, then make your way up," Xander advises us. "And make it count, ladies."

We all smile at him, and James punches him lightly on the arm. "Let's do this."

We do our traditional fist bumps, but we each have our own superstitious rituals as well. Ollie cracks his neck to each side, and then crosses his chest, even though he's nowhere near Catholic. Rob kisses his father's dog tags that he's had since he was killed in combat during the Gulf War, and James always bows his head and says a silent prayer before kissing his index finger and raising it to the sky. I of course pull my locket out, close my eyes and kiss it twice, once on each side. Then I give it a squeeze and put it back in my pocket.

"Let's go," James says, once the MC finishes and we all get our game faces on as we walk out into the blazing afternoon sun.

CHAPTER 9 - SYDNEY

"So, Ollie's even better looking in person," Lacey states calmly – too calmly – as they finally reveal themselves to us on stage, and I gape at my friend.

Ollie? Lacey likes Ollie? The tattooed, hip-hop loving, free-spirited member of the group?

"What?" she asks with a shrug when she sees me staring.

"You didn't tell me you were an Ollie fan," I scold. "As a matter of fact, you didn't tell me you were a London Boys fan at all."

"I'm not, really," she claims, with her usual nonchalance. "I know tons about Simon, thanks to you, but I thought it would help if I educated myself on the other three as well, so I did a little research before the trip. Honestly, their music isn't half bad. I can see the appeal."

And Lacey shocks me once again.

"I think I may love you even more now," I confess, and we both laugh. "But why Ollie?"

Lacey seems more like a James fan to me, or Rob. Yes, definitely Rob – gorgeous, but in a clean cut, all manners, conservative kind of way. Much more Lacey's speed.

Lacey shrugs again. "I have a thing for tattoos. Is that a big deal?"

"Oh, it's huge," I inform her with a gasp. "How could you have not told me about this before?"

Lacey and tattooed boys? I didn't see that one coming.

"It's art. What's not to like?"

"Especially when it's Ollie's art?"

"Yes." Lacey gives me a shy smile, then looks back to the stage. "Ollie's art is...*very nice.*"

Oh my goodness! There's hope for my Lacey girl yet!

"Ollie's fantastic," I agree as we both look back at the guys, but of course I can't focus on Ollie. My eyes are trained on only one person standing on the main stage in front of us, and frankly, I don't understand how anyone could notice anything else when he's around.

Simon looks beautiful, so much happier and carefree than he did last night. He seems relaxed now and vacation ready in Converse with no socks, tan shorts, a gray wife beater and a light blue, short-sleeved shirt, unbuttoned and blowing behind him in the ocean breeze. His smile is bright and wide, and his shaggy hair is curled slightly from the humidity and whipping around his perfect face.

"Too bad Jameson is married," Lacey says in my ear. "He's ridiculously hot, too."

I finally pull my eyes away from Simon and notice all of the guys do look amazing. It's the first time I've seen them live since I was thirteen, and they all look just as good now as they did then, maybe even better. They all obviously take great care of themselves, especially James who is by far the most muscular of the bunch. But they each have tight bodies, killer smiles and seriously great hair.

"This is going to be so much fun!" I squeal, feeling myself slowly finding that thirteen year old fangirl inside of me. "I can't believe we're here! I can't believe this is my job!"

Lacey hugs me with an adorable "squeee" in my ear. "And we're just getting started!"

Just then, James grabs a mic and starts to speak.

"So, did everyone enjoy Miami? Hot enough for you?" he asks, and the crowd goes wild. "Well, I hope you're ready to party with The London Boys this weekend because we're sure ready to show you a good time."

I look over and see Simon's laughing now and waving to the crowd. I feel like I may burst with happiness.

"How about we sing you lovelies a song?" Ollie suggests, and the screams for him are ten times louder than they were for James.

Growing up, no one compared to Simon of course, but Ollie was always a close second – especially on days like today, when I get to look at him in a snug white tank top that shows off all of his colorful "artwork". Plus, he has these adorable dimples when he smiles, white-blonde hair and crystal green eyes that will render you speechless if you stare too long. And to top it off, he has a carefree style and attitude that make him that much more attractive.

I still can't believe he's someone Lacey would go for, but you never know. The girl has been full of surprises lately.

While the fans scream away, the guys start up their first song. There are four catwalks coming from the main stage, with four smaller stages at the end of each of the catwalks. Lacey and I snag a spot next to one of the smaller stages where the guys will essentially be standing in the middle of the crowd. *Incredible*!

The first song is an oldie, but a goodie – *Girl, You've Got It* – and I swear it's like some kind of religious experience. The fans start singing along and dancing to the upbeat music, and I smile as I feel every worry I have slip away into the cloudless blue sky above us.

Work officially starts after this, so I decide to let myself get out all my fangirling until I have to meet with the guys after the show. It's better than sitting here, stewing over the meeting – and how in the hell I'm going to handle the "Simon Situation" – which would most certainly cause me to lose my breakfast.

Lacey and I sing and scream our little hearts out along with the rest of the crowd, until the first song ends, and the guys start moving toward the catwalks. I hate it, but I have to reel it in a bit up close with the guys. Can't let my fangirl show to our clients, now can I?

The guys each take their places on one of the smaller stages before the second song starts, and to my dismay, Simon is two stages away from where we're standing. But we have Ollie, so Lacey is ecstatic.

As they start to sing another one of their more upbeat tunes – *Graffiti* – Ollie starts doing his signature dance moves, and I laugh as Lacey grabs on to my arm for support. All of the guys can dance, but Ollie and Simon are unquestionably the most talented in that arena.

Ollie's looking down into the crowd, and when he notices Lacey, I feel like I'm reliving my concert experience through her. I watch as Ollie's eyes widen and he kneels in front of us, still singing the song. Lacey's smile is so big I think her face may split in two, as Ollie holds out a hand, inviting her onto the small stage with him.

I refrain from jumping up and down and squealing as he helps Lacey on stage, and Lacey's confidence surprises me yet again as she stands next to Ollie and lets him sing to her. Ollie will be in for a surprise in our meeting later, but at least Lacey's keeping it professional. Ollie, on the other hand, is looking at her like he wants to peel those old lady clothes off her body piece by piece and have her on the stage in front of everyone.

I glance over and see the other guys smile as they notice what he's doing, and when my eyes finally land on Simon, I'm confused by the look on his face. He's still singing, but I catch a brief flash of dread cross his features as he stares at Ollie and Lacey. Is it possible he recognizes her from last night? There's no way. She looks entirely different, now that she's in business mode. But in the midst of my doubting, his eyes start frantically searching around the stage where we are and when his gaze finally locks on to mine, time seems to stop. Even from far away, I can see his remarkable smile and between that and the sweltering heat, I think I may actually melt away.

Unfortunately, his face goes from excitement to frustration – *or was that fear?* – in no time at all. The next thing I know, Simon is walking back toward the main stage and when the guys see him leaving, they all follow suit. Ollie helps Lacey back down, but not before whispering something in her ear. She's all cool confidence in front of him, but when she finally turns her eyes to me, she looks like a lovesick puppy.

The guys retreat back toward the main stage, and quickly start another song. As they sing, all of the guys make their way to each of the catwalks to mingle with the crowd. All of the guys, except for one.

After they finish the third song, they spend a lot of time signing autographs and taking pictures with fans. James and Rob even come back down the catwalks again, but Ollie and Simon are so covered up in fans near the main stage, they never make it back out. Lacey and I move away from the small stage, letting the other girls have their chances with James and Rob, knowing we'll officially have the pleasure of meeting them within the hour.

I try to catch Simon's eyes again as we get pushed around by the crowd, but he never even looks in my direction. He's in the zone as he works the fans, but I can tell his smile has a slight edge to it now, or maybe I'm just imagining things. Either way, the other fans don't seem to notice as they reach and scream for him.

When they're done, James grabs the mic again. "Thank you so much!" James yells over the crowd. "Everyone, get settled and we can't wait to see all of your lovely faces for dinner!"

The guys go to leave, and Simon leads the group as he all but sprints off the stage. *Interesting.* I know I didn't imagine *that.*

I turn to Lacey and see her staring after Ollie with a grin on her face. I try to push back my questions about Simon for the moment and concentrate on the epic event that just happened to my friend.

"No way, Lace!" I shout at her, since the crowd is still roaring for an encore. "What did he say to you?"

Lacey tries to seem indifferent, despite the enormous grin on her face. "He told me I was beautiful and asked me to find him later after dinner."

My mouth pops open in shock. "He said *what?*"

Lacey finally breaks and a giggle bursts from her lips. I hug her against me and squeal with delight. I know we're supposed to be here on business and all that jazz, but I think Ollie singling Lacey out in the crowd is worth a squeal or two.

When we finally get over our fangirl moment, Lacey grabs my arm and we make our way through the crowd. Looking around the lido deck I remember nearly having a panic attack getting onboard earlier, but I forgot about my fear of boats as soon as Simon took the stage. I didn't even realize until now that the ship had started moving.

"I'm kind of excited to see how Ollie reacts when he finds out who you are," I tell Lacey with a smile. "Looks like we may both be facing an awkward situation in this meeting."

"It will be so worth it." Lacey gives me a dreamy smile, and I smile with her.

"I would have to agree."

"I didn't do anything stupid, did I?" Lacey asks me, and the alarm on her face is endearing. "I was so shocked when it happened. I kind of lost my head for a minute there."

"You're usual poise was in full effect," I confirm. "As a matter of fact, your confidence level is off the charts these days, my friend. I'm impressed."

"Whatever." Lacey smiles and shakes her head. "Don't get too excited. I may have seemed poised, but I was sure I would pass out and fall to my death on that stage. I mean, have you seen Ollie's eyes?"

"Oh good Lord." I give her arm a squeeze to break her from her trance. "You're already smitten."

"I am not," Lacey tries, but she still can't stop smiling. "I think he's a nice looking guy. What's wrong with that?"

"Nothing at all." I smirk, letting her off the hook for now.

I consider telling her about the awkward eye contact between me and Simon, but instead we walk toward our cabin a while in silence, muscling through the excited fans. "So, what do you need from me in this meeting?" Lacey asks when we near our cabin.

"I have some notes, but I just thought I'd take this first meeting to introduce myself, shake hands, that kind of thing."

"So I'll just be there for support then, take some notes if needed," Lacey confirms. "I think you'll do great, Syd," she adds after glancing over at me. "Even if he does remember, I'm sure things will be fine. Everyone makes mistakes, and Simon seems to make lots of them."

"Ouch."

"Sorry. Of course I didn't mean *you* were a mistake. I just meant...well, you know what I meant."

"Yeah. I get it."

But I hate associating the word *mistake* with what happened between Simon and me last night. I realize that's the truth of it, but it sure didn't feel like a mistake. Not to me.

"Are you going to wear that to the meeting?" Lacey asks me, and I'm grateful for the subject change.

"Probably." I look down at my red dress and shoes. "I may change into heels, and freshen up a bit, but I'm most likely going to stick with this dress."

"I'm thinking I should change." Lacey's quiet voice causes me to glance her way.

As soon as she sees me eyeing her, she snaps to attention. "I know there's nothing wrong with what I'm wearing, but I'm just...well, I think I may be a little warm in this skirt. I was thinking I'd put on one of the new dresses I bought. Cotton would be much cooler, and then we would be dressed more alike. A uniformed front, right?"

Hmmm...should I let this one slide, or no?

"You should wear that light green dress that you bought. It would look good with those nude heels, and green is always a fabulous choice for you."

"You think?"

"Absolutely."

"Okay then. The green dress it is," Lacey says with a wide smile, and I go in for the kill.

"I think Ollie will love it."

"Oh hush up!" She slaps my arm as we finally make it to our cabin. "I'm just too warm in this outfit. That's all."

I give her another smirk, letting her know I'll play along, but she's not fooling me. This trip may be more fun that I hoped. Ollie and Lacey? This will either be a complete train wreck, or one of the hottest couplings this world has ever seen.

CHAPTER 10 - SIMON

Of course she's a fan. *Of course*!

She said she knew who I was last night, but I didn't expect her to be on the goddamn cruise!

Pacing in my suite, I try and figure out how best to handle this situation. What is it about this girl that leaves me in knots? I don't need this right now. Simple. Simple is how I like it, and little Ms. Sydney is anything but simple.

Shit. I need a drink.

I move to the kitchen area and pour myself a whiskey. I down it in one gulp and swiftly pour another. I stand and enjoy the warmth as the liquor slides down my throat, then I move to the sofa and take a seat. I wish I could ignore the gorgeous face continuously flashing through my mind now like a neon sign, but I can't. It felt good to see her again. Really good.

I'm. Totally. Fucked.

I can't let this woman get inside my head. Just a few minutes with her last night, and I knew she would be trouble. And here I am, trapped on a damn boat with her, unable to escape for the next five days!

I close my eyes and take a deep breath – and another large sip of whiskey – trying my best to think rationally.

There are several hundred people on this ship. Avoiding her for the next five days may be easier than I thought. Very doable. And if I do see her, I'll make sure all walls are up. My usual charms will most likely have a fiery girl like her running in the other direction with no problem. Sure sent her running from me last night.

So, it's decided. I'll work this cruise, business as usual. I'll bide my time until I can get off the boat, then make my way back to California and figure out what the hell I'm going to do with myself now that the guys have kicked me out. That's where my head should be right now. Not on some random girl I met in a bar.

I take another sip of Jack and just as I'm about to finish my glass, there's a knock on my door.

I slowly stand and make my way over. Looking through the peephole I see it's Ollie, so I open the door for him, then make my way to the kitchen area for another drink.

"What's up, Si? Why the rush back to your suite?"

Fucking Ollie. What's with all the concern lately? And he thinks *I'm* the one going soft?

"I'm fine. It's just hot as hell out there."

Ollie nods. "That's the truth. Good crowd though, yeah? Did you see that hunny I pulled up on stage with me? Not my usual type, but she had this school teacher look that totally did it for me."

Ollie's smile is wide as he relives the memory. Mine, however, is not.

"She was a good one, mate."

We both squirm a bit as the silence between us grows uncomfortable. Thankfully, Ollie decides to leave, rather than press it. I'm sure he thinks my unease is still about what happened with the guys yesterday, as it should be, and I'll let him continue to believe that for now.

"Okay, well I'll see you at the meeting then?" he asks, moving back toward the door. "James's suite in a half hour, remember?"

"Yeah, see you then."

Once Ollie leaves, I top off my glass and move back toward the sofa. I nearly fall down into it – the lack of sleep, the liquor and the adrenaline all hitting me at once. I take another large sip from my glass, waiting for the alcohol to rid her from my thoughts.

Looks like I'm going to need a few more bottles of whiskey.

By the time the meeting rolls around, I've got quite a nice buzz going. Amazingly enough, I did manage to get myself a shower and into some dry clothes as I polished off nearly half a bottle of Jack.

Getting wasted before a business meeting probably wasn't one of my better ideas, but what the fuck do I care? I'm as good as out of the group anyway, so no need for me to get overly involved in a meeting that's all about planning for the future, right?

With a glance at the clock, I realize I'm a bit late. I slam back the remainder of the whiskey in my latest glass and make my way to the door. Just as I open it, Ollie appears on the other side.

"We got a problem, Si."

The grave look on his face sobers me a bit, but I assume the problem he's referring to is me. It's always me.

"I know I'm late, but it's only a few minutes. James can sod off."

Ollie puts his hands on my shoulders and blocks my path to James's suite. "It's not that. It's the girl, the one I pulled on stage."

"What about her?"

Ollie takes a deep breath. "She's one of our new PR reps."

I narrow my eyes, trying to decide if my liquor filled brain heard him correctly. "I'm sorry?"

"The girl." He runs a hand roughly through his hair. "The girl I was hitting on at the concert earlier is one of the new fucking reps! Can you say *awkward*? I bet she thinks I'm a total wanker! I can't go back in there, Si. I can't even look at her."

I feel the anxiety settle in, but it's not about Ollie's dilemma. Oh no. I've got problems of my own. Big ones.

Because if Ollie's girl is one of our new PR reps, then that means...

"I will say though that the other girl? The one in charge? She's a beauty, mate," Ollie happily confesses as my alarm continues to grow. "Blonde hair, blue eyes and the body of a goddess. Figures James would keep that bit of information to himself, if he even noticed."

For a moment I think how funny it is that Ollie would use the exact description of her that I chose last night – Venus, an absolute goddess. But as the truth of the situation settles in, I close my eyes and start to pray. *Oh dear God, no. Please tell me this isn't happening. Please tell me my luck isn't this bad.*

"You okay, Si?" I hear Ollie ask, and I squeeze my eyes tighter, not sure how to answer.

"Ollie, I'm a total cock up. Big time."

I think about how nervous Ollie is about this situation when all he did was pull a girl on stage. Me? I yelled and threw a fit like a pouty child, then attacked her with my mouth. Brilliant.

I'm about to give Ollie the short version of what happened last night when James walks out of his suite and stomps toward us in the hallway. "What in the hell is going on out here?"

My eyes pop open to find James's face blood red with anger. Or embarrassment. Most likely both.

"Sorry, James." Ollie steps up, probably to cover for me. "I was telling Si about the unfortunate happenings between me and a certain new PR rep. We were coming right in. I just—"

But James is not hearing it, as usual. "You handle your personal shit on personal time. We have a business meeting to attend." He tosses an angry thumb back in the direction of his suite. "And I suggest you get your arses in there before I toss you both off the side of this bloody ship."

James walks back toward his suite, mumbling curses at us as he runs his hands through his hair.

"Good thing that bastard's in such good shape," Ollie says when James closes the door. "Otherwise I'd worry about a stroke or heart attack."

"Right," I reply, but I'm not really listening. The horror of my situation, mixed with the whiskey, has numbed me out completely.

"What were you about to say?" Ollie reminds me, but I shake my head.

"Never mind," I tell him as I start walking slowly toward James's suite. "I'll talk to you about it later."

Ollie follows behind me, and I say another little prayer when my fingers grasp the door handle. Then, out of nowhere, the urge to see her again up close, to be near her in any way I can, takes precedence over everything else. *What the hell*?

"You gonna open the door, Si?"

I blink a few times and turn back to Ollie. "Yeah. Sorry."

I slowly open the door, and my eyes immediately dart around the room, searching her out. Her head rises at the sound of the door and her eyes lock with mine. I can't believe how incredibly beautiful she is. Ollie confirmed it. She's an absolute goddess.

We make our way to the table, and the girls both stand as we approach. I notice Ollie's school teacher has had a bit of a makeover. She's now in a short green number with her hair down, and her full, pink lips are currently turned up in an attractive smile. I glance over at Ollie to see he's obviously noticed as well. This should be interesting.

"Ladies, you've met Ollie. And this is Simon Young." James does the introductions. "Simon, this is Sydney, our new account rep from White and Associates, and her assistant Lacey."

"Sydney Campbell," the goddess says, as she extends her hand to me.

There's worry in her eyes, so I give her my best reassuring smile. "It's lovely to meet you, Sydney."

I watch as she shakes my hand and I catch a discreet exhale. I'm still smiling when the other girl extends her hand to me.

"Lacey McIntyre," she says, and I reluctantly release Sydney's hand to shake Lacey's.

"Nice to meet you."

We all sit, and when I glance over at James his eyes are narrowed in confusion. I quickly look away.

"So, what did we miss?" I ask, hoping to break the tension. "Sorry for being a bit late."

Sydney clears her throat. "It's no problem, Mr. Young."

"Simon," I correct her. "Please, call me Simon."

"Okay, Simon," she smiles, and my entire body warms at the sight. "I wanted this meeting to be a casual get-to-know-you, since I've only had the pleasure of meeting James so far." She clears her throat again and looks down at the table briefly. Goddess needs to work on her poker face. "As for the next few days, I'll be spending some time with each of you, getting your thoughts and ideas about the direction you see for the group. I even plan to speak to a few fans, maybe do some off-record polling. Might as well, since we have a great mix of long-time and new fans on the ship."

"Sounds good," I say, but again, I wasn't really listening. I was too busy starting at her mouth – full and soft, perfect for nibbling.

"Sydney's actually a big fan of ours," James tells us, and my eyes move from her mouth as her cheeks redden.

"Guilty," she laughs. "That's one of the many reasons I was so excited about this account."

"What were the other reasons?" I ask, before I can stop myself. I feel the stares as they shift my way, but I don't care.

Sydney's eyes snap back to mine, her face a careful mask. "Well…" she pauses and glances around at the rest of the guys at the table. "As James knows, and as all of you may know by now, you're my first client with White and Associates. I'm very eager, thrilled about the opportunity and the possibilities. And as a fan, it's an honor to work with you all, but being a fan also gives me incentive. Your future and livelihood are…personal to me."

Sydney's eyes linger on mine for a second too long with that last sentence, but before I can question it, James pipes up again.

"I think you were a great choice, Sydney. I can't wait to hear your ideas."

"Thank you," she says, and I take a moment to admire her sincerity. It's obvious she will take this job very seriously, giving me all the more reason not to screw things up for her.

I sit back in my chair as Sydney gets bombarded with questions from the group. It's the ideal opportunity to admire her, and that's exactly what I do.

I quickly note her confidence. It's hard to miss. That's not always an admirable trait, but in Sydney, it's a huge turn on – probably because it's not cockiness or conceit. It's confidence. And it's genuine. And it's incredibly sexy.

I gaze at her a while longer, switching my eyes from her to the guys a few times, pretending I'm following the conversations, but I haven't a clue what's going on. Even before I walked in the door, I was pulled toward this beautiful woman, with just the memory of her alone. Now that I'm only a few feet away, I'm absolutely enchanted.

And then, like being doused with ice water in a hot shower, I'm yanked from my musing when I hear this come from her lovely mouth.

"As I told James before, I personally feel like you would be making a huge mistake losing any members of the group. It would be professional suicide, and I don't think you can afford that right now."

I was analyzing her features so closely before, I have no idea how I missed the change. When I blink and refocus my eyes, I see bright red cheeks and a slight sheen of sweat on her forehead. Something struck a nerve big time, and since I wasn't listening to the conversation, I have no idea what that may be. But after her last comment, I can only assume they were talking about me.

My eyes immediately find James. He *told* her? I wonder what else she knows. I wonder what she must think of me now. After I practically molested her in the bar last night and now *this*?

I can feel the heat in my own cheeks, the sweat now forming on my own brow. I glance over at Ollie and see that everyone's eyes are shifting back and forth, nervously. Then something from Sydney's statement pops into the front of my brain. She said, "as I told James *before*". When was "before" I wonder? Most likely not today, so was it when James met with these people last week? Now the conversation I overheard between James and Ollie yesterday in the suite makes more sense. It must have been last week, and if that's the case, Sydney knew all of this about me last night.

This entire situation is becoming some jumbled mess of anger, embarrassment and a ton of other unsavory emotions crowding my head. And just as I start to feel the impact of it all, my eyes find Sydney's again, and I see the worst thing I could possibly see in her beautiful blue eyes. Pity.

Fuck. That.

I stand and head for the door without looking back, until I hear James's voice. "Si, where are you going?"

I'm nearly choking on my anger as I turn back to him. I have no idea what to say...well, that's not exactly true. There are a thousand things I would like to say right now, but none are appropriate in mixed company.

However, I don't think manners will be winning out this time.

"We've been together for fifteen years, James. Fifteen. Fucking. Years. And this is what we've become? You don't have any more respect for me than *that*?" James moves to interrupt, but I lift my hand to stop him. I hate that it's shaking. "I get it. I know what you think of me, what you all must think of me. So, to keep up appearances, I'm going back to my suite to finish my bottle of Jack. You know where to find me, should you need to feel better about yourselves."

I turn back to the door, open it and slam it shut behind me, like the coward I've become. But I can't bear to look at any of them any longer, especially Sydney with all of that sympathy clouding her pretty face.

Before I can shut the door to my own suite, Ollie's there. "I'm sorry, Si. I don't think James should have gotten that personal with them either, but it's not a big deal. We're all going to smooth this over soon, yeah?"

"Either way, I don't think I can be in there anymore."

As much as his optimism makes me want to vomit, I don't feel up to hurting Ollie right now. And I'm also not really feeling up to sharing.

"I understand." Ollie's now staring a hole through the floor. "I just wish everything wasn't so fucked up, you know? I miss the old days something awful."

I think for a moment about comforting Ollie, but I'm too rattled...and still a little drunk, but not nearly as drunk as I want to be.

"Go back in there, Ol. I'll be fine. See you at dinner." And with that, I close the door on my friend's face.

I know. I'm a horrible, horrible bastard.

But it seems just when I think something good may come into my miserable life, that gets tossed back in my face like dog shit hitting a front door. The thought of Sydney knowing I was getting the boot when I met her last night sends cold chills prickling up my spine. Hell, that whole thing could have been scripted, just trying to see how I would react – some kind of test to see how far she could push me, verify what James told them about me so she could make a more educated decision. And after my pathetic performance last night at the restaurant, it's no wonder she wants to keep me in the group. No wonder that pity was all over her face. She feels sorry for me now, and that's the last thing I need.

Well, fuck her. Fuck James. Fuck every one of them.

Now, where's my whiskey.

CHAPTER 11 - SYDNEY

"Is he okay?" James asks Ollie as he re-enters the room.

My fingers are clutched so tightly together in my lap, my knuckles are white. It's all I can do to stay in this chair and not go rushing after Simon and apologize to him for even dignifying what Xander said with a response.

I look over at Lacey, and she glances back at me with wide, questioning eyes.

I lean toward her ear. "I'll tell you what I know later."

When James filled us in on the plans to kick Simon out of the group at our meeting last week, I promptly told him then that I didn't agree with the idea. But it's more than my long time crush on Simon that helped me come to that decision. Everyone knows that Simon is the true talent behind the group. He has the best voice, he's the best song-writer and even with all of the ridiculous drama he's been through with the press over the past few years, he's still the fan favorite.

I didn't mention any of this to Lacey because frankly, I didn't think it would come up on the cruise. James told Lena and me that we should keep that news in the strictest of confidence because he hadn't even told Simon about it at the time. I will admit that James didn't look very happy to deliver that news to me and Lena. He actually looked downright heartbroken, which gave me hope. But that hope evaporated when I saw the look on Simon's face after Xander brought it up just a moment ago. I wonder if that's the first

Simon has heard about it. If that's the way the news was broken to him, Xander is a total bastard.

"Of course he's not okay." Ollie points a heated look at Xander. "What the fuck was *that*?"

"What?" Xander shrugs, and I squeeze my hands together even tighter. "It's not like it's news to him, and I feel like everything needs to be out on the table if we're going to get serious about making a change."

"But you shouldn't have brought it up like that in front of everyone." Ollie is fuming, as he paces by the table without taking his eyes off Xander. "You knew we had this conversation with him just yesterday. Why would you bring it up again now?"

I'm thankful this wasn't the first Simon had heard about their decision, but as I continue looking at Xander, the look that he exchanges with Ollie is a real eye-opener. He wants Simon out, and he'll force things if he has to, so they go his way. Total. Bastard.

"I agree with Ollie, Xander. That was out of line," James says in a tired voice. "I told Simon we would table that discussion until after the cruise, and he also had no idea that I had told the group at White and Associates. You blind-sided and embarrassed him. And you probably just made all of our lives a living Hell for the next few days."

Xander shrugs his shoulders again, and my hands are starting to go numb I'm squeezing them so hard, but at least I haven't punched anyone yet. "You know my thoughts on this." He gives James a meaningful look, but James shakes his head.

"Now's not the time," he tells Xander and then looks over at Lacey and me. "Ladies, I'm sorry you had to see that. I would like for things to proceed as we discussed. I'll try and speak to Simon, but

94

until then, please leave him out of this – not because I don't want his input to be included. His head is simply not in the right place at the moment. I hope you understand."

I'm starting to really like James.

I glance over at Lacey and she gives me a nod. "We understand, and please don't worry about this. I'm confident everything will work out as it should."

"Thank you, Sydney," James says with a sigh. "I appreciate you being so optimistic and accepting. Perhaps we should call it a day. We'll see you both again at dinner, and just let me know when you want to schedule time to speak to each of us privately."

"I will." I stand and gather the few things I brought to the meeting. I extend my hand to James and he takes it. "Thank you for taking a chance on me, James. I appreciate it more than you know."

James smiles. "I'm looking forward to hearing your ideas. I think you will be an excellent fit for us."

I smile back and shake Rob's hand next. "Nice to meet you, Sydney," he tells me. "And thanks for not running scared after that." Rob has a nice laugh.

"You'll have to do better than that to scare me off," I ensure him, then turn to Xander. He shakes my hand, and I suppress a gag at the feel of his sweaty palm in mine. "Pleasure," I say to him with a tight smile.

"Ms. Campbell," he says with a smile to match mine. "I look forward to working with you."

I drop his hand as quickly as I can without being too obvious and wait for a moment while Lacey shakes hands as well.

"I'll see you ladies out," Ollie offers as we wait for Lacey by the door.

"Thanks." I smile up at him, but his eyes are trained on Lacey. *Very interesting.*

"It was nice to...officially meet you," Lacey says to Ollie when she approaches, but he cuts her off.

"I'm walking out with you," he tells her. "Shall we?"

Ollie's smile is semi-relaxed for Lacey, but I can see the anger still simmering in his features. He's obviously close to Simon and eager to protect him. And if I didn't love Ollie before, I certainly do now.

"I'm sorry you ladies had to see that as well," Ollie says, as soon as the suite door closes behind us. "But I'm not apologizing for Si's behavior. I'm apologizing for Xander's."

"It's okay." I glance around at the doors while we walk and wonder which one is Simon's. "I think you'll find that we Southern girls are pretty tough-skinned."

My teasing brings a more genuine smile to Ollie's face. "I think I'm going to like you," he winks, and I concentrate on keeping my inner-fangirl from bubbling to the surface. "Can't wait to see you lovelies at dinner."

Ollie stops when we reach the security guards at the end of the hallway. I extend my hand for a shake, but he pulls my knuckles to his lips instead. I should be caught off guard, but it's such a natural move for Ollie. And when he reaches for Lacey's hand and does the same, I wonder for a moment if he only kissed mine so he could kiss hers. It looks that way.

With a wave, Ollie turns and heads back down the hallway, and Lacey looks like a lost puppy dog as she watches him leave. I grab her arm to turn her back toward our own cabin. "Come on, Juliet."

"I'm sorry." Lacey gives me a sheepish smile as we walk. "But he is dreamy."

"*Dreamy*?" I smile at her pre-teen vocabulary. "Yes, you're right. They're all pretty dreamy."

"Except for that manager of theirs," Lacey adds. "I can't believe he did that to Simon. Poor guy."

"I know. I felt awful for him. Hopefully, the guys will talk to him and he'll be okay."

"So, you knew before the cruise?"

"Sorry for not telling you," I wince. "But I didn't think I'd have a need. James told us to keep it in confidence because he hadn't told Simon at the time. I never thought it would come up on this trip, or I would have told you."

"It's no problem," Lacey assures me. "I'm just glad you're going to fight for him. I'm not as big of a fan as you, obviously, but the little I know tells me Simon is an important part of this group."

"And I think the rest of the guys feel the same," I add. "This all seems more like an ultimatum to try and scare Simon into making some changes. I'm not sure if that's the best approach or not. I guess we'll see."

As we approach our cabin, Lacey nudges my side. "I can't believe you're going to force me to bring it up."

I give her a confused look and open the door. "Bring what up?"

"Well, we can start with the way Simon was looking at you during the meeting. Let's just say that the hope of him not remembering you is no longer a possibility."

"Oh God, I know." I lie back on my bed and close my eyes. "But we still don't know if it was a memory he wants to remember or forget."

"Are you serious?"

I feel Lacey plop down beside me, and I open my eyes to find her staring at me. "Yes?" I question because her green eyes are fierce, and honestly a little scary.

"Sydney, give me a break. I thought he was going to crawl across that table and rip your clothes off any minute," she says, her voice almost bored.

Was it really like that? I could feel Simon watching me a few times, and I even caught his eyes once or twice, but I didn't get the vibe Lacey is talking about. She's obviously just trying to make me feel better.

"Lacey, even if he was thinking that, it doesn't matter. He's my client, and this is my first account. If I screw this up, not only will I probably lose my job at White and Associates, but it may ruin my reputation in the industry all together."

I'm not afraid to admit to myself that I would love nothing more than experiencing Simon Young on an unprofessional level. But I can't...

Whatever. It. Takes.

No. Nope. No need to discuss it any further.

Lacey looks like she's going to argue with me, then slumps her shoulders in defeat. "God. You're absolutely right. And that absolutely sucks."

"Sucks for me, or sucks for you?" I smile and turn on my side to face her. "I actually think you may be able to get away with some private time with Mr. Sutton. You know I wouldn't tell."

Lacey looks from side to side as if she's contemplating my suggestion, then frowns. "No way. In my wildest fantasies, maybe. But in reality, it's not going to happen."

"Why not?"

"Mainly because I know what his reputation is like, and I don't think I would be a match for the women he's accustomed to."

"And that's a bad thing?" I ask, and Lacey shrugs. "Maybe he could use a change. Doesn't seem like his usual holds his interest, as the man has never in his life had a serious girlfriend, at least not that I've ever heard about. You could be his first."

"Oh, stop it." Lacey pushes my shoulder, and I laugh. "I would be nothing more than a plaything to that man, and you and I both know it."

"And that's a bad thing?"

Lacey smiles at me and I smile back because I like seeing Lacey like this. She looks like a million bucks in her new dress. Her hair is down and her make-up is light, but more than she usually wears, and right now she's sitting on the bed with me, legs crossed, a pillow in her lap, chewing on her fingernails. This casual behavior is so un-Lacey like and so wonderful at the same time. It feels like she's getting comfortable with herself for the first time since I've met her, and you just can't help but to smile at that.

"What are you wearing to dinner?" Lacey asks me, and I keep smiling. Lacey being concerned about clothing options is just another sign of some epic change she's going through.

"I was thinking one of my little black dresses. You?"

"Not sure. Will you help me find something?" She looks away from me. "I want to look nice."

"You bet I will. Will you let me do your make-up too? I promise to keep it light."

"Okay," she agrees, which is another positive sign. "I like that lipstick you've been wearing today."

"The red?" *Three for three!* "Well then let's get started, Juliet. Your Romeo awaits!"

CHAPTER 12 - SIMON

By the time dinner rolls around, I'm completely hammered, which is perfect for me, but the rest of the guys seem to have a problem with it. What the hell do they care anyway? I'm out after this, so I may as well go out with a bang.

"You all right, Si?" Ollie asks, as I accidentally stumble on our way to dinner. Wasn't my fault. Must have been a bump in the carpet or something.

"Yeah, mate. Totally fine."

I start concentrating a little more on my walking, so the guys will stop giving me the *eat shit* looks. They're killing my buzz.

When we finally make it to the banquet room door, James stops and turns to face the rest of us. *Splendid*, I think, as I prepare myself for one of his speeches.

"This is important," James starts, "at least to some of us," he adds, glancing over at me. "These fans paid a lot of money to be on this cruise, and I think we owe it to them to make sure they have the best vacation imaginable."

I give my head a shake, trying to rid it of the fuzziness. I need food. Food will help. I'll feel better after dinner.

"Did you hear me, Simon?"

I lift my head, searching for whoever just said my name, but they're all looking at me.

"What?" I give them all a look, until James finally hangs his head.

"I know you're angry, but can you just try and behave?" James requests in a weary voice. "We can talk later, when you sober up, but for now, for the fans...please just try."

If I wasn't so full of whiskey right now, I probably could have been adult about this. I probably would have said something like "Sure. I'd do anything for the fans." But instead...

"Fuck you, James." I turn and look at Ollie and Rob. "And fuck you both as well. And fuck you too Xander!" I yell back to our fat arsed manager, Xander, but he barely looks up from his iPad to acknowledge me. "How about you all stop pretending like you give a shit about me? It's becoming quite irritating."

James's face is resigned, and I'm not drunk enough to handle all of that disappointment. So I shove past him and make my way into the banquet room. I guess the MC was supposed to announce us because he starts scrambling when I enter. Oh well.

Someone approaches me, and I stop so I can focus on her face. She's quite a beauty, so I give her a smile.

"Hello, Mr. Young." She sighs and I toss her a wink. Damn, they make it too easy. "Let me show you to your table."

She moves in front of me to lead the way, and my eyes slide down to her full hips. *Hell yeah.* I could deal with some of that later on.

I lean toward her a bit as we walk. "What's your name, love?" I ask, and she turns her head slightly with a shy smile.

She's attractive – nice build, sexy brown eyes and dark red hair – but I have a feeling this one isn't as shy as she may have me think.

"Layla," she tells me and gives me a wink as we approach what I assume is my table.

I repeat her name and extend my hand. "Hopefully, we'll meet again soon."

Layla takes my hand and gives me another deceivingly shy smile. "I hope so," she says, then turns to walk away. I watch her for a moment, just long enough to see her throw me a look over her shoulder that is far from shy. Yeah, I'll certainly be on the lookout for Ms. Layla later this evening.

I'm about to turn back to my table when my eyes are drawn to a flash of blonde hair not far to my right. Up until now, I had temporarily forgotten the reason for my recent obsession with the hair color. And unfortunately, also thanks to the liquor, my brain is too slow to tell my eyes not to go there.

Fucking Jack Daniels. I thought we were friends, mate?

The worst part is, by the time my drunken brain catches up, I realize she's staring straight at me and I can't look away. My eyes lock with those aquamarine beauties, and I nearly fall to my knees, spellbound, eager to soak up all of the warmth and comfort those eyes are giving me. What is it about this woman?

A small part of me – a very, very small part – knows I need to turn and greet the people at my table. I'm here for a reason, even though I may not be one hundred percent sure at the time what exactly that reason may be. I think fans are involved? Dinner maybe? I have no clue. All I know is that Sydney looks stunning. Her long, blonde hair is down and draped over bare shoulders. Since she's sitting down, I have no clue what she's wearing, but it doesn't matter, as long as I can see those gorgeous eyes. I do notice her cheeks are flush as she stares at me, and her lips are perfectly pink, perfectly kissable.

Just as I'm about to move toward her, Sydney looks down, breaking our eye contact and thankfully breaking the spell, but I can't seem to entirely rid myself of that moment. *Shit.* I need more liquor. Or food. Something.

I take a deep breath and finally turn to my table. It's filled with a dozen or so fans, all watching me intently, looking like they may lose it soon if I don't do something.

"Good evening, my lovelies."

I watch as everyone smiles and relaxes into their seats. That was easy enough.

I force myself to sit without taking another glance over at Sydney, which takes way more effort than I can afford at the moment.

"So, what are we eating? I'm starved," I tell the table, and they all giggle and start filling me in on dinner.

I look down to see a salad in front of me, and it seems some form of chicken is coming at us soon. Sounds good because it's going to take a constant stream of alcohol to keep my Venus out of my head all night.

I somehow managed to get through dinner without glancing back at Sydney once. I also don't think I upset any of the fans either, but it's hard to tell. Despite the four-course meal, I'm still royally pissed. But everyone seemed to be having a good time, and I made sure to kiss hands and toss out a few winks and smiles for good measure.

Thankfully, we don't have to perform tonight. Making it through a show right now would take a miracle. Instead, we have a welcome party that normally lasts through the night. I kind of wish I could skip the damn thing, head back to my suite and drink myself to sleep, but unfortunately I have to make an appearance. And besides, I think I may like to pick myself up a tasty treat for the evening, never mind my earlier thoughts about taking a break from women. Maybe shagging another girl senseless will help rid my mind of all things blue eyes, blonde hair and warm smiles. Seemed to work fine last night.

I'm waiting now with the other guys in a small room as the party gets going. We're to be announced before we enter, and I already got scolded for jumping the gun at dinner.

Ollie's sitting next to me, but no one's talking. I know they're angry with me, but I really don't give a shit. Not right now.

I rest my elbows on my knees and lay my head in my hands, knowing that I will give a shit soon enough. Tomorrow, when the alcohol's all gone, I will definitely give a shit. And based on several thousand past experiences, I know it's going to hurt something awful.

That thought sends me to a right nasty place, just in time for Xander to tell us it's go time. Wonderful. This party should be a fucking blast.

CHAPTER 13 - SYDNEY

"When are they getting here?" Lacey asks anxiously at my side. "It felt like dinner lasted forever."

I smile, feeling so happy for her and all of the flirty looks she got from Ollie during dinner. I wish I could share in her enthusiasm. The one odd look I shared with Simon at dinner didn't exactly leave me hopeful. And I could tell he was wasted. I recognized the familiar behavior from the restaurant last night.

I swear I felt him undress me with his eyes though. Those soulful, brown eyes. I've never had anyone be able to level me with a look like he seems to do, and I'd be lying if I said it didn't scare me a little.

Just as I'm about to share my thoughts with Lacey, someone speaks into the mic.

"All right everyone, I think I have something to help get this party started!"

The entire crowd starts screaming, and Lacey and I are no exception.

"Why don't you all help me welcome your party starters – The London Boys!"

The roar of the crowd is unbelievable as the guys make their way into the room. This party is being held in one of the restaurants on deck, and Lacey and I are seated at a high-top near the bar area which, due to a lucky coincidence, happens to be just feet away from where the guys are entering.

Ollie immediately finds Lacey and gives her a huge smile and a wink. *Swoon.*

Simon is walking behind everyone else, head down, hands in his pockets. My heart flutters at the sight of him wrapped in dark jeans, a black t-shirt and his trademark Docs, but I can tell he's wrecked in more ways than one it seems.

I look at the other guys and they're all smiling, but if you look closely, you can tell something's wrong. And I have a feeling a drunk Simon may be the root of the problem.

As they approach the stage, Simon finally looks up and does a quick scan of the crowd. His eyes are heavy and he's wearing a lazy smile, which happens to be ridiculously sexy, but it wouldn't take a genius to see it's alcohol induced.

Simon takes one hand out of his pocket as Ollie hands him a mic. All of the guys are waving and I notice the crowd is getting thicker in here by the second. I hold on to the table so I don't get knocked off my stool.

"I love you Simon!" Some random girl yells at the top of her lungs, and all of the guys laugh.

"I love you too," Simon says with an adorable grin.

"I wanna fuck you Simon!" someone else yells, and a collection of gasps and cheers fills the room.

Lacey looks over at me with wide eyes and we both can't help but to gape at the person's boldness.

"Find me later, love," Simon says into the mic, and a strange feeling surges through me. Jealousy.

God, this is going to be a long five days.

James says a few words, as soon as the girls finally calm down and stop drooling over Simon, then the announcer grabs the mic before the crowd has a chance to get going again.

"Now remember everyone," the announcer starts, "these guys want a chance to meet as many of you as possible tonight, so please be courteous and respectful of their time. You have four more days with them, so I promise you'll have your turn at some point. At the end of the day, we're all here to have a good time, right?" Everyone cheers loudly as a waitress walks onto the stage and hands each of the guys a drink. "I hope you all have a great evening! Cheers!"

The announcer raises his own drink as everyone takes a moment to toast, then the guys find their way off the stage and into the crowd. I sit on my stool and watch as Simon and Ollie are swarmed by dozens of salivating females.

Ugh. Why am I being so catty? I'm better than that, and I keep repeating those words in my head as I watch Simon work the crowd once again. Slowly, the bitchiness and jealousy turn to appreciation. I love the way his warm smile calms and reassures everyone around him, making it obvious Simon gives his whole heart to his fans. He's incredible. Just incredible.

As I'm lost in my adoration, Simon glances up from his harem and his eyes find mine. I'm puzzled by the longing I see there, as if he's begging me to come to him, to save him. I can feel my own face mirroring his for a moment, but after everything that's happened between us already, I don't want to embarrass myself any further. I quickly rearrange my features and give him a small smile – a suitable, professional smile – and a wave.

I'm confused when Simon's face suddenly hardens and the side of his mouth quirks up as he stares at me. The devious grin makes my skin crawl. *What in the hell?* I continue to watch as he takes a large sip of his drink and wraps his arm around the shoulders of a blonde girl standing next to him. He leans and whispers something in her ear, and she giggles as she gives all of the other girls her best "I win" smile.

I feel sick. I think it's obvious at this point that Simon remembers me from last night, but wishes he didn't. Maybe he feels betrayed, after discovering who I am this afternoon. Maybe he's still pissed off at the guys. Or maybe, by some long shot, he felt something there between us last night the same way I did and maybe that scares him.

Regardless of what the case may be, I need to get any hope of that last "maybe" out of my head.

"Are you okay?" Lacey asks, rescuing me from my thoughts.

"I'm great."

I fake a smile for my friend. No need to bother Lacey with my irrational Simon obsessing.

Lacey smiles back. "Do you want to go dance or something? Maybe talk to some fans?"

"Let's get another drink first, okay?"

Lacey nods excitedly, but before we can leave our table, up walks Ollie with a huge smile on his face. He looks amazing tonight in jeans, Nikes and a light green t-shirt that matches his pretty eyes.

"Hello, ladies." *Goodness*, those accents are sexy. I look over at Lacey to make sure she's still breathing. "Having a good time so far?"

Lacey smiles widely at him, and I watch Ollie's eyes soften as he stares at her. It seems he's just as smitten, and I couldn't be happier for Lacey.

"We're having a great time," she tells Ollie. "We were about to go get a drink and do some dancing."

Ollie takes her hand in his and kisses the top. I know Lacey must be trembling all over because I can feel the heat from his stare and it's not even directed at me.

"Save one of those dances for me?"

"If you're lucky," she tells him with a wink, and I smile.

Un-freaking-believable what a hot dress and a pair of killer heels will do for a girl's confidence.

"Well, lucky for *you*, I'm a gambling man. I'll find you later, love." Ollie waves at us both, then turns and makes his way back through the crowd. Once he's out of sight, Lacey's cool demeanor disappears.

"Good Lord," she breathes as she puts a death grip on my hand. "Did that just happen?"

"Lacey, the way he was looking at you...that man's got it bad."

"Whatever," she brushes off my comment, back to the old Lacey I know and love. "He's only offering as a courtesy to us as business partners. I'm sure James told him to make sure we have a good time on this trip. He's only being nice."

I don't know why I'm shocked by her statement. It's typical Lacey, but what shocks me is that she really seems to believe it. Could she really be that *blind*?

Lacey laughs. "Doesn't mean I can't have some fun with it though, right? The guy is gorgeous, and even if it is a courtesy from him, I'll still enjoy being pressed close to him for a song or two."

I decide to leave it alone for now, but I'll talk some sense into this girl one of these days, even if it kills me. "Our friendship is officially over if you don't take advantage of that opportunity. Have I taught you nothing?"

Lacey grabs my face and kisses my forehead. "Let's go get some drinks and get this party started!"

I dance with Lacey for a while, and decide I need some air. Lacey chooses to stay on the dance floor with some new friends we've made, so I make my way out of the restaurant and head toward the pool area.

I'm disappointed to see it's really crowded, so I decide to take a detour. I find some steps that lead me up to the very top deck, which is vacant at the moment, probably because everyone is still partying hard a floor below me. And really, there's not much up here except a few games – shuffleboard and paddle tennis – and a couple of rows of deck chairs on either side. To my left I see an observation deck, and I head that way, stopping several feet from the railing. I take a few deep breaths, trying to reason through my fear, but as I'm trying to relax, images of Simon's tongue sliding up and down some lucky blonde's neck come popping into my head. Oh well, at least that temporarily takes my mind off my fear of boats.

I stay backed up against a wall and remove my heels, dropping them to the floor. I look out over the ocean, and the peaceful sounds help me to relax a little.

After a few minutes of feeling hopelessly sorry for myself, I wipe a lone tear from my eye and groan. Why in the hell am I crying? *Oh for goodness sake, Syd*. No tears. Not now. I need to focus. I need to focus on my livelihood and stop with all of these ridiculous fantasies. I close my eyes. *Focus, Sydney. Focus!*

I stay a while longer, trying in vain to clear my head, and when I finally decide to head back to the party, I hear soft footsteps coming toward me. Assuming it's Lacey, I make one last swipe at my eyes to make sure all evidence of my personal pity party have been erased.

"Hello?"

My eyes go wide at the unexpected greeting...well, not so much at the greeting as the voice.

"How about some company?" Simon asks, and even though I will my body to relax, it's not happening.

When I feel him near me, I turn to my left and he's standing there, looking very wasted...*again*...but still heart-stoppingly beautiful. I reluctantly pry my eyes from his and look back out at the ocean.

"Want some company?" he asks again and all I can think is that I really hope my knees don't give out. I should have picked a spot with chairs.

"Why not." I shift back and forth on my feet, trying to get some feeling back in my legs. The next thing I know, I'm stumbling and Simon is quick to reach a hand out to help me.

He grabs my upper arm, keeping me on my feet and I close my eyes, wondering how many more times I can humiliate myself in this man's presence.

"Sorry about that," I mutter. "And if you can believe it, I'm completely sober."

Simon laughs, and it's a nice sound. "You know, if you were looking for a way to touch me, we could have worked something out. No need to put yourself in danger, love."

Although the conceited smirk that follows is rather sexy, I snag my arm back and concentrate my stare back out at the ocean. His comment was just another reminder of what an absolute jerk he can be. I feel like crying again.

"If I wanted to touch you, I doubt you would have objected," I snap, surprising myself. "I'm breathing and I have breasts – just your type."

"Ouch."

I look at him out of the corner of my eye and I'm surprised to see he looks genuinely hurt. The man is a walking contradiction.

"I'm sorry. I shouldn't have said that. I'm just feeling a little stressed out. A little...overwhelmed at the moment. No need to take it out on you."

Simon pauses, as if considering my statement. "No problem. I can be very overwhelming."

I continue to look straight ahead, deciding not to respond to that one. Mainly because he's exactly right.

"Look, Sydney..."

"It's fine, Simon," I quickly interrupt. "I have no idea what you were about to say, but just save it, okay?"

Simon chuckles, causing my blood to boil. He obviously thinks this is all a joke, thinks *I'm* a joke. Well, he can think again.

I turn to face him, and I can feel my nostrils flaring and my eyes narrowing as my anger sets in. I have no idea why I'm so angry right now. All I know is I can't let him get to me this time, with his perfect hair and his perfect face and his perfect...*everything*!

"I'm starting to..." I stop, unable to say the word "regret" because it doesn't feel right. "Simon, I'm not sure what happened between us last night, and I feel like I should thank you for not outing me in the meeting this afternoon, but I want you to know something. I came on this ridiculous cruise, even though I'm terrified of boats, because this is a wonderful opportunity for me, and I want to help you guys the best I can. You owe me nothing but your cooperation and some professionalism. No more heated stares, no kissing, no touching, no apologies needed. Let's just forget it ever happened. Agreed?"

My chest is heaving by the time I'm done. And I wait impatiently, hands on my hips, for a response, but Simon just stands in front of me with that sexy smirk back on his face.

"So, I can't even look?" he asks, and I gawk at him.

"Excuse me?"

"Why don't you like boats?"

That's it. I start to walk past him, ignoring his question, but he reaches out and grabs my hand before I can get too far.

"You didn't answer my question." I turn back to face him, and he glances down at his hand holding mine, then back up at me. "Why are you afraid of boats, goddess?"

Wait. Did he just call me *goddess*?

"Simon..." I give my head a shake to try and clear it. "Out of everything I just said to you, that's what you think is most important? Really?"

"No, no." Simon gives me a sad laugh. "I heard everything loud and clear, but I genuinely have no response for the rest at the moment. However, I think I can help with this whole boat thing."

"I doubt it."

Now I'm extremely aware of his thumb slowly stroking the top of my hand. He obviously missed the "no touching" portion of my speech.

"Let me ask you this," he starts, a thoughtful look on his face, "what would happen if you stood at the railing of this boat with me?"

"I may die."

Simon smiles. "Not likely."

"Well, I would probably pass out or have a panic attack." I shudder. "'I may have one just thinking about it."

"Okay." Simon looks deep in thought now, and I start to wonder where he's going with this. "But would a panic attack kill you?"

"Of course not."

"So, if there's no chance of death or even bodily harm, what are you afraid of? A little panic attack?" he tsks. "I could induce something similar without you even getting near the side of this boat – no fear necessary."

"What do you mean?"

"Well, as I was saying..." Simon leans in closer and laces his fingers through mine. "A silly panic attack is nothing to be afraid of. It's just a physical reaction to something that frightens or overwhelms you, right?" I manage a nod. "Well, what if you associated that same reaction, those same symptoms, with something a little less scary? Maybe then, the next time you were afraid of something, your reaction would trigger a different feeling like excitement or exhilaration instead of fear."

Okay, I have no idea where he's going with this, but I've said my peace, and he's being a little too friendly now. *Way* too friendly, as a matter of fact, and I don't need to fall into this trap again. I need to walk away. I need to politely say goodbye and walk...

Simon squeezes my hand and *God* how I love the feel of his long fingers tangled with mine. And by the look on Simon's face, he's very aware of that fact.

"So, the first thing that happens is your pulse quickens, yeah?" Simon brushes the fingertips of his free hand from my temple to my chin, then down my neck to the base of my throat.

My eyes flutter closed. Quickening pulse? Absolutely.

"Excellent," Simon whispers, as he places his hand over my heart. My eyes pop open just in time to watch him lean closer so we're cheek to cheek.

Dear God, I need to get out of here. *Leave, Sydney! Walk away!*

"Next your breathing becomes erratic." He tugs gently on my earlobe with his teeth. "And you may start to feel a bit dizzy," he breathes, while raining feather-light kisses from right below my ear to my bare shoulder.

Screw it. I'm not going anywhere.

A soft whimper escapes my lips, and I feel Simon smile against my shoulder. He releases my hand and puts an arm around my waist, pulling me against him. "Now, close those beautiful eyes for me," he commands, and I do as he says.

When I feel him take a step backward, I wrap my arms tightly around his waist and bury my face in his chest. Simon continues to pull me toward the railing of the boat, and I breathe in the smell of his cologne and try to concentrate on the feel of his arms around me as he walks. It helps a little, until Simon stops and moves to pull my arms from around his waist. I squeeze tighter. *No.*

"I'm between you and the edge, goddess," he assures me. "I won't let anything happen to you. I promise."

I take a deep breath and allow him to place my hands on the railing, so he's now the only thing standing between me and one of my worst fears.

The moment my fingers touch the railing, I feel all of the air escape my lungs in one quick gust. I keep my face pressed against his chest, eyes closed, trying to find the place I was in before – the smell of his cologne, the feel of his body against mine – but it's not working.

I start gasping for air against him, and Simon wraps his arms back around me and pulls me in closer. He tries to move me back toward the wall, but my fingers are gripping the steel bar so tightly I hinder his efforts.

He falls back against the railing, and holds me close. "It's okay," he soothes. "I shouldn't have pushed you. I'm so sorry."

Simon starts pushing me back toward the wall again, but I'm determined now to face this fear and rescue this moment with him.

I slowly lift my face from his chest and move my eyes directly to his. I don't have to see the railing or the water behind him. I want to focus solely on his face.

I'm much shorter than he is with no shoes on, but it doesn't matter. Simon is staring intently into my eyes, and my first thought is that there is no better view than the one right in front of me.

"I'll protect you," he whispers. "I want you to believe that."

And I do. I don't know why, but I do. Maybe it's his surprising sincerity in this moment, his eyes desperate for me to believe him, to trust him. Or maybe it's because for some unknown reason, I really do trust Simon. I have no rational explanation, but like most things with him, I just *feel* it.

I remove one hand from the railing and press it against Simon's lower back, palm flat. I steady myself then move my hand slowly around, and Simon inhales sharply when I slide my fingers over his tight stomach, up to his chest, then around his neck. *Oh God,*

Sydney. What are you doing? Now I'm more scared than ever, but it has nothing to do with boats.

Simon looks at me warily, as if he's afraid he's crossed the line with his little stunt, but I kind of love him for it. I know now that not even one of my worst fears or my job apparently, can come between me and my need to be close to him.

I remove my other hand and quickly place it on his shoulder. And just to prove to him that my fear no longer seems to exist in his presence, I turn slowly in a circle and pull him with me, until I'm the one wedged between him and the ship's railing.

Simon's eyes go suddenly wide, but then something dark and feral replaces his shock and I shiver at the sight. He leans in closer, his arms wound tightly around my waist, as he presses me hard against the railing. It doesn't bother me in the least. I welcome the pressure and the heat.

Simon's nostrils flare, as his gaze roams my face. And my breathing stops all together when he puts his sweet lips on mine.

I know I shouldn't let him kiss me. I should be angry with the way he's treated me so far, like I'm some kind of plaything so easily discarded. I should be angry with myself for allowing this to happen – for falling prey to his player ways, for possibly hurting my friend Ethan by not taking my career more seriously.

But when trembling hands clench the silk fabric of my dress and pull me close, I know there's no way I can refuse him – in any way, for any reason. And as if he wanted to bring that point home, his tongue slows its assault and starts gently massaging mine, and the rhythm has my head spinning Nascar style.

I wrap both my arms around his neck, searching for some stability, but once my hands reach the back of his hair, an extremely sexy sound rumbles deep in his chest and leaves me anything but steady.

"*Fuck*," Simon rasps against my lips as he pulls me backward, and this time I let him take me.

He pushes me against the wall, and as soon as I feel the cold surface against my back, he grabs the back of my thighs and lifts me up. My legs eagerly wrap around him, my traitorous body obviously intent on obeying his every demand.

I whisper his name as his mouth slides down my neck, causing that sexy sound to vibrate deep in his chest once more. I know my voice seems needy and desperate, but I've had a weak spot for Simon for years. And now, with everything that's happened over the past twenty-four hours, I'm completely defenseless.

Simon grinds against me, pushing me further into the wall as his mouth moves back to mine, tantalizing me with its insanely seductive movements. If I were to compare the moments between us, this one seems different from last night. Last night, it felt like Simon was looking for comfort from someone, anyone. But right now, it feels more like he was looking for...*me*.

All too soon, Simon pulls away, leaving me with some more of those delicious nibbles he likes to give my bottom lip. After a few quiet minutes to catch our breath, Simon lowers me back down with a sweet smile, but keeps a firm hold on my waist. I start moving my fingers through his hair and grin inside at the instant effect it has on him.

He dips his head down to give me better access to the back of his neck, and with his face right next to my mouth, I can't resist. I turn and brush my lips lightly across his cheek, and he stills for a moment before burying his face into my neck. His hands move slowly up my back, and we find ourselves in yet another heated embrace just enjoying each other's warmth and touch and nothing else.

CHAPTER 14 - SIMON

Oh God, what am I doing? I can't keep playing with this girl's head. Or is she playing with mine? Intentions seem blurry at best as she runs those gentle fingers through my hair. Her presence alone is more soothing than any drink or drug I've ever tried, but her touch...her touch makes me feel like a new man.

I inhale shamelessly, taking in her delicious scent, as I trail greedy fingers down her back – mostly exposed by this barely-there dress she has on. Sydney trembles, and I hold her close, wondering if it's the after effects of that amazing kiss that's giving her the shakes or maybe she's still working through her fear. It could even be the fear of losing her job I suppose, but there's no need to worry about that. I'd be willing to lie, cheat or steal to have this woman in my arms. Her secret is safe with me.

"Are you all right?" My eyes roam her beautiful face, waiting for an answer.

"I'm perfect."

I keep my arms around her and start to walk backward, teasing her. And I'm surprised when she goes willingly, smiling as we go.

"I'm okay, Simon. Promise."

"You must really trust me." It's supposed to be an observation, but comes out more like a question.

"I do trust you," she says as we reach the railing, and I can see on her face that she's telling the truth.

And just like that, my lungs shut down, and I feel like I'm falling. A panic attack of my own starts building in my chest.

I don't deserve her trust. I don't deserve *her*.

"You don't even know me," I claim. "How can you trust me?"

"No idea. I just do." She gives me a small smile, her voice barely audible over the sound of the wind and the pounding of my heart. "Otherwise I probably wouldn't be risking life and limb on this moment."

"I like that you trust me."

I wince, silently punishing myself for my liquor-induced response. I see the surprise register on her face, and suddenly her touch feels like a branding iron that I'm foolishly holding on to knowing sooner or later, I'll have to let go.

I unwillingly drop my hands to my sides, and oddly enough, the pain doubles away from her touch. But I don't let her see that, no matter how much I may want to let her in.

"I have to go."

I look down at my boots and take a deep breath, wondering if maybe I should explain. Maybe someone like Sydney would understand. Maybe I could confide in her, tell her my secrets. Maybe I could tell her why I can't be with someone like her. I don't have to leave her this way. She deserves an explanation.

But when I look up, expecting anger, I'm met with disappointment instead. And just like her pity, it hurts more than anger ever could.

I'm speechless as Sydney closes her eyes and wraps her arms around her waist. "Look, Simon. I'm not sure what's going on between us, but what just happened...well, it can't happen again." Her eyes open but only so she can stare at the ground. "I shouldn't have let you do that, and I'm sorry if I led you on in any way, but this has to stop. I'm your business associate, not some groupie, and you can't play with me like this. I can't allow it."

Her tone grows firmer toward the end, until finally, she drops her arms and her eyes meet mine. The disappointment is gone now, replaced by a steady resolve, and fuck me if I'm not completely mesmerized by this incredible creature.

"You don't take my shit," I practically mumble, barely able to form a coherent sentence. "Why do I like that so much?"

Without thought, I take both of her hands in mine and dip down so our faces are level. "Sydney, it's extremely important that you know...the last thing I would want is for you to feel like anything other than the intelligent, kind, respectable lady that I know you are. You deserve nothing less."

"You don't know anything about me," she snaps, pulling her hands from mine, but I'm not giving up hope. Not yet.

"I know enough. And you should know that things aren't always as they seem." I lean in and give her a soft kiss on her cheek. I'll take the fact that she didn't pull away, or try and punch me, as a good sign. "Until tomorrow, goddess."

I put my hands in my pockets as I turn and walk away and wrap my fingers around the locket. I take a deep breath and squeeze it tight. I sure could use some luck right about now.

CHAPTER 15 - SYDNEY

I watch, dumbfounded as he walks away from me.

Things aren't always what they seem? Could he have been any more cryptic?

I stay on the side of the boat, trying to keep the tears out of my eyes for several minutes after Simon leaves. What kind of person plays with someone's mind like that?

Oh, who am I kidding? I'm just as guilty as he is.

I grudgingly slip my shoes back on, cringing as they grip my swollen feet like a vice, but I need to find Lacey before she calls out a "missing persons".

I finally make it downstairs and back toward the restaurant. "Sydney! Over here!" I hear my name called and sigh with relief at the sound of Lacey's voice.

"Sydney, what's wrong?" she asks as soon as I'm in front of her on the dance floor. "Are you okay?"

"I'm fine. I just went to get some air and got a little spooked when I took a step too close to the side of the ship."

I try and smile convincingly, and it seems to work. Lacey bursts out laughing and pulls me in for a hug. "Oh, what we're willing to do for our careers, right?"

I shrug my shoulders and start to dance, wanting to end the conversation. Lacey takes the cue and starts dancing along with me. I try and concentrate on losing myself in the music and dancing Simon Young right out of my head.

I spend another hour or so on the dance floor with Lacey until I can't stand being in these dreadful heels any longer.

"I think I'm going to call it a night," I tell Lacey. "Do you want to stay?"

"No, I'll go with you."

We both start to exit the dance floor, but before we can get past all of the gyrating bodies, Ollie comes walking toward us with a huge grin on his face.

"So, I'm feeling lucky," he says to Lacey when he reaches us. "What do you say, love?"

Lacey looks to me and I smile. "Go. Just be careful, and I'll see you later."

"You be careful, too. I'll see you later."

Lacey gives me a hug and a wave, then turns toward Ollie and wraps her arms around his neck. I'm so happy for her that I'm smiling like crazy as I continue to make my way through the crowd and hopefully toward some pajamas and a nice comfy bed.

I take one last look back at Lacey before I exit through the restaurant doors. I can barely see her through the crowd on the dance floor, but I do catch a few glimpses of her dancing with Ollie. I don't think I've ever seen her look so happy.

I turn and continue through the doors and onto the pool deck. The crowd is thick out here as well, but I push through all of the happy party goers as fast as my sore feet will take me.

"Hi Sydney," I hear as I'm nearing the elevators and my heart sinks. It's James, and he doesn't sound happy.

I quickly collect myself and turn toward him. "Hi James. How's it going?"

"It's good. Have you been enjoying the party?"

Scared that I may be wearing this Simon nonsense all over my face, I check his features trying to see if there's some kind of accusation in his eyes, but there's nothing there.

"The party's been great." I force another smile. "Lacey and I chatted with some fans here and over dinner. We think we're gathering some great information to get us started. I look forward to talking with you guys though and getting your ideas."

"Definitely," James agrees. "We'll get that started tomorrow."

"Perfect."

James smiles, but a frown quickly follows. "Sydney, I just want to apologize again for what happened earlier at the meeting. I haven't had a chance to talk to Simon yet. I'm sure you've noticed he's not in a good state this evening, but I hope to have a chat with him tomorrow." He runs a hand through his dark hair. "I want you to know Simon really is a good guy. He's having a hard time of it lately, and after we discussed our plans for him leaving the group...well, of course he didn't take it well."

"I understand, James. I really do," I interrupt him, not wanting to talk about Simon anymore tonight. "As a fan, I'm aware of what he's been through, and the kind of person he is. I promise to handle him carefully."

"Yes, well it's also important that you know this was no easy decision for me or the rest of the guys."

Break. My. Heart. Why don't you?

"I can't imagine it would be. Let's just hope everything works out for the best."

James gives me a sad smile. "Goodnight, Sydney."

"Goodnight." I wave goodbye and walk away, happy that conversation is over.

By the time I reach the elevators, there's hardly a soul around, and I'm grateful for the quiet. When I make it to our cabin, I remove my horribly painful shoes and toss them in a corner. I fall onto my bed and lie on my back, then stare at the ceiling and wonder how in the hell I'm ever going to make sense of these random encounters I've had with Simon – each one a little more confusing than the last.

I hate myself for giving into my weakness for him, and I'm angry with him for taking advantage of that weakness. But ultimately, what frightens me the most is how I seem to lose myself with even the slightest touch from him. I immediately cave, like there's no choice in the matter, and that loss of control, that loss of self, it's not something I'm used to and it's certainly not something I'm comfortable with. It's obvious Simon is wrong for me in so many ways, but it seems I can't resist him. And I'm not sure I want to anymore.

I curl onto my side and continue to try and make sense of the situation, but my eyes start to close and I eventually fall into a restless sleep before I get anywhere close to a solution.

CHAPTER 16 - SIMON

Well, this is new.

I'm lying in my bed, with a beautiful girl wrapped around me, her tongue eager and warm as it glides along mine, but I feel nothing. Absolutely. Nothing.

You would think that feeling, that nothingness, would be welcome since that's exactly what I've been trying to achieve all day. But it's not. It's not welcome. It's horrible because I'm tired of feeling nothing. It seems my senses have recently been reawakened, and this poor girl's company is not the company I'm seeking.

It's Sydney. She's ruined me.

I've tried flirting. I've tried drinking. I've done everything I could to get those blue eyes out of my head, but I can't do it. Even now, as this random stranger runs her hands through my hair and down my back, I'm envisioning Sydney – Sydney's slim fingers brushing my neck as they comb through the back of my hair, Sydney's velvet lips moving slowly, timidly against mine. My hands still tingle from caressing her soft skin. The sound of her voice, as she whispered my name, is still ringing in my ears.

Every time she's around me, I'm drawn to her like a moth to a flame. I swore to myself I wasn't going to mess with her again, but my body followed her out onto that deck tonight by its own will. I tried to talk myself out of it, but it seems Jack Daniels betrayed me once again, working hand in hand with my dick and ignoring everything else. I've got to quit that rat bastard.

I'm trying to pretend. I'm trying to forget. But nothing's working. It's obviously time to accept the fact that the fantasy is simply not enough. Nothing but the real thing will do.

"I'm sorry." I push the girl away and sit up in bed. I don't even remember her name. I'm such a dick.

"What's the matter, Simon?" she asks, and I can't bear to look at her.

"I'm sorry, but I can't do this." I scrub my hands over my face and stand up. "You're lovely, but I think...I'm just too wasted. Maybe another time."

I move to the kitchen, in search of a bottle of water, still unable to look in the poor girl's direction. Soon after, I hear her get up from the bed and pause behind me, but I don't turn around. I close my eyes instead, wishing she would just leave already so I can pass out and forget this fucking day ever happened.

Finally, I hear her walk toward the door and I breathe what I hope is a discreet sigh of relief. She opens the door and when I don't hear her close it, I turn my head slightly in that direction, still not fully allowing my shameful eyes to meet hers.

"You don't have to lie, you know."

"I'm sorry?"

"Look, Simon." The girl shakes her head with a shrewd smile. "I know coming here with you after seeing you with several different girls tonight may seem pretty desperate of me, but I'm not an idiot. I know what I want, and I was willing to do whatever it took to get it. Too bad you can't say the same."

And with that, the remarkably insightful girl closes the door behind her without looking back.

I stand at the counter a moment longer, letting that little zinger settle in. Believe it or not, I feel strangely sober now and if possible, like even more of a shit. I move over to the sofa and take a seat as I start playing through today's and tonight's events in my head. The first thing to note is I've spent the last twenty-four hours trying to get Sydney out of my mind, and no matter what I do, it's not working.

Sure, she's gorgeous, and I'm obviously having quite a time keeping my hands off her. But there's something else there, as if just being around her is satisfying enough.

I guess she could at least serve to keep my mind off what's going on between me and the guys while we're on the cruise, but now that I think about it, the idea of only having a few days with her makes me anxious. *Dammit.* This is all very foreign but totally fascinating, and I know for certain it's going to take more than one night with her for me to figure this out.

I wonder if I still have a chance to make things right. Not in a million years could I ever be a good enough person to deserve what I feel when I'm around her, but I want her. *No.* It's stronger than that. I *need* her. And if it's too late, so be it. But I at least have to try.

After nearly two hours of tossing and turning in my bed, I realize sleep is going to be a waste of time tonight. I think about polishing off another bottle of whiskey, but I just don't have the stomach for it. I decide instead to give up on sleeping and hope I can catch a nap at some point during the day.

Sitting up in bed, the one thing I know for certain is that I need to escape the confines of this room, and I need a little more space than even my balcony will allow. I get up and throw on some shorts and a t-shirt. I slip on my Converse, run a hand through my hair and make my way toward the door. I hate the thought of possibly running into fans in such a state, but at nearly five in the morning, I hope most everyone will most likely still be down for the night.

I slowly exit my suite and the hallway is dead silent. The security guards are seated at the end of the hall, one playing with his phone, the other reading a newspaper.

They both turn toward me when they hear my door close. "I'm going for a walk. I'll be back in a bit."

"You may need an escort," the dark-haired one says to me. He stands and drops his paper in his chair. "I'll accompany you."

"No, I'll be fine," I assure him. "I doubt many people are out and about at this hour."

The guard nods once in agreement. "We have security stationed throughout the ship. If you need anyone, you shouldn't have to look too far."

"Thanks, but I'm certain I'll be fine."

I walk for a while and just as I suspected, the ship is pretty much deserted. I make my way up a couple of flights of stairs to the main deck. I smile politely at a few staff members scurrying about to prepare for the day, but they couldn't be less interested in me.

I continue walking toward my destination – the observation deck where I had my encounter last night with Sydney. It's still dark out, and the sound of the boat rushing through the water is incredibly soothing. When I finally reach the deck and stand at the railing, I wrap my arms around my chest bracing against the wind as the boat travels on, probably nearing our destination for today. I close my eyes and let the sounds and smells rush through me as I try my best to clear my head. I'm sober now and have a much clearer picture of how my emotions got the best of me last night, yet again. And as usual when that happens, the weight of the regret is a lot to bear.

I'll have to find some time today to apologize to the guys. I'm still angry, of course, but they didn't deserve what I gave them last night, especially Ollie. And hopefully, I'll find some time to apologize to Sydney as well. I'm not sorry for kissing her. I could never be sorry for that. But I did come on way too strong, thanks to the alcohol and how she seems to illicit these bizarre, uncontrollable urges when I'm around her. She probably thinks I'm a complete head case with all of my crazy mood swings, but it's because I've been fighting my feelings for her, and that stops today, if she'll have me.

I realize our business relationship may complicate things, but I'm certain we can find a way to work everything out. I have to at least give this a shot. I have no idea what the outcome will be, but it's been so long since I've wanted someone like this. It's terrifying, but I feel alive again, and it's quite the addictive high.

By the time I decide to head back, there's a hint of pink on the horizon announcing the sunrise. I glance around, thankful that at least the top deck is still deserted as I start to walk quickly, not wanting to be late for the breakfast this morning. But when I round the corner heading back toward the stairs, a familiar flash of blonde hair catches my eye.

There's no way this is possible.

I blink a few times and rub my eyes. It has to be a dream. Sleep walking would not be out of the question.

I take a couple of steps closer squinting in her direction. She's still several feet away near the stairs, but she was heading in this direction. Even from this distance, I can see she's looking right at me and she looks...*amazing.* Casual now, in short pink shorts and a sweatshirt to match, she's positively stunning. Her long hair is blowing wildly across her beautiful face, and her arms are wound tightly around her middle, except for every few seconds when she reaches one hand up to push one of the buttery-colored strands behind her ear. As I stare, her cheeks slowly flush and I smile.

I move toward the stairs and a few steps closer to my goddess, but just when I'm within speaking distance, she turns on her heel and starts walking in the opposite direction. *Fuck.* As if I needed any confirmation, that move tells me everything I need to know. I've ruined things, and I'm not sure there's any amount of charm or begging that will bring her back to me now.

I hang my head and sigh, resting my hands on my hips as I mentally punish myself for yet another selfish, ignorant act that ruined what could have been something special. *Par for the goddamn course, Simon.*

I start walking toward the stairs, head still down, trying to give myself a pep talk so I can at least make it through breakfast. But after a few steps, something pulls at my insides begging me to look up. So I do. And there she is.

I stop, now only a few feet away from her, but it's obvious something's changed in the air around us. I can feel it, and when I study her face I can see it. It's in her eyes. Something's changed. And my heart starts thumping in my chest when I realize it's a *good* change.

Her baby blue eyes are warm now as they caress my face, and I watch mesmerized as her gaze falls to my mouth. She slowly pulls her fingers up and brushes them along her bottom lip. *Christ*, I've never been more envious of a couple of fingers in my life.

Sydney's eyes move back to mine and she rewards me with a smile that's worth more than any words. The smile tells me I was wrong. It's not over. I doubt I'm forgiven, but I'm not yet forgotten and that's enough for me. At least for now.

I don't move from my spot until after Sydney is back down the stairs and out of sight. I remain standing a moment, soaking up what just happened between us, feeling wide awake and lighter than I've felt in years. I take off toward my suite with a huge grin on my face, eager to get this breakfast over with so I can start winning back my goddess.

CHAPTER 17 - SYDNEY

"So, how did things go last night with Ollie? Or are the glassy eyes and dreamy smile all I'm going to get out of you this morning?" I tease Lacey as we sit at breakfast, or brunch, I should say. We both had a hard time getting going this morning, and I haven't had a chance yet to really talk to her about last night.

"Ollie is a lot of fun," she tells me. "And he's an excellent dancer. My legs are so sore, but it was worth it."

"Well, how did you leave it? Hugs? Kisses? Marriage proposals?"

"Stop it." Lacey rolls her pretty green eyes. "You're going to have to give me at least a couple more days for a proposal," she adds with a wink.

"Who are you, and what have you done with my friend Lacey?"

Lacey smiles. "Actually, he was dancing with a lot of girls last night. Not just me." Then she adds, very nonchalantly, "but he did ask me to sit with him at dinner tonight."

"Are you serious? Like a date?"

"No, silly." Lacey laughs. "I'm sure it's to discuss business."

She's trying hard to hide it, but I can see the disappointment on her face.

"Lace, let me explain something to you," I start, eager to give her yet another lesson on how the male brain works. "I'm the account rep, so if he wanted to discuss business, don't you think he would have invited *me* to sit with him? If he made asking you seem like a business gesture, it's because he's trying to be polite so you don't get in trouble due to our working relationship."

I can see the doubt in her eyes, but she doesn't give me a chance to comment. "It doesn't matter either way, right? We *are* business associates, so nothing can happen between us, regardless."

I tense and shift uncomfortably in my chair, praying Lacey doesn't notice. "Lacey, I think he has the hots for you, and I don't think it's a huge deal to explore that. Just keep it quiet, at least until we get off the cruise. We'll figure the rest out later."

I glance down at my lap and wonder if I'm trying to convince Lacey of this because it would make me feel better about my own situation. In which case, I am a heinous bitch.

But I know that's not the case. I love Lacey, and I want her to be happy. Although it may be best that she keeps any PDA to a minimum on the cruise, she won't be working directly with Ollie in the future. I'm sure we can talk to Jasper and work something out when we get home.

And now I'm feeling very jealous.

Ugh. I suck at this "being an adult" nonsense.

"So, what about you?" Lacey asks, as she peruses the menu. "Anything exciting happen after you left me last night? And why were you up before dawn this morning?"

Hmmm... Am I ready to talk about all of this mess? I was up half the night thinking about it, and spent the other half being upset with myself for worrying so much over it. Most of the time, I'm pretty good at not overcomplicating things, but this whole situation has thrown me for a complete loop. And just when I think I have a handle on things, I'm slung right back into the whirlwind that is Simon Young and his fantastic kisses.

When I saw him on deck this morning, I'd been wandering around for a couple of hours, sifting through the details from last night and possibly making some headway on how to handle all of this chaos. But then I decided to go back to the observation deck – to return to the scene of the crime, so to speak – and there he was, looking so incredibly beautiful that every sensible thought I had just spent hours mulling over shot straight out of my head. How am I supposed to resist that? It's pointless to even try.

And that's the final conclusion I came to after seeing him this morning. I'm going to stop trying to resist. It's no use and I don't care anymore if I'm nothing but just another one of Simon Young's many one-night stands. If that's the only way I get to spend time with him, I'm all in. And if I accept the fact up front that that's all this will be, I should be fine. I'll keep my expectations low, and no one gets hurt, right? Right.

And I'm sure we can keep things a secret. It's just sex, which can be done late at night away from watchful eyes. Or in the middle of the afternoon in a broom closet somewhere. Or maybe if we found a really secluded spot on the beach in the Bahamas...

"Sydney?"

My eyes snap back to Lacey's. "Sorry. Must have zoned out for a second there."

"What were you thinking about just then?" she asks, but again doesn't give me a chance to answer, or in this case, come up with a good lie. "What happened last night, Sydney?"

I look around nervously, but luckily the room is pretty empty. Most everyone is already out enjoying the island, and the few remaining late risers, like Lacey and me, don't seem to be paying us any attention.

Just as I'm about to start, the waitress comes by for our orders. Lacey orders quickly, but my brain is doing nothing quickly at this point. I finally decide on oatmeal and fruit, realizing it doesn't matter because I probably won't be able to eat anything anyway.

"No more suspense," Lacey says after the waitress leaves. "You had better spill it. Now."

"Okay, okay..." I know I better hurry or I'll never get this out. "Simon and I had an...encounter last night."

Lacey's eyes and smile widen. "*Encounter*? Please, do tell."

"Well, when I left you on the dance floor that time to get some air, I went up to the top deck and I think Simon followed me."

"And what exactly happened on the top deck?"

"It wasn't a huge deal."

"Liar. What happened?"

I sit up in my chair and lean toward her so no one overhears. "We just talked a bit. No big deal."

"You're lying. Again."

"Okay we kissed," I add but throw my hand up to stop the explosion of excitement that I'm sure is about to come. "It was incredible, Lace. It truly was, but the way we left things was confusing to say the least. He laid some ambiguous line on me then gave me one last, really sweet goodbye kiss and off he went."

I look over at Lacey and she's smiling at me with a goofy look on her face. "Say that last part again."

"What are you talking about?"

"I just want to see your face again when you say that last part about the goodbye kiss. It was adorable."

"Stop it," I giggle. "Anyway, I'm not sure what to think about everything that's happened between us. I'm embarrassed to admit

I've put a ridiculous amount of thought into this over the past twelve hours or so, but I think I've come to a conclusion."

I look at her and wonder if I should confide in Lacey. It's not because I can't trust her. I'm just not sure I should involve her in this. What if something happens and she's guilty by association? I would never want to do anything to hurt Lacey or her future with the company.

"I don't want to get you in trouble."

"Don't even go there." Lacey waves a finger in front of my face. "You know that job is a means to an end for me anyway."

With a deep breath, I decide to give it a shot. "I'm not sure you're going to like my decision, but I could use your advice."

Lacey narrows her eyes at me, then gives me a small smile. "Go ahead."

I proceed to tell her about this morning with Simon and my resulting epiphany, and she's quiet the entire time. When I'm done, I wait for her to start scolding me loud enough for the entire boat to hear. Instead, she leans back in her chair, looking thoughtful.

"Sydney, if I'm being honest, I kind of love this decision. I love it so much I could jump on top of this table and announce it to the entire restaurant. But obviously I won't," she says, as my eyes go wide in horror. "However, I want to make sure...I want to make double, triple, quadruple sure you know what you're doing here. Are you sure you can handle this, Syd?"

Wait. What?

I know she's my friend, but I thought she would certainly shoot me down. It's career suicide, if nothing else.

"You think this is a good idea?"

"Sydney, this is the man of your dreams, and he has been since you were a young girl. If you have any kind of chance at romance with him, as your friend, I could never steer you away from that opportunity."

"But what about my job?"

"Why does anyone have to know?"

Lacey's face is so convincing, so calm and casual that I feel the hope continue to spring up inside me.

"I'm nervous. I have no idea if I can handle this," I openly admit. "But I do know I want more of him, and I'll take him any way I can get him. Does that sound horrible? That sounds so horrible."

Suddenly the chorus of Beyoncé's *Naughty Girl* is on repeat in my head. *Oh God.* What am I doing?

"That doesn't sound horrible." Lacey gives me a huge smile. "And I think you may be surprised. I don't think everything is as it seems with Simon Young."

My head pops up as she basically repeats his words from last night. Was that what he was referring to? Himself? That things are not what they seem with *him*? That idea opens an entirely new realm of possibilities that will surely keep me up all night tonight as well.

"I just want you to be careful," Lacey tells me, "and not just on the professional side."

"I understand," I smile. "But nothing's happened yet, and I actually have no idea if he'll even talk to me again. The man's mood swings are enough to keep my head spinning for days."

"Oh, he'll talk to you again."

"Do you really think so?"

"Most definitely."

"Why do you think so?"

"Because he's walking toward you right now."

I gasp, as Lacey's eyes look over my shoulder, presumably at Simon approaching us. My heart starts fluttering in my chest – a warm up before heading into a full sprint.

I take a deep breath, just as Simon pulls out the chair next to me and takes a seat.

"Good morning, ladies." His deep voice and sexy accent have goose bumps popping up across every inch of my skin. "Late breakfast?"

"It's vacation." I smile. "We slept in. Is that a crime?"

"I can see you're going to make this hard for me," Simon grins. "But I promise I *will* change your mind about me before we get off this boat."

I say nothing, but continue to smile at him as I take a sip of my water.

"And I know for a fact *you* didn't sleep in," he tells me. "You were up with the sun, same as me. And what a lovely morning it was, yeah? So incredibly beautiful, captivating, really. I've never experienced anything like it."

"You've never seen a sunrise before?" I ask, trying not to get lost in those sparkling brown eyes. This close up, I notice there are tiny flecks of gold in them.

Simon's mouth curves into a wicked grin as he leans in and places a kiss on my cheek. The kiss is brief, but the promise it holds thrills me to my core.

"You know I wasn't talking about the sunrise, goddess," he says, and after tossing a wink at Lacey, he stands and leaves the table.

"Wow. Just...*wow*," I hear Lacey say, but I'm barely paying attention as I turn in my seat and see Simon's still in the room.

He's talking to another table full of fans who are obviously excited about their unexpected guest, and just as I'm about to turn back to Lacey, Simon turns his head and I'm busted for staring. A genuinely happy smile spreads across his face as we gaze at each other, and I smile back at him before finally turning back around and facing my friend.

"You're really going to do this, right?" Lacey's face is deadly serious. "Because after that line he just dropped on you, I'll have to admit, I understand. Resisting that man would be impossible."

CHAPTER 18 - SIMON

"Simon, what's going on?" Ollie asks, but I continue my pacing. "You've been a bit dodgy the past couple of days. Well, dodgier than usual, at least."

I came back to my suite after seeing Sydney in the restaurant, hoping to work some things out in my head before I see her today on the island. This situation with Sydney has left me feeling good but edgy, and I wanted some time alone to think about my next move. So much for that.

"Is this still about what happened with the guys? Are you sure we should let this linger until after the cruise?" Ollie asks with a frown.

"I don't give a shit about that right now," I interrupt him, while raking my hands nervously through my hair.

"Well then what in the hell's going on?" Ollie takes a beer from the refrigerator, opens it and takes a drink. "I mean, last night you were acting like a total dick for example, but then today you seem fucking ecstatic. You taking the happy pills again, mate?" I grin as Ollie narrows his eyes and points a finger at me. "Or was it that waitress from last night? I saw you leave the party with her. Is she the reason for all your smiles today?"

When I don't answer, Ollie takes another swig of his beer waiting for me to explain. I move to the bedroom and throw myself down onto my bed. I feel spent from the lack of sleep last night, my recent pacing and of course the several near heart attacks I've suffered since meeting Sydney.

"You had better start talking, Si," Ollie commands from the living area.

"It's Sydney," I mumble, still not sure I want to talk about this, but...fuck it. "I thought I'd never see her again."

"Did you say *Sydney*? As in our new PR rep, Sydney?"

"That's the one." I pull myself up into a sitting position on the bed and face Ollie. "I met her for the first time the other night in Miami."

"Miami?" Ollie moves to the edge of the sofa. "What are the odds?"

"I didn't know who she was at the time," I confess. "And let's just say I didn't exactly keep things...professional."

"Ah shit, Si." Ollie blows out a harsh breath while running his hands down his face. "That's why you were acting so strange around her yesterday? We all noticed, but I just thought it was because she's a beauty."

"Wait." I stop Ollie right there. "What do you mean, *we* all noticed?"

Ollie shrugs. "James asked me last night after our meeting if you had ever met her before. I told him I didn't think so, but we both agreed you were acting weird around her. *Jesus*, Si," Ollie scrubs his face again with his hands. "What are you going to do? James will go ballistic if he finds out about this. You saw how pissed he was about me pulling Lacey on stage."

"That's why he won't find out," I say quickly. "So there's no need to tell anyone about this. More than anything, I wouldn't want to get Sydney in trouble."

Ollie studies me with narrow eyes. "You're going to see her again, aren't you?"

"I don't know what's happening," I admit. "That night in Miami...*God*, one minute I was chatting up some girls, and the next minute she was there. Once I saw her, I had to talk to her. It was like I couldn't think or do anything else until I met her."

I pause to remember that fascinating pull she had on me that night, but Ollie is impatient for the story, apparently. "You can't stop there. What the hell happened?"

I get off the bed and move to sit next to him on the sofa. I know I'm setting myself up for what will most likely be months of relentless hazing after I say all of this, but hopefully he'll take it easy on me. I need to talk to someone and out of all of the guys, I'm closest to Ollie. And I'm confident he'll keep quiet about this which is the most important thing at the moment.

"I got up and went to speak to her," I continue. "She looked gorgeous that night, in this tight pink dress and killer heels. And I swear those beautiful blue eyes somehow penetrated straight through to my dark soul." I sigh and lean back into the sofa, thinking about those eyes. "For the first time in a long time, I was nervous to talk to a girl, Ol. She knew who I was, and I assume she probably would have explained her relationship with us if I had let her, but I didn't really care at the time. It never occurred to me that she may be on the cruise, let alone our new rep."

"Rotten luck, mate," Ollie chimes in.

I hate the thought of getting Sydney in trouble with her job. I would never want to hurt her like that, but damn if I can seem to stay away.

"I was hammered that night in Miami, trying to be cool, but stumbling all over the place and she made a comment about how I had probably had one too many." I still can't believe the harsh things

I said to her. "After everything that happened that day with you guys, it just set me off and I said some pretty awful things."

"Like what?"

"I don't really want to relive it," I tell him. "The point is she didn't take my shit, like most other girls would. She stood up to me and it was liberating. I couldn't let her walk away." I take a deep breath before I get to the really shameful part. "I went after her to apologize, but when I grabbed her elbow to get her attention something came over me. I swear to God that one touch was like the most powerful drug imaginable. I instantly needed more, so I...kissed her."

Saying it out loud now seems kind of barbaric, like I was staking my territory or something. But when I look at Ollie, he doesn't seem affected in the least.

"Go on," he says, eyes wide, and I smile.

"Honestly, I was waiting on someone to come and bounce me out of the place for essentially tackling her with my mouth, but then she started kissing me back, and I nearly lost it. I had to pull away, but she kept her arms around my neck and just held me. I swear Ollie, it was like nothing I've ever felt before. It was like I've known this girl my whole life. It was like..." I stop and remember how right and familiar she felt. "It was like finding the answer to every question I've ever had – like every broken piece of me was fused back together, suddenly repaired. Just one touch from this girl and I felt whole again, Ol. Just *one* touch."

Ollie turns away from me then and leans back into the sofa. "Huh," is all he says, as we both sit and let the story seep in.

He's never going to let me live this one down.

"Of course I never thought I'd see her again, but then she's on the cruise and I panicked." I drag my hands down my face with a groan. "*Fuck.* This girl has me so rattled, I can't think straight. I'm surprised she's even speaking to me with how crazy I've been acting around her."

"Wait...are you referring to the meeting yesterday, or have you seen her since?"

"At first, I had decided to act like it never happened," I continue on, ignoring his question for now. "The vibe I got from her in the meeting was that she wanted things that way too, and I knew avoiding her would be the best thing for both of us, but staying away from her has proved to be difficult. There's just something about this girl and I have to find out what that something is."

"Well, well..." Ollie shakes his head. "Even though I believe I will have to officially revoke your Man Card after all of that sappy mess, I have to say that I'm happy for you, my brother. Just don't ever unleash that kind of girly shit on me again. I have a reputation to uphold, thank you very much."

I laugh as I rake my hands through my hair. If that's as bad as I'm going to get from Ollie, I'll take it.

"What am I supposed to do, Ol? This is new territory for me, and I don't know if I'm up for it," I confess. "And you're right about James. He's going to go apeshit if he finds out about this."

"You know what? I say go for it, Si and to hell with James." Ollie gets up and tosses his empty beer bottle in the trash. "Sorry to be harsh brother, but at this point you have nowhere to go but up. And if what you say about this girl is true, especially the part about how she doesn't take any of your shit, then maybe she's exactly what you need."

I get up and follow him to the door, knowing the reason his words sting so badly is because they're true.

"You know I'll hurt her, Ollie," I whisper, as my worst fears start to surface. "I barely know anything about her other than her name, but I can sense she's good."

"Are you really afraid of hurting her?" Ollie asks, as he reaches for the door. "Or are you more afraid of *her* hurting *you*?"

I close my eyes and sigh. Fucking bastard. I hate it when he's right.

"Just keep things on the down low," he suggests. "James's head is normally so far up his arse, he'll probably never even notice. And you know I got your back. Just try not to cock things up with her too badly, or we'll both be screwed."

"Yeah. Thanks, Ol."

Ollie gives me a smile and a shoulder punch. "So you ready to go or what? James is probably foaming at the mouth since the crew was late setting up the stage today."

"Let's go."

I make sure the locket is still in the low pocket of my cargo shorts, before following Ollie out.

CHAPTER 19 - SYDNEY

Lacey and I have already finished one margarita and started on a second, when Ollie comes up behind us at the bar.

"What are we drinking, ladies?" Ollie asks, as he tickles Lacey's sides from behind. She lets out a very un-Lacey like squeal that makes me nearly choke on my drink.

"Margaritas. Care to join us?"

"Of course." Ollie spins Lacey around on her stool to face him. "Let me make a few rounds first, and I'll be back to you shortly. Deal?"

Lacey smiles. "Saving the best for last?"

She winks over at me, and I smirk at her boldness. I'm starting to think Ollie is making more progress with her in twenty-four hours than I've made in months.

"Always." Ollie grabs her hand and places a kiss on her knuckles. "Be back in a flash."

The minute Ollie walks away, he's surrounded by several girls who were seemingly waiting in the wings while he spoke with us. Lacey and I both smile before turning back to the bar to finish our drinks. We're ordering margarita number three by the time Simon finally comes around.

He slides up to the bar a couple of seats down on my right with girls hanging off of him. He gives me a wide-eyed grin, obviously asking for some assistance, but I shake my head and refuse. It's too much fun to watch him squirm. His eyes narrow at me, and I can see I might be paying for this later. I can hardly wait.

"Sydney, you're evil," Lacey tells me with a smile.

"Maybe so," I shrug. "But he needs to spend some time with the fans. He should be mingling around like the other guys. It's important."

I turn my head slightly to glance at Simon who's turned now in his stool so he can chat with the flock of females surrounding him. His smile is sincere and bright and I really love watching him like this. It's where he seems happiest and I like seeing him happy.

"Maybe he doesn't want to spend time with other fans," Lacey says, and I turn back around to face her. "Maybe he only wants to spend time with *one particular* fan."

"They paid for this cruise. They deserve his attention more than me. Besides, we need to keep things professional. Remember?"

"Right. Unless you're behind closed doors, of course."

"You know you love–" I start to say to Lacey, when I'm interrupted by someone tapping my right shoulder.

I turn to see a girl around my age standing behind me with a huge smile on her face. She's a tiny thing with blue eyes and short red hair. Her smile is sincere, and her sweet, pixie-like face warms me to her immediately.

"Hi," she says and extends a hand.

"Hello." I shake her hand and glance over at Lacey when the lady doesn't do anything but smile at me. Lacey shrugs as she turns in her seat to face us and I turn my attention back to the mystery woman.

"I'm so sorry." She seems embarrassed now. "I'm Amy, and I know this may sound crazy, but I just had to ask you a question."

"Okay..." I give her a nervous smile. "Ask away, Amy."

"Well, since you're the official nurse for the guys, I have to know. Have you really seen all of them naked? And if so, are the rumors true about Simon? Is he really...you know...hung like a horse?"

I burst out laughing at the same time Lacey nearly spits out her drink. When I finally recover, I notice the woman is staring at me looking irritated.

"I'm sorry. Who told you I was the guys' official nurse?" I ask, but when I glance over Amy's shoulder, I have my answer. Simon's standing in the distance with a few fans, looking my way, a mischievous smile spread across his handsome face.

Okay then. Two can play this game.

"I was just talking to Simon and he mentioned it." Amy tells me, her sincere smile back in place.

"Ah, yes. Well, he told you the truth. I am in fact the nurse for the guys and travel with them everywhere. Tough job, right?"

Amy and I laugh together now. "You're so lucky!" she squeals. "Simon said he thinks you make up excuses to see them all naked, which I personally think is kind of genius. I would so do that too."

I laugh with her again, mainly to hide the shock on my face. "Well, they're all fantastic of course, but to answer your question, the rumors you've heard about Simon are unfortunately not true."

Amy stares at me open-mouthed, waiting for me to continue. I take another quick glance at Simon, and he has the decency to look worried now. Good.

"Yeah, not so much." I extend my pinky finger, making sure I'm in Simon's line of sight when I do it.

"No!" Amy gasps when she sees my finger, then turns quickly to stare back at Simon.

I can barely contain my smile as I watch Simon excuse himself from his harem and start walking toward us.

"Oh my God! Did he see you do that?" Amy asks, and I shrug. "He's totally coming over here!"

By the time Simon makes it over to us, Lacey's about to burst from trying to hold in her laughter. The poor lady in front of me looks like she's about to face a firing squad, while I sit relaxed on my barstool, arms crossed staring now into the most beautiful brown eyes I've ever had the pleasure of knowing.

"And what lies has the good nurse been telling you, my love?"

Simon puts an arm around Amy, and she gives me a conspiratorial wink before gazing up at Simon. "She was telling me about Rob," she says with a poker face I would kill for as she wiggles her pinky finger at Simon.

Simon throws his head back in laughter. "Is that so?" He flashes me his million dollar smile. "Well, don't believe a word this woman says. She's the worst kind of manipulator."

Amy glances up at Simon, and with an air of superiority, she looks back at me. It's obvious that with only one word from Simon, my brief kinship with this charming lady has officially ended.

And just to add fuel to the fire, Simon leans down and whispers something in her ear, topping it off with a kiss on her cheek. She reaches up to give him a hug and walks away, and I don't even get a second glance.

"That was Amy by the way." He gives her a final wave over his shoulder as she moves back to her friends near the pool. "She's the president of one of my fan clubs. Lovely girl."

"Poor Amy," I tsk. "I thought you loved your fans. How could you lie to her like that?"

"She knows I was playing a joke on you, and she was more than willing to take part. So loyal, my fans."

"Good grief. Could your ego get any larger?"

"I'm sure you'll keep it in check for me."

"Gladly."

"All right, that's enough for me," Lacey says with a smile. "I'll see you guys later."

Lacey winks at me, then hops off her barstool to head toward the pool. "Have fun, Lacey." Simon tells her but keeps those playful eyes on me.

"Will do," she sings, as she strides toward Ollie, who I notice is currently doing some insane jumps off the diving board.

"Team nurse, huh?" I tease. "Did you know I wanted to be a nurse? Or was that just a happy coincidence?"

"Lucky guess," he confesses. "Happy to hear it's true though. I think that's wonderful."

"Thanks. I'm currently taking a break from school, but I hope to go back soon." I try and hide my unease, but Simon seems to notice so I quickly change the subject. "You know I actually don't think I'd mind the *Team Nurse* title. Is there an opening?"

"No." Simon shakes his head. "Absolutely not."

"And why not? Don't think I'm good enough?"

Simon moves a little closer. "Oh, I'm sure you'll be a great nurse, but I'm not about to share you with the other guys. Selfish Simon." He points to his perfect chest and I smile.

"What if they need medical attention?"

"They can find their own sexy, blond nurses. You're mine."

"Yours?"

"Mine."

Wow. I really love the sound of that.

CHAPTER 20 - SIMON

My God, she's beautiful. Being on the beach today has added a soft glow to her already tanned skin, and her eyes shine like blue diamonds in the sun. Her hair is pulled up and away from her face today, giving me a great view of those spectacular eyes and the new dusting of freckles across her cheeks and nose.

"So, what are the plans for the show tonight?" Sydney asks me, pulling me from my daze.

My lips automatically turn up in a smile, but my thoughts start drifting. I still feel torn in two every time I'm around her – one side of me wanting to be open with her because it feels good to let someone see that part of me. It's been so long since I could just let go.

But the other side of me is fighting that release. Hard. And for the same reasons. It's been so long since I've let anyone in, but this girl is threatening to change all of that. And it's scaring the shit out of me.

And then of course I have the capability of possibly ruining her life by destroying her career. But she did just mention she wants to be a nurse. Maybe I'd be doing her a favor in the end.

Nice try, Simon.

"Simon?" Sydney reaches out and brushes my arm with her fingers. "Are you okay?"

"I'm fine," I tell her as I take a step back. "Tonight's just a concert. No big deal."

A hurt look cuts across her face but she quickly hides it, crossing her legs, forcing me even further away. I wish I knew why she just did that. Does she realize I need the space, or is she pissed off? *Fuck.*

I want to say something. I know I need to explain things to her, but I don't know if I fully understand what's happening myself.

"I'm sorry." I'm not exactly sure what I'm apologizing for, but Sydney sighs seeming to understand. "I'm such an arse."

I scrub a hand down my face, hating the distance between us now. I want to touch her in some way, but I don't want to frighten her. My mood swings are hard to understand these days, even for me.

"It's okay," Sydney says, but she looks away from me, disappointed. "I have a meeting scheduled with Rob in a bit, then Lacey and I probably need to go get ready for dinner. I'll see you then?"

"Sure." I try for an honest smile, but I know it doesn't come off that way. "Sydney..." I grab her arm as she jumps off the stool before she can walk away. "I'm trying. I really am, but this is not going to be easy for me."

Holy shit. What just flew out of my mouth? When I opened it to say something, anything to erase that disheartened look on her face, I didn't expect the honesty to come that easily. But then Sydney smiles at me. And her smile is reassuring. Because it's sincere. And it's positively breathtaking.

"Maybe you should stop trying so hard, Simon. There's no need to rush anything." She places a hand on my cheek and as always, her touch seems to bring this flood of contentment right along with it. "I'll see you later, okay?"

"Can't wait."

"Me neither."

Unable to resist since I'm still holding her arm, I pull her in close and give her a quick kiss on her cheek. "Farewell, goddess."

I release her arm and Sydney gives me a graceful curtsy making us both laugh before she walks away. I'm not quick to take my eyes off the back of her as she searches through the crowd for her friend, and after a few steps, she glances over her shoulder and smiles when she sees me watching her. And just like that, my worries completely vanish.

I continue watching her until I eventually lose her in the crowd, then I turn around and order a bottled water from the bar. I down my water just as some fans approach me, and I start talking to them politely as usual. But in all honesty, I'm only going through the motions until I can see my goddess again. Dinner can't get here fast enough.

I came back to my suite about an hour after Sydney left me at the pool, and I haven't stopped thinking about her since. Now here I am pacing again, gripping my locket while trying to figure out what to do about that fact. Away from her and her touch, I'm more anxious than ever – that same feeling of unease creeping back in and threatening to eat me alive.

Damn. I've got it bad.

"You in there, mate?"

Ollie startles me when he pounds on my door causing me to stumble as I pace.

"Looking good, brother," I say as I open the door.

I crack a smile at his outfit – a black tuxedo vest, white t-shirt, plaid bowtie with jeans and red high top Nikes that probably cost more than the rent at my flat. His hair is styled into some kind of Mohawk, and he's decorated with his signature diamond studs in each ear and a wrist full of the rubber bracelets his niece makes for him.

I gesture to my go-to outfit of jeans, a t-shirt and Docs. "I feel underdressed."

"Well, some of us have to work harder at it, yeah?" Ollie smiles at me. "So, are you ready? Rob and James are waiting by the elevators."

"Born that way."

I put the locket in the pocket of my jeans, before shutting my door and following Ollie out.

"So, who's this date I heard you talking about earlier?" James asks Ollie, as we wait for the elevator to head down to the banquet room.

Ollie glances at me and clears his throat. "It's Lacey, actually. And it's not really a date."

"Lacey with the PR firm? That Lacey?" James doesn't look too happy.

Ollie clears his throat again. "Just a friendly business gesture. You know."

"Right," James says in reply, but it's clear in his tone that a "business gesture" is all it better be. "Who will Sydney be sitting with then? Perhaps I should ask her to sit at my table."

"I'll make sure she's cared for." I try not to wince, since the words slipped out of my bloody mouth without my permission.

"You?" James sizes me up, but I don't cower under his scrutiny. It's too important that I have some time with her, and I can't let James of all people find out about us. "All right then," James finally says as the elevator arrives. "I suppose that's fine."

I say nothing more and the silence grows uncomfortable, until Ollie does me another solid and opens his big mouth.

"Hey, you guys don't think having Lacey sit with me will look bad, do you?"

"Look bad?" Rob asks. "What do you mean?"

"Well, I wouldn't want the other ladies to think I'm taken. That could ruin my time on the cruise and more importantly my reputation."

We all look at Ollie for a moment in shock before we burst out laughing. Ollie laughs along with us, tossing me a wink over his shoulder that only I can see. I fucking love that bastard.

As we exit the elevator, I pull on Ollie's arm causing us to fall in step behind everyone else.

"Should I invite Sydney to sit with me?" I whisper to him. "Or should I maybe just visit her table? Or perhaps I should sit at *her* table? But I can't do that. Can I? Are we allowed to switch tables for the entire dinner, or just for a few minutes at a time after we eat? I forget the rules."

Ollie turns to me with a huge grin. "Damn, Si. You are truly messed up over this girl," he says excitedly. "Since when is Simon Young all nervous and needing my advice on how to ask a girl out? This is priceless!"

"Shut up, Ollie," I chide. "I'm not asking her out. I've just messed with her head too much already, so I have to take this slow. She's special."

"*Special*, huh? Well then I'll put in a good word for you with Lacey. We can all meet up for drinks after the show. You can thank me later."

He smiles, gives me a rough pat on the back, and rushes to catch up with the other guys. I stay behind trying to get my breathing under control. Truth is, I'm nervous as hell to spend time with her again. Being interested in a girl for more than a night or two is something I haven't experienced in years.

We finally reach the banquet room and the MC announces us, before we enter. I can hear the fans screaming our names, and consequentially, my adrenaline kicks into gear – this time for more reasons than one.

Since I'm actually sober for dinner tonight, I'm able to glance around and take in my surroundings. The room is enormous – a sea of round tables full of happy, chattering fans. On past cruises, we didn't get to have dinner with the fans due to the larger crowds, but on this ship we each have a place designated at one of the guest tables based on the near outrageous cost some fans paid for that particular privilege. I hope the fans at my table last night didn't feel slighted by "Drunk Simon".

As I get led to my table for the evening, my hands start to shake. The room is packed and even though I'm not searching her out, I catch Ollie out of the corner of my eye as he finds Lacey and motions for her to join him. Knowing she's close, my eyes involuntarily move to find Sydney, and I find her in no time. She's standing near her friend, smiling and looking irresistible in a short black dress that causes a low growl to rumble in my chest.

There's an extra seat at every table. They're supposed to be used by us, as we're encouraged to move around to various tables and mingle toward the end of the dinner, but Ollie ushers Lacey to the empty seat by him and I smile at the unpleasant reaction of the other fans at his table.

As I approach my own table, I say a quick hello to the fans there, but before I sit, I once again seek her out. It's because the thought of her being alone – since her friend is with Ollie – bothers me. At least that's what I'm telling myself for now.

She's taken a seat at a table a few down from mine, and as I'm staring, she looks up at me and back down quickly. Her cheeks turn a beautiful shade of pink and I smile. That's been her standard reaction each time she's caught me staring at her today, and it's more adorable each time.

As much as I want to invite her to sit with me and have her close, I decide against it. I still haven't formulated exactly how best to handle things with her, but I know one thing for sure: resistance is futile. I'm certain at this point there is no amount of women, drugs or liquor that will suffice to get this girl out of my head.

CHAPTER 21 - SYDNEY

As I sit and eat a delicious dinner of salmon and mixed veggies, I keep sneaking glances of Simon out of the corner of my eye. He's been engaged with the fans all night, laughing and smiling at each of them. He has everyone at his table eating out of the palm of his hand, and why wouldn't he? Not only is he poised and charming when he wants to be, no man wears a t-shirt like Simon, and tonight it's a navy blue v-neck, exposing just enough of that smooth chest to leave you wanting more. His faded jeans hang low on his hips and who can resist a man in Docs? It's a weakness of mine, for sure.

Simon happens to be the talk of the table I'm sitting at and more than once, I have to bite my bottom lip to keep from lashing out at some of the girls making rude comments about his promiscuity. I have no idea why people insist on putting celebrities on such pedestals.

Even though I can still fangirl with the best of them, I think a celebrity's personal life should be of zero concern to anyone but maybe their own friends and family. Don't get me wrong. I'm the first to soak up all available knowledge on Simon Young. However, it doesn't change my opinion of him at all. Not even his erratic behavior over the past couple of days has worked to change the way I feel about him. The fact of the matter is I don't know him personally – as much as I wish I did – so I have no idea what he's really going through or how that's affected the person he is today. What I do know is that ten years ago, he took a chance on a chubby, thirteen year old girl and changed her life forever. He can screw half the world's population, which he's basically done it seems, and it won't take away from his brilliant talent or the way he cares for his fans.

One of the girls makes yet another comment about how many diseases Simon probably has, and I groan. As the group's new PR rep, I should be working to diffuse this situation, to turn a negative into a positive, but....

"Pardon me, ladies, but let me give you some insight," *Sydney, don't make a scene. Don't make a–* "Perfect doesn't exist. Want proof? Take a look in the mirror."

I grab my purse and head for the ladies room. *Dammit.* I shouldn't have done that, but my patience was worn thin. Catty bitches.

Good God, Sydney. Who's the pot and who's the kettle?

I don't even chance a look in Simon's direction. I don't want to risk getting busted again, but I do try and catch eyes with Lacey on my way out. Of course she doesn't notice me because she's mesmerized by Mr. Sutton, and I smile as I see he seems to be just as charmed by her. *You go girl.*

The banquet room is huge, so I have to walk a ways to reach the exit. When I finally make my way out of the room, I see the rest of the ship is a ghost town.

Opting for a little more fresh air than the bathroom can provide, I decide to head somewhere outside. I let my mind drift as I walk, and I don't realize where my legs are taking me until I'm there – back to the observation deck. *Hmmm.*

I quickly remove my heels, lean back against the wall and stare out over the ocean. My thoughts instantly turn to Simon, and I can't help my smile. Just for curiosity's sake, I keep a clear image of

Simon front and center and start slowly approaching the ship's railing. The wind is strong and nearly knocks me off my feet at one point, but I keep moving continuing to smile as I think of kissing him last night in this very spot. Or even better, his triumphant face when I saw him here this morning.

When I get half way between the wall and the railing, my hands start shaking but I'm still giddy with pride over my small accomplishment. So giddy in fact, that I don't hear Simon when he comes up behind me.

"Look at you."

I jump, startled by his deep, sexy voice and when I turn to face him, his smile takes the sexiness up by a few thousand notches.

"Aren't you proud of me?"

"Very," he laughs. "But sad as well. Looks like you'll soon have no need for me anymore."

"Oh, I can think of a few other uses for you."

Oh my God. Did I just say that out loud?

Simon steps closer and slowly pushes me backward with his body until his hands are gripping the railing and he's caging me in with those strong arms of his. "Goddess..." He leans in and kisses the side of my neck. "You can use me any way you want."

Sweet. Heavens.

Impulsively, I wrap my arms around his neck and kiss him. Thoroughly. And his answering moan makes my decision well worth it.

"How did you find me?" I ask, after I've had my feel...*for now.*

"Followed you out."

"I'm glad you did."

Simon closes his eyes when I start stroking the back of his hair. "Me too."

We stay like that a moment, then Simon takes my hands in his. "I have to get back," he tells me. "I just wanted to make sure you were all right."

"Thank you." I give him a smile for his good manners. "Actually, I was going to the bathroom but decided I needed some fresh air."

"Ah, I see. Well then, may I escort you back or do you still need the loo?"

"I can skip the restroom," I tell him. "I really just wanted a break."

Simon grabs my shoes and starts leading me back toward the stairs. Have I mentioned how much I love the way his hand feels in mine?

"You know, goddess," he starts, and I bite back a sigh. His voice is definitely one of his sexiest assets. And what's with this *goddess* business? No doubt, I love it. "I'm still a little shocked about you being on the cruise. I never thought I'd see you again."

"Well, I was going to tell you who I was that night in Miami, before your...ummm...fit of rage."

"Yes, that was unfortunate." Simon flinches, and I feel bad for bringing it up. "But if I remember correctly, I did try to apologize."

"I see. And you've been trying to apologize ever since?"

"Something like that," he smiles. "I hope I'm forgiven?"

"Well, those were *some* apologies."

Simon lets out a nervous laugh that makes me relax even further. The fact that he might also feel unsure about everything that's happened between us is refreshing.

"Yes, well, if you're going to do something, do it right," he jokes. "I'm surprised I haven't frightened you away."

I look up at him, and his eyes are examining me intently. "Honestly, your mood swings have kept me on my toes," I confess. "But don't worry. I don't scare easily."

"That's good to hear," he says, his sweet smile meeting his eyes. "But if I may, I'd like to try a more traditional apology, so as to prevent any further confusion."

I stop and turn to him, and he grins as he takes both of my hands in his. He's still carrying my heels, so he dips his head low until his eyes are even with mine.

"I'm very sorry, Sydney," he starts. "I'm sorry for being a horribly indecisive, mental arse since the moment I met you in Miami. I promise to figure out some way to make it up to you, to prove to you that I'm actually a fairly decent guy and not a complete lunatic."

I laugh and glance down at my bare feet. When I bring my eyes back up to his, the energy between us quickly shifts, like it always seems to do when we're this close to each other, and the words are out of my mouth before I can stop them.

"I think I like your other method of apology better."

Simon's eyes flame wildly, his grin turning more toward the wicked variety, as he places a hand on my cheek. "In that case, I'll probably be messing things up quite a bit, just so I can beg for forgiveness."

I turn my head into his hand and place a soft kiss on his palm. "I might like the sound of that," I whisper, and he takes a deep breath as he hooks my arm through his.

We head toward the elevator, and as we're waiting, Simon turns to me. "Meet me after the show tonight? Please?"

"Sure."

My response was quick and Simon smiles brightly. "I don't know what the plans are after, so just stay by the stage, and someone will be there to give you instructions. Sound good?"

"I'd like that."

"Me too." Simon releases my arm and kisses the top of my hand just as the elevator arrives. "I'm going to go meet the guys, but I'll see you soon."

"See you soon."

I get on the elevator and we're both smiling as the door closes between us.

CHAPTER 22 - SIMON

We're already on our second song when I see Sydney coming into the theater. She and Lacey are arm in arm, smiling and laughing and I smile too as I sing. I'm startled by the rush of relief that floods through me at the sight of her. I was thinking maybe she ran, even though we're on a boat and there's really no where for her to go. But there's a part of me that knows this girl is way too good for me. I wouldn't be surprised if she stood me up this evening. She should. She should run from me at top speed, but I certainly hope she doesn't – more than anything, I pray she doesn't.

She moves toward some seats not far from the stage, and as she gets closer her eyes find mine, and her smile widens. I don't even feel bad for getting caught staring. She's fucking beautiful, and I could spend all day looking at her, especially in that dress.

By the time she sits, we've wrapped the second song and now it's time for requests. This is one of my favorite things to do because it means we actually get a little break from the norm.

"All right everyone," James says into the mic, as stools are brought out, along with our instruments. "It's time for some requests, so give us your best shot."

Ollie steps away from the turn table and grabs his bass, Rob takes his guitar, James settles himself behind his drums and I take a seat on the bench in front of the small piano they rolled on the stage. It's nothing like my beloved baby grand at home, but it'll do in a pinch.

I smile at the obvious appreciation from the audience as we take to our instruments. Everyone loves a musician, right? And that's one thing I can say about each of us – we may be a pop group, but we're all true musicians at heart. We can all play multiple instruments, and *all* of us are song writers, despite what James thinks.

I take a quick glance at Sydney, unable to keep my eyes away. When I see she's watching me, a pleasant heat rushes through me and I notice her squirm a bit in her seat when I smile at her.

Hmmm. It seems my goddess is into musicians as well.

Our first request comes from an adorable girl, who can't be a day over eighteen – the cut off age for the cruise, and I'm glad. I laugh quietly to myself thinking about what Ollie said during the first cruise – "At least we know they're legal, right?" But the truth is the fans can get kind of raunchy some times during our shows, and I would hate to think of young girls here witnessing that. Luckily, most of our fans are twenty-somethings – lifetime fans from our glory days – and no matter what James and his shitty attitude may think, I love them. Every one of them. Their loyalty is what's kept me going over the years.

The first request is one of our own – *Just You and Me* – and I notice Sydney sit up straighter in her chair when we start the song. She's smiling brilliantly, and her eyes are only for me. *Perfection.*

As I stare at her and sing, this strange feeling of déjà vu hits me. It's her eyes. Those eyes seem so familiar, but how could I not remember her or those stunning blue eyes? I *would* remember. The woman ripped me wide open the first night I met her, and she's continued to leave quite the impression on me since. I could never forget her. Never.

We get request after request, everything from The Beatles to Aerosmith to Willie Nelson, and we happily do our best to accommodate. Some songs we don't know, which is where the comedy comes in – Ollie's forte. He's a riot as he makes up the craziest lyrics and the faces in the audience are red with laughter, including Sydney's.

God, she's beautiful when she smiles.

Suddenly I find myself trained on those full lips, eager to have them on mine, and I'm so thankful I'm seated and no one can see just how eager I really am.

I get back to my piano as we finish up a horrible rendition of Jimmy Buffet's "Why Don't We Get Drunk and Screw". This song is requested often, so why we don't take the time to actually learn it is beyond me, but Ollie never disappoints with his ridiculous ad-libbing and the fans go mad.

"All right everyone, we're going to take a quick break," James tells the crowd. I smile at how the ladies react to him, even if he is married with kids. "We have something special in store for you in a bit, and it involves Ollie in a bikini, so don't go anywhere."

Everyone has a laugh, and I look over at Sydney hoping to catch her smiling again. I'm rewarded with not only a smile, but her eyes are on me and she winks. My mouth pops open in shock. She just winked at me. And it was sexy as hell.

She giggles and puts her hands over her face, which is quite adorable. I laugh out loud as I exit the stage with the guys, smiling so widely my cheeks hurt. And here I am again, counting the seconds until I can be near her. That moment never seems to come soon enough.

We finally finish the skits we had planned, which were a huge hit as always, but they are my least favorite part. We do it to get the crowd going, but I'm not much of an actor, so they always make me a little uncomfortable. I prefer being on stage with a mic in my hand and a guitar or piano in front of me.

Still, all of us are high from the energy of the crowd, laughing as we head back stage again. It feels like old times, before things went sideways, before my life turned to shit.

The thought makes me frown, and Ollie notices. "What's up, Si? I saw your lady checking you out on stage."

The mention of Sydney helps bring a smile back to my face. "I told her to meet me after. What about you and Lacey? Any plans?" I wag my eyebrows and Ollie smiles.

"I told her to save me a dance at the party. Why don't we all hang out? Grab a drink together?"

I shake my head. "No way, mate. I'm not going to watch you get drunk and divulge all my dirty secrets to Sydney." I smile, but Ollie sees through my weak excuse to be alone with her.

"All right then. I get it." He gives me a mock salute as he walks backward toward the dressing room. "I'll catch you later, Si."

"Hey Ollie..." A sudden thought hits me. "Do you think James will be suspicious if I don't make it to the party? Especially if he notices Sydney's not there either? I think he may already be on to me after my big mouth episode before dinner earlier."

"I'll cover for you, brother. Don't worry about James."

"Thanks, Ol."

Ollie smiles, then turns his back to me. "Have fun tonight. Don't do anything I wouldn't do," he calls over his shoulder.

"That doesn't leave me with a lot of options."

"You're one to talk."

He's got me there.

In my dressing room, I take a quick shower to wash off the make-up we used for our "London Girls" skit. Yes, it was quite embarrassing having Sydney see me dressed like a woman, but every time I looked at her, she was smiling and laughing like crazy which made it all worth it.

I dry off and toss on my clothes and shoes as fast as I can. I'm anxious to get back to her and her smiles.

"Are there lots of people left?" I ask one of our security guards, Greg, as I walk back around toward the stage.

"No, just a few stragglers trying to stake out the exits to catch one of you."

I bite my bottom lip as I move away from Greg, trying to figure out how to get to Sydney. Deep in thought, I'm startled when Ollie comes up behind me.

"You going to meet Sydney?" he asks and I nod.

"I was just thinking of what would be the best way to get to her."

"Maybe she and Lacey should come back here. That wouldn't look too suspicious. Then you can take the back entrance back up to the suites."

"I hadn't planned to take Sydney to my suite. I don't want to freak her out any more than I already have."

Ollie looks at me like I'm crazy. "Are you feeling okay, Si?"

I push his hand away before it reaches my forehead to check for a fever. "Stop being a dick. She's different. I told you that."

172

Ollie shrugs. "Look brother, you're not going to have any privacy anywhere else," he explains, and he's right. "How about you guys hang with Lacey and me? We can all skip the party and go to my suite or yours. All of us together may ease her mind."

I sigh, knowing he's right, and hating it. "Fine, but please don't do anything stupid."

"Me?" Ollie points at his chest. "Don't be silly."

I shake my head and turn back to Greg. "There are two girls by the stage outside or at least there should be." I describe them both and what they were wearing. "Their names are Lacey and Sydney. Can you find someone to bring them backstage for Ollie and me?"

Greg nods, as this is a fairly normal routine. "Yes, sir. I'll go get someone on it."

"Thanks," I say, and Ollie and I move toward the wall to wait. "Do you think Lacey will be with her?" I ask Ollie. "Hopefully, she is."

"Yeah, I'm sure she will be. And if she's not, I'll go grab her from the party and meet you somewhere."

"Sounds good, but please Ollie, remember this one is different, okay? I don't want the regular shit to go down."

"I got it. I got it," Ollie holds his hands up in surrender. "I actually like Lacey, too. "

"She seems cool," I agree, "probably too good for you," I add, and Ollie punches my arm. I laugh and punch him back, but before it becomes a full on wrestling match, we hear the click of high heels approaching.

We both straighten, just in time to see Lacey and Sydney rounding the corner, once again arm in arm and smiling widely.

Greg gives Ollie and me a wink, then turns away and heads back toward the stage, leaving us alone with the girls.

"Fucking hell." Ollie voices his approval and I have to agree.

Fucking hell, indeed.

"Hi."

Sydney's soft, sweet voice immediately draws me in.

"Hey." I move slowly toward her. "How did you guys like the show?"

"I'm glad you showered," Sydney says, and I smile.

"It takes a real man to wear make-up," Ollie adds, and both girls quietly giggle. "So, shall we head out? I was thinking we could all skip this after party and maybe go have a drink together."

Lacey leans into whisper something in Ollie's ear, while I stand there staring at each one of them, feeling like I'm being left out.

Ollie looks at me and smiles as Lacey whispers, and now I know I'm being left out. Just before I'm about to pull Ollie away and get some answers, a warm hand grabs my elbow and tugs. Sydney pulls me toward her, away from Ollie and Lacey, and I move without question.

"No offense to Ollie…" Her voice is so low I have to lean down to hear her. She takes advantage and pulls up so her mouth is at my ear. "I would rather spend time alone with you, if that's okay."

A shiver escapes me as her warm breath slides across my skin. *Holy shit.*

I pull away and see her smiling shyly. I'm not certain if she wants alone time for the same purposes I do, and for some unknown and extremely baffling reason, I'm okay with that. Honestly, I think I'd be happy to stay up all night and do nothing but get to know this beautiful woman, sit close to her and maybe sneak a kiss or twenty.

174

I smile as I take her hand and turn to tell Ollie our plans, but they're already gone. "If you're worried about Lacey, don't," Sydney tells me. "She can take care of herself."

"Good to know." I nod, as we start heading toward the back exit. "Ollie's actually a pretty good guy. Not all rumors are true."

"I know," she answers quickly, and I have a feeling she's not talking about Ollie. "Things aren't always what they seem."

I stop walking and look at her. Yeah. Definitely not talking about Ollie.

"You remembered. Good girl."

Sydney gives me a knowing smile and I smile back as we start walking again.

"Where are we going?"

"I was just walking, actually," I lie. I was headed for my suite, but I shouldn't assume she's okay with that. "Did you have something in mind?"

"Don't you think we should go to the after party? You should probably make an appearance."

"I probably should," I admit. "But I'm not obligated, unless you'd like to go."

She puts a finger on her chin, an endearing gesture. "I hate to sound catty, but I would rather not have to fight girls off of you all night. Is there any place we can get some privacy?"

Here goes nothing. I stop again and face her.

"We could go to my suite," I suggest, but the uncertain look on her face makes me immediately rethink that idea. "I promise not to try anything, Sydney, unless you want me to, of course," I add with a wink. Old habits die hard. "It's just the only place on the boat we're guaranteed privacy."

"Your suite is fine," she replies with a nervous smile, and I feel like a shit.

She obviously knows my reputation, and I've done nothing to prove it wrong since I've met her. She thinks I want in her panties, which I do. *God I do.* But this girl *is* different. She's good. She's sweet. She's kind. And she ignites things inside of me that have been dormant for a very long time. I can *feel* again, which is both exhilarating and terrifying, but I'm enjoying both emotions at the moment. Anything is better than the robot I've become over the last few years.

Just to make double sure she's okay with my suggestion, I take both her hands in mine. I lean down a bit so our faces are level, and I nearly get lost once again in those baby blue eyes.

"Sydney, we can do anything you want tonight. I just want to spend some time with you." I feel her hands relax in mine, which urges me on. "I know these are not ideal circumstances, and I truly am sorry for the way I've acted since we met. I wish I had a good excuse for that behavior, but I don't. What I can tell you is that I feel like something good is happening between us. I have no idea what exactly that may be, but I'd like the opportunity to try and figure it out, if that's all right with you."

Sydney's smile is radiant, and I feel my shoulders sag in relief. She seems overly pleased with what I said, which makes me extremely happy. I think I'd do just about anything for that smile.

"Your suite is perfect." She's smiling more confidently now, and that smile is so amazing it makes me physically ache.

I drop one of her hands, and we start walking again toward the back exit. I hold her other hand firmly as we walk and to my surprise, she laces her fingers through mine as I open the door to the stairwell. She looks up at me as if asking if that was okay, and I smile and give her hand a squeeze as I lead her up the stairs.

We get through one flight before Sydney tugs on my hand. "Can we stop a sec?" she asks, then lets go of my hand to remove her shoes. "Sorry. These things are killing me."

I reach and take them from her, then quickly grab her hand back in mine. She's much shorter than me out of those sky high heels, but I love it. Maybe it's the barbarian in me coming out again, but I like the way I tower over her now like a protector, even though this girl hasn't needed much protecting so far.

We finally reach my floor and I stop at the door, hesitant, wondering if there may be some fans waiting on the other side.

Sydney notices my pause and moves in front of me. "I'll take a peek."

She seems almost excited, as she lets go of my hand and opens the door a crack to peer out.

"See anything?"

Sydney closes the door and turns back to me with a huge smile on her face. "I think we're all clear."

She turns to open the door again and takes my hand back in hers as we rush out into the hallway toward the suites. I nod at security as we pass praying to God they keep their mouths shut about seeing us, and right before I'm about to enter my key into the door, we hear some girls chatting excitedly down the hall.

Even though we're safely behind the security guards now, I still try and hurriedly open the door hoping to save Sydney from the rumors that are sure to spread quickly around the boat, but I fumble with the key. Sydney starts cracking up laughing as she takes the keycard from my hand, and we make it in just as the gaggle of fans round the corner. They scream my name and I give a quick wave before shutting the door.

"Good grief." Sydney's fit of laughter finally subsides. "Does that happen all the time?"

"Not really," I confess. "This ship is full of fans, so they're everywhere. In my everyday life, our fans aren't everywhere. At least not anymore."

"Well, we're going to change that," Sydney states proudly and I give her a wide grin.

As she turns and walks further into my suite, I follow the leisurely sway of her hips as she walks. It's going to be tough to keep my hands off her all night, but I'll do whatever I have to do to prove to her I'm not a complete arsehole – whatever it takes to keep her happy and keep her close.

Don't fuck this up, Simon. Please don't fuck this up.

CHAPTER 23 - SYDNEY

My goodness, this suite is fantastic! My nervousness is nearly forgotten as I walk around and admire the place.

"This is really beautiful."

I run my fingers along the granite countertop in the kitchen as I walk a little further into a small living area with a huge flat screen TV hung on the wall. Then I notice the bedroom to my left, and my pulse jumps, reminding me of my naughty hopes for this evening and at the same time, screaming at myself to reconsider. But I can't. And I won't. I want this. I want *him*.

I keep walking, taking a few indiscreet breaths in an effort to calm my nerves, until I realize I'm getting closer to the balcony. My lingering fear causes me to stop short before reaching the door, but I do notice that the balcony is huge, stretching across into the bedroom as well. Nearly the entire side of the suite is covered in glass.

"Do you want a drink?" Thankfully, Simon pulls me back to the here and now.

"Sure."

"What do you like?"

"What do you have?"

Simon ducks into a small refrigerator. "Beer, wine or Jack Daniels."

"Wine would be nice."

I turn back toward the glass, wishing I wasn't so terrified of boats. I do love the sight and sounds of the ocean. Who doesn't love the beach? And I bet the view is outstanding from Simon's balcony, while relaxing in one of the two plush lounges it offers, preferably wrapped safely in Simon's arms.

And with that thought, my fear starts to slowly subside. *Wow*. I can't imagine being afraid of anything when I'm snuggled close to that man.

I turn and watch Simon's smile as he approaches me with our drinks. His snug, white t-shirt makes his newly tanned skin look even darker, and his hair is still a little damp from his shower. My fingers literally ache to touch it.

"Would you like to sit on the balcony?" he suggests, and a quiet laugh escapes me.

"Can we stay inside?" I offer, but I can tell Simon isn't going to let it go.

"Still afraid, goddess?" he asks, and when I don't say anything he grins widely. "I thought we put that fear to rest."

I smile as I remember being on deck earlier with his arms around me and his lips on mine. "I'm still working on it."

"I'll take it easy on you then...for now."

"Thanks."

Simon hands me my drink and we both take a seat on his sofa.

"So, since we've skipped over a lot of the 'getting to know you' part," Simon starts, "how about you tell me about yourself?"

"What would you like to know?"

"Everything."

Sweet heavens. That *smile*.

"Lately, I've been extremely busy with work." I take a sip of my drink, trying to ignore how close his thigh is to mine. "A friend of mine was kind enough to get me the job with White and Associates, and I've been trying really hard to do well and work my way up so I can make him proud."

Simon clears his throat. *"Him?"*

"Yes. My friend, Ethan, is the one who got me the job, but he's just a friend," I tell him, putting him out of his misery. "He's actually my friend Sam's boyfriend. He's a great guy."

"Oh, that's good to hear." Simon smiles back at me. "So, I know you said you hope to be a nurse someday, and I'll say again I admire you for that decision. I know I could never do it."

"Too selfish?" I interrupt.

"But of course," he proudly admits. "And because I know I could never do it, I'm curious to know why or how you would choose that field."

"Well..." I take a deep breath. "My grand mom passed away from cancer when I was fourteen and I had a very hard time with it. She had in-home hospice care toward the end and I became close with one of the nurses. She suggested a therapy group for me to go to after Grammy died and I went. They were helpful, but what helped me more was when I was old enough, I started volunteering for the hospice care group at a hospital in my hometown. I loved the nurse who tended to my Grammy in those last few weeks of her life. She treated her with such loving kindness, and I wanted to give that back somehow. The first person I helped was an elderly lady who had a grandson that was having a hard time letting go. The situation was so similar to mine; I just knew it was a sign that hospice care was what I was meant to do for the rest of my life. I've been volunteering when I can ever since, and hopefully I'll get back to school one day so I can do it full time. It may seem like a depressing job to some people, but it's more rewarding than you may think."

"I guess I could see that," Simon says in a quiet voice, and when I look over at him, I'm humbled by the expression on his face. "It's a very honorable profession, Sydney. And not everyone could be a part of something like that and look at it the way you do. You should make going back to school a priority if you feel it's your calling."

"I'll get there eventually," I assure him. "I'm able to save quite a bit working at my current job, and I actually enjoy PR more than I thought I would."

Especially lately.

"That's good." Simon takes a quick sip of his drink. "So, moving on...where are you from originally? If I had to guess based on your accent, somewhere in the Southern states?"

"That bad?"

"It's beautiful, really. I could listen to you speak all day."

Ditto.

"I'm actually from Georgia."

"Born and raised?" he asks, turning his body to me, and I love how he's giving me his undivided attention.

"Yep. I grew up in a small town called Delia." I take another sip of wine. It's rich and kind of spicy and I love it. "I only recently moved to Atlanta when I got the job with White and Associates."

Simon nods, with a thoughtful expression on his handsome face. "Atlanta is a great city. We've played there several times. The fans are some of my favorites."

"You're really good with the fans, you know," I tell him, and he gives me the most adorable, shy smile.

"That's my favorite part of all of this."

"The fans? Really?" I tease. "Isn't that what you're supposed to say?"

"I suppose, but honestly, I've just learned to grab on to the things that make me happy and hold on tight."

"The fans make you happy?"

"They never disappoint," he explains. "Every single indiscretion is plastered all over the papers, online or on television. And no matter what I do, no matter how hard I try to push them away, they never give up on me. I'm not naïve enough to think they actually care about me personally, but they act like they do, and that's good enough."

"That's not necessarily true. I think a lot of your fans genuinely care about you."

"They don't really know me," he says, but his eyes are curious. "How can you truly care about someone you don't know?"

I pause, not sure how to answer, and also because I can't decide if he's asking himself that question or if he's asking me.

The truth is, I care about Simon – much more than I should. And all I really know about him is what I read in magazines or online and in my experience, only about half of that information is true. But still...

"I think it's possible," I admit. "I definitely think it's possible to care about someone without knowing them fully."

"Yes, maybe it is."

The tender look in his eyes has me thrown, and I take another sip of wine hoping it will calm my nerves. I may need multiple glasses.

"Simon, I love how wonderful you are with the fans. It's an admirable quality, but I'm sure you have people in your life that care about you too. It's not like you have to rely solely on the fans."

"You'd be surprised," he sulks. "I'm pretty hard to love."

"I don't believe that. The guys in the group love you."

Simon gives me a pointed look. "I think you and I both know that's not the case. Not anymore."

Yikes. This conversation just became extremely uncomfortable.

"Well," I start again, "I obviously have no clue what all went down between you and the other guys. I only know what James told me, which I will tell you seemed like it was killing him to mention out loud. So maybe it's not the guys hating you. Maybe it's just *you* hating *yourself*. And maybe they're tired of watching that."

Simon's head pops back as if I punched him. "Excuse me?"

"You heard me." I put my wine on the table in front of us and cross my arms as I settle back into the sofa. "Look, I try not to judge others. It's my mom's favorite lesson. But it seems to me like *you* push *them* away, not the other way around."

I watch nervously as Simon's face goes from fuming to resigned. He sighs and looks away from me. "You're right. I've been pretty tough to deal with for the past few years, and I'm not proud of it. But at this point, I'm not sure there's anything I can do to make up for everything I've done."

"Is that what you were upset about the other night in Miami?"

I know I'm fishing and shouldn't be, but Simon looks surprisingly amused.

"Aren't you the intuitive one, my goddess," he says with a smile. "But I'd rather not talk about that night right now. As a matter of fact, can we just pretend we only just met – forget how crazy I've acted with you over the past couple of days, and start over? I would really appreciate that. More than you could ever know."

Truthfully, I'm happy to start over with him as well, but I refuse to forget everything that's happened between us, especially the kissing. Certainly not the kissing.

"If that's what you want."

"Well, the dirty bits I'll hold on to, if you don't mind," he teases. "But I would really like to start over and get to know each other a little better. Maybe I'll show a little more chivalry this time."

"I'm all for second chances." Especially when it comes to those *dirty bits*. "And I believe everyone is capable of change. You just have to want it badly enough."

Simon smiles at me. "And what about you?"

"Me?" I point to my chest.

"Yeah. What about your fear of boats?"

"What about it?"

"Don't you think it's about time you got over that fear? Time for a *change*?"

Nice transition. Very smooth.

"My fear of boats doesn't negatively impact my life or the people around me on a daily basis."

Simon is shaking his head before I even finish, his messy hair falling into his eyes. "That's not true. I would like nothing more than to stand on the balcony right now, look out over the ocean and relax as the breeze blows my cares away. But I can't because you won't join me, and it would be rude to leave you here alone."

"You have my permission to go on the balcony, if you wish."

"But Sydney, we've been through this." He's trying to keep a straight face, and his humor regarding my panic is irritating me. "It seemed to me like you had overcome this silly little fear. Shall we reenact the scenes? Perhaps that will help you remember?"

Hmmm...Now that sounds like a plan.

I stand and reach my hand out for Simon to take, and like before, my fears seem to simply float away when I think about having him close to me again.

He places his drink on a side table and grabs my hand. "Where are we going?" he asks with a crooked smile, but I don't reply.

When he stands up from the sofa, his face is close to mine. I smile up at him as I reach back and slide the glass door open. Then I take both of his hands in mine and walk him backward toward the balcony.

"Well, look at you, goddess. You've gone and gotten fearless on me."

"No," I correct him and continue to walk until my back presses against the railing. "I think I've become fearless *because* of you."

Simon's eyes go wide with my admission, and I'm kind of shocked I said something like that myself, but it's the truth. He gives me strength. I'm not sure how or why, but I feel it when I'm around him.

Simon moves my arms around his waist, then palms my face with his warm hands. "I don't understand why you believe in me so much," he breathes, as he stares into my eyes. "The worst part is that you're starting to make me feel like I'm worth it."

"Maybe you are."

Simon slowly drops his hands from my face and grabs the railing on either side of me. He seems almost pained by my words, as he presses against me, so I don't hesitate to comfort him. I reach my arms up around his neck and run my fingers through his hair. His eyes close and his broad shoulders sag with relief, and when I stand on my toes to pull his face toward my neck, Simon comes eagerly. He wraps both arms tightly around my waist, and I savor the warmth of his body now flush against mine.

But despite the warmth, I can feel us both trembling in each other's arms, and I start to wonder if Simon is feeling what I'm feeling in this moment. And if so, I'm more excited than ever to see what the night may bring.

CHAPTER 24 - SIMON

Christ, this woman is going to be the death of me. My emotions have gone haywire. I'm shaking like a leaf, on the brink of an orgasm with just her fingers in the back of my hair.

I'm struggling between wanting to carry her to my bed and have my way with her, versus wanting to take this slow because the thought of not being around her – not touching her in some way – is becoming more painful by the minute.

"Simon..."

Her sweet, warm breath is against my ear, and I close my eyes letting the pleasant sensation flood through me. When I pull away from her, it's only by a little. There's no way I'm taking my hands off her any time soon.

"Yes?" I ask in wonder, when she doesn't say anything further.

She's staring up at me now with those brilliant blue eyes that are shining brightly in the moonlight, and it's obvious she's torn about something. I'm about to reassure her that even though I may not be letting her go any time soon, tonight will be at her pace, but she speaks before I can get it out.

"Kiss me?" she asks, and I nearly come undone. *Holy shit*...this enchantress and the spells she weaves.

I move my hands slowly to either side of her face, and I'm so crazy for this girl right now, the steady movement is no easy task. She moves both arms back around my waist as she waits, and I'm nervous about a kiss for the first time since I was a lad.

I brush my lips against hers, softly at first, but when she opens her sweet mouth for me, giving me entry, I gladly take it. Not only does kissing Sydney feel like a new experience every time, but each time seems to be better than the last.

I want her. Every part of her. That's for certain. But I don't deserve her. Giving into my feelings for this woman would be criminal in so many ways. Even with her lips moving so perfectly against mine it's like they were made for me; I know I can't do this. But *dear God*, she tastes better than ice cream. How do I resist?

As if sensing my turmoil, Sydney pulls me toward her, pressing my mouth harder against hers and giving me my answer. Her tongue is swirling slowly with mine, silently showing me her desires. I feel I may explode if I don't have her in my bed soon, but I'm determined to let her lead this time.

We stay on the balcony for a while making out like teenagers, and although my head is swimming with visions of her naked beneath me, I'm loving every minute of kissing her, of holding her and just being close to her. It's been so long since I actually enjoyed this part. I'd forgotten what it could be like. And with Sydney, it's even better than I remember.

I'm prepared to spend the rest of my life kissing her on this balcony, when she pulls away unexpectedly and buries her face in my chest. "Simon," she breathes, and I realize I'm still trembling against her.

She pulls her face away from me and looks down at her feet. *What's this?*

I reach to pull her chin up so I can see those beautiful eyes. "What's wrong, goddess?"

I'm terrified now that I may have crossed the line once again, but before I can say a word, her mouth is back on mine. "Please," she begs onto my lips. "*Please*, Simon."

I pull my face slightly away from hers. I can't seem to get enough of those eyes, and I need to catch my breath. Her quiet plea has left me reeling. *Fuck*, I can't stop shaking.

"What do you need, Sydney?" I ask, and she's adorable as she narrows her eyes at me. "I need to hear you say it," I whisper in her ear. "Tell me what you want."

I put my mouth on her neck enjoying the taste of her as I wait for an answer, but it never comes.

When I pull away again, she traces my bottom lip with her fingertip and kisses me once more.

"How about I *show* you?" she offers with a sexy smile, then releases everything but my hand and leads me inside.

Holy shit. I think I'm in love.

CHAPTER 25 - SYDNEY

I know I keep saying "I'm not that kind of girl", but that make out session with Simon has left me in urgent need, and I'm pretty sure I'll die if I don't have him soon.

I reach up and touch my lips as I lead him back into the suite. They're swollen from all the delicious kissing, and I smile against my fingers. If Simon Young is even half as good in bed as he is at kissing, this is sure to be the most memorable experience of my life.

The minute we reach his bedroom, Simon spins me around and pulls me against him. I know I want him more than anything I've ever wanted before, but it's been a while and my body keeps betraying me. Showing my nerves, I'm shaking in his arms again. I can only hope he takes it as excitement, because it honestly is. It's fear and excitement and a million other emotions all wrapped into one.

Before I can think any more about it, Simon's mouth is back on mine. He moves his hands slowly along my back, savoring me, making me feel like I'm his favorite meal and he's taking his time to enjoy the flavor.

"Sydney," he breathes against my neck. "Please tell me you're sure about this. Please God, tell me you're sure."

I pull his face away so I can look into his eyes. "I'm certain."

His breathing is ragged and his eyes are wild as they move over my face, from my eyes to my lips and back again and again. I want to tell him how long I've waited for this moment. I want to tell him how he makes me feel. I want him to know that even though I don't actually know him, I do care about him, and whatever happens tonight won't change that. I want to tell him so many things, but it's not the time, and I'm terrified of scaring him off. My need for him tonight has reached the point of desperation.

"I was trying to be a gentleman this time," Simon teases in a whisper.

I smile up at him. "I'm from the South, Simon, and I can confirm that chivalry is overrated."

Simon smiles back as he holds me, and I watch as his breathing slows and his eyes settle intently on mine. Then my chest aches as that familiar pain returns to his face. What did I do? What did I say? *Please tell me I haven't ruined this.*

"Is this about our working relationship?" I have to ask. It's the only reason I can think of for his hesitation.

Simon shakes his head. "As long as you're okay with it, I couldn't give a fuck about that part in all of this."

"I'm okay with it." I don't even hesitate because right now my job is the least of my concerns.

Simon studies me closely, running a hand through my hair and down my back. "I'm not sure I can give you what you want, Sydney, what I know you deserve."

"How do you know what I want?" I ask, but my heart is suddenly in my throat and I can't believe how quickly things turned from light to dark.

"I guess I shouldn't assume," Simon says, the hurt still in his eyes. "But you have to know, this is all I'm good for. I don't know anything else. Not anymore."

I move my fingers through the back of his hair trying to figure out what to say to salvage what we've built so far. I know Simon is broken. And I know I'm probably not the person to piece him back together. But I want this moment with him, and I don't give a damn about the consequences.

"Simon…" I'm hopeful as I watch his eyes flicker to my mouth when I speak. "I want you to know that I believe you're capable of just about anything, but tonight, I'll take whatever you're willing to give. No expectations, okay? I just want to be with you."

Simon's mouth and hands are all over me, before I can say another word. He pulls me firmly against him, moving fast now, no longer savoring. It's time to devour.

But as much I want him, I *do* want to savor. I want to enjoy every minute I have with him, knowing I may never have this opportunity again.

I slow his mouth with mine and to my surprise, he doesn't fight. He moves with me, lets me lead, and that only makes me want him more.

I spin him around and push him gently down onto the bed. I move to stand between his legs and reach for the bottom of his t-shirt. He lifts his arms as I pull it over his head, and my eyes are immediately drawn to the swirly black ink that covers the upper left side of his chest, across his shoulder and down his upper arm. The size and design of the tattoo are impressive, and I'm so excited to finally see it up close, I feel obligated to take a moment to appreciate its beauty.

I trail my fingertips along the thick black lines on his shoulder, until Simon grabs my waist and pulls me to him. He places a kiss on my belly, over my dress, and I wish the fabric wasn't there separating his lips from my sensitive skin.

Simon looks back up at me, and I lean down to kiss him briefly before kneeling and removing his sexy boots.

"Did I mention I have a thing for Doc Martens," I tell him, as I undo his laces.

"Me too. Please don't tell me you have a pair." The growl in his voice echoes low in my center.

I look up at him from my knees after I finish removing his boots and socks. "My knee high lace-ups are my most prized possession."

Simon's eyes widen before turning positively savage. "*Christ, woman,*" he breathes, and I gasp as he reaches under my arms and pulls me swiftly to the bed. He moves to hover over me, and buries his face in my neck, his breath warm and tempting. "I can't take anymore. Let me have you, Sydney. I *need* you."

Once again, the mood went from playful to frantic in an instant, but I'm finding his intensity thrilling. I want him, and he wants me, and that's all that matters right now.

"I'm yours," I whimper, as he sucks and bites at my neck. "I'm yours, Simon."

He groans against my shoulder and soon we're back to reckless and wild, instead of slow and steady. But I no longer feel the need to take things slow. I want this just as much as he does. And we have all night.

His hands are fast and rough at first as he moves over my body, down to my thighs pushing up the bottom of my dress. I think he's about to rip it off me, but instead he places a hand at the small of my back and gently rises onto his knees, pulling me with him until we're both kneeling on the bed. His hands tremble as he pulls down the zipper on the back of my dress, but he keeps his eyes on mine, as he pushes my dress straps down over my shoulders. As soon as my black, lacy bra is exposed, I hear a low growl and I smile, slowly remembering what it's like to feel wanted like this.

He continues pushing my dress down and I move to help him get it completely off, exposing my matching black undies. "You're a goddess. Do you know that?"

"So I've been told."

He smirks as his eyes drink me in. His hands rove slowly up and down my sides, then move to my breasts. He moves his soft lips to kiss the center of my chest, and I'm lost in Simon once again – lost in his words, his touch, the feel of his lips on my bare skin. I can barely control my emotions. I feel like screaming. I feel like crying. My breathing is wild as he removes my bra and explores my breasts with his mouth. I grab on to his hair again, needing something to keep me grounded, but my entire body is shaking, and I don't know how much longer I can wait.

"Simon," I beg, my voice barely a whisper.

His head slowly rises and glittering brown eyes lock with mine. "What do you need, love?" he asks, as he moves to place tender kisses along my cheek. "Do you need *this*?"

His mouth moves to my neck, as he trails a finger down my chest to the waistline of my undies. He pushes two fingers inside and I moan. *Sweet heavens.*

"*My* goddess," he breathes against my neck, and it's nearly my undoing.

Simon continues taunting me with his fingers, and the feeling is exquisite. He has me wound so tight, and it's been so long that I'm already close. I try and hold on, but his practiced touch is hitting the perfect spot, and I can't hold out anymore. I cry out his name, trembling against him as I spin, then fall blissfully down from my orgasm.

Simon guides me gently down onto the bed and moves in beside me. He caresses my face, as I continue to shiver from the aftershock of what just happened. "That was extraordinary," he whispers in my ear, and I'm stunned to feel the need for him returning again so soon.

I lie there a few minutes longer, just enjoying the feel of Simon's tender touch. "Forgive me," I smile shyly as I turn on my side to face him. "It's been a while."

Simon laughs deep in his chest. "I'm sorry to hear that. So glad I could be of service."

I smile as I climb on top of him, and Simon settles his hands loosely on my hips. "May I repay the favor?" I ask against his lips, giving him a seductive smile as I spread his legs with my knees and move between them.

My hands are trembling still, but I'm slowly able to get his jeans unbuttoned. I wish I could say I'm shocked to find he's not wearing any underwear, but I'm not.

"It only gets in the way, love," he jokes, and I smack his tight tummy with my palm, causing him to laugh out loud as he rubs the spot where I hit him. "Damn. Remind me to never make you angry."

Still smiling, I pull his jeans off his legs and drop them on the floor. I once again find myself gawking at the fineness that is Simon Young as I climb back between his legs. Every single inch of him makes my mouth water.

"*Sydney...*" He hisses my name as I lean down and slowly move my mouth over him.

I wait for him to grab my head or tell me what he wants, to guide me as I pleasure him, but he never does. And when I peek up at him, I find him braced on his elbows staring down at me, watching me – his eyes hooded and dark, as he grasps the comforter of the bed holding on for dear life.

When he sees me look up at him, he throws his head back. "*Fuck*...Sydney..." he growls, and I start moving faster, knowing what's coming. Simon tries to pull my head up, but I resist, wanting to taste him, and I'm not disappointed.

Feeling satisfied but still thirsting for more, I crawl slowly up him, placing soft kisses along the way. Simon's quiet laugh shakes his body beneath me. "Ticklish," he mumbles, as I kiss his belly.

I pause to smile against him, but don't stop my kisses until I reach his mouth. And when my lips touch his, he rolls me over so he's on top. I expect him to relax against me, satisfied with what I just gave him, but instead I feel him ready and willing between my legs.

"I can't seem to get enough of you," he breathes into my mouth. "I think I could do this all day and all night and never get my fill."

Simon hastily removes my undies, then jumps up to retrieve a condom from his suitcase. I miss his touch the second he removes his body from mine, but he's back in no time, as if he couldn't stand to be away from me too long either.

"Put it on me?" he asks, handing me the condom and I gladly accept the challenge.

I rip the package open with my teeth and Simon smiles before assaulting my mouth with his. I roll the condom down his length slowly, swallowing Simon's appreciative sigh with my kisses.

"Do you want me inside you, Sydney?" he asks, and I whimper as he pushes halfway in, then quickly pulls back out. "Say it. Say you want me inside you. Because I can't think of any place I'd rather be right now."

I look up at him and to once again prove I'm more a woman of action rather than words, I dig my heels into his backside and force him in. "*Goddess...*" he gasps, and buries his face in my hair at my neck.

I wrap my arms around his shoulders, and claw at his back as he starts moving slowly inside me. The feeling of fullness, combined with his steady, penetrating rhythm, has me at the brink again faster than I thought possible.

"Simon," I call out his name as he quickens the pace, knowing I won't last much longer.

"Come for me, Sydney," he commands against my neck in a soft whisper. "I'm right there with you. Come for me, love."

And with that, I find myself crying out his name once again as I spiral blissfully down into oblivion. I can barely keep my eyes open after that mind-blowing experience, but I do see Simon squeeze his eyes closed before falling right along with me.

He collapses on top of me, and the weight of his body is welcome as we both tremble uncontrollably. We stay like that a moment, coming down from the high, but Simon is running his fingers along my side, down to my hip and up and over the top of my thigh, making it hard for me to stop the shaking.

Eventually Simon rolls onto his back, pulling me with him. I gladly sprawl across his naked chest, his silky smooth skin damp with sweat and pulled tight against his muscles. There's hardly a blemish, besides a freckle here or there. He's literally perfect.

The door to the balcony is still open in the living area, and the sound of the ocean is creeping into the bedroom as we lie in silence. I close my eyes and run my fingers lightly across his chest, basking in the peacefulness.

"Will you stay with me tonight?" Simon asks.

I raise my head to look at his face. There's worry and indecision there, but I want to stay with him, and he asked me to, so I will.

"Of course," I whisper back. "If that's what you want."

Simon pauses, but only for a moment. "I would love for you to stay. Please stay."

"Okay," I tell him, and he seems to relax a bit with my smile. "Have any pajamas I can borrow?"

Simon gives me a delightful chuckle as he rolls back on top of me. "Pajamas won't be necessary."

It's hard to believe he wants more, but I find I'm just as eager and more than willing to oblige.

"Sounds good to me," I manage before his mouth meets mine once again.

CHAPTER 26 - SIMON

"So, how'd you make out with the goddess last night?" Ollie yells at me from the bathroom, as I sit on the sofa waiting for him to get ready for another breakfast with fans this morning.

I smile to myself, but say nothing.

"That good, eh?" he asks with a smile, as he leans out the door.

I continue to remain silent, but it's going to take a miracle to remove the shit-eating grin off my face.

"Well, Lacey is fantastic," he says, stepping back into the bathroom. "But since you and I are playing the silent game, I refuse to tell you anything further, other than she did say she liked my tattoos. I'm hoping she won't mind exploring them further at some point. *All* of them."

I have a laugh, knowing Ollie has tattoos in extremely indiscreet places on his body. I'm sure he would most definitely appreciate the favor.

"Glad to hear you had fun," I say, and Ollie quickly appears in my eyesight again as he stands outside the door.

"You're seriously not going to tell me anything, Si? What the hell?"

"Just let me enjoy this, yeah?" Ollie gives me a ridiculous pout and I wish I had something to toss at him. "I need some time to get my head around this one."

"Get your head *around* it? Or *in* it?" Ollie rubs his chin, thoughtfully. "You should have just said you couldn't seal the deal. No worries. I hear it's common with old age."

That's it. I grab the nearest object – a drink coaster – and send it flying toward his head. Unfortunately, the prick dodges it and starts cracking up laughing before walking back into the bathroom and starting the shower.

I move to wait on the balcony, as my mind crowds with thoughts of last night and the beautiful woman that shared my bed. The only way I could even leave her this morning was remembering the promise she made me last night before we finally drifted off to sleep.

"May I see you again tomorrow...or *today* rather?" I asked her, laughing as I realized how late it was.

She laughed with me, her breath whispering across my chest as she cuddled into my side.

"Sure," she said quietly. "You can see me whenever you'd like."

God, I love the idea of that so much more than I should.

She looked heavenly this morning lying in bed, wearing my t-shirt, with her long blonde hair wild across the pillows. She snores a little when she sleeps, and I found it absolutely adorable. *Fuck me*. I even think her snoring is sexy.

I thought I may have ruined everything at one point last night. I wanted to take things slowly with her, wanting her to see I could spend time with her without jumping her bones like a maniac, but like every other time I'm around her, I could barely control myself. I crave her touch like an addict, and I had to fight all night to keep my impulses in check. If she didn't think I was mad before, she probably does now.

All I know is I have to see where this goes. Last night was incredible. Sex with Sydney is hot and sweet and playful...completely mind-blowing, and the Neanderthal in me can't resist that, if nothing else. But there's plenty more I want to explore with her.

We spent time talking a bit last night, her opening up more than me, of course. She told me about her family, her friends, where she grew up, more about her current job and her dreams of going into nursing. We even discussed her beauty pageant days and our shared love of ice cream, and I soaked up every word out of that delectable mouth. She's kind, passionate, ambitious, brilliant. And learning all of these things about her only makes me want her more.

Hopefully, she's not angry with me for not saying goodbye this morning. I didn't have the heart to wake her, so I pray the note I left will suffice. We planned to meet again tonight after dinner, but I know I won't be able to resist her until then. I'm mad with need just thinking about seeing her in a bikini again today, and now I've seen that gorgeous body naked, so that's saying a lot. This girl is too good to be true. She has to be.

"I'm all set, mate!" Ollie shouts at me, and I turn and walk toward him ready to get this breakfast over with, so I can see Sydney again.

"It's about time."

"Wait. What the fuck happened last night?" Ollie asks me as I approach him, and I raise an eyebrow in confusion.

"What do you mean?"

"I haven't seen you smile like this in ages." Ollie shakes his head. "This one has you by the balls, doesn't she?"

"Hell no," I lie. "Sydney's great. She really is, but you know me. I don't do serious."

Ollie tries to catch my eyes, but I move around him heading for the door. "Lying bastard," he mumbles, and I smile, knowing he can't see me as I open the door to his suite.

I also don't argue because he's right. Sydney has indeed triggered something inside me that I haven't felt in a long time. As a matter of fact, I've been running from it for years. But with her, I don't know if I want to run anymore. I'm not even sure if I can.

CHAPTER 27 - SYDNEY

"Spill it!" Lacey shouts at me as soon as I walk into our cabin. "I want to hear every raunchy detail."

Smiling widely, I fall down on the bed and kick off my shoes. I had to do the "walk of shame" this morning in my little black dress and heels, but I did steal Simon's t-shirt that he let me sleep in last night. Hope he doesn't mind.

"You first," I tell Lacey, as I rise up on my elbows so I can see her face.

She's sitting in the chair at the small desk in the corner putting her hair up into a ponytail, and her smile is as wide as mine.

"Fine," she agrees, as she narrows her eyes at me. "But don't think you're holding out on me, Sydney. I can only assume that piece of clothing you have locked in a death grip belongs to one Simon Young."

"Tell me about Ollie." I laugh.

"Well, after last night..." Lacey sighs and I giggle again at how smitten she is already. I know the feeling. "I can confidently say that Ollie is more than just a great dancer. He also has incredibly sexy lips. Plus, he's sweet and totally hilarious. He had me in stitches most of the night. I had a blast."

"Okay, hold up," I interject, as I pop up on the bed to stare her down. "You *kissed* him?"

Lacey's smile is blinding as she bobs that pretty little head up and down.

"Oh my God!" We're both squealing like little girls, which is extremely out of character for Lacey, but I of course have all fangirl rituals down to a science. "I'm so happy for you, Lace!"

"Me too." She gives me a shy smile. "I think he may have been a little disappointed that I didn't want to go back to his suite with him, but it just didn't feel right. Not yet."

"That's okay, and I'm sure he understands," I try and reassure her, while simultaneously feeling like a huge slut. "Ollie Sutton is probably not used to girls turning him down. It will most likely make him fall madly in love with you."

"Shut up," she says and we both laugh. "By the way, you know what I heard last night from another fan? We were agreeing that we all love Ollie's tattoos, and one girl said he has one on his...you know..."

"No way!" I gasp. "I had no idea, but I guess I shouldn't be surprised."

"True. But is it bad that I think that's insanely hot?"

"Not. At. All," I happily declare. "It makes me proud to call you my friend."

"Only you." Lacey shakes her head at me. "And now it's your turn, Syd. I'm not waiting a minute longer."

I sigh, close my eyes and lie back down on the bed. "Oh Lacey, what am I going to do? He's so much better than I ever could have imagined. We may not have gotten off on the right foot, but he more than made up for that last night. He was charming and considerate and ridiculously sexy, of course," I laugh. "You know he keeps calling me *goddess* for some reason, and that's exactly how he treated me last night. He worshipped me like a *goddess*."

I open my eyes to find Lacey standing over me, her arms crossed over her chest.

"Dear God, you are so gone," she grins. "How did this happen, Syd? You're in so deep."

I sit up in a panic. "I am not. I barely know him."

"So what?" Lacey shrugs. "I've never seen you like this before. You're glowing, and you can't even talk about him without smiling."

"Oh, stop it." I stand up to move away from her and her accusations, but I can't help the smile that spreads across my face as I grab a water bottle from our tiny refrigerator. "It's just a little teenage-dream-come-true scenario. That's all. In fact, he told me last night that he couldn't give me anything more than sex, and that's perfectly okay with me. It will be best that way." I fiddle nervously with the paper around my water bottle as I remember that particular part. With a troubled sigh, I sit back down on the bed. "Simon's completely damaged, Lace, and I don't need the distraction right now, especially considering what this could potentially do to both of our careers. I mean, even though the sex was...*oh my God* I don't even know what to say about the sex, but Simon isn't the settling type. He's the type of guy that could break my heart into a million pieces, and I would probably never recover."

Lacey sits next to me, and drapes an arm around my shoulders. "Simon may seem like a train wreck in the public eye, but Ollie brought him up last night, assuring me that he's a really good guy, and I believe him. Everyone knows Simon's had a rough time of it, but maybe you're exactly what he needs, Syd. Maybe you and Simon are destined to be together. Maybe you always have been. Ever think of that?"

I look up at her and roll my eyes lovingly. "Thanks Lace, but I don't think the moon and stars stuff is what I need right now."

Lacey laughs and pulls me closer. "All right, I'm sorry I made a big deal out of things. I just want you to be happy, Sydney." I wrap my arms around her waist and hold her close. "Seems like whatever's going on with Simon is making you happy right now, so go with it. Who cares how long it lasts? Just enjoy your time with him while you have it, okay?"

"I plan on it," I mumble into her chest. "Are you seeing Ollie again?"

Lacey kisses my forehead before she releases me and heads back over to the desk to finish her hair and make-up. "I'll see him at the concert today on the island, and hopefully we can meet up again at the party tonight."

"What concert?" I question, not remembering what was on the itinerary for today.

"We're in the Bahamas today," Lacey reminds me. "The guys are doing some kind of event and then we can explore the island, remember? Or has Simon got your brain?"

"Haha. Very funny."

But he actually does have my brain. And my heart, I fear.

"Did he ask to see you again?"

I smile as I think about the note he left me this morning. "I told him he could see me anytime he'd like."

"Girl," Lacey drawls. "You are at Simon Young's beck and call for the next few days. Things could be worse."

I laugh as I stand and remove my dress. "Just curious, but why are you, of all people, putting on make-up only to sweat it off on the beach all day?"

Lacey gives me a guilty look. "Just trying to look professional. We *are* here on business, in case you forgot."

I give her a look that lets her know I see through her lie, as I make my way into the bathroom. I desperately need a shower, but I kind of hate the idea of washing the smell of Simon off my skin. At least I have his t-shirt, thanks to my thieving ways.

I take my time in the shower – shaving and buffing every surface to a shine. When I come back into the room after I'm done, Lacey is sitting on the bed playing with her iPad. She looks gorgeous in her white bathing suit with little hot pink hearts all over it and high-waisted khaki shorts.

"Is this too much?" she asks, as she stands and turns for me.

"You look fantastic," I tell her. "Ollie's going to die when he sees that swimsuit."

She stands and wraps a white button down around her shoulders, tying the front in a knot. "Well, it's not for Ollie. It's just the one that's not wet at the moment."

"Mmm hmm."

"Anyway..." She drags out the word in annoyance. "You don't think I look...slutty?"

"Seriously, Lace. You look amazing," I assure her. "And cleavage does not equal *slut*. We have to get your stereotypes in check."

"I'll work on it," she giggles. "Which suit are you going to wear?"

I move to peek in my suitcase at my options. "My super slutty red, halter-top bikini with the tiny white polka dots."

"I do love that one," Lacey smiles. "And you can wear those short denim shorts you brought – the faded cut-offs."

I pull them out, along with the bikini. "Look at you giving me fashion advice! I could cry right now, I'm so proud!"

I smile at Lacey's dainty middle finger, then dig to find a white tank top. I pull everything on and slip into my brown flip-flops as I move to the bathroom to do my hair. I know it will be up eventually, with the wind and crazy heat, but I think I'll leave it down for now. I add a little mouse and scrunch as I dry. My new cut gives me great volume for the perfect beach waves.

As I'm drying my hair, I think I hear an "Oh my God!", but I'm not sure, so I keep drying. The next thing I know, Lacey is next to me with a piece of paper in her hands. She's waving it at me with wide eyes.

"What is *this*?"

I put the dryer down so I can see what she's holding. "Lacey! Why do you have this?"

I quickly snatch my note from Simon out of her thieving little hands.

"I went into your purse to borrow your pink lip-gloss and I found it. Sydney, I'm not going to lie. This is so romantic I can barely breathe."

I smile at her as she pulls me into her arms holding me close.

"It's not what you think," I tell her, remembering again what he said last night about it only being physical between us and nothing else. "He tried to help me overcome my fear of boats. It's like a private joke. No biggie."

Lacey grabs the note back out of my hands and starts reading.

My sweet goddess, even though leaving you looking this incredible in my bed is agonizing, I take comfort in knowing I get to see you again soon. I look forward to working through more fears with you this evening – yours and mine.

Simon

Lacey looks up at me with wide eyes. "He called you his *sweet goddess*. Sydney, he's so into you."

"I'm not sure what's up with that nickname," I admit, but I know I *love* it. "But Lacey, you should know enough by now to know that Simon isn't into anyone but himself, at least not long term."

As I speak the words they feel wrong, but I have to keep telling myself that. I can't fall for Simon Young. I just can't.

Lacey narrows her eyes at me. "Fine. I'll let you win this one. Let's go get some breakfast."

I give her a grateful smile and follow her out of our cabin door.

"I should probably eat some oatmeal and fruit," Lacey frowns, "but pancakes sound so damn good."

"It's vacation, remember? You can splurge. I won't tell."

"Pancakes it is," she says with a smile.

"I thought I was going to have to twist your arm."

"Haha. What are you getting?"

"I think I'm going with an omelet," I decide, just as Lacey kicks my leg under the table. "Ouch! What was that for?"

"Simon's here," she informs me, staring over my shoulder. "I think he's looking for you."

Unable to resist seeing him again, I turn in my seat and my eyes find him immediately. He's standing in the doorway of the restaurant in navy blue board shorts, a tank top and flip-flops. His tattoo is on display for everyone to see, which makes me jealous now for some reason, and his hair is perfectly shaggy and unkempt, just the way I like it.

I watch him scan the crowd a bit until he finds what he's looking for. His brown eyes meet mine, and he gives me a quick wink before he's swarmed by waiting fans.

Ollie and the other guys are close behind him, and as soon as they arrive, some of the heat is taken off Simon as the fans start mingling among the rest of the group, but a large gaggle of giggling females is still surrounding Simon. The guys spend about twenty minutes chatting and taking pictures, then they start to spread out and come by the tables to chat with those of us that didn't rush them at the door.

Simon and Ollie walk directly to our table, both with huge smiles on their faces.

"Good morning, my lovelies." Ollie slides into the chair next to Lacey and gives me a quick glance and a smile, but then all of his attention is back to Lacey.

"Good morning," I say, looking over at Simon as he sits in the chair next to me.

He leans in, like he's going to whisper something in my ear, but plants a soft kiss on my neck instead.

"Good morning, goddess," he breathes against my neck before pulling away, and I glance around to make sure no one important witnessed that exchange. James and Rob are still by the door with fans, and it's obvious they didn't notice. Thank goodness.

"I wanted to let you know that I may not have the opportunity to spend as much time with you today as I would like." Simon slides a lazy fingertip along the top of my thigh under the table. "But I do plan to fantasize about you all day. Hope you don't mind."

The look he's giving me from under those long lashes is downright sinful.

"Depends on what you're fantasizing about," I tease and watch the lust cloud his eyes.

"Well, I'm hoping *your* mind will be on the same things, so you tell me." His finger slips up the inside of my shorts, and I gasp. "I'll see you later, goddess."

With a wink, Simon moves to the next table and Ollie leaves shortly after. I reluctantly move my eyes away from Simon to pay attention to Lacey for a moment. I hope her time with Ollie was as promising as mine.

"He's becoming more irresistible by the second." Lacey bites her lip as she studies the object of her desire.

I turn to take another look at Simon, and he glances up at me at the same time. A sexy smile spreads across his face before he returns to the people at the table.

"Tell me about it."

"This is insane. You know that, right? If James ever finds out, we're probably both toast. And not only that, but neither of these guys are the relationship type and no other man will probably ever compare to them. We're screwed, Sydney. We are so screwed."

"Pardon the pun?" I smile at my friend, and she smiles back. "That may be true, but like you said earlier, we're going to enjoy it while it lasts."

"You're damn right we are." Lacey holds up her mimosa and proposes a toast. "Here's to broken hearts."

I clink my glass with hers. "Amen to that," I agree, then down the entire glass.

CHAPTER 28 - SIMON

I can't even fucking concentrate with Sydney in the same room. I'm trying to give the fans my undivided attention, as always, but she's so beautiful I can barely keep my eyes away.

Although as I steal quick glances of her now and then, I can't pretend it's just my dick thinking. I'm excited to see her again. It feels good to have her close to me. I hadn't realized how much I missed her until just now. It's like a weight's been lifted off my chest now that I know she's nearby.

"So, Simon…"

I turn back to the table I'm at and meet the eyes of a short-haired brunette with fierce brown eyes – dark and dangerous looking, nothing like my goddess. "Yes, love?"

The girl looks at her friends at the table, and I notice the blonde sitting next to me widen her eyes in apparent disapproval. But when I look back at the brunette, she seems more determined than ever and I stifle a groan.

Before she even speaks, I know what's coming. And like always, I feel my heart slowly inching up into my throat, threatening to choke me. *Please don't do it*, I beg her in my mind. *Please. Don't.*

"So, Simon, how have things been going lately?" she asks, and I breathe a sigh of relief. Maybe this won't be as bad as I thought.

"I've been great," I tell her. "Even better now, surrounded by all of you ladies."

I see the blonde next to me smile widely and they all titter at my comment. Unfortunately, it seems that wasn't a good enough answer for the brunette.

"I'm so glad you're doing better now," she starts, with a load of fake sympathy on her face. "I know how the...accident must have affected you. I can't imagine I would ever get over something like that."

She reaches across the table and grabs for one of my hands. I let her take it, although I instantly feel sick. It's obvious what she's doing, and unfortunately, it's been done before. Many times.

"That's what whiskey is for, yeah?" I know it's a horrible thing to say, but honestly, who does this shit? Pretending to care about someone's pain and heartache, just so you can get closer to them?

Please don't make me lose faith in my fans, I silently plead with her again. *They're all I have left.*

To my dismay, no one seems to notice my rising panic. Instead, they all seem to think I'm okay now with this subject, so the other few girls at the table start pawing at me as well, continuing to ask questions.

"Weren't you driving the car? You poor thing," one of them says, but I don't even have a chance to respond before someone else speaks up.

"It wasn't your fault, Simon. It could have happened to anyone."

I try to smile. I try to play along. I try and fight my way through it, but I can't. I feel myself start to shake, and I know things are about to get ugly. This conversation is never an easy one, and with my nerves already spent from everything that's happened recently with Sydney, I can't find it in me to sit and listen any longer.

I remove my hand from the brunette's and quickly stand. "Please excuse me, ladies."

I make my way toward the deck or somewhere, anywhere but here, and I try and walk casually toward the door to the restaurant, but I can hear the silent whispers and sympathetic "awwws" coming from the table I just left, so I start walking faster.

"Are we done here?" Ollie asks, a confused expression on his face, as he catches up with me at the door. "I didn't think the event started until noon. We've got a couple of hours."

"I'm done," I mutter and keep walking. "I just had to get out of there."

Ollie grabs my arm, stopping me mid stride in the hallway. "What's up, Si? What's going on? Someone say something?"

Naturally, he assumes someone brought up Melissa. That's the obvious conclusion. It's been known to happen and my reaction is normally similar to this – *escape*. But I don't want to talk about it right now.

"No," I tell him. "I just need some air. I may go back to my suite for a bit."

Ollie studies me a moment. "All right then. I'm going back inside. I want to spend a little more time with the fans before the show."

"Sounds good. I'll see you later."

"Want me to say anything to Sydney for you?"

I pause, keeping my back to Ollie. I'm not sure I want Sydney to see me like this.

"No. Just tell her I'll see her later."

I don't wait for Ollie to respond. I walk as fast as I can back to my suite. My mind is wrestling with all of these bullshit emotions I haven't dealt with in so long. I nearly forgot I even had them.

By the time I near my suite, I'm jogging at a brisk pace. I was somehow able to avoid other fans on the way, or maybe I just didn't notice. I have no idea.

I open the door to my suite and close it behind me. I slide down the back of the door and pull my knees up. I'm breathing heavily, and not from the brief run.

I pull the locket from the pocket of my shorts and hold it tightly in my palm. Lowering my head to my knees, I try and inhale deeply, in and out, over and over again. I'm just starting to come down when a soft knock against the door rattles my back.

"I'm fine, mate. Stop worrying," I mumble, assuming it's Ollie coming to check on me.

"Simon? It's Sydney."

Oh shit.

I shoot up from my perch on the floor and turn to stare at the door. She knows I'm in here, so I can't avoid her.

I return the locket to the safety of my pocket, then place a hand on the door where I imagine her face would be.

"Simon, are you sure you're okay?" she asks, and I can hear the worry in her tone. "Ollie brought me here. I didn't want to bother you, but he insisted."

Fucking Ollie.

I hear a clink against the door near my face, and I realize it was probably the ring Sydney wears on her right hand, as she put a hand on the door to match mine. I can't stand it any longer, knowing she wants to be close to me, and I want nothing more than to be close to her right now.

I open the door, and Sydney's hand falls back to her side. Her face is concerned, her lips parted as if she's about to speak, but I don't give her time to say another word.

I grab her waist and pull her to me. As soon as the door is shut, I press my mouth fiercely against hers, aching to taste her again. This morning she tastes of oranges and champagne. Mimosas for breakfast, it seems. *Delicious.*

I pull her in even closer until nearly every part of her is pressed against me, but it's still not close enough. I push her against the door, and press my body so hard against hers I feel her gasp on my lips.

I know I'm being rough with her, but I can't stop. I keep waiting for her to push me away but she doesn't. Instead, she pulls her arms up and wraps them around my neck. She runs her fingers gently through the back of my hair, always the perfect complement to the war of emotions inside me – her calm to my storm.

Relaxing into her touch, I move my mouth slowly along her cheek down to her neck. I feel her shiver against me, and the feeling I get inside is pure, unadulterated pleasure. Once again, I'm torn between wanting to rip her clothes off with lightning speed and bury myself inside her to wanting to take my time and cherish every inch.

Her fingernails scratch lightly down the back of my neck and along my shoulders, and I moan, wanting her even closer. I put my hands underneath her thighs and lift her up, hoping she'll wrap those smooth legs around my waist. I'm delighted to find she seems eager to comply.

"Sydney," I whisper against her chest, as I press into her. I love saying her name.

"Yes?" she asks in a barely there voice, and I love that she seems just as affected as I am.

When I don't answer, she pulls my face back up so my eyes meet hers. She's searching my eyes for God knows what, but I can't have her looking too deeply. She's successfully broken down several of my walls in a very short period of time. I can't afford to lose anything more.

I pull her full lips back to mine, hoping to stop her invasion, but she pulls away moving her mouth to my ear.

"You feel so good, Simon."

I nestle my face in the soft skin of her neck, bracing my body with hers against the door. My legs are shaking so badly, I'm afraid I may drop her.

"I need you, Sydney. Please."

"I'm yours," she breathes, weaving her arms tightly around my neck, her hands back in my hair and my answering sigh is deep and long.

I'm yours. She said these words last night as well, and I find I'm loving them more and more every time I hear them.

I want to carry her to my bed, but I'm scared I may not make it in my current condition. As if she senses my dilemma, Sydney pushes that beautiful bottom down on my hands, wanting me to release her. I let go and she slides slowly down the front of my body, but this move is crazy sexy and does nothing for my fragile state.

With a warm smile, she grabs both my hands in hers as she walks backward. When we reach the bed, Sydney stops and wraps her arms around my waist and I stroke a petal pink cheek before pressing my lips lightly against hers. I stick with slow drugging kisses until I feel some stability return, then I lay her gently down and quickly move beside her, never allowing those lips to leave mine. Sydney turns to face me, tangling our legs, and starts sweetly caressing the sides of my face as we kiss. A low growl glides up my throat as this very foreign feeling of contentment bursts inside me. At the sound, Sydney pushes me onto my back, her hands back in my hair as her soft lips continue moving slowly against mine. Her touch is so loving and sincere, I know I have to take back the reigns or I'm going to start bawling like a baby in front of her, which I'd rather avoid.

I push her onto her back and hover above her. I snake my hand up her shirt and grab a handful of her full breast, while dragging my tongue down her sweet-smelling neck. She mimics my low growl from just moments ago, and I smile against her skin, as I glide my fingers down her bare stomach to the top of her shorts and undo the button. I pull down the zipper and move my fingers under her barely there bikini bottoms.

"Always so ready for me," I whisper, loving the look on her face as I please her.

My goddess never looks away or closes her eyes. She just gazes at me hungrily, making soft, sexy noises as she arches her back and pretty soon, I can't take anymore. I have to have her.

Urgent now to be inside her, I try to get her shorts off, but I'm shaking again and I can't seem to make it happen. Sydney sits up, forcing me to kneel in front of her. She puts both of her hands on either side of my face, and I'm instantly calm.

"Relax, Simon. I want you inside me just as much as you want to be there...maybe even more."

After that, I have those tiny shorts off in no time, along with the rest of her clothing. She helps me get my shirt and shorts off too in record speed, which is perfect because I don't want to waste another minute.

I fumble through my suitcase for a condom, making a mental note to make these more readily accessible next time, then I climb back on the bed.

"You want do the honors, my lady?"

"I was hoping you would ask me that."

Sydney pushes me on my back and moves between my legs. I look up to see her about to take me in her mouth, and I slam my head back down hoping I can last.

"*Sydney*," I grind her name out between clinched teeth, wanting her to keep going and wanting her to stop because I'm dying to have her. *All* of her.

Sydney gives me one last squeeze with her mouth before rising up and putting on the condom. She climbs on top of me and slowly lowers herself down, both of us gasping with the new connection.

Sydney's face is radiant as she looks down at me – her long, wavy hair shrouding her shoulders, her soft hands kneading my chest. Always wanting her close, I sit up and pull her chest against mine. I see on her face she must like this position, so I switch my selfishness off to fulfill her needs for a moment. And I enjoy every second of it. Immensely.

"*Oh God*...Simon."

I grab her waist and pull one perfectly round breast into my mouth. She cries out and moves her fingers back in my hair, but there's no gentle stroking this time around. She grabs a chunk in either hand and pushes my face against her.

"So fucking gorgeous." I breathe in her luscious scent. "I could do this all day."

I flick with my tongue, suck with my mouth, nibble with my teeth, and with a whimper, Sydney puts her hands on my shoulders to steady herself as she quickens her pace. She trembles against me with every nip, every taste, and it only fuels my fire. I have to hear her scream my name.

When I feel she's close, I pull her face down and ravish those plump lips with mine as I move my hand between us. "Simon...*yes*..." she cries, as she buries her face in my neck. And then she's screaming my name as she convulses in my lap and that's all it takes for me, before I'm lost in this beautiful woman once again.

Sydney's head is on my chest, and I'm inhaling the strawberry scent of her hair, feeling better than I've felt in a very long time.

"I guess we should get back, right?"

"Probably." I'm happy to hear the reluctance in her voice. "But I'd like to continue this later, if you don't mind."

"Not at all," Sydney sighs and cuddles closer into my side. "Simon?"

"Yes?

"I realize we're just getting to know each other, but...please know that I'm here...if you ever need anything."

"I know." I give her waist a squeeze, as her words just did to my heart. "And I appreciate that, but it's nothing you should worry about."

Sydney raises her pretty head and her eyes meet mine. "Ollie mentioned you were really upset earlier, and I'm not pressuring you in any way, but I'm willing to listen, if you ever want to talk."

I push a few strands of hair behind her ear and smile. "Thank you."

"No problem," she smiles back at me, then places a soft kiss above my heart. "Now, I'm going to get dressed."

I grumble my disapproval, as she starts pulling on her bikini.

"What? You don't like this swimsuit?" Sydney asks with a smile as I watch her get dressed.

"I like it better on my floor," I tease, and she gasps before grabbing my shorts and tossing them at me.

"You're incorrigible."

"You like my dirty mind, goddess. Admit it."

Sydney's smile makes me feel warm and cozy inside, and I realize then she's "Jekyll and Hyde", just like me. On the outside she's a fighter, and in the sack, she's a tiger. But there's a softer side to her that I can tell she rarely let's other people see. I feel honored she lets me in, even if it is in small doses at a time.

"I do like your dirty mind. I like it a lot," she adds in her insanely sexy, sweet Southern voice, and I have to fight the urge to pull her back onto the bed with me.

She finishes getting dressed and heads to the bathroom, as I hop off the bed and pull my clothes back on. I would love nothing more than to spend the rest of the day locked in my suite with Sydney, but a glance at my clock tells me I have about fifteen minutes until our "pre-show" meeting in James's suite.

"So, what are you guys doing on the island today?" Sydney asks from the bathroom. "Another concert? Do you get to do any sightseeing?"

"It's just the concert, I think. We don't really have time for sightseeing," I tell her. "I'm sure James is going to talk a little about his charity, and Ollie is going to embarrass all of us with his stand-up."

"Ollie's hysterical. He'll be great," she says, and I can sense the smile in her voice.

"He can be riot. That's for sure," I agree. "So, what's up with him and Lacey? How are they getting along?"

Sydney comes and sits beside me on the bed, looking appetizing. She's fully dressed, which is unfortunate, but her cheeks are rosy from all of the fantastic love-making, her baby blue eyes are bright, and that beautiful hair is pulled away from her face. I smile as I stare at her, and she smiles back.

"What is it?" she asks, bringing me back down to Earth.

"Huh? Oh, nothing," I lie. "Just admiring your smile."

Sydney's already rosy cheeks flash a deeper shade of pink. "Yeah? Well, I like yours too."

I lean over to kiss her, forgetting about whatever it was we were talking about. I realize Sydney has a tendency to make me forget about everything but her when she's around.

"Lacey likes Ollie, a lot," she tells me after our kiss, reminding me of the question I had forgotten about asking. "But I'm hoping she doesn't get too attached. I don't get the idea that Ollie's the relationship type."

Hmmm. If she thinks that about Ollie...

I know I told her last night it was only about the physical, but damn if I didn't love waking up with her next to me this morning. And the way she came to my rescue today? I'm starting to crave her nearness more and more, and I'm not sure how to feel about that.

"Ollie's a good guy." I'm quick to defend my friend.

"I agree. I know I don't know him like you do, but from what I've seen, he seems great."

"He is," I confirm, knowing it's not only Ollie I'm defending. "He's been a good friend to me over the years, better than I deserve really."

Sydney stands up to slip her sandals on. "And I love that about him, but Ollie's kind of a *walk on the wild side* for Lacey. I just want her to be careful. After the cruise, Lacey goes back to work and you guys go back to touring and promoting. The fantasy will be over. Right?"

"Is that the way you feel about us?" I'm not sure I want the answer, but I had to ask.

Sydney turns to me and searches my face. I both love and hate that look. I love the way her eyes seem to touch every piece of me inside, but I'm so afraid she'll find that part of me – the evil part, the self-loathing part, the part that doesn't deserve her. If she finds that part, it will break us both.

I try and keep my expression impassive as she stares at me. I want an honest reply from her, not one that is influenced by what my face might be giving away.

After several beats she finally speaks. "Sure. I think it's best to keep things...uncomplicated. Don't you?"

I wish this response didn't leave such a foul a taste in my mouth, but it does. In fact, I feel my black heart shatter into a thousand tiny pieces with her words, but I'm careful not to show it. My only saving grace at the moment is the indecision I see on Sydney's face. I don't think she actually believes what she's saying any more than I want to hear it, but I decide to give a vague, but truthful answer for the time being.

"Uncomplicated works."

Sydney mirrors my half-hearted smile and reaches out her hand to me. "Come on. You don't want to be late."

With a deep breath I take her hand in mine, and let her lead me to the door.

CHAPTER 29 - SYDNEY

"Are you crying?"

Dammit! I was hoping Lacey wouldn't follow me out of the banquet room.

I sniff and wipe away at the tears on my cheeks before I turn to face her. "I'm fine," I tell her, but she narrows her eyes and stalks toward me.

"Oh Sydney, please talk to me. What happened between you two? I thought everything was going really well."

"I'm actually not sure what's going on."

And that's the truth. The only thing I can think of was the last conversation we had when I left his suite earlier today. He essentially asked me how I felt about "us", and I wish now I was honest with him so that no matter what happened, he would know how I really feel. But instead I told him what I thought he wanted to hear, what I thought he needed to hear, so I could prolong my time with him. I thought if I confessed my feelings for him, he'd run screaming, but it looks like he did that anyway.

Lacey sighs and takes a seat next to me in a lounge chair. The poolside is empty, since everyone else is still at dinner or headed to the show.

"I'm sorry Syd, but I just don't understand it. After everything's that happened, and that amazing note he left for you? His behavior doesn't make any sense."

I wonder for a moment if I would feel better talking about it, and I decide I would. I have nothing to hide from Lacey, and maybe she'll have some good advice.

I take a deep breath before I begin. "When Simon and I were together this afternoon, it was...intense."

Lacey smiles and waits for me to continue. "But that's good right?"

I tilt my head up and look to the sky. For what? Answers? Good grief, this man has me all kinds of confused.

"It was good," I confirm. "And Simon is kind of intense in general. But he sort of attacked me when I went up to his suite."

Lacey's eyes widen, her jaw tensing. "What exactly do you mean by *attack*?"

"Not in a bad way." I wave off her alarm. "He didn't hurt me. It was sexy, kind of animalistic, but at one point, he was shaking so badly I thought he may lose it."

I notice Lacey has moved in even closer to me. "Lose it? What was wrong with him?"

"I have no idea. We all know he has some serious baggage, but..." I trail off, not sure I want to go there, even with Lacey.

I look up to find Lacey giving me a death glare. "You cannot leave me hanging like that, Sydney."

I take another deep breath. "Well, it was the strangest thing. He seemed so upset when I first got there, but then it was like I calmed him down, just by being near him. Actually, I've gotten that feeling with every crazy encounter we've had. I know this sounds insane, but I feel connected to him, Lacey – physically, emotionally, spiritually, you name it. I've gone crazy, right? You think I'm nuts?"

I watch as a slow smile spreads across Lacey's face. "I don't think you're crazy."

"You don't?"

"Of course I don't. I'm not sure what's going on between you guys, but it's something more than just chemistry."

"You think so?"

Lacey leans back a little and crosses her arms across her chest. "Yes I do. And you should too."

"But he agreed with me that this was just a fling," I sadly admit.

Lacey looks confused. "He did? What exactly was said?"

I don't want to tell her we were actually talking about she and Ollie at the time. "We were basically having the same conversation that you and I had this morning – that this is just a 'fun while it lasts' kind of adventure. I told him I didn't want things to get too complicated."

"And what did he say?"

"His exact words were 'uncomplicated works'."

"He doesn't think this is a fling," Lacey says with a confident smile.

"Did you not just hear my story?"

"I heard every word, and I'm telling you, this means more to him than just a fling."

I stare at Lacey's adamant face. "Why do you think that?"

"Because he didn't agree with you, Sydney," Lacey explains, as if I'm a toddler. "That answer was incredibly vague. I mean, what person wants a *complicated* relationship?"

I hadn't thought about it like that, but Lacey's theory is giving me more of that dangerous hope that I shouldn't be having, especially since he hasn't even glanced at me since our little *sexcapade* earlier.

I put my head in my hands, and Lacey pats my shoulder. "What am I doing, Lace? I don't do random hookups, especially with clients for God's sake! I can't be this girl. This isn't right."

"Yeah, you keep saying that." Lacey pulls my head up so I'll look at her. "But for starters, I think we're way past the work issue. And do I have to tell you that Simon Young is not *random*?"

"Okay, so maybe *random* was a bad choice of words, but what about the rest of it?" I ask, praying she has an answer. I need an answer. "I'm taking some pretty big risks here, Lace. Don't you think it's time I started acting like an adult for a change? Maybe it's time I grow up and start denying myself a few things, rather than thinking I'm entitled to whatever I want all the time."

"Do you honestly think that's what's going on here? That being with Simon is some selfish reward to your inner spoiled brat?"

"No," I admit, truthfully. "When I'm with him, it all seems so right, but that's even scarier."

"Why is that scary? Why is it scary to be happy, Sydney?"

"It's not about being happy," I correct. "Simon is turning me upside down, and I don't know if I can handle that right now."

"Well, get ready," Lacey commands. "Because despite this mess you've been going through with Simon you're nailing this account. The guys love you, and I don't think James would give you up at this point, even if he found out about you and Simon. You're on a roll. You're more confident than ever, and it's for all the right reasons. You *have* grown up, Syd. You're respected by your clients for being great at your job, and you're having a perfectly acceptable adult relationship with a man that, no matter what you may think, is much more than some silly fantasy come to life.

"Please don't take this the wrong way, but I think you've prided yourself on your looks for way too long. You're more than that, and I think Simon recognizes that fact as well." Lacey notices my eyes watering and she leans in to put a hand on my leg. "I'm not trying to upset you, girl. I'm just trying to make you see the truth. Your life is changing for the better, and I know it seems crazy, but I feel like Simon could be a part of that. I think taking a risk on him is well worth it."

"Since when are you the smart one," I sniff, and Lacey laughs.

"I've always been the smart one."

"That's so true," I agree with a smile. "Thanks Lace."

"My pleasure. Just promise me you won't give up on Simon."

"I won't. I promise."

I'm not sure how or why, but somewhere along the way I underestimated Lacey. I feel silly now for thinking I was changing her for the better by giving her fashion advice and dating advice that she clearly doesn't need. The student has definitely become the teacher. Actually, she may have been the teacher all along.

CHAPTER 30 - SIMON

Dinner was a fucking nightmare.

I could see Sydney looking at me out of the corner of my eye throughout most of it, and as a result, I barely paid attention to any of the fans at my table. I was totally off my game, and I hate disappointing the fans.

With about twenty minutes left of dinner, I saw Sydney get up from her table and leave. Lacey followed soon behind her, and I didn't miss the look Ollie gave me when they left.

Ollie shrugged, silently asking me what the hell's going on, but I ignored him. I used the last few minutes to try and save face at my dinner table now that Sydney was no longer a distraction, but her leaving only made things worse. I was worried about her, and I felt like a complete shit. She deserves more. She deserves an explanation, and that's what I'm trying to get up the nerve to do now as I sit back stage, waiting for the show to start.

I can't believe how much I've allowed myself to care in such a short period of time. All I can think about now is what she said earlier, about how she feels about us. It shouldn't bother me that she would look at this for what it is...what it *should* be.

But it does bother me, *dammit*. It bothers me and I hate it. This whole situation is making me uncomfortable and vulnerable and I simply can't have it. I have to trust my gut, not my heart. I need to end this. It's not right. I'm not right for her. I'm not right for anyone.

"You want to talk about it, Si?"

I put the locket back in my jeans pocket and look up at Ollie. I didn't even hear him come in.

He looks concerned, as he should be, I guess. I wish I could talk to him. I wish I knew what to say, how to explain this, but I don't.

I take a sip of my whiskey and shake my head. "No worries, mate."

"Did something happen with Sydney?"

"No."

Ollie's intense scrutiny is making me very uncomfortable, so I return to staring at the ground, sipping my Jack.

"Si, I know something's going on." Ollie raises his voice, forcing me to look up at him. "You ignored her at the event this afternoon and again at dinner. I thought this morning things were good between you. That's why I told James."

What the hell? My emotions shift from nervous to pissed off in an instant.

"You told *James*? How could you do that to me?"

"He's okay with it," Ollie tells me with a shrug. The fucker actually has the nerve to look delighted. "I told him she makes you happy, and he wants that for you, just like we all do. Plus, he loves her too," Ollie adds, and my eyebrows shoot up. "From a business perspective, of course. Thinks she's brilliant. Says he'll talk to the big boss at the firm, figure out a way to keep her on board."

"You must be joking."

"That's what he said," Ollie confirms. "And he agrees you're different with her, Si. Maybe things are finally turning around."

Okay, so I'm a little shocked that James is apparently fine with all of this, but Ollie's gone completely mad, if he thinks James's approval is the solution to all my problems.

232

"Seriously, Ollie? For starters, I don't think a woman is going to erase four years of living on the edge of misery, especially one I met less than seventy-two hours ago."

Ollie crosses his arms and looks away from me, knowing what's coming, but I stand up and move in front of him, making sure his eyes stay on me. I need to make sure he hears this loud and clear.

"And secondly, why don't you and James and the rest of the fucking planet stop worrying about me and every goddamn move that I make. I'm nearly thirty years old for Christ's sake, not a child. And if memory serves, I'm already out of the picture anyway, so give it a bloody rest!"

Ollie takes a deep breath and glances down at his shoes. "When are you going to get it? We worry because we care, you fucking arsehole."

And with that, he swipes a hand through his hair and turns and walks away, leaving me staggering and emotionally wrecked.

I sit back down in my chair, grab my drink from the floor and down it in one gulp. This is why I haven't allowed myself to care in years. It hurts. It hurts too damn much.

How am I supposed to accept other people's forgiveness when I can't forgive myself? It's impossible, and it's killing me, little by little, day by day.

And to top it all off, now I've gone and involved this wonderfully innocent girl into my sordid, muddle of a life. I knew from the moment I laid eyes on her things wouldn't end well, and here we are. I'm as fucked up as ever and still a total bastard – a wretchedly selfish bastard because no matter how badly I knew this would end, I still took what I wanted. Regardless of how she feels about me, I should never have slept with her. I shouldn't have even approached her at that restaurant in Miami. I should have left her alone, happy and safe in her world, exactly where she belongs. Because now, she's mixed up with the devil himself, and if I don't figure out a way to let her go, I'm afraid I may drag her down to Hell right along with me.

CHAPTER 31 - SYDNEY

I tried to fight it, but Lacey demanded that we go watch the show tonight. So here I am, following her to the theatre, watching her stumble around in another pair of impossibly-high heels I made her wear.

"I'm wearing flats the rest of the trip," she grunts, as we make our way downstairs toward the theatre. "These shoes are killing me."

"Like hell you are." She may have the upper hand in relationship advice, but I still have the say when it comes to fashion. "I'm keeping you looking sextastic this entire trip. There's beauty in pain, my friend."

She narrows her eyes at me and I smile as we trudge on.

When Lacey opens the door to the theatre, we're met with a burst of laughter. I look to the stage and see Ollie standing alone, finally getting the chance to do his comedy routine it seems.

"Isn't he adorable?" Lacey squeals in my ear, but I can barely hear her over the crowd.

We don't even try to get down front this time. Instead, we take a couple of seats on the back row and watch as Ollie does his thing. He pulls some of the other guys on stage a few times, including some of the crew members, but mysteriously, Simon is never one of them.

Ollie gets a standing ovation before the rest of the guys join him on stage. Simon walks out last, and I sigh with relief at the sight of him. I'm not sure what I thought was wrong or where he was, but seeing him in the flesh makes me feel better.

"How about some requests?" Rob asks, and several people stand and rush the mics throughout the theatre to give their suggestions.

Lacey and I watch as the guys run through a couple of oldies but goodies, including a hilarious version of *Sexy Back* by Justin Timberlake, where the guys imitate Justin's falsetto throughout the entire song.

They all appear to be having fun, but it's obvious something is bothering Simon. I'm not sure if anyone else is studying him like I am, but I can see the tension in his shoulders and the half-hearted smiles even from the back row.

"Who's next?" James asks, after they finish up the last request, and a girl standing at one of the back mics starts to speak.

"I have one," she says, and her voice sounds strange, almost seductive.

When I look back at Simon, the surprise and absolute horror on his face has me looking back in the direction of the girl that just spoke. I can't really see much of her from here, since the theatre is dark except for the spotlights on the stage, and she's standing on the opposite side of the theatre from where we're sitting.

I glance back up at the stage, just in time to see James shoot Simon a worried look. At the same time, Rob puts his bass down and quickly heads back stage. *What in the world is going on?*

"Go ahead." Ollie squints his eyes, trying to make out the face of the girl speaking.

Simon is now frozen in his seat at the piano, staring in the general direction of the girl.

"How about *Sweet Melissa* by The Allman Brothers," the girl says, causing an audible gasp to roll through the theatre. "Or maybe

Crash by the Dave Matthews Band," she adds, but she doesn't get out anything further.

Even in the darkness, you couldn't have missed the commotion caused by the security guards as they come to remove her from the theatre.

I look back at Simon, and his head is turned away from the crowd. He knows all eyes are on him, and after a few seconds, he stands and makes his way backstage, just as Rob returns. The three remaining guys all exchange a look and I see James nod to Ollie, giving him permission to go after Simon.

Unsure of what to do, but knowing I need to do something, I stand in my seat, but Lacey grabs my arm and pulls me back down.

"Where are you going?" she asks, and I can barely hear her over the crowd now as people have all started chatting about what just happened.

I don't get a chance to answer before James starts speaking into the mic. The chatter stops instantly.

"I'm so sorry about that everyone. Just a little unexpected interruption there, but let's move on, shall we? I'm sure Rob and I can entertain you. How about a few more requests? Duets anyone?" he adds with a laugh and the crowd seems to relax a bit.

Everyone except me.

I try to stand again, but Lacey refuses to let me go. "I don't think you should go after him right now, Sydney. I know you want to help, but he has Ollie, and I think Ollie may be a better candidate to deal with what just happened."

I sit and try to push away the sting of Lacey's words, but she's right.

It's obvious that girl was an ex of Simon's out for revenge. That's all fine and good, but the fact that she had the nerve to bring up Melissa like that...well, Lacey's right. I'm not what Simon needs right now. He doesn't need to get laid. He needs a friend, and I unfortunately don't think I fit that description at the moment.

CHAPTER 32 - SIMON

Oh dear God, make it stop. Please make it stop.

"Holy shit, Si! Was that Tricia? That fucking bitch!"

Ollie's voice sounds far away, due to the ringing in my ears, but I know he's close behind me. I continue to walk toward...I have no clue where I'm going, or what I need right now. An image of a stunning blonde goddess with light blue eyes flashes in my head, but I shut it out. I shut her out.

I need to sit down.

I see an open room behind the stage to my right and make my way inside. I hear Ollie's muffled footsteps following me, but I can't seem to concentrate on any one thing at the moment.

I sit down in the first chair I see and drop my head into my hands. I immediately start gasping for air. I'm so sick of this fucking feeling.

"How the fuck did she get on this ship?" Ollie's voice still seems far away from me, as the ringing in my ears escalates to a dull roar. "Hey, you okay, Si?"

I focus on trying to catch my breath, hoping that this isn't the straw that breaks the proverbial camel's back. I may be finally losing it. I thought I had hit rock bottom before, but maybe not. Maybe this is it.

"Si?" I hear Ollie ask again, and then I feel his hand on my shoulder. I jump at the contact and he removes it. "Si, do you need me to call a medic? I'm getting worried over here."

I'm together enough to notice Ollie's sat down in a chair next to me, being graciously silent now, and I appreciate that more than he probably knows.

A few beats later, and I find my voice. "Sorry, Ollie."

"You don't have to apologize to me. It's not your fault that piece of shit somehow got on the boat."

"Yeah, but it is my fault that she decided to tear me apart in front of hundreds of fans."

I look up to see a small smile on Ollie's face. "That bad, mate?"

"No note. No phone call. Nothing. I just disappeared, and that was before she found out I'd been sleeping with one of her roommates."

"Aces," Ollie laughs. "Still hate she got to you. Security caught her, though. I assume she'll be in 'cruise ship jail' until we get back to Miami."

I hate that it happened as well, but what's upsetting me the most is that it happened in front of Sydney, or at least I assume it did. I saw her leave dinner early, so there's a chance she may not have been at the show. But with my luck, I'm certain she saw the whole damn thing.

"I wonder if there will ever come a time when my past doesn't keep biting me in the arse."

"Maybe when you stop letting it?" Ollie smiles. "Or maybe when you learn how to stop making such bad decisions in the hunny department?"

"Can't argue that," I agree with a smile.

"But I think you're finally headed in the right direction. Or at least, you were. May want to try and salvage that one. Try and do something right for a change."

"I can't," I admit, and it physically hurts to push those words out. "She's too good for me. I deserve girls like Tricia, not like Sydney. Trust me."

"I do trust you, Si. And I truly am sorry about what happened tonight." I watch Ollie as he leans up in his chair and looks down at his feet. "But I'm going to be honest with you. I agreed with James's decision to let you go mainly because I don't want to watch you do this to yourself anymore."

I go to interrupt, not wanting to hear this right now, but Ollie holds up a finger to stop me as he continues to stare at his shoes.

"Four years of watching you plod through the deepest, darkest circles of Hell...well, it's killing me too, you know. There's obviously nothing any of us can do to help you, and it's frustrating. For everyone. Not just you." Ollie takes a deep breath and looks up at me. "I'll always be your friend, Si, your brother. But what happened tonight shouldn't have bothered you like it did. You reacted like Melissa died four months ago, instead of four years ago."

I stand and start to leave, eager to do anything that will make him stop all the bloody talking.

Ollie stays in his seat, and I turn to face him before I walk out the door. "I get it Ollie. Honestly, I do. But it was *my* fault. I was driving the car. Remember? It's my fucking fault she's dead. And I'm sorry that I'm bringing you down, but I don't care if it's been four months, four years or forty years, I don't think the fact that I took my fiancé's life will ever get any easier."

"Si, you didn't–" Ollie starts, but that's all I hear.

I turn the corner, toward the same staircase that I took last night with Sydney. I walk up the first flight, but by the time I reach the door to my floor, I'm in a near sprint. I fling the staircase door open, not caring who may be on the other side, and continue to run past security down to my suite.

I'm panting as I pull out the key, and my hands are shaking so badly I can barely open the door. Luckily, I make it inside my suite before I lose it completely.

CHAPTER 33 - SYDNEY

"So, tonight was a little crazy," Lacey says, as I remove my make-up in the bathroom, trying in vain to keep my mind off of Simon.

"Agreed."

"I hope Simon's okay. You're not mad at me for not letting you go to him are you?"

I pat my face dry and open my eyes to find Lacey standing close to me in the doorway of our tiny bathroom.

"Of course I'm not mad at you," I tell her. "You were right. What could I have done to help him? I'm sure Ollie's with him, or he's at least made sure Simon's okay."

I watch Lacey in the mirror and she stares at me thoughtfully, as I move from washing my face to brushing my teeth.

"I'll ask about Simon when I see Ollie later at the party."

"No, don't," I say anxiously, with a mouth full of toothpaste. I finish up, then turn to face her. "Or at least don't let him think it's me that's curious. I don't want to seem needy."

"I don't think caring about people makes you seem needy, Sydney," Lacey argues. "It means you're a good person. And why shouldn't Simon know that you care about him? Maybe he needs a little more of that in his life."

"You can go ahead and go to the party, if you want," I tell her for the hundredth time. "It'll be more fun than hanging out with me. I promise."

"Don't worry about me. I don't have to go to the party right now." Lacey moves back to the bed and plops herself down. "If you wanna know the truth, the eighties theme is as tempting to me as an endless supply of road-kill," she smiles. "I'd rather hang out with you for a bit. I'll go to the party later. Should we rent a movie?"

She starts flicking through the channels with the remote, as I change into my pajamas – a pair of one of my ex's boxer briefs that I kept because of the wonderfully soft material, and a black tank top.

"Are you mad at me, Lacey?" I ask her, as I slip under the covers of my bed. "For not going to the party with you? I should go, shouldn't I? I should go and mingle with you. It probably looks bad if I stay in tonight."

"Of course I'm not mad at you, Sydney," she says with a smile. "And I don't think it's a big deal if you skip the party. You're getting your work done. That's what matters. The guys don't think you came on this trip to party."

"Good," I smile back. "Because I feel kind of beat, and a movie sounds awesome."

"So, what movie should we watch?"

"You choose. Just nothing scary."

"You got it."

Lacey gets up to turn off the lights, then kicks off her heels and hops back on the bed. I'm half-heartedly watching the television as Lacey chooses a movie, but I can't seem to get Simon out of my head.

The next thing I know, the credits are rolling, and I look over to find Lacey's in front of the bathroom mirror freshening up. A quick glance at her new true-to-the-decade outfit tells me she must be about to ditch me for the party. I hadn't even noticed her get up.

As Lacey prepares for what I'm sure will be a wonderful evening with Ollie, I'm restless under the covers and wide awake, wondering if I'll ever get to sleep tonight. Maybe I should go to the party. Maybe Simon will be there. I want to see him. I need to make sure he's okay.

I reach for the remote and turn off the television so Lacey can hear me, but just as I'm about to tell her I think I'll join her after all, there's a light knock on our door.

"It's probably Ollie," I guess, but Lacey shakes her head.

"I'm meeting him upstairs. I didn't want him to have to leave the party."

We both look at the door again just as another soft knock fills the quiet of our cabin.

"I'll get it." Lacey wipes her hands down the front of her denim skirt and moves toward the door.

A quick glance at the clock tells me it's nearly one in the morning, and since I have no idea who this could be, I pull the covers up to my neck, not wanting whoever this is to see me in my braless state.

I watch as Lacey peers through the tiny peephole, and my heart comes up through my throat as she turns quickly to face me, her hand flying over her mouth.

"It's Simon!" she whispers urgently, and I suddenly feel faint.

We stare at each other in shock for a moment, until I thankfully come to my senses.

"Open the door," I tell her, but my voice is quivering and unsure.

Lacey turns back to the door and opens it slowly. At first, her body is shielding my view, and I can't see him. But I can hear him.

"Sorry to bother you so late, but is Sydney here?"

Simon's voice is soft and slightly slurred, and instead of answering him, Lacey opens the door wider and moves to the side so he can see me.

I have to stifle a gasp at his appearance. His hair is a mess – he's obviously been running his hands through it for hours – and I can tell his eyes are heavy and rimmed in red, even in the dim lighting. He's wearing dark shorts and a white t-shirt, and I notice the collar of his shirt looks stretched, like he's been pulling at it, as if it's been choking him.

I sit up in the bed when our eyes meet, and I don't know how to process the emotion I see spring into his eyes. It's unmistakably *relief.*

"May I come in?" he asks, and I nod.

Simon crosses the threshold, and I move to get out of my bed to greet him.

My legs are shaking slightly as I try and get to my feet. I can't believe he's here. What's he *doing* here?

I don't have much time to think about it. Simon moves quicker than anticipated, and as soon as he reaches me, he bends to bury his face in my neck and wrap his arms tightly around my waist.

My arms immediately go around him, and I feel him relax even further into me as I begin to run my fingers through his hair. When I look back over at Lacey, she has a hand over her mouth, but even in our dimly lit cabin I can see the smile behind it.

She gives me a small wave with her free hand and winks before leaving and closing the door behind her.

Simon is rocking us both back and forth, which I think at first is a calming gesture. Then I smell the alcohol on his breath as he breathes against my neck, and I realize he's actually swaying very unsteadily on his feet.

"Simon, are you okay?" I ask him. "I was so worried."

I manage to get a hand on either side of his face and push gently, wanting to see his eyes. He slowly lifts his head and sad, tired eyes meet mine briefly before he closes them.

"I can't sleep, Sydney," he whispers, burying his face back into my neck. "And I'm so tired. So fucking tired."

"Well then, let's get you some rest," I whisper back, my heart breaking for him.

I move to sit down on the bed, and seeming unwilling to let me go, Simon follows me down until we're lying next to each other, his arms still around my waist and his head now on my chest. I pull the covers over us both, then adjust my body so I have one arm around him, cradling him against me as I run my fingers through his soft, blonde hair.

Simon curls himself into me, and he's sound asleep in seconds, making it hard to believe he was having any trouble sleeping.

I continue to try and soothe him in some way, even after I know he's asleep. I play with his hair, stroke his back, kiss the top of his head, whatever I can do to make it better.

I was awake when Lacey came in at some point during the night, and now I'm awake again as the sun starts shining in the tiny window of our cabin. Simon is still sleeping – still curled against me, and seemingly peaceful.

Lacey tiptoes out of the bathroom and gives me a smile. "I'm going to grab some coffee," she whispers. "Do you want anything?"

I shake my head in reply, not wanting to risk waking Simon.

"I'll take my time." She winks and heads out the door.

As soon as Lacey leaves, my attention is back on Simon. I pull away from him slightly and notice he has a light shading of blonde stubble on his jaw that I can't resist. I should feel exhausted, but I feel the complete opposite as I move to brush my fingers across the soft hairs on his cheek. He moans quietly with the contact, making me smile. I brush my fingers down his cheek again, eliciting yet another faint sound, this time more like a whimper that tugs at my heart.

The arm I have wrapped around him has been asleep for hours, but I can't make myself care. I move my free hand gently up his arm and push up the sleeve of his t-shirt so I can see the piece of his tattoo that's poking out more clearly.

This is the first time I've had a chance to really study it, and the dark lines still don't make much sense to me. It's kind of chaotic – erratic shapes and lines all blurred and connected to each other. I think I see some letters mixed in, but I can't make out any words.

As I'm working to figure out one of the intricate designs, Simon stirs in my arms, and a brief flash of panic registers. He was obviously drunk last night. What if he regrets his decision to come see me? God, that would be so embarrassing.

But I don't let myself get sidetracked by that thought. I decide instead to enjoy the feel of him in my arms, as he continues to stir until sleepy brown eyes meet mine.

Simon and I stare at each other in silence for a few moments. His eyes aren't quite as miserable as last night, but the darkness is still there. I give him what I hope is a reassuring smile, and it seems to work. He closes his eyes and pulls me close, once again burying his face in my neck, like he's carving out a space for himself there. He inhales deeply and sighs.

"Did you sleep well?" I ask him as we hold each other close.

"I did. Thank you." His voice is deep and raspy from sleep. "What time is it?"

"Almost eight."

"Good," he says with another sigh.

I remember the itinerary saying there was another show on deck today, but I don't think there's anything happening before noon. I assume from Simon's obvious relief at the time of day, he doesn't have any obligations beforehand.

We sit in silence for a while, just holding each other and with each minute that passes, I'm more and more relieved that he obviously doesn't regret his drunken decision last night.

"Sydney, I'm so sorry about yesterday." Simon lifts his head to find my eyes. "I don't think it's a mystery I'm a little mixed up in the head right now. I've been trying to decide if I want to risk bringing you into my fucked up life, but after last night, and the way you always seem to..." I watch as Simon's eyes glow with intensity. "I can't seem to get enough of you, goddess. I know in the deepest, darkest part of me that I don't deserve you, but I don't want to fight it anymore."

"Well, then don't," I interrupt. "Don't fight. Let's just spend time together, okay? I like spending time with you. It doesn't have to be this complicated thing, Simon."

"Right. *Uncomplicated.*" I wince as he repeats the word from our disturbing conversation yesterday. "I guess I feel like I wasted time yesterday, not spending it with you."

I smile as I caress his cheek. "We still have today and tonight. You can make it up to me."

"Oh, I plan to," Simon promises. "In fact, we don't have an appearance until noon. I'd like to spend the morning with you, if that's all right."

"Shouldn't you be mingling around the boat? Talking with the fans?"

"You're a fan." Simon smiles, and places a gentle kiss on my lips. "We'll just think of it as an exclusive engagement."

"I feel so honored."

"I would never want to disappoint a fan." Simon kisses me softly again. "So, breakfast then?"

"That sounds good," I tell him, still smiling. "Mind if I get a shower first?"

"Not at all," he whispers. "As long as I can join you."

CHAPTER 34 - SIMON

It's official. Sydney is my latest vice, and I'm wholeheartedly addicted.

I pull her closer as we kiss, so my chest is pressed firmly against hers. "Shower," I mumble on to her lips, but I have zero desire to move from this bed anytime soon.

"Or bed," Sydney suggests, and a growl escapes me as I grab the back of her hair and pull, giving me access to that irresistible neck.

Sydney lets out a whimper as my tongue trails leisurely across her jaw. I love pleasing her. She's so beautiful like this – aroused and fully abandoned. It's spectacular to watch.

Wanting to push her further, I slide my fingers from her hair, across her collarbone and take a handful of her breast. *Absolute perfection.*

I've been a selfish lover for a while now. I'll admit it. But pleasing Sydney is energizing, empowering almost. It truly is like a drug, and I'm weak and defenseless against its potent effects.

Listen to that. I love the sounds she makes as I slowly move my hand down her tight stomach to between her thighs.

"Yes, Simon. Please," she begs, and I'm dying to give her what she needs.

That's right, goddess. Anything for you.

"Tell me what you want, Sydney," I command, mostly because I just can't get enough of that sexy, Southern voice. "Talk to me, love. I'll do whatever you want. Just tell me."

by Melinda Harris

She pulls away from me, her face flush and her sparkling blue eyes wild with lust.

"I want you inside me, Simon," she says, caressing my face. "I want to feel you inside me."

Christ. This drug has me positively euphoric.

I close my eyes for a moment, concentrating on her soft hands brushing my face. I know that if I would have had these same hands on me last night after what happened with Tricia, I would have been fine. I wouldn't have needed the whiskey. I would have been safe and warm beneath these hands, just like I felt when I finally got up the courage to come to her. Just like I feel now – happy and safe.

I move to hover above her, and I'm amazed by how perfectly I fit, cradled between her thighs. I lean down and kiss her sweet lips and swallow up her sighs as I press against her.

She grabs at the bottom of my t-shirt and, eager to have her hands on my bare skin, I lift up but only for a moment so I can help her. My lips are back on hers as soon as possible and I remove her top and bottoms without ever breaking our kiss. I reach a hand between us now and find she's more than ready for me and I fucking love it. Nothing can describe the way it feels, knowing this incredible creature wants me, needs me, as much as I need her.

"Simon, please," she begs again, and I can't deny her – or myself – any longer.

She moves her hands to my hips and lingers there, grasping my shorts, waiting for permission, as if she needs it. I pull my lips from hers and humor her with a smile, giving her the permission she needlessly seems to be requesting.

She smiles back, and pushes my shorts down my legs. "Condom?" I ask against her neck, praying she has one. *Please God don't make me stop. Not now.*

"I trust you."

I exhale against her skin as my heart flutters in my chest. It's not the first time she's said those words, and although her trust in me is most undeserved, it feels so damn good, regardless of subject matter.

"I'm on the pill." She looks slightly embarrassed now and totally adorable. "I trust you, Simon. And I need you. *Please.*"

I continue to stare at her a moment. Can she be real? Am I dreaming? I have to wonder because it's been so long since I've felt this way about a woman. Honestly, I'm not sure I ever have.

"I'm clean," I tell her. "I promise. I get checked regularly, because, well..."

Sydney places a hand over my mouth. "Let's not get into that right now."

"Yes," I agree, with a smile. "I would like to get into you, however, if you don't mind."

"Sounds wonderful," she moans and closes her eyes as I slowly enter her.

Oh, sweet relief.

I move leisurely, but with purpose, as I make love to someone for the first time in what feels like an eternity. Once again, my emotions overwhelm me, and I start to tremble in her arms, but it's not about need this time, or fear. I realize that in this moment, I'm surrendering myself completely to her. And I realize just as quickly that it's probably a mistake, but I can't make myself stop. It feels too good.

When it's over, Sydney and I are both shaking silently while we hold each other, my face finding its new favorite spot, buried beneath her thick, blond hair, nestled comfortably against her sweet smelling neck.

And as I come down from what had to be the best orgasm of my existence, I realize I've waited forever to feel what I just felt with Sydney, and no matter what happens between us, I know this moment will be etched in my mind as one of the best experiences of my life.

"Simon, that was…"

I lift my head when she doesn't continue so I can see her face. Her cheeks are flush and her face is glistening from our recent love-making. She's so unbelievably sexy.

"Yes?" I ask, my eyes drawn to her lips which are a beautiful shade of pink and swollen from my kisses.

But before either of us can say anything further, we hear a click near the door. Looks like Lacey's back. *Dammit.*

"Oh my God!" Sydney cowers beneath me, and I roll off of her, laughing. I pull her into my chest and cover us both with the sheet.

"We can hide," I whisper. "She'll never know we're here."

Sydney smiles widely as she wraps her arms around my neck and kisses me sweetly. *Christ*, how much more of this can I take? I'm a slave to this girl. In every way.

"Good morning, you two."

"Good morning, Lace," Sydney says, smiling at me under our makeshift tent.

She gives me one more quick kiss, then pulls the covers back to reveal our faces. Lacey is still standing by the door, arms across her chest, grinning widely.

"I'm going to grab a shower so you two can get decent," she tells us. "Take your time."

Lacey moves into the bathroom, and Sydney and I turn back toward each other. "How about we get cleaned up in your suite?" she suggests, and I smile, loving the sound of that. "Get dressed, and I'll grab some clothes, okay?"

I give her one more kiss, then get up to find my clothes. I could stay attached to her lips every day for a month and still not get enough of that taste.

I dress quickly and watch Sydney as she pulls on some skin tight workout pants, a tank top and some trainers. She smiles back at me as she pulls her hair into a ponytail and I feel like my face may split in two at any moment from all the ridiculous grinning I've been doing this morning – quite the change from my state last night.

"Let me just get my things from the bathroom, and we can go, okay?"

"Sure." I'm barely able to speak after watching her move around in those tight pants for the past ten minutes.

"Ready?" she asks when she returns.

"Ready."

I stand and move toward her, and she extends her hand to me. I willingly grab for it, craving the stability her touch seems to bring.

Sydney pauses before we reach the door and looks up at me. "Do you think we should go separately?" she asks. "What if someone sees us?"

She tries to drop my hand, but I refuse. Instead, I take both her hands in one of mine and use my other hand to pull her chin back up so she'll look at me.

"Let me make this clear," I start, about to tell her that there's really no need to hide anymore, but something entirely unexpected comes out instead. "As of right now, I don't give a shit what other people think. And if people find out that we're spending time together, I'll proudly confirm it, if that's your wish. And I *will* hold your hand because I want to, and I enjoy the way it feels in mine. You make me happy, Sydney. I feel good when I'm with you. I feel safe. And I haven't felt that way in a very long time. I know I don't deserve you, but if you haven't already noticed, I'm horribly selfish. I'm afraid you may be stuck with me for a while, goddess."

Sydney looks down, and I pull her eyes back up to mine, just in time to see a tear roll down her cheek.

"Sorry," she says smiling. "I'm a total sap."

"It's endearing, and you're lovely." I lean down and kiss the tear from her chin. When I find her eyes again, they're closed and I smile. "And besides, apparently James and the rest of the guys already know about us. There's not really a need to hide anymore."

Sydney's eyes pop open wide with fright. "What did you say?"

"James said he's happy, if I'm happy," I tell her. "There's no need to worry."

"But Simon, this means that...*oh God*...what will he tell Jasper and Lena?" Sydney's frantic. And not surprisingly, I find that quite adorable as well. "I don't think Jasper will be okay with this. What if I lose my job? What will I do?"

I put my hands on her face and force her to look at me. "Sydney, the important part in all of this is that James is okay with it. If James doesn't have a problem, Jasper won't have a problem." Sydney starts nodding slowly, but I'm not sure I've convinced her quite yet. "And James loves you. He told me so. He wants to keep you on the account, so please don't worry. He'll talk with Jasper and everything will be squared away, yeah?"

Sydney continues to nod, but her eyes are still wide and unfocused. I pull her face to mine and kiss her once more, trying to bring her back to me. I feel her relax a little in my arms, but I continue to kiss her deeply, reverently, and when I hear her sigh, I know I have her.

I pull away and find a dreamy smile on my goddess's lips. "Better?"

"Better."

"Good. Now, how about that shower?"

Sydney smiles up at me with a new light in her eyes. "I'll race you," she says playfully, before tossing open the door and bolting down the hall.

With my own smile firmly in place, I take off after her. Little does she know, I may chase this woman to the ends of the earth, if she'll let me.

CHAPTER 35 - SYDNEY

"Don't you play guitar as well, or is it only the piano these days?" I ask Simon, as he wheels over the room service cart so we can eat our breakfast on the sofa.

He appears to be in a much better mood now, and I smile, hoping I had something to do with that. Personally, I'm still reeling from the news that James and the guys all know about Simon and me. And even more shocking is that they're okay with it.

Simon keeps assuring me everything will be fine, but James giving us his blessing makes this all seem too good to be true. And that makes me very nervous.

But I've decided not to think about that right now. Honestly, it's hard to think about much of anything when Simon is wandering around in loose cargo shorts, a black wife beater and hair still damp from our shower. I smile, remembering what he did to me in that shower...pressing me against the back wall and slamming–

"What are you thinking about?"

Simon interrupts my naughty thoughts and I smile wider. "The shower," I shamelessly admit.

"It was quite nice."

"*Nice*?" I feign offended. "That's the best you've got?"

Simon leans down and kisses me soundly. "It was mind-blowing, incredible," he whispers, staring deep into my eyes. "And if I could do that every minute of every day, I would be the happiest man on earth."

"Much better," I smirk, as he moves back to arranging our pancakes and fruit.

"And to answer your question, I do still like playing guitar and even the drums on occasion," he informs me. "And in case you didn't know, I'm sometimes known for playing women as well."

I toss the small pillow from the sofa at him, and he uses his arms to dodge the blow as he laughs.

"Smartass."

"I know," he says, then joins me on the sofa. "But you have to clarify these things. I can be rather dense, you see."

Simon wraps both arms around my waist and pulls me onto his lap so I'm straddling him. I smile and caress his left temple. "I know for a fact, you are far from dense. Magic happens in this beautiful head of yours."

"Oh really?" He closes his eyes with my gentle touch. "And what makes you say that?"

"Your songwriting, for one," I say automatically. "You're a poet Simon, and forgive me for saying this, but I think your talent surpasses what's needed to keep a boy band successful these days."

"What are you suggesting?"

"I'm not suggesting anything. I just...well, I'm a little biased, but I think you're the most talented member of the group in a lot of ways. You write and you play multiple instruments. You can fit into any genre. There's nothing you can't do."

Simon studies my face a long time, so long that I repeat my last words in my head, wondering what I could have said that was so thought provoking. I'm running through them a second time when Simon's features abruptly change, and he lets out a resigned sigh.

259

"Some of that may be true, but my poetry writing days are in the past, I'm afraid," he says in a sad voice. "I haven't written any music in a long time."

"Why not?"

Simon shrugs. "I've lost my inspiration, I guess."

"That one's too easy. I'm not buying it."

"It wasn't a line or an excuse," Simon chuckles. "It's the truth. Life has been kind of heavy for me the past few years. I'm afraid I've become a bit blocked."

"Say what you want. That's an excuse," I disagree, trying not to get distracted by Simon's thumbs moving back and forth across the top of my bare thighs. "A lot of artists do their best work at some of the lowest times in their lives. If you're not writing anymore, then it's because you don't want to, not because you can't."

As soon as the words are out of my mouth, I know I've overstepped my boundaries. "Simon, I didn't mean–"

Simon pulls my face to his and presses his lips tenderly against mine. "Maybe you could inspire me, my goddess."

"Me?"

His eyes roam my face as he lightly brushes my cheeks with his fingers. "Maybe you already have."

Oh wow.

Technically, you could say I've been in love with Simon Young since I was thirteen years old. But that's fangirl love – love inspired by dreamy boy band physiques and catchy tunes. This, however, is not fangirl love. *This* is different.

Since I first laid eyes on him in Miami, my feelings for Simon became this living, breathing, tangible thing. And despite the "I don't wanna grow up" conversation I had with Lacey recently, I'm mature enough to know the feelings I have for this man are not possible in two days. Just. Not. Possible.

But here I sit, in the lap of my teenage dream, staring into his chocolate brown eyes as he looks into mine with unmistakable adoration. I keep telling myself this can't be real, but it is. And as he moves his lips back to mine, I realize something else is also very real about this moment.

I'm falling in love with him.

I'm falling hard and fast for the compassionate, loving person I've found him to be. That part of him may have been shut down to the rest of the world for a while now, but it's still there and for some inexplicable reason, he's showing that side of himself to me. I seem to be helping him find that person again. And that feeling is....

"Why are you crying?" Simon's soft voice pulls me from my revelation, making me feel exposed. My entire body starts to tremble in his arms. "Sydney? Are you all right?"

I wipe at the tears I had no idea were falling and quickly jump from his lap, knowing I can't explain what's wrong and terrified by even the thought of saying it out loud.

"I have to go," I tell him, as I move to gather my things. Of course Simon doesn't take my departure lightly.

"What do you mean?" He stands and moves toward me. "Where are you going? What the hell happened, Sydney? I don't understand."

"I just have to go," I repeat, not knowing what else to say. "I promised Lacey I'd spend time with her today. I'll see you later, okay?"

"Sydney, please," he begs, his voice so desperate that I feel a new swell of tears forming in my eyes. "Look at me," he commands, and my body automatically obeys.

I move my eyes to his and the desperation that was in his voice is lying tenfold on his face.

"Don't do this," he says quietly, approaching me like I'm a wild animal he's trying to trap in the woods. "Whatever happened, whatever I said, let's just talk about it please?"

I shake my head slowly as tears continue to roll down my cheeks.

"You didn't do anything," I admit. I don't want him to feel guilty. "I just...I'm sorry, Simon. I'm starting to feel a little overwhelmed. That's all."

Simon rakes his hands through his hair in frustration. "Overwhelmed? What did I do?"

"It's nothing you did," I repeat. "You're wonderful. I just can't..."

I have no idea how to explain or what to say in general. I just know I have to get away from him before I sell my soul completely, with no chance of ever getting it back.

But before I can make my move toward the door, Simon is in front of me, blocking my path.

"Talk to me," he pleads. "I've made you cry more in the past few days than I'd ever care to see and it's breaking my heart. Please talk to me, Sydney."

He grabs my hand and places it on his cheek. "I don't know what happened, but I can't have you leave me like this. You're upset, and if I had any part at all in causing that....*again*...I won't be able to live with myself. You can leave if you want, but not without an explanation. Please."

I contemplate telling him the truth, but I know I can't. Not now. Probably not ever. So I decide to do the one thing I know will give me the best chance of distracting him.

I drop my bag to the floor and wrap my arms around his neck. I pull my fingers through the back of his hair. "I'm sorry," I say again, and Simon sighs deeply, pulling me close as he buries his face in my neck.

"Don't do that to me again," he whispers. "Ever."

"I know this sounds silly," I start, as I lay my forehead against his shoulder. "But it feels like none of this is real. When I think about being with you, spending time with you, it can be a little overwhelming."

Simon kisses my neck gently before raising his head to look at me. "What's overwhelming?" he asks, with sincere curiosity in his eyes. "Whatever it is, I'll help make you feel better about it. And please don't tell me it's the celebrity thing. We may be popular on this boat, but outside of here, I'm able to lead a relatively normal life if I choose. Trust me."

I smile and continue to move my hands through the back of Simon's soft hair, soothing us both.

"I'm not star struck," I tell him, but Simon cocks a very sexy eyebrow in question. "Okay, maybe a little."

"So what's the problem?" Simon laughs, and I'm happy to feel him relax against me. "Why'd you freak out on me just then?"

I take a deep breath and look into his beautiful brown eyes. I focus on the feel of his strong arms wrapped around me and realize how much I want to enjoy these moments I have with him, knowing they're probably numbered.

"Simon, you have to understand that this isn't something I do all the time...or ever, really, for that matter. I've never slept with someone without being in a relationship first. This is all very new to me, and once you add in who you are and everything that comes along with that, it's a little hard to swallow for a small town girl like me."

Whew. I exhale, feeling satisfied with my quickly contrived excuse.

"Uncomplicated." Simon smirks. "Your word, not mine."

I smack him playfully on the arm, and I love the sound of his laugh, the feel of his solid chest vibrating against mine as he holds me close.

"What's so funny?"

"I'm just glad it wasn't anything I did, at least not this time. Seems I have a few more go's before I completely fuck this up."

"Oh, stop it." I roll my eyes. "You're not going to mess anything up, but you might have to help bring me back down to reality periodically, if that's okay."

"Gladly." Simon licks slowly into my mouth and caresses my tongue with his. A soft moan escapes me and he smiles. "Just don't try and run away from me again. Promise me." I nod my head, unable to speak after that kiss. "Good. Now, shall we have a bit of breakfast? You're going to need some energy for what I have in mind this morning."

"Breakfast sounds good." I smile as we walk back to the sofa hand in hand. "Almost as good as these plans you have for me."

Simon whips around to look at me. "I'm willing to let you in on my plans sooner, rather than later, if you're game."

"Who needs food?"

And before I even have a chance to laugh at the shocked look on Simon's face, he has me in his arms and his mouth is on mine once again.

CHAPTER 36 - SIMON

Today was phenomenal. It started out great and just kept getting better. After that one frightening episode this morning in my suite, Sydney seemed to be fine the rest of the day. Even though there were concerts and meet-and-greets keeping us apart, I searched her out every chance I had and never missed an opportunity to touch her in some way, even if it was a simple brushing of my arm against hers.

Now I'm sitting back stage, preparing for the last concert of the cruise and thinking about the possibility of this being my last night with Sydney. I hope it's not, and if I have any part in the decision, it won't be.

I can't wait to see her outside of this chaos. I look forward to spending some quality time with her away from the band, away from the fans – just the two of us, enjoying each other's company in peace. I'm going to learn everything about her. I want to know everything she loves, so I can try and provide at least one of those things to her on a daily basis. And I'll make sure to find out her dislikes as well, so I can avoid anything that causes her unhappiness. I plan to make pleasing this woman my full time job. And I'm going to enjoy every minute.

"Are you serious about this, Si?"

I grin at the nervous look on James's face as he pokes his head in my door. "I think they deserve an apology tonight, don't you?"

James sighs as he walks into the room, raking a hand through his hair. "An apology, yes, but you've never done anything like this publicly before. Why now?"

I study James for a moment, not sure what to say. I still haven't quite figured all of this out yet myself, but I know I want to do this tonight. It feels right, and if I've learned anything the past few days, it's that I need to start following my heart again. It's worked with Sydney. And that's all the reassurance I need.

"I know it's a little unexpected." I give him a serious look. "But I need to do this, and I want you guys there when I do. It only seems right."

"Okay. It's on you then," James says without another thought. "And we'll be there to support you. Do what you have to do."

"Thanks James." I reach out to give him a one-armed hug, and he reluctantly complies. James hates affectionate gestures like that, which makes me want to do it even more.

"You smell really nice," I taunt, and he swiftly pushes me away.

"Arsehole," he smiles, and I smile too, feeling lighter than air at the moment.

James goes to leave my small dressing room back stage and I pick up my guitar to practice a bit for what I have planned for this evening. When I don't hear the door open or close, I look back over to find James standing at the door staring at me.

"What's up, mate?"

"I'm just...well, I hate to sound like an old man, but...I'm proud of you, Si."

James gives me a small smile and a wave, then turns to leave. I sit with my guitar in hand for several minutes after he leaves, lightly strumming, feeling each emotion instead of trying to push them away. It's a tough exercise, but necessary and much easier, knowing my goddess isn't far away.

"Let's go, Si," I hear from behind my door and James knocks once, letting me know it's time to hit the stage.

I take a deep breath. One more night with Sydney. That may be all I have left, and I intend on making it count.

I fasten the shoulder strap of my guitar around me as I stand, and with one more calming breath, I open the door and meet the guys as we walk toward the stage. I say a silent prayer, praying I can get through what I'm about to do. But deep down, I know all I have to do is find a pair of sweet, blue eyes in the crowd. Every time those beauties meet mine, it feels like I can make it through anything.

"Good evening, my lovelies," I say into the mic, as I take a seat on a stool with my guitar in hand.

The guys and I agreed I should just get this out of the way first off. That way I don't have to brood over it the entire show.

The cheers from the crowd after my greeting are encouraging. I smile on stage as I wait for them to simmer down. When it doesn't seem like it's going to happen, I lift my hands and give the crowd a calm-down gesture. And when the screams start to trail off, I lean into the mic again. My heart's racing like crazy, and I'm worried I won't be able to keep my voice level through this, but it has to be done.

"I just wanted to give you all a quick apology for what happened last night," I start, and the theatre grows so quiet you could hear a pin drop. "It was an unfortunate circumstance, but I can assure you...I deserved it."

I have a laugh, and I'm relieved when the audience laughs with me.

"But enough about that," I continue with a casual wave. "What I really want to talk about is the *topic* of last night's outburst and my subsequent early departure from the stage." *And another deep breath.* "I haven't really spoken about this publically in a while, so forgive my struggle to find the right words."

Shit. I can't do this. What was I thinking? Nearing a full on panic attack, I decide to seek her out in the crowd. When I find her, only a few rows back to my left, she gives me a warm, reassuring smile which is exactly what I needed. I smile back and resume my speech.

"As most of you know, I lost someone very close to me a few years ago. The pain of that day will forever be etched in my memory, my heart and my soul. It took me to such a deep, dark place I thought I may never see the light again." I pause and look back at my goddess once more. "Recently I've been treated to a happiness that I'm certain I don't deserve, but I've decided to say fuck it and enjoy it any way."

The crowd laughs along with me again, but my eyes are focused only on Sydney now. She's just too hard to ignore when she smiles like that.

"The best part about this happiness is that I'm starting to feel...hopeful. I'm being reminded that good things are still possible for me. And for the first time in a long time, I feel like the pain may one day be manageable – that maybe someday, I may find a way to remember the good times, instead of focusing solely on the bad. Maybe someday, I'll be able to find some...*peace.*"

I have to look away from Sydney when I notice a tear fall down her cheek as she watches me try and keep my own emotions in check.

The rest of the guys are sitting quietly on stage, silently supporting me, silently urging me on. I turn briefly to see Ollie and Rob trying to stifle their smiles, but I understand why. They've all been waiting for this moment for a very long time now.

I look over to find James with a similar expression, but it's mixed with a sort of fatherly pride. Oddly enough, that's what nearly sends me over the edge. In spite of our differences, and there are many, I've always looked up to James like a true big brother. I've missed his friendship and support these past few years, more than I'd like to admit.

James gives me a small smile and tilts his chin toward the mic, urging me to finish. I turn back to the crowd, and have to take yet another deep breath before I can start again.

"I'm sorry for leaving you all last night," I say. "But I want you to know that no matter what kind of crazy shit gets pinned on me – and most of it's true, by the way – you guys are the only reason I'm sitting here on stage tonight. You have kept me alive for the past few years, so it's only fitting that I'm baring my soul to you now." I glance over at Sydney again with a smile, then look back into the crowd. "I'm sure it's no surprise that music has a large influence on my life. There are a few artists I've found over the years that work well to keep the demons at bay, and this next song was on repeat for several months after the accident, working to do just that. If you don't mind, I think I'd like to sing it for you tonight. It's not going to be easy, but I'd like to try my hand at saying goodbye."

The sniffles throughout the theater echo in the silence when I stop speaking to adjust my guitar. When my eyes find Sydney again, she's looking at me like she can't believe I'm real, like she's watching some kind of miraculous transformation happening. It truly does feel like a miracle, and little does she know she's the guiding light behind it. I give her the grin I reserve for only her, then laugh to myself as the most beautiful shade of pink rushes her cheeks.

Then I close my eyes, trying to find the zone, as I start to strum my guitar. The chords of Ray LaMontagne's *A Falling Through* come easily, as I've played it a thousand times. I'd know it in my sleep.

I work my emotions into every word as I try to say goodbye to my first love. I try to imagine Melissa looking down on me now, watching as I lay my heart at my feet. I want her to know how sorry I am. I want her to know how much I miss her. And I want this audience to feel that too.

I keep my eyes closed the entire time, concentrating on the words, thinking about Melissa's face as I lose myself in the song and in the memories.

When I finally finish, I hang my head for a second or two until the roar of applause and appreciation fills the room. I wipe at the wetness under my eyes and when I look up, I see everyone is on their feet, cheering for me, encouraging me.

I turn and share glances with my bandmates before getting up and hugging each one in turn. The crowd gets even louder when this starts happening, especially the hug shared between me and Ollie.

I eventually move back to the mic to address the crowd. "Thanks again." My voice is unavoidably thick with emotion. "I'm going to take a quick break, but I promise to be back this time."

I take one last look at Sydney, then turn to walk off the stage. There's only one thing I need right now, only one thing that will make what just happened on stage actually seem real.

I grab our security guard, Greg, the minute I walk off the stage and give him instructions to bring my goddess to me. Immediately.

CHAPTER 37 - SYDNEY

Simon smiles at me and turns to walk off stage, as everyone falls back to their seats. I wish so much that I could go back stage with him, comfort him and tell him how proud he should be of himself for doing something like that. But I guess I'll have to wait until later. Small sacrifice to make, in the grand scheme of things, I suppose.

"All right everyone, how about we get this party started?" James asks into the mic, and the audience agrees with a chorus of applause and cheers.

When the music starts, I look over at Lacey with a huge grin on my face. Her smile matches mine, as we silently relive what just happened. I'm about to chat with Lacey about it, when someone taps me on my shoulder.

"Sydney Campbell?" the man asks in a very charming British accent, and I nod. "Please come with me."

I turn to Lacey and she mouths "Simon" at me. Suddenly, I'm jumping out of my chair ready to follow this man anywhere.

I follow the rather large man in a professional looking black suit toward the back of the theater. I get a few looks from the crowd, probably assuming I'm getting tossed out or something, and I might be.

"Excuse me, sir? Where are we going?"

The man turns to me and smiles. "You don't have to call me *sir*. My name is Greg, and Mr. Young wants to see you."

"Thank you, Greg. I was hoping you might say that." I smile up at him, and we continue walking.

"You know, this is none of my business..." Greg starts, and then stops walking when we reach a side door, outside of the theatre. "But if it's you that had something to do with what happened tonight, I would like to say thank you. I've been with these guys a long time, and tonight I think we all felt like we saw a glimpse of the old Simon again. It was nice to see."

"Thank you." I blush, staring up at my new friend, Greg. "I'm not sure what part I played in it, if any at all. But I've been a fan of theirs for a long time, and I agree that it was wonderful to watch what happened tonight."

Greg smiles down at me, then enters a code outside the door. When it opens, Greg gestures down a short hallway. "He's in the room two doors down on the right. He's expecting you."

"Thanks again." I give him a brief smile and a wave before making my way toward Simon.

The door I was directed to is closed, so rather than barging in, I decide to knock. "Simon?"

I barely get his name out before the door is slung open and I'm in Simon's arms.

The door closes behind us, as we stand in the small room and hold each other. "I'm so proud of you," I whisper, as I run my fingers through the back of his hair.

Simon doesn't say a word. He just holds me tight, his face buried in his favorite spot, and I can feel the wetness on my neck from his tears.

Eventually, he raises his head and looks at me with a smile as I wipe the remaining tears from his cheeks.

"We don't have long. I probably need to get back out there," he tells me, and places the sweetest of kisses on my lips. "I just wanted to..."

Simon searches my eyes for a moment, and I stare back, trying to figure out what exactly he's looking for.

"Just wanted to what?"

He shakes his head and smiles down at me. "I just wanted...to hold you."

Oh dear God.

"I'm available for holding any time," I giggle lightly, but my heart is pounding hard in my chest.

This man is like fire in my veins, and sometimes, I think the intensity of it all may consume me. But when I'm wrapped around him like this safe in his capable arms, fear is the last thing on my mind. I feel exhilarated. I feel alive. I feel...like I'm in love with him.

Yes, that's it. That's exactly it. I'm hopelessly, shamelessly in love with Simon Young. There's no more denying it.

Simon leans down for another kiss, and I happily oblige him.

"I'm so happy to have met you, Sydney." He sighs as he places his forehead against mine. "So very happy."

He places a long, sweet kiss on my forehead, then takes both my hands in his and smiles. "I need to get back, but you'll wait for me after, yeah?"

I nod a little too enthusiastically, eliciting a happy chuckle from Simon.

"Brilliant," he says, then turns to leave.

"Simon, wait." He turns back toward me with a confused look on his face. "I'm happy to have met you as well."

"Thank you, goddess." He leans in and kisses my cheek. "Not as happy as I am, though. Don't even try it."

"Equally happy, then?" I suggest, but Simon obviously disagrees.

"I said don't even try it." He smiles and pulls on my hand. "I have to get back, but be thinking about plans for later. We can join the party, if you'd like. We don't have to stay cooped up in my suite all night."

"Honestly, I'm not really the partying type," I tell him, as Simon leads me back toward the stage. "And I happen to enjoy being cooped up with you, if you don't mind."

Simon stops just before reaching the stage and turns to me. He wraps both arms around my waist and pulls me close. "I was hoping you'd say that," he admits and kisses me – long and hard this time, a taste of what I have in store later on. My entire body tingles with anticipation. By the time we break away, we're both breathless.

"You can stay back here and wait, if you want. I can send Greg for Lacey."

"Sounds great."

Simon leaves me a moment to talk to another black-suited man that I didn't notice was nearby. "She'll be back here in a bit," he tells me when he returns. "Later, goddess."

Simon places a kiss on the top of my hand, then heads to the stage.

I stand on the outskirts and prepare to watch the guys play as I wait for Lacey. I have no idea what's going to happen after this cruise is over tomorrow. I don't even want to think about that right now. But I know one thing is for certain. Lacey was right again. From now on, every other man will have to live up to this standard.

Best of luck to them.

Simon and I decided to make a brief appearance at the party. I hung back with Lacey a few times while Simon spent some time with the fans. But for the most part, he wanted to be next to me, and I didn't mind that one bit.

I didn't really see the other guys much at the party — awkwardness avoided for now, but I'm going to have to deal with it sooner or later. I've decided to try and be optimistic about it all and pray that everything will work out as it should. If Simon feels good about things, then I will too.

After about an hour at the party, Simon went around saying his goodbyes, and then he was back at my side, leading me to the elevators.

A few people join us now on the elevator, and Simon charms the wits out of them in just the short ride to his floor. The girls look longingly at me as I exit with him, and I give them a small wave. I can't blame them. I would envy me too.

"Do I really have to go back home in a couple of days?" I whine as we approach the door to Simon's suite. "This trip has gone by so fast."

Simon pulls me into his side, as we walk through the door. "I don't want to hear another word about this going home business."

He leans over to kiss me on the cheek, then moves to the kitchen to make us a drink. I follow him and wrap my arms around his waist from behind.

"We still have tonight," I whisper, feeling miserable with the thought of leaving him.

"And tomorrow morning," Simon adds, rubbing my arm with a free hand. "And I'll be spending the night in Miami tomorrow evening as well before we leave for L.A. We should spend it together."

"Hmmm, I like the sound of that," I agree, pressing my face into his back and inhaling deeply. I want to soak up as much of him as I can while I still have the chance.

Simon finishes our drinks, and I let go of him so he can lead me to the sofa. I kick off my heels with a sigh of relief as we sit.

"Shall we enjoy our drinks on the balcony?" Simon asks with a mischievous grin and I laugh.

"Sure," I challenge, standing with my drink in my hand and making my way toward the glass doors. I wish I felt as confident as I sounded.

Simon stands and follows me, reaching around to slide the door open. He gestures for me to take a seat in one of the large, cushioned lounges under the covered portion of the balcony and I do as requested. He then places our drinks down on a small table and with a smile, pulls on my arm and then moves in behind me. I gladly snuggle into him as he wraps his arms around my shoulders and holds me close.

"I'm going to miss you," I say suddenly, and Simon kisses the top of my head.

"I'm going to miss you too."

I turn to my side, so I can wrap my arms around his waist and bury my nose in his chest. I inhale that luscious scent once more, trying to figure out what I'll miss most about him. There are so many things.

"Sydney," Simon whispers, holding me tight. "We don't have to say goodbye, you know. This doesn't have to end with the cruise. As a matter of fact, I would prefer it didn't."

I close my eyes and breathe in his words. I've been thinking it, but he just said it. He wants *more*, and I can't even begin to describe how that makes me feel. But the reality is that Simon is too far removed from the real world and I'm deeply entrenched. We live on opposite sides of the country, and he's busy and traveling all the time, guaranteeing we'd barely see each other. I've thought about it more than I care to admit over the past couple of days, and I'm yet to figure out how we could ever make this work.

But for now, I just want to enjoy our last night together on the boat, so I decide to keep my depressing thoughts to myself.

"I'm not saying goodbye," I tell him, and it's true. I know now more than ever that no matter what happens I'm not sure I'll ever be able to fully say goodbye to Simon Young. "I'm only saying I'll miss you." I give him another truth. "These past few days have been amazing. I'll miss being close to you."

I press my lips to his and move my hands slowly up his chest and around his neck. As soon as my fingers find his silky, blonde hair, Simon's hands are on my backside, pulling me into his lap. My tight, black skirt bunches around my hips as I straddle him, and I can already feel his need for me against the thin material of my undies.

"What I said on stage tonight..." Simon's words are a hum against my neck, as he places gentle kisses there. "About finding peace...I've already found it."

I move my hands to his face and pull his eyes to mine. "What do you mean?"

Simon places a hand over mine and pulls my palm to his mouth, kissing the center. "Just being near you...it gives me strength. And your touch..." Simon presses his cheek into my other palm, still cradling his face. "I don't know how, or why, but when you touch me..." he pauses again with a deep breath, "There's a welcome silence in my head. You bring me peace. You *are* my peace."

A tear rolls down my cheek and Simon wipes it away. "*Christ.* I'm always making you cry."

Caught up in the moment, trembling, with no idea what to say, I stare into Simon's shining brown eyes as I bring his mouth back to mine. His words have left me feeling powerful and reassured and...*loved*. And the fact that it's Simon Young making me feel that way makes the moment all the more surreal – not because he's a celebrity, but because I feel like I've been in love with him my whole life. Maybe meeting him on stage all of those years ago meant more than I ever thought possible. Maybe we are written in the stars.

Simon presses into me, deepening the kiss, and I don't object. As he sits up, pulling me flush against his solid chest, I welcome the warmth, even though my shivering has nothing to do with the cool ocean breeze swirling around us.

I try and put my feelings for Simon in this kiss, since I couldn't respond with words before. I try to convey those thoughts now as I let my lips melt into his. I run my fingers through the back of his soft hair, exactly the way he likes, hoping in some way it helps him understand how he makes me feel.

After a while, even though we're pressed tightly against each other without an inch to spare, I realize it's just not close enough.

"Take me to bed," I breathe against his lips, and Simon quickly stands, keeping me in his arms, his mouth still moving against mine.

He walks leisurely to his bed, and I'm grateful for the slow pace. I don't want to rush tonight.

He sits on the end, with me still wrapped around him, and we stay like that for a while, continuing our kissing from the balcony, but hands are moving more freely now and with purpose.

"We're going to stay like this all night," Simon whispers his promise. "You pressed against me. Me holding you there."

"I like that plan," I tell him, as he trails his lips along my skin, and I feel his smile against my neck.

When I pull his face and lips back to mine, Simon turns us and guides me slowly down onto the bed. He shifts his body to the side, sliding one long leg between mine, as he drags his fingers from my thigh, up the center of my body until they're tangled in my hair. He presses his nose into the other side of my neck and nuzzles me, inhaling deeply. "You always smell so wonderful, like strawberries and springtime. Absolutely edible."

I turn into him, tangling my legs with his. "Take a bite," I tease, and then jump when Simon actually does it. Well, not a real bite, more like a nibble, making my toes curl in response.

Simon rolls me over and nestles between my legs and I moan as he presses his hips down, loving the feel of his weight on me. I don't know if it's because it's our last night together on the cruise, or if it's what Simon went through tonight on stage, but the way he's holding me right now, the way he's kissing me, all gentle strokes and sweet caresses...there's no rush, no urgency, just deep, loving movements. He truly does seem at peace.

And that same unhurried passion continues for what seems like days, or weeks even, until we're finally skin to skin. Simon enters me easily, gently, taking care to make sure I feel every inch of him as he glides in and out. He keeps me close as promised, while we make love – kissing me, nuzzling my neck, whispering my name, telling me how good I feel and how he can't get enough.

My orgasm is so powerful, I feel my eyes swell with tears, but I'm careful not to let them fall. Simon has made it clear he doesn't like to see me cry, and I would never want to do anything to spoil this beautiful moment between us. Simon is close behind me. His mouth is on my shoulder, lightly biting down as he growls through his release.

"I don't want to let you go, Sydney," Simon murmurs against my chest when it's over. "I can't let you go."

"Don't worry." I run my fingers through his hair. "We're together now. We'll figure the rest out later, okay?"

Simon lifts his eyes to mine. "Agree to see me again after all of this is over. I won't make you promise anything further, but please at least give me that. Say this isn't over when we leave Miami. Promise me."

His voice grows more urgent with every word, so I answer without thinking, just wanting to give him whatever will make him happy in the moment.

"I promise."

Simon kisses me softly and pulls me with him as he rolls to his back. He keeps both arms around me, holding me tight against his chest. I fight his hold slightly so I can place a few kisses above his heart.

"May I ask a question?"

"Anything."

"What's the meaning behind your tattoo?"

Simon looks over at it as if he forgot it was there. He pulls one arm behind his head, and stares up at the ceiling, as I trace along the lines with my fingers.

"Have you ever had a thought that plagues you? Something you can't seem to get out of your head, and you mull it over a million times, in a million different ways, to the point where you think it may actually drive you mad?"

"Of course, but I'm sure that happens to everyone from time to time."

"I'm sure it does," Simon agrees. "But it happens to me *all* of the time, and usually I can get some of the thoughts out on paper in a song. Of course, I haven't been able to write in a while, so I had the idea to get some things out this way. It's actually several different tattoos, pieced together over time."

"Did it work?" I wonder out loud, as I continue my tracing. "Did you feel better, once you got things out?"

"For a while," he admits. "But it's obviously not the same as song writing. Plus, it's not truly my work, just my idea. It's not the same, I guess."

"But why get your troubling thoughts made into a permanent reminder? Wouldn't it be better to get them out onto something you don't have to look at every day?"

"Who said the thoughts were troubling?"

I look back down at the tattoo and try to examine it closer. At first I still see the same swirly, misshapen lines and random letters that I've seen before, but as I stare, letting my eyes adjust to the dim lighting of the room, I start to make out some of the designs. There's a rustic outline of the Union Flag, tons of music notes and staffs, a flower – maybe a mum or a daisy? – and everything is all connected and beautifully laid out. You have to look closely to make out some of the images, but now that I've seen a few, they start to come easier.

I notice Simon watching me from the corner of his eye as I continue to study the lines. I find what looks like an engagement ring, a guitar pic and some numbers that are possible dates or times but it's hard to tell. There's also another piece of abstract looking jewelry, maybe a charm or a locket of some kind.

"These are happy memories," I murmur, as I start to realize what I'm looking at. "These are things you didn't want to forget."

"The bad stuff started taking over. I was trying to find a way to remember the good things."

"Will you add me to the mix somehow? I would be honored," I try and tease, but for some reason, the idea makes me sad. I don't want him to forget me, but I also don't want to be just a memory.

Simon pulls his arm from behind his head and places a warm palm on my cheek. "How could I ever forget you, goddess?"

Trying once again not to cry, I snuggle back into Simon's chest and hold him close.

CHAPTER 38 - SIMON

After I hand over yet another little piece of my soul to the beautiful woman lying next to me, she snuggles into my side, and we stay like that for a while, just breathing each other in. I don't want to move. I could stay like this for the rest of my life and be perfectly content. I try and remind myself that this isn't the last night I'll spend with her. She promised. But I'm still fighting the urge to keep my hands on her every second so she doesn't disappear on me.

"I'm thirsty," my goddess says in a sleepy voice.

"I'll get us some water," I offer, wanting to keep her in my bed.

I reluctantly let her go and pull on a pair of shorts. I grab two water bottles from the refrigerator and as I'm getting the waters, Sydney wraps her arms around me from behind. Maybe she doesn't want to let go of me either.

"Mmmm...I like you close," I share my thoughts. "You're so warm."

"That's your fault. You get me all hot and bothered."

"My pleasure." I turn around in her arms to face her. "And I plan to keep you that way all evening."

"Now that's something to look forward to."

I kiss those delicious lips, then grab her hand to lead her to the balcony. "You're doing much better with this," I notice, as I sit our waters on one of the small tables. "I'm very proud of you."

I drop into one of the lounge chairs and pull my goddess onto my lap. I situate her so she's facing me, and she looks radiant in the moonlight with mussed up hair, bright eyes and wearing nothing but a blanket and a sexy grin.

"Maybe I was never afraid of boats. Ever think of that?" She has such an adorable smirk. "Maybe I just played the 'damsel in distress' role to get you in bed."

I have to laugh as she starts showering me with kisses all over my smiling face. "If that's true, then I would have to say that I like you even more now."

Sydney's bubbly laugh shakes my body in the most delicious way. "You would."

"And I would also have to say..." I pull the comforter away so it falls to her waist. "That there was no need to try so hard, goddess."

Sydney whimpers softly as I move my mouth over her breasts, her fingers tangling in my hair. "But I know you didn't make it up," I continue between kisses. "Because you're too sweet...too innocent for something like that."

And it's true. She's the perfect antidote to my broody bitterness, and I've become wholly addicted.

"I'm not that sweet and innocent," she breathes, as I grab at her hips, moving my lips to her neck.

"No? Then what are you?"

I look up at her when she doesn't answer, and she immediately pulls my mouth to hers. I love it when she takes control like that. It's such a turn on.

"I don't know," she confesses, as we take a breath. "I don't know who I am when I'm with you."

Those words startle me, and I instinctively pull her close. "Is that good or bad?"

"Not sure. I've been trying to figure that out."

286

"Any luck?"

"I don't know whether it's good or bad, but I like it. Does that count for anything?"

I gently palm her warm cheek as she smiles down at me. "That's everything."

You're everything. That's what I feel like telling her. *You. Are. Everything.*

"I like that I can tease you without you getting upset with me," she continues. "I like that you share my affection for Ben and Jerry's."

"You can't trust people who don't like ice cream."

Sydney smiles and cuddles closer. "I like that we share control when we're together."

And with that, she leans down, grabs the back of my head and pulls my mouth to hers as if to prove her point. I clench her hips harder, but let her lead, as she swirls that delectable tongue around mine, then nibbles a bit on my bottom lip. *Fuck. Me.*

"What else do you like?" I ask, somewhat light-headed from the kiss she just gave me.

"I like..." she pauses, like she's not sure she should continue. "I like that you needed me last night after the concert. It felt good to be needed like that."

I can tell she regrets what she just said, so I smile at her honesty, reassuring her. Because she's right. I did need her. I still do.

I lean in and take her lips with mine, rocking her hips against me. Now she won't have to question my need for her. I'll let her *feel* it.

Within minutes, we're both sweaty and panting. Sydney reaches between us and pulls down my shorts, springing me free. Lucky for me, she's already naked, and she doesn't waste any time pushing me inside. As always, she feels amazing.

I moan into her mouth when she starts moving. I love when Sydney takes control, I do, but for some reason I'm struggling not to take it right now. I want to know I'm the one responsible for making her feel good. I want to work her until she's screaming my name again.

I dig my nails into her hips, fighting against my urge to takeover, but once again, she seems to sense what I need. Sydney stops moving and leans down so her lips are at my ear. "Take me, Simon," she whispers, and I don't hesitate.

I lift her slowly, then slam her back down – over and over, again and again – and the feeling is magnificent.

By the time I give back the reigns, I'm breathing hard against her neck and she grabs the back of the chair, quickening the pace.

"*Christ...Sydney....*"

I'm holding on by a thread as I watch her gorgeous body move on top of me, and I try and hold onto her, my hands seeking purchase on the slippery skin of her back, but finding none. I settle on her hips again, as she finds her release, and I explode into her shortly after. She whimpers my name into my neck instead of screaming it, but the intimacy of the moment – the sound of that sweet, sultry voice and her breath on my sensitive skin – has me shaking beneath her. And that's when I know. That's the moment I know I'm in love with her. And I never want to let her go.

✦ ✦ ✦

I wake up to the sound of waves lapping against the side of the ship. Sydney and I fell asleep in each other's arms, lulled by that same sound only minutes earlier. I'm exhausted, but in a good way. A very good way.

I look to my left and see my goddess curled into my side, her head on my shoulder, her arm draped around my waist. I close my eyes and smile, quietly laughing at how much I love that sexy little snore of hers.

I reach to brush a lock of hair behind her ear that was blowing with the ocean breeze, and she sighs contentedly and snuggles even closer, a small smile playing across her lips. I've never seen anything more beautiful.

And just like that, as I stare at the phenomenal woman lying in my arms, the words come to me.

There go my walls.
Now I stand bare before you.

Before I realize what I'm doing, I'm sliding out of the chair, careful not to wake my goddess, and moving into the bedroom to find my guitar. I pull on a pair of shorts and search for a pen and paper. I find what I need in the drawer of the nightstand, and with guitar in hand, I start to write. My blood starts pumping through my veins as the song pours out of me like it's been waiting to escape for centuries.

Exposed, I cannot hide
All the pain that's left inside.

I have no idea how long I've been writing when I look up to see Sydney standing in the entryway to my room, still wearing nothing but a blanket. That and the smile on her face are enough to take my breath away. It may be the happiest I've seen her yet.

"Are you writing?"

She's going for nonchalance, but she can't seem to pocket that adorable smile completely.

"I am," I stand and reach out my hand to her. "Come sit with me."

Sydney takes my hand, and I pull her onto the bed.

"Can I play it for you?" I ask her, and I hate that I look up and find tears in her eyes. Even though I know they're happy ones, it still hurts to see her cry.

"I would love that," she whispers, and wipes at her eyes. She moves so she's facing me on the bed with her legs crossed, and her face is so eager, I have to laugh.

I take my guitar back in my hands, and I'm just about to start when Sydney leans in and kisses me.

"What was that for?" Not that I mind her kisses, of course.

"I'm just so proud of you." Another tear rolls down her cheek, but she quickly brushes it away. "I can't wait to hear it."

And I can't describe the feeling in my chest when she tells me she's proud of me. It's been so long since I've heard those words.

"I hope you like it." I lean in and steal a kiss of my own. "Because it's about you."

Sydney sighs deeply. "You better start, before I become a total blubbering mess over here."

"Okay," I say with a laugh. "Here goes."

I haven't worked out all of the kinks yet, but I play her the couple of verses I have down so far. I watch her face the entire time, and I love what I see there. Sydney is a fan, after all. And I do love my fans.

"It's...incredible. *You're* incredible," she tells me when I'm done, and I place my guitar on the floor next to the bed, ready to have my hands on her. She giggles as I push her down on the bed and hover over her. "We're messing up your papers."

"That's okay. I'm thinking I need to do a bit more research, anyway."

She wraps her arms around my neck, and I slide in between her legs. I pull the papers from underneath us and toss them to the floor.

"Oh really?" Sydney gives me that sexy smirk that I adore. "And how exactly am I going to help with that?"

"Well, you're my muse, goddess." I love the feel of her trembling beneath me as I kiss along her neck. "So inspire me."

The next thing I know, I'm on my back with a beautiful woman smiling down at me. "You're the inspiration, Simon Young. Not me."

I love you, I tell her silently in my head, still afraid to say the words aloud, but knowing I feel them loud and clear.

"You've been inspiring millions of people for a long time," she continues, "and I'm confident that will never change. But thank you for my song," she adds with a shy smile. "I wish I knew how to tell you what it means to me."

I sit up in the bed and pull her close, as I stare into those dazzling eyes. There are so many things to say, and I have no idea where to start.

I want to thank her for showing me how to live again, or at least pointing me in the right direction. I want to tell her how much it means that she believes in me, how she trusts me, without even really knowing me. And as a result, I just spent time writing a song – something I haven't done since Melissa died.

There are a million things I'm dying to tell her, a million things she needs to hear, but there will be plenty of time to show my gratitude and I plan to shower her with it for as long as she'll have me.

So for now, instead of pouring my heart out to her like I so desperately want to do, I take a deep breath and smile. "You're very welcome for your song, and you can bet there are tons more where that came from."

"Maybe a little more research first?" Sydney leans in to kiss my cheek.

"Most definitely," I growl, as she moves her soft lips down my neck. "Lots and lots of research."

CHAPTER 39 - SYDNEY

The ship is already docked at the port in Miami but Simon and I refuse to remove our lazy selves from bed this morning. Truth be told, I have no desire to get off this boat, and I never thought I'd be saying something like *that*.

But then again, I never thought I'd be waking up in the arms of Simon Young, either.

"It's not goodbye," Simon says to me for the millionth time as I cuddle closer into his side. "We still have tonight in Miami, and then we'll see each other again soon. Promise me."

These promises are making me uneasy, no matter how badly I want to make them. I just have no idea how to make this work without a lot of heartache and disappointment involved. Sure, Ethan and Sam made it work, but he gave up his acting career for her. I can't expect Simon to do something like that for me.

Plus, there are things I need to work through at home. Hopefully, I still have my job when all of this is over, and I want to finish school. I can't just pick up my life and relocate it for Simon and I wouldn't want him to have to do that either. Regardless of how I feel about him, we only just met. I have to try and be an adult about this.

I sigh into his chest, realizing I'm getting a little ahead of myself. Certainly Simon wouldn't want those things after only knowing me a few days. What's wrong with keeping in touch with him? You never know what could happen down the road. And the thought of never seeing him again...well, I'm not sure that's an option for me.

"I promise," I say, because whether it's two days, two weeks or two years, I know I have to see him again.

Simon sighs contentedly, and pulls me closer. "So, what should we do in Miami today? Were you able to sightsee before the cruise? It's a great city with lots to do. I could take you around."

"I'd like that." I move my lips to place a kiss on his bare tummy. "I have to meet with all of you at some point this morning to go over the next steps, but that certainly won't take all day. We should have plenty of time this afternoon and evening to do some sightseeing."

"Sounds perfect."

We lie there for a few more minutes before Simon speaks up again.

"Well, as much as I hate to move, I think we should probably make our way to the hotel."

"No," I pout, as I squeeze his waist and tangle my legs with his. "I don't want to get out of bed."

"Come on, sleepyhead," Simon chuckles but makes no effort to move me. "Do you want to shower here or at the hotel?"

"I can wait until the hotel," I tell him. "But only if you promise to join me."

"Oh, that's a given," Simon laughs and rolls on top of me. "Now, let's get up and get going or we won't be making it anywhere today."

Simon leans down and....*mmm*. He's the best kisser.

I wrap my legs around his waist and my fingers find the back of his hair. Simon kisses me hard, then quickly pulls back with a growl. "You're testing my willpower, goddess, and I don't have much to start with when it comes to you."

I give him a devilish smile and run my fingers along his scruffy cheek. "Okay, fine," I concede. "My willpower is a bit lacking when it comes to you as well. Obviously."

After one more sound kiss, he rolls off of me and out of the bed. He reaches a hand out and I reluctantly take it. I don't want to leave our comfy little cocoon, but the thought of spending at least one more day and night with him in Miami helps to ease my mind.

As soon as I'm up, Simon pulls me to him and playfully kisses my face, my ears and my neck.

"Maybe just one more taste." He gives me a final peck on my lips, and I sigh. "That should hold me over for at least a minute or two."

I watch his fantastic, naked backside walk into the bathroom, and when he throws me a wink over his shoulder, I nearly collapse. *Sweet heavens.*

I toss on my clothes from last night, while Simon is in the bathroom. "I have an extra toothbrush for you on the sink," he informs me when he comes out. "And you're welcome to anything else you need in there."

"Thank you," I say, immensely grateful for the opportunity to brush my teeth.

Simon pulls on a pair of shorts and a t-shirt. "I have to chat with the guys before we go. I'll be back in a few."

"Should I wait here?"

"You better be here when I get back."

"I'll take that as a *yes.*"

Simon leans down and kisses me one more time. "I'll be back soon, goddess."

He gives me a wink, then moves toward the door. Smiling, I make my way to the bathroom to brush my teeth. God, that feels so good.

Unable to find a brush, I use my fingers to comb through my tangled hair and I'm able to get it somewhat tamed. I splash a little cold water on my face to help wipe off the residual make-up from last night, but it does nothing to remove the flush in my cheeks or the glow on my skin and I'm thankful for that.

I make my way back out to the room and find a hairband in my purse. I pull my hair into a ponytail and walk out onto the balcony. Simon's suite is on the side of the ship that's facing the ocean, rather than the dock, so I sit in one of the lounge chairs and make myself comfortable.

As I wait for Simon to return, I start to reminisce about the past few days. I think about how much has changed, how much has happened, and at first those thoughts bring a huge smile to my face. But after a while, I start to feel uneasy. *What am I doing?* His words from last night about me being his "peace" are kind of unnerving in the light of day. A lot of responsibility comes along with words like that, and I'm worried I can't live up to those types of expectations.

I put my face in my hands and take a few deep breaths. I just want to get through this last day with Simon, and I can worry about the rest later.

"Miss me?"

I remove my hands from my face and turn quickly. I smile up at the ridiculously gorgeous man standing leisurely in the doorway to the balcony, his arms gripping the top of the doorframe, causing his t-shirt to ride up and tease me with a sliver of his tight tummy.

"Ready to go, goddess?" he asks, and I stand to move toward him. "I'll walk you back to your room so you can pack up."

I wrap my arms around his waist because I have to touch him when he's close to me. Simon releases the doorframe and wraps his arms around me, and we kiss for a while on the balcony.

Simon eventually takes my hand to lead me inside, and I grab my clutch on the way out, but decide to carry my heels instead of wearing them.

Lacey's in our cabin when we get there with a sad look on her face. "I so don't want to leave," she admits as she continues her packing.

Simon and I both sigh in agreement as we enter the room. "Ollie and I will be back to get you both in a half hour. Get everything packed and leave your bags by the door. I'll have someone come get them and bring them to the dock for you."

I reach my arms around his neck and kiss his lips. "I'll see you soon."

"Don't miss me too much."

"I'll try not to."

Simon gives me one last kiss, then turns to leave. "Hi Lacey. Bye Lacey."

"Bye Simon." Lacey waves as he closes the door. She tosses herself on the bed, and I move to sit beside her. "This trip has been unbelievable. I hope you've enjoyed yourself."

I give her a look as if she's crazy for even having to ask, and Lacey smiles in return. I get up to change out of my dress and into some shorts and a tank top. I rethink the shower for a moment when I'm done packing my things, but I decide against it, preferring the idea of sharing one with Simon later on.

Thirty minutes on the dot, there's a knock on our door. Lacey moves to open it as I slip on my flip-flops.

"Damn, you get more beautiful every time I see you," Ollie gushes from the doorway, and when I look up, I see Ollie kissing Lacey's hand and Simon trying to wiggle past them.

At the same time, someone comes for our bags, and Ollie and Lacey instruct him as Simon wraps his arms around my waist and kisses my forehead.

"All packed up, goddess?"

"Why do you call me 'goddess'?" I speak loud enough so only he can hear. "Don't get me wrong. I love it. But I was just wondering why you always call me that."

Simon smiles as he shrugs. "Maybe so I'll remember to treat you like one?"

"Very funny."

"What do you want me to say? It just fits. You're as beautiful as Venus, as desirable as Aphrodite. Why wouldn't I call you *goddess*?" he teases and I laugh along with him, but then he continues in a more serious tone. "Actually, you're better than both of them because you're beautiful inside and out. You've had my respect and adoration since the moment we met, even though I may not have treated you as such. But believe me, you've had it. You still do. That and more."

I gaze into his heartfelt eyes, stunned by that answer. "Thank you," I finally manage, and I'm rewarded with a warm smile.

"Let's get going," Lacey says, coming up behind Simon and tugging on my hand. "I'm starving."

I'd almost forgotten she and Ollie were even in the room.

I move with Lacey, and Simon takes my other hand and moves along with us toward the door. Lacey lets me go and moves next to Ollie once we're in the hallway.

"I booked an additional suite," Simon puts an arm over my shoulders and I wrap my arm around his waist as we walk. "The guys and I would normally share a room on a night like tonight, but if it's okay with you, I thought maybe we could have some privacy."

"That news makes me very happy," I confess, smiling up at him. "But what about Lacey?"

Simon rolls his eyes. "Ollie exchanged her room for a suite as well. Said it wasn't fair that she be 'left in coach while everyone else gets to ride in first class'."

"Well, that was very sweet of him," I smirk.

"Mmm hmm."

"Lacey can take care of herself, you know."

"I know," Simon sighs. "I just hope he's a gentleman."

I glance up at Lacey and Ollie walking in front of us. Ollie's hands are in his pockets, shoulders slumped, as if he's concentrating hard on not touching her. And the clenched fists at Lacey's sides give off the exact same message. It's almost painful to watch.

"You know, I have to disagree." I grab Simon a little tighter around the waist and give him a happy kiss on the cheek. "I kind of hope he's not a gentleman."

"So, exactly what genre of music are you suggesting?" James asks me as we all sit around the living room of his suite, munching on lunch during our meeting.

"You would still be considered pop, but with an edgier, more sophisticated style. You're older now, more mature, and your music needs to reflect that. The good news is that your fans are older now too, and they'll appreciate the change – first because they're your fans, but also because their tastes have probably changed somewhere along the line as well. You'll always have the hits that everyone knows and loves, but you have an opportunity to branch out now that you didn't have fifteen years ago. You were pigeon-held into a look and feel that would sell the most records back then, and it worked. But now I think it's time to showcase who you really are, to show your strengths and individuality to the world. I think you'll be pleasantly surprised at how successful you all will be, just by being yourselves."

I glance at each of them, hoping I haven't spoken out of turn. I'm still not sure I should be handling an account like this, but I figure if I just stick to honesty, I can't go wrong. These guys deserve that.

I start to relax when I see they all have smiles for me – Simon's is the widest, of course.

"That sounds...like a dream come true," Rob says, and I relax even further. "We've waited a long time for someone to tell us to do our own thing. And you really think people will buy it? You don't think we're going to look like an over-aged boy band trying to reinvent the wheel?"

"Not at all," I say with confidence. "Marketing you appropriately will be the key, but I think you'll be respected for finally dumping the stereotype and doing what you do best. You're all extremely talented, and each of you has something unique to bring to the table. Ollie's a magician when it comes to mixing." I gesture to Ollie, and when he winks at me, I have to suppress my fangirl giggle. "And James is a closet heavy metal junkie, and I think you should incorporate some of those sounds into your new material. It will give it a nice hard edge, which I think will attract a lot of new fans, since it will be such a deviation from what people are used to from you guys."

When I look over at Rob, he smiles at me and I still can't believe I'm sitting at a table with them, let alone giving them advice. "Rob is a brilliant guitarist," I continue. "But I don't think that's been recognized enough in the past. The first time I've ever really seen you guys with instruments was on the cruise, and that has to change."

"And I'm good at everything, of course," Simon pipes up, and I turn to him with a smile. "So I'll just sit back and watch."

All of us laugh, and I'm loving the energy in the room. Everyone is relaxed and comfortable, but excited and ready for a change. I feel like these guys could take on the world right now if they set their minds to it.

"We all know your best strength, Simon," I start. "But I don't think hitting on women is relevant to the current conversation."

"Yes!" Ollie shouts, and the rest of the guys start cackling as Simon smiles at me. The look in his eyes tells me he wants to eat me alive for that comment. I couldn't be more thrilled.

"Sydney is signing a lifetime contract with us," Rob says through his laughter, and James gives him a fist bump in agreement.

"Simon, we all know your songwriting is incomparable," I say, once the laughter dies down. "I'm sure you felt restricted in the past, but this is a new era. You have nothing to conform to, and personally, I can't wait to see the results."

Simon's smile is spectacular now as he gazes at me from across the table, and I smile back, unashamed, because I may be biased when it comes to him, but everything I just said is true. He's a poet, and I think the surface has barely been scratched when it comes to his song writing potential.

"When this tour is over, I want you in the studio with us, Sydney."

My eyes shoot over to James, wide with disbelief. "Really?"

"Of course. I want your opinion on what we come up with. You can make sure we stay on track."

I clap excitedly and bounce a few times in my seat, not even trying to contain the fangirl this time. "Sorry," I wince, but they're all still smiling at me. "That is just such a huge honor, and I'm flattered that you would even ask. I would love to be there."

"Great," James gives me a nod. "We'll keep you updated on our progress between now and then, but we should be able to work on some new material through the remainder of this tour. We can schedule some studio time in the next few months."

"That sounds perfect," I tell him. "I'll work to put some marketing ideas together at the office, so we can get that ball rolling as well."

"Well, I feel really good about this." James starts to gather his notes from the table. "And this cruise was more like a vacation than the others, due to the smaller crowd, so I'm almost feeling rejuvenated over here."

"Told you the smaller crowd would be nice," Simon smirks, and James rolls his eyes.

"Sydney, can we treat you and Lacey to dinner for your last night in Miami?" James asks, but Simon answers for me.

"I've already requested that privilege of Sydney, and lucky for me, she accepted."

I can feel the heat in my cheeks as all eyes turn to me, including Lacey's. We are yet to discuss mine and Simon's relationship with the guys, and the awkwardness is as awful as I'd imagined it would be.

I chew my bottom lip and look to Simon for help, but he offers me nothing but that adorable grin of his.

"You are a lucky man indeed," James tells Simon, while giving me a sincere smile. "How about you, Lacey? Dinner tonight?"

"That would be wonderful," she replies. "Thank you."

"It's the least we can do," James says. "Plus, I'm sure Ollie would love to spend more time with you before you head back tomorrow, but he's probably too terrified to ask."

There's a chorus of gasps all around, followed by Ollie choking on his drink. "You arsehole!" he screams at James, but by then we're all laughing so hard you can barely hear the remaining string of profanity.

James punches Ollie in the shoulder. "Come on, Ol. Give us a smile."

Ollie rubs at his arm while glaring at James, but then he looks at Lacey and smiles. I look over to see Lacey studying the table like it's going to reveal the secrets of the universe, but the smile on her face is as wide as Ollie's.

"All right, I think I've had enough of all of this lovey dovey nonsense," James says. "Let's get settled then before dinner, yeah?"

We all start cleaning up the various papers and messes we've made over the past few hours, and after a few minutes, Ollie comes to give me a hug goodbye. "Not sure if we'll see you again before you leave tomorrow."

"I'll see you again soon," I assure him with a smile. "Don't worry."

Ollie smiles back and gives me a wave as he and Lacey leave together. *Hmm.* Wonder what they'll be up to between now and dinner.

"It was great to meet you, Sydney," Rob tells me. "I think you'll be the perfect addition to the group. I can't wait to get excited about all of this again."

"I'm already excited, Rob. You guys are going to be better than ever, and as a fan, nothing makes me happier."

Rob leaves shortly after that as well, leaving James, me and Simon alone in the suite. "On a serious note," James starts, "and I hate to be all business on this, but Sydney, we probably need to take a moment to discuss how best to handle what's happened between you and Simon. I'll go ahead and say I have no problem with it, and I would still like to work with you."

"Thank you, James." It's nice to hear the approval from his own lips. "But I am a little worried about how this will look to Jasper."

"Don't worry about Jasper," James cuts me off. "We go way back, and I'm confident I can make him see things my way. I just want to make sure you and Simon are comfortable with all of this, and that it won't interfere with the work we have coming up."

Simon has a stunned look on his face, so I figure he must be as surprised as I am about how cool James is being about our situation.

"I think Simon and I can remain professional, no matter what happens," I answer, since James had originally directed the comment at me. "I appreciate your understanding."

"I would never want to stand in the way of what makes my brother happy."

Simon and James share a quick hug, and both pairs of eyes are glistening when they pull away.

"Well, enough of your sappy shit," Simon jokes and we all laugh, shaking off the tension. Simon takes both of my hands in his, and pulls me toward him. "We can discuss this more in the morning. Until then, Sydney and I are going out to have some Miami-style fun we'll never forget."

"Sounds good." James pats Simon on the shoulder. "Sydney, please do stop by and say goodbye before you go tomorrow."

"I certainly will," I promise him. "And thank you again for taking a chance on me. I'm so happy to work with you and very excited to see what the future holds."

"I think we all feel the same."

Simon and I leave James's suite hand in hand and head toward ours. "We have a couple of hours to kill before dinner," Simon gives me a very mischievous smile once we enter the room. "Any ideas?"

"Loads," I wrap my arms around his waist and pull him close. "How about that shower you promised? I'll get the water going."

"Sounds heavenly. Let me check my messages, and I'll be right there." Simon kisses me deeply, then ushers me toward the bathroom with a pat on the ass.

I'm only in the bathroom a couple of minutes when I remember something I was supposed to give to James. I poke my head out the door to find Simon standing by the window on the phone, looking about as sexy as sexy gets. "Simon?" I call and his head whips around, a smile already in place.

"Yes?"

"Sorry to interrupt, but could you do me a favor?"

"Anything, goddess."

Sigh.

"Could you take that blue folder," I point at the object I'm referring to, "and pull out a copy of the signed contract for James? I forgot to give it to him at the meeting, and I don't want to forget again before I leave. If you don't mind, just sit it out on the desk, so I'll remember?"

"No problem."

I blow him a kiss and close myself back in the bathroom. After nearly fifteen minutes, I start to wonder what's taking Simon so long.

I step out of the shower and grab one of the plush robes hanging on the back of the door to cover my naked body. I make my way back out to the suite and look to the bed, hoping to find Simon there, but that's not where I find him.

His back is to me, but I can tell he's studying something in his hands. And I can tell by the tightness in his back and shoulders that it's not the contract. And then, with a stuttering skip of my heart, I realize exactly what he's looking at. *Oh God, no.*

I rush over to the desk, but it's too late. He has my emails. The ones from Lena. The ones telling me to do "whatever it takes" to make this client happy.

"Such a fucking idiot," Simon mutters when I approach, but he doesn't look over at me. He continues to study the emails instead, as if they're a transcript of his worst nightmare.

"Simon..."

What the hell do I say? The only things coming to mind are so cliché. *Simon, I can explain. Simon, just hear me out. Simon, you don't understand.* But I don't say any of that because Simon's jaded past makes this situation far more critical, leaving me at a complete loss.

All I can do is hope Simon knows that I would never hurt him, but when he drags his blank, distant eyes over to me, that hope vanishes in a flash.

"You're everything I've ever wanted," he whispers, and his voice is just as distant as his stare.

"Simon, please..." I pause again, still not sure what else to do but beg. "Please."

I'm surprised when his unfocused gaze snaps swiftly into awareness. "No, I get it. You used me to make sure you get your precious promotion. Is that it? Or is this all some kind of set up? Were you sent to try and save me, Sydney? Save the group? Who else was in on this? James? Xander? Not Ollie. Please God not Ollie."

Simon starts to pace, crumpling the papers in his hands as he claws his fingers through his hair. I watch him pace for a moment, embarrassed and honestly quite horrified that he would jump to those conclusions so quickly. The fact that he was so quick to judge me breaks my heart. I thought he saw more in me than that. I guess I was wrong.

Still I want to try and save what we have. It feels too important to end over some ridiculous misunderstanding.

"Simon, let's talk about this." I reach for his arm to stop his pacing. "It's not what you think."

Simon stops his pacing and pulls his arm well out of my reach. My heart starts beating like a freight train as I watch Simon's control slide further and further down the slippery slope that is his sanity. Although his words cut deep, I know the reason he's lashing out is because of how many times he's been hurt in the past. He's barely holding it together, and I'm starting to get scared I won't be able to calm him down this time, or have a chance to explain.

His brown eyes are stone cold as he glares at me, and I feel my freight train of a heart hit a brick wall with an impact that makes tears spill over and slide down my cheeks.

"Simon, I can–" I start again, but he doesn't let me finish. Of course he doesn't.

"Don't. Even. Think. About. It," he seethes, then drops the emails to the floor and walks toward the door of the suite.

His harsh words and lack of trust are ripping me apart, but I chase after him and manage to grab his elbow right before he reaches the door. He stops and swings around to face me. "Simon, please," I beg, more tears rolling down my face. "Just let me try and explain."

And I see it for a split second – a glimpse of hope crosses his face, but then it's gone. "You surprised me, *goddess*," he sneers, as he yanks his arm once again from my grasp. "How gullible am I? I should have known better."

"Don't do this, Simon." I try pleading with him again, but I know I'm fighting a losing battle, and the frustration is making it hard for me not to lash out as well. *Listen to me, dammit!*

Simon leans in close, his face inches from mine, and in a last ditch effort, I place my hand on his cheek. Although I'm shaking like a leaf, I try calming him with my touch like I've somehow done before, and when he closes his eyes, I start to think it's working.

"God, Sydney," he whispers as his shoulders slump, and I feel mine relax as well.

"It's not what you think." I place both my hands on his miserable face. "You have to know that, Simon. I was appalled by those emails. I would never do something like that to you."

Simon squeezes his eyes shut and takes a deep breath. "I don't want to hear this, Sydney. I don't want to hear it because I can't trust that what you're saying is true. I can't...*trust* you."

He sounds so defeated, and my heart beats double-time in my chest at the thought of this being over, at the thought of never seeing or talking to him, never kissing him again.

He can't possibly think I would intentionally do something to hurt him, right? He's letting his past dictate his current actions, and I refuse to let that happen. I have to make him understand how I feel, and since he isn't going to listen, maybe I can show him.

I swing my arms around his neck and pull his lips to mine. My fingers strum through the back of his soft hair, as I put everything I have into this kiss. I let my lips plead with him to know me, to understand who I am, to show him how much I care about him and no one else. Simon doesn't respond at first, but I hold strong to my resolve, until I eventually feel his arms wrap around my waist and pull me close. "I would never hurt you, Simon," I breathe against his lips. "Never."

Simon pulls away briefly, then leans back in and places a few more soft kisses at the corner of my mouth, my cheek, my nose and a last one on my lips. He stares at me a moment and the pain on his face brings a fresh set of tears to my eyes.

"I deserve this," he tells me. "I feel like such a hypocrite because God knows I've done my share of hurting other people, but it was only because I didn't care before. Then I met you, and..." Simon glances at the floor, and when he looks back at me, the resolve is clear on his face. "You're not who I thought you were. And I can't change that now. There's no going back. It's over."

As he plunges that final knife into my already bloodied chest, I have no idea what to say or do. He's not going to believe me. He doesn't trust me. The hope is gone.

I pull my hands up over my mouth, as the tears continue to stream down my face. Simon looks down at me one last time, then quickly leaves the room.

As I stare at the back of the closed door, I move my arms around my waist and try to hold it together, but it's no use. I collapse on the floor and let the sobs shudder through me, realizing I've been reduced yet again to nothing more than just another pretty face, and by the only man I ever thought could possibly love the real me.

In just a few short days, I've wrecked my heart, most likely my career and maybe even the future of a beloved boy band, so I believe this makes it official.

I'm a complete and total...failure.

CHAPTER 40 - SIMON

There's no way this is happening.

I put my heart on a platter for that woman, and she hands it back to me, sliced, diced and mangled into a million pieces.

But that's what I get. That's what I get for taking a chance, for putting myself out there, for opening up again. I knew better, but I did it anyway. I thought she was different, but it seems this was all just another sick joke to remind me that my life is obviously meant to be spent in the same cold, dark place I've been rotting in for the past four years.

So much for trusting my fucking heart. I'll be sticking with my gut from now on.

I can barely see a foot in front of me as I stumble my way into a cab. My eyes are filled with unshed tears, and I hate it. I hate how weak she's made me, forcing me to drop my walls, to bear my soul and now, I'm a spineless heap in the back of this cab, unable to stop the tears no matter how hard I try.

"Where to?"

"A bar," I mumble and wipe at my eyes. "Any bar."

"You got it."

I lean back against the hot vinyl seat and cover my face with my hands, but all I see is the wretched, tear-soaked face of my goddess, and my gut twists in agony.

I want to believe her. *God,* I want to believe her, but I've been in this business nearly my entire life. I know how things work. I know how business mingles with pleasure to produce the desired monetary results. Hell, I've been on the giving and receiving side of that nightmare before – one more reason I should have known to keep my guard up. I shouldn't have let that beautiful face, that soft voice, those kind gestures get into my head, but I was so certain she was real.

It looks like I'll have to get used to the fact that the things I want most are the things I'll never have.

"Here we are," the driver tells me. "Hey, you all right, man?"

I won't even justify that one with a response.

Instead, I pull out a twenty, certain it's more than enough for the ten minute ride and tell him to keep the change. I hop out of the cab and look up at the restaurant sign in front of me. *Golden Venus* the sign reads, and I stand in the middle of the sidewalk, as pain ripples through my chest, squeezing my heart. Interesting. I thought I left my heart in that hotel room.

When I finally make my way inside, I head straight for the bar. "Jack. No ice," I tell the man waiting for my order, as I feel the tears start to well back up in my eyes. I grip the bridge of my nose, begging them to stay down, at least while I'm in public for Christ's sake.

Instinctively, I reach into my pocket and wrap my fingers around the locket. It's no match for this kind of hurt, but I continue to hold it tight as I down one drink then order another. As the alcohol starts to slow my reflexes, images of my goddess start popping in my head again and I scrub one hand down my face, silently cursing this bizarre need for her. I'm about to down my third drink, when I hear a voice beside me.

"Mind if I join you?"

312

The voice is female, but it may as well be razor blades slicing through my ears because it's not the sweet, Southern voice I'm aching for. It seems the goddess has ruined me. It has to be *her* voice, *her* touch, *her* kiss now. Nothing else will do.

I swipe angrily at my eyes, pissed off because I can't seem to hold it together. I take a deep breath, trying to get my temper in check, but then I decide fuck it. Anger is better than any of the other alternatives at the moment.

I look up at the friendly stranger, and any other day, I would think this woman was quite attractive. She looks a few years older than me – mid-thirties, maybe – with long, dark hair hanging down to the middle of her back. Her shapely figure is hugged by a tight, black dress, and her full lips are covered in red, her green eyes glowing with possibilities.

However, this isn't any other day. And this woman doesn't appeal to me at all. Not even on the basest of levels. But with my anger and resentment front and center, I answer her.

"Sure."

I pull out the stool next to me for her to sit, and she waves the bartender over. He winks at her, informing me she's a regular here, in one capacity or another, but I honestly couldn't give a shit either way.

"You look upset," she says, as she turns back to me. "Girl trouble?"

I glance at her but don't say anything because I know it would be a horribly sarcastic remark, and this woman doesn't deserve my wrath.

"I'm still trying to get over my last one, too," she tells me, as the bartender brings her drink and she orders me another. "Love is about equal to insanity in my book."

I couldn't agree more.

"This one's on me," she informs me as the bartender brings my next drink, and I raise my glass in thanks.

"Simon." I extend my hand and she takes it with a smile.

"I'm Sophia. It's nice to meet you, Simon," she grins and takes a sip of her drink. "So, what's her name?"

I consider telling her my sad, pathetic story, but I can't even find it in me to say *her* name out loud right now. Instead, I shake my head, hopefully letting her know I don't want to talk about it.

"Well, if there's anything I can help with..."

When I look over at her again she has a wicked smile on her lips, and my stomach turns. I couldn't be more turned off, but she doesn't seem to notice, or simply chooses to ignore my disinterest.

"You know, you look familiar. Have we met before?"

Oh, please. Not this.

"I don't think so."

"Wait it minute!" she practically squeals and I groan. "You're Simon Young from The London Boys! Wow! I used to be such a huge fan."

Used to be a fan? Perfect. As if I needed to feel worse about myself or this situation.

I glance around to see if anyone overheard her discovery, but the bar is pretty much deserted. Not surprising, I guess, since it's not even lunch time yet.

"I can't believe it. Simon Young," she muses. "It must be my lucky day."

I sigh and take another sip of my drink. *Luck*? I wouldn't know anything about that.

I look over at Sophia, neither confirming nor denying my identity, but it's too late. She knows the truth, and like all the rest, her entire demeanor changes once she learns who I am. She starts slowly inching closer to me, her eyes bright and excited, as if I have something special to offer her now that I didn't have before. Fucking bullshit.

She orders us both another drink, then leans in close. "I can help you forget her, Simon," she whispers in my ear. "I can help take away the pain. We can help each other. All you have to do is ask."

Wonderful. It seems my reputation has preceded me once again.

But despite the fact that I don't really find myself attracted to this woman at all, I do like the sound of those words more than I should.

Forget her...Take away the pain.

With a sigh, I close my eyes and start to surrender to the inevitable.

Empty.

Cold.

Alone.

I remember this place well. This is where I live, and this is where I'm going to stay. It's safer in the dark, where beautiful, soul-ripping goddesses can't find me.

But when I pull back and look into the eyes of the woman sitting next to me, I quickly lose my resolve. She wants to help me forget, but what if I don't want to forget? I look away and take down my drink in one gulp. Out of the corner of my eye I see her signal the bartender again, probably ordering me another. She's going to have to start injecting me with this shit if she expects me to forget about Sydney any time soon.

The next thing I know, there are two more drinks in front of me, and I down them both without thinking. My new drinking buddy hasn't said another word, but I know she's sitting there just biding her time until I'm drunk enough to accept what she has to offer. Part of me hopes it'll be soon, but deep down I'm not sure if I'll ever get there. How could this woman even compare to what I've been spoiled with these past few days?

But as the alcohol starts to work like truth serum in my brain, I realize none of that really matters because Sydney was more than I could ever ask for or deserve. Her one betrayal, her one minor indiscretion, is nothing compared to the years of torment I've brought to the people I love most. I'm practically a monster compared to her. I don't deserve her. I never will.

And isn't that one hell of an epiphany?

The ache in my chest spreads like wildfire, but I ignore it. I shut it out, like I've done a million times before and my bleary eyes look over to my left. I lick my lips, trying not to picture Sydney's face as I focus on my distraction. I remind myself again that I'm no good for her, and I'm getting exactly what I deserve.

The misery brings a quiet sort of calm, a blissful numbness that allows me to seize the moment. I lean over and pull the stranger's mouth to mine. She tastes like gin and cigarettes and I want to gag, but I push past that too and kiss her harder. Her hand slides between my thighs and moves slowly upward until she's cupping me through my jeans. I may feel excited to her, but on the inside, I feel nothing. And I grab hold of that familiar feeling and hug it tight, knowing it's the only thing that will keep me safe from now on.

"I'm only a couple of blocks from here," she whispers against my lips, and I don't hesitate.

"Let's go," I command, noticing the strain in my voice as I slur the words, but the stranger – *what was her name again?* – doesn't seem to mind.

She's smiling as she takes my hand and starts pulling me toward the exit. I glance over my shoulder at the restaurant sign as she leads me down the street. *Golden Venus.* I close my eyes a moment, and when I open them again, I inhale a ragged breath and turn my head back around, knowing I'll never be the same again, as I leave my goddess and the memory of her behind me for good.

CHAPTER 41 - SYDNEY

Just another night – just another horrendously depressing night of sitting alone on my sofa, while the rest of the world moves around me as if nothing has changed.

Can't they see it? Don't they understand that my heart basically stopped beating two months ago? Why so selfish, world?

I plop down on my sofa with my Ben and Jerry's, but I don't even bother turning on the television. There's nothing that interests me there, and I'm always afraid I may see something I don't want to see.

I thought it would be impossible, especially for a gossip hound like me, to avoid all things electronic for the last couple of months. But shifting myself back into the dark ages has been easier than I thought. I've had to combat intrusions from friends a few times, but after a couple of weeks or so, everyone seemed to get the hint.

Needless to say, I've been a mess since that fateful day in Miami.

After Simon left, I sunk into the bed of the hotel room and cried until the only things left were empty sobs. But at some point during all of that, I somehow convinced myself to try again, to go after him.

I cleaned myself up and searched the hotel first. Then I checked with the guys, but Simon was nowhere to be found. I didn't tell anyone at the time what had happened, hoping I could still fix things between Simon and me. Of course I wasted all that hope for nothing.

I eventually made it back down to the lobby and started asking around. I managed to find the cab that had driven Simon to a restaurant nearby and I remember laughing at the name when the driver told me. I remember thinking maybe it was a positive sign. Wrong again.

I was about to step out of the cab in front of the restaurant when Simon came stumbling out of the door with some strange woman locked around him. I watched as he looked over his shoulder at the restaurant sign and shook his head as they started to walk away. My heart sank, but I wasn't going down without a fight. I opened the cab door and started walking purposefully toward him. I would make him listen, dammit. I would make him see that I loved him, and things were not as they seemed, but I only made it a few steps.

Simon turned to the woman that was draped around him and pushed his mouth against hers, kissing her so deeply I felt it on my own lips. I knew then it wasn't just a matter of time until he would listen. He would never listen. He had been hurt too many times, and there was no hope or trust left in him. And that revelation took the rest of the hope right out of me.

Two hours. That's how long it took for him to leave me behind for someone else. In *two hours*, he decided that what we shared those days on the cruise wasn't worth fighting for. Two. Fucking. Hours. That's how long it took him to forget about me.

I wish I could say the same.

After crying my way back to the hotel, I sat in my room for a long time, until I could pull myself together and figure out how to get back home. I wanted to get out of there and the sooner the better.

By the time I got around to calling Lacey, she was sightseeing with Ollie. I was able to keep it together long enough to give her the low points and ask that she and Ollie please not say anything to James until I had a chance to speak with him.

"Oh, Sydney," Lacey said, her voice sharing in the sadness I felt. "I'm so sorry. What a mess."

"I don't want to talk about it right now," I told her. "I just wanted to let you know I'm leaving. I'm going to get a cab to the airport and I'll get my flight changed there."

Lacey tried to talk me into staying, and I could even hear Ollie in the background. "Simon will cool off, and he'll be back. They can talk. Tell her to stay," he said, but I answered before Lacey could repeat his idea.

"I don't think Simon will be back to the hotel tonight," I regretfully admitted. "And it's too late to try and explain. It's over."

"Sydney, come on," Lacey begged one last time. "Don't do this. Don't give up."

Even then, I didn't want to give up on him, but she didn't see his face. She didn't see the determination when he kissed that horrible woman. She didn't see him officially letting me go.

"I'm sorry, Lace." Tears were streaming down my cheeks again. "Be safe getting home, and I'll see you tomorrow, okay?"

"I'll just come home with you, Syd. I can't let you leave like this."

"Please stay with Ollie. It's just one night, and I really want to be alone right now. I'll be fine, and I'll see you tomorrow. Don't worry."

Lacey's sigh was sad but resigned. "Call me when you land, and we'll talk about this when I get home, okay? I love you, Sydney."

"I love you too."

After we hung up, I sat a few moments longer and cried an ocean or two more until I finally had myself together enough to ask the front desk to retrieve my bags from the room. Less than twenty minutes later, I was in a cab on my way to the airport and I bawled my eyes out the entire way home.

Just the memory of that day brings tears to my eyes, but I force them back and dive into some Chubby Hubby goodness. Unfortunately, I'm barely able to get even a few bites down.

Is it really possible for someone's life to change so drastically in less than a week?

Before I went on that dreaded cruise, I was a strong, confident woman with a great job and a promising future. Now, every day is the same exhausting exercise of waking up and trying not to cry all day at work. Then I come home and try to sleep, but I'm usually awake well before my alarm goes off and then I have to do it all over again.

Wake. Cry. Sleep. Repeat.

And work has been brutal, now that I'm back to my old assistant job. I lied to Lena and told her I wasn't ready to be an account rep, and James must have kept his mouth shut because there was barely any fall out. I get the feeling Lena has been dying to say "I told you so", but thankfully she's kept her mouth shut too. Jasper has actually been handling the account personally, so I'm sure the guys are happy and well taken care of.

Sometimes I think of telling Lena what really happened on the cruise. Part of me wants to blame her, but as much as I hate to admit it, it's not her fault. After talking with her when I backed away from the account, I think I may have misinterpreted her message as well. Lena is indeed a hard-ass, but at the end of the day, she's a decent person. I should have known better than to think she would ever stoop to that level for an account, but past experience led me to believe otherwise. So how can I blame Simon for jumping to that conclusion when I did the same damn thing?

Tears begin to fill my eyes again, but I barely notice them anymore, as I pick through my chocolaty vice. When my phone rings, I know it's probably Liz, and I think for a moment about not answering it, but I've avoided her the last few times she's called.

I peel myself off my sofa and move to the kitchen where I left my phone on charge. *Hmmm*. Not Liz. I actually don't recognize the number, but since I'm already up, I may as well answer anyway.

"Hello?"

"Sydney? It's Ollie." I grasp the countertop to stay upright, as the air starts flying out of my lungs. "I'm sorry to be calling you like this, but it's Simon. He's in trouble, and I'm at a loss. I was hoping you may be willing to help."

Of course I'm dying to know if Simon's okay, but I can't speak. Shocked would be an understatement.

"Sydney?"

"I'm here." My voice is barely recognizable. The words were such a struggle. "I'm here," I say again, after I clear my throat. "Wh-What's going on?"

Ollie takes a deep breath, and the pause makes me want to jump through the phone and strangle the answer out of him.

"It's bad, Sydney. The drinking is off the charts. For the first time ever, he came to a show the other night completely pissed. James is done. He's going to kick Si out for good. Simon's going to lose everything, and I can't watch that happen." Ollie's voice is full of desperation, and I can only imagine what his face must look like on the other end. "I've tried talking to him, on the rare occasion he's sober, and he keeps telling me things will get better, but nothing's changed. Sydney, I never would have called you if I wasn't desperate. The last time I saw him happy was with you. I don't know what else to do. Please help me."

Simon. Oh God, Simon. This is my fault and that's why I'll go to him. I'll go and try to fix what's broken – or at least the part I had a hand in.

"What do you need me to do?"

"We have a show in Memphis this weekend," Ollie tells me. "Do you think you could come? Maybe talk to him?"

"Do you seriously think he's going to want to see me?" I have to ask the obvious question.

"Well, I won't tell him you're coming. He may...."

"Run?" No need to dance around the truth.

Ollie sighs. "I'm sorry, Sydney. I know this is hard for you, but if you can help him in some way, I...we....all of us would be forever in your debt. He's like a brother to me. I hate bringing you into this, but I'd do anything for him. Anything."

"I know, Ollie, and I'm so sorry for the part I caused in all of this."

I feel like I'm reliving everything bad that happened between Simon and me, and it's seems to hurt worse the second time around, which is hard to believe.

"Fuck me. I'm not trying to make you feel guilty." Ollie pauses again. "Look, Sydney, what happened between the two of you is your business. Simon won't really talk to anyone about it anyway. I just know that there was something about you that seemed to...well, you were good for him."

The fact that we're talking about me being good for him in the past tense only makes the tears fall harder. I *was* good for him. Not anymore.

"I'll do what I can, but I can't make any promises. I'm sure I'm the last person he's going to want to see."

Ollie sighs heavily into the phone. "Thank you so much, Sydney. The concert is Friday night. It's at The Pyramid. I'll get you a plane ticket there and even book you a room. You don't need to worry about a thing."

"That's fine, but I would prefer to just stay the one night." I'm not sure I'd be able to handle anything more.

"That's fine. I'll take what I can get," he says, and I'm surprised to hear a smile in his voice. "I'll get all the details to you tomorrow. Text your email address to this number, okay?"

"I will."

"Thanks again, Sydney."

"Ollie?" I stop him before he hangs up. "Do you really think this will work? He hates me, Ollie. Why do you think I have a chance at bringing him back?"

Ollie's quiet for what seems like forever. "I don't know if it will work or not, but one thing I do know...you did it before, Sydney. You brought him back. Maybe you can do it again."

We say our goodbyes, and I sit on my sofa and ponder that last statement for the rest of the night, on up until the morning.

I didn't save Simon on that cruise. Maybe I played a small part, but ultimately, he saved himself. And he showed me what real love was in the process. So I'll go to Memphis. I'll try and right my wrongs in this, and I'll make sure at some point to thank him for saving me too – not just once, but twice.

"I'm on a nine o'clock flight," I tell my bestie Liz, as I careen through morning traffic like my life depends on it.

"I think you're doing the right thing," she says to me. "Regardless of the circumstances, the two of you shared something on that cruise. And I know better than anyone that you have enough confidence and strength for the two of you. He needs your strength, Sydney."

Dammit Liz. I want to cry, but tears aren't going to do me any good now.

"I hope you're right."

"I'm always right."

"True," I agree with a smile. "Let's just hope he doesn't try and murder me or something before I even get a chance to talk to him."

"I think you may be surprised by his reaction. Based on what you told me, I doubt he's over you any more than you are over him. You never know. He might be happy to see you. He *should* be happy to see you."

I think about that a moment. What will I do if he's actually happy to see me?

"Look, Liz," I sigh. "We've been over this a million times, and I understand your point and Lacey's. But the fact is I hurt him, and with Simon, there may be no coming back from that. I just pray Ollie's right and that maybe I still have a chance to convince him off the edge somehow. I would give anything to see him happy, Liz. That's all I want."

"Well, well. Look who's all grown up."

"Oh hush," I say, as my lips curl into a sad kind of smile. Why does being a grown-up have to come with so much heartache?

"If you want to see him happy, then that's what you'll get," Liz tells me. "But I think this is your chance to reconcile things, your opportunity to explain. We all know you have plenty of confidence in yourself, but you need to have confidence in the way you feel about him, too. Stop being afraid of it. And don't let anything – and I mean, *anything* – derail you. Things will work out. I promise."

"How can you be so sure?"

"I'm not," she admits with a laugh. "But I believe in you, and I believe in happily ever after's. This may be yours, Sydney. Don't give up."

"Thanks Liz. I better go."

"Okay. I love you, Syd."

I repeat the words to my friend and hang up, concentrating once again on dodging and swerving through traffic so I don't miss my flight.

I'm not sure I want to think about the possibility of a positive outcome in all of this for Simon and me. I love Liz, but I can't afford to go there right now. I need to keep my head in the game. I need to keep Simon's needs at the forefront.

Thankfully, I arrive at the airport with time to spare, but I'm going to be cutting it close if the security line is out of control.

When I check in, I find I'm flying first class – seems Ollie went all out, allowing me to take the short line through security, even giving me time to stop for coffee before my flight. I owe Ollie for that one big time.

But now that I have this extra time – and two extra shots in my coffee – I'm as jittery as ever, thinking about what tonight will bring.

I was hoping Lacey would be able to come to the show with me, but she has a make-up session in one of her art classes tomorrow morning, and I couldn't let her skip that. She was so sweet about wanting me to try and help Simon, but what if I can't help him? What if he rejects me or laughs in my face?

No. I can't think like that. I have to at least give this a shot because no matter what I try and convince myself of when I look in the mirror each morning, I'm still in love with him. So very much. And if I have to suffer through something like an embarrassing public rejection, it's a risk I'm willing to take. He may listen. He may be happy again. So I have to try.

I arrive in Memphis around the same time as I left Atlanta, thanks to the time change. The wait and plane ride were excruciating – those few hours seeming like eons. And now, I'm at my hotel in Memphis, waiting for Ollie with sweaty palms and shaky knees. But I am pretty excited to see Ollie again as well. I've missed him.

Just as I sit down on the bed from my most recent pacing stint, there's a knock at my door.

I open the door to a grinning Ollie. "Aren't you a sight for sore eyes?"

He pulls me into a huge bear hug, and it feels amazing.

When I pull away, I have to smile as I take in his appearance. He's wearing jeans, beat-up Converse and a black, NWA t-shirt, and his white blond hair is styled into a faux hawk, which looks adorably sexy on him.

"How was your flight?" he asks, as he walks into my room. "Everything okay? Car show up on time?"

"Everything was perfect. But this waiting is going to kill me," I admit and Ollie's smile vanishes.

He takes a seat at the desk, and I sit near him on the end of the bed. "I'm sorry again, Sydney. I know you don't want to do this, but I'm so glad you're here. I actually feel better now that you're here. I feel hopeful. Maybe this can work."

I look down at my shoes, hating that he's hopeful. I want to feel the same. I really do. But this is a stretch and hope seems just out of reach.

"Ollie, I'll do what I can, but he was so angry with me. I can assure you, he's not going to be happy to see me."

"I wouldn't bet on that," Ollie says, and my head pops up out of curiosity. "You don't know him like I do, Sydney. He's hurting. That's what this is. And it's not just one thing. Si's a pro at letting it all pile up, then he has a hard time finding the light at the end of the tunnel." Ollie holds my eyes with his. "You're his light, Sydney. He told me that on the cruise. And I don't think whatever happened between the two of you that day in Miami changed that. I truly don't."

Okay, so the whole "light" comment was a little unexpected. *Don't cry, Sydney. Dammit.*

"Well, I'm glad you're so confident, Ollie, and I promise I'll try. I care about him too."

"I know you do. I wouldn't have asked you to come, otherwise." Ollie stands, and I follow. "Now, how about some breakfast? I'm bloody starved, and we've got a long day ahead of us."

Eating? Not likely. If I'm able to get anything other than coffee and water down today, it will be a miracle.

"There's a nice restaurant here at the hotel, actually," Ollie mentions, as I grab my purse and we head toward the door to my room. "We can eat and then chat about the plan."

"What is the plan exactly? And don't you need security or something?"

Ollie laughs as we walk down the hall. "This isn't the cruise. I may get noticed, but I'm not going to get mobbed or anything. You'll see."

"Okay," I smile at him. "And the plan?"

"Oh right." Ollie furrows his brow. "Well, we'll eat, then I can take you to Simon. Easy as that."

"Wait, what?"

I freeze as Ollie presses the down button at the elevator. I didn't think I would have to see him until tonight. I thought I'd have more time to prepare. I'm not sure how much good that would do, but still.

"Problem?"

"I just...I thought I wouldn't see him until later," I stutter out, as we enter the elevator.

"Yeah...right...well, I thought about waiting until later, but when I spoke to James, he agreed that we shouldn't wait. Even if Si gets pissed and blows off the show, it'd be better than what happened last time. We don't have much to lose, either way."

"So, James and Rob know I'm here?"

I find it hard to believe I've been a part of any kind of *positive* conversation between the guys after everything that's happened.

"This was all James's idea, actually. James loves him too, Sydney," Ollie tells me, as the shock registers on my face. "I agreed to make the call, made all the plans, but James was the one that initially mentioned the idea of you trying to help him."

"No pressure," I mumble to myself, but Ollie hears me and laughs.

"There's no pressure." He pulls me into his side and gives me a squeeze. "If this doesn't work, I'll keep trying. I won't give up on him, even if everyone else does. I promise."

Ollie's words are soothing. I like hearing that someone will always be there to take care of Simon. It does take the pressure off, if only a tiny bit.

"We can strategize over pancakes." Ollie smiles. "Miracle working is better done on a full stomach."

I take a deep breath and smile back as we exit the elevator. Here goes nothing.

CHAPTER 42 - SIMON

I open my eyes briefly and see it's still dark. Why is it still dark? And where the fuck am I?

I close my eyes and try to take a deep breath, but my chest hurts constantly these days. Breathing has become a chore.

I try and find a clock for the time, but quickly decide it isn't worth the effort. I'll just stay in the dark for now.

I toss my leg over the side of the bed and place my foot on the floor to try and stop the spinning. It seems I drank so much last night I couldn't even sleep it off. Brilliant.

"Simon?"

The groggy female voice startles me, but I keep my eyes closed and rub my temples, not even bothering to respond. I don't give a shit who she is or what she needs. I just want her to get the hell out.

Yep. Total bastard. That's me.

"Simon, are you awake?" the voice asks as a warm arm slides around my waist.

If I keep my eyes closed and concentrate, I can pretend it's someone else's arm – a familiar, comforting arm, instead of whoever I drug home with me last night.

But my cloudy brain won't let me concentrate hard enough at the moment, and I'm tired of pretending.

I gather enough strength to push the stranger's arm away from me, then I roll out of the bed and make my way to the loo. I find some jeans on the floor on my way and pull them on, stumbling a bit in my efforts, but I eventually get to my destination and lock the door behind me.

I take a seat on the edge of the bathtub and put my head in my hands, not even bothering to turn on the light. It seems no matter how much I drink, the pain just won't fucking go away.

"Simon? Is everything okay?"

The voice is back and knocking on the bathroom door, and I feel every rap as it echoes in my pounding head.

"Please, just go," I say in a low voice, not sure if she can hear, but I hope to God she can.

"You're kidding me, right?"

Now the voice is angry. I should care, but I don't. I don't care at all.

"Get the fuck out." I try and make my voice louder, but I can't seem to get it much above a raspy whisper.

I hear a few sounds of exasperation and a string of curses, as the stranger moves through my room, hopefully getting dressed. "You're an asshole, Simon Young! And I'll make sure every reporter in the country knows it!" she shouts right before she opens and then slams the door to my suite.

"Wonderful," I mumble to myself once the door slams.

I stay on my perch at the edge of the tub until the dizziness sets back in, then I move to the floor. The cold tile feels good, so I curl up and sooner or later, I fall back asleep.

When I wake up for the second time I'm still in the dark, but I can see a sliver of light coming from under the door. I lie there a moment, making sure the dizziness has at least faded to a dull spin, before I decide to get up in search of some coffee and maybe a shower.

I stretch my arm above my head, and that's when I realize there's a pillow there. I grab at it wondering if I brought it with me last night, but I know without thinking too hard there's no way I did something like that. However, I can't remember last night with much clarity at all at the moment.

Was there a woman in my bed last night? Is she still there? Maybe she brought me the pillow?

I rise slowly, pulling the pillow into my blanket covered lap – *a blanket too?* – as I gradually start to recall what happened sometime in the middle of the night.

Nope. There's no way that girl did anything nice for me.

I drop the pillow to the floor as I pull myself to my feet. If it wasn't the girl from last night, that only leaves one person. Ollie. I swear that bastard's a glutton for punishment.

When I turn on the light, I have to close my eyes to stop what feels like the scorching of my goddamn retinas. I open them again slowly and cringe at my reflection in the mirror. I don't know why I'm surprised. I shouldn't be shocked that I don't even recognize the person staring back at me. His face is pale and ashen. His chin hasn't seen a razor in days, and his eyes are so bloodshot you can hardly make out the actual color. I've brought him to the edge of death multiple times over the past few years, but looking at him now, I'm afraid I may be a step too close this time. I think his nine lives may be about to run out.

Fuck it. What do I care anyway?

I use the loo and wash up, then decide to splash my face with a bit of cold. I run my fingers through my hair and brush my teeth, hoping that will take away the urge to vomit, but it doesn't work. I take a deep breath before I go and face Ollie and his annoying persistence. I can't seem to convince him to give up, even though part of me understands. I would do the same for him. I truly would. But he can't help me this time. I'm done. I'm lost. And I'm too tired to try and find my way back.

I open the bathroom door slowly and notice the room is bright with sunlight. Knowing I would never voluntarily open the drapes, it's obvious someone has been here, but when I walk into the bedroom there's no one around. I decide to change into some gym shorts before walking into the living room of the suite to find Ollie.

"Stop worrying. I'm fine, mate."

I look around the room, but no one's there. *What the hell?* Maybe he stepped out for some breakfast? Or lunch? I have no idea what time it is.

I'm about to take a seat on the sofa to wait for him to come back when someone answers me from the balcony.

"Glad to hear it," the familiar voice says, but it's not Ollie. It most definitely is *not* Ollie.

No, that voice...that voice stops me mid-step, and I feel the after effects of last night's bender exit my body in a rush. Suddenly, I'm stone cold sober, awake and revived.

But just as quickly as the new energy floods in, it floods right back out replaced with things like anger, regret and sadness.

Why is she here? And how could she do this to me?

I'm as still as a statue in the middle of the living room refusing to look her way. I'm afraid with one look I'll be lost forever, and my mind is barely hanging on as it is.

"Simon?"

That beautiful voice calls out to me like a siren's call, and I hang my head in defeat. I don't even have to look. With just a few simple words, I'm completely under her spell. *My fucking Venus.*

I still can't bring myself to look at her, or even speak, but I hear her moving slowly toward me, and as she gets closer, I catch her scent – her lovely, flowery scent – and I feel like I've been given fresh blood in my veins.

"I...I know...you probably don't want to see or talk to me, and I...well, I can understand that," she says from behind me, and I close my eyes tightly hating how much I'm enjoying just the sound of her voice. "I only wanted...I just...."

I raise my head when she stops speaking and turn toward her. She pulls her hand to her mouth, probably shocked by my appearance. I can't fault her for that. I know it's awful. I wish I cared.

"Why did you stop?" I ask, and she blinks in confusion, but I can't seem to find any other words. It took everything inside me to get those few out.

"T-Talking," I finally stutter. "Don't stop talking," I plead as I study her face.

Oh God, she's gorgeous. But I'm surprised to find her mirroring my appearance in a few areas – thinner, pale face, bloodshot eyes.

I watch as Sydney slowly removes her hand from her mouth. Christ, that *mouth.*

"O-Okay," she says. "Ummm...I just...I wanted to see how you were doing."

I continue staring at her, greedily soaking up her features, until what she said last finally registers. She wants to know how I'm doing? Is she *serious*?

I easily snap back into the angry, self-destructive persona I know and love, as I watch her face become more and more hopeful by the second. Fuck hope.

"Oh, I'm perfectly fine, love," I give her as much snark and sarcasm as I can muster. "And you?"

"I've been awful, actually." Sydney's face falls, and I feel her pain mingle with mine. "But this isn't about me." She tilts her head to look at me, and I cross my arms across my chest feeling the sudden urge to protect my heart. "I came to talk to you. Ollie asked me to come. He hoped...he hoped I may be able to..."

I watch her, waiting. And I'm about to go in for the kill. I'm going to tell her how she and Ollie need to get the hell out of my life and worry about theirs, but just as I'm about to ruin this moment with her and send her away for good, I see a glimpse of something flash across her face.

Steadfast. Determination.

She stands up straighter and moves a step closer to me. I want to back away, but I can't. Apparently, I still crave her closeness, so I keep my arms wrapped tightly around my chest, just in case my body decides to do something stupid.

"Look. I screwed up, Simon," she tells me. "And I'm so, so sorry. I should have fought harder, but there's no going back now and doing things differently. If I could, I would have been honest with you in the first place. I would have told you how much..."

Sydney's blue eyes burn into mine, and I take a step backward, doing whatever it takes to resist that potent touch. I know there's no way I can tolerate her hands on me in any way. I'll be a goner for sure.

"I've come to try and explain," she says. "I want you to be happy. You deserve that. I know you don't think so, but you deserve happiness, Simon."

I shake my head and continue backing away from her, still trying to digest all of this. I slowly uncross my arms and move to the sofa. I have to sit down before the weight of her being here causes me to collapse. I don't know if I can take this today. I'm going to kill Ollie. He's stepped way over the line with this one.

"Won't you say something, Simon? Anything?"

Sydney's taken a seat on the edge of a chair next to me, and tears are pouring out of her eyes. *Fuck.* I hate seeing her cry.

"Honestly, I don't know what to say. I'm...I'm a little shocked that you're even here."

Sydney looks down at her shoes again. "I'm sorry for that. I should have reached out sooner. I just thought that after Miami you never wanted to speak to me again..." She pauses and looks at me as if she's reliving some terrible pain, then shakes it off. "But that's no excuse. I still should have called to try and explain things, to make amends."

I watch, heartbroken as the tears continue streaming silently down her beautiful face.

"Was I right?" she asks me in a whisper. "Do you hate me, Simon? I gave up on us, so you should hate me I suppose, but it would still hurt."

I try to formulate an intelligent response. I'm not sure I want to risk my feelings again, but the truth is...

"I don't hate you," I admit without thinking. "Not even a little."

I watch Sydney's shoulders relax as she exhales, but she doesn't appear any happier than she was before my answer.

"That's good," she breathes. "But I have to say that the more I think about it, the more I'm starting to think that what we had on the cruise was...well, I've never experienced anything like it, and I'm certain I never will again. But it wasn't reality."

"Felt pretty real to me," I snap, feeling the anger settling back in. "Especially the part afterward when you lied to me."

"I didn't lie," she tells me, with unexpected venom in her voice as well. "And you would have known that if you wouldn't have walked away from me, which seemed extremely easy for you, by the way."

She did *not* just say that.

"You think it was *easy* for me to walk away?" I feel my face heat up, right along with my words. "I trusted you, and you betrayed me. I thought you were different, but you're the same as all the rest, just in it for yourself, no matter who you hurt."

"You supremely selfish bastard! It's not always about *you*!"

I can tell by her expression she hadn't intended to shout at me, but I'm glad she did. That passion means she cares.

With a frustrated groan, Sydney stands and moves toward the balcony door. She winds her arms tightly around her waist, as she looks through the glass and out at the city. I can sense her trying to hold it together, as I know the feeling well.

"I'm sorry for getting upset. That wasn't my intention." Sydney's voice is quiet, full of sorrow. "But how do you think it made me feel to find out you were no different than the rest either? Maybe I didn't fight hard enough for you, but maybe you should have fought a little harder for *me*. You read those emails and automatically assumed I would do something to hurt you. I know we haven't known each

338

other long, but I thought what we shared...I thought you knew me, Simon. How do you think it felt to find out I was wrong?"

Defeat has replaced the passion in her voice, and the thick cloud of despair left in its wake threatens to suffocate me. And as I struggle to breathe, clarity hits me like a wrecking ball. *Oh God. What have I done?*

Sydney turns back to me, her arms still wrapped firmly around her tiny middle, her stare pointed at the floor. "The truth is, Simon...we're both selfish. I've been told it's not always about me a million times over, but I think it's finally starting to sink in, because for the first time..."

With a determined look back on her face, Sydney comes and sits next to me on the sofa. I inch away from her, still afraid of giving into her touch, but I immediately regret the reaction, especially when she breathes a dejected sigh, looks down at her lap and says, "For the first time in my life, I found someone to care about more than myself. Your happiness means more to me than my own."

The bitter taste of panic rises up my throat like bile.

"Sydney, I—"

"I'm not finished." She tosses a shaky hand up to stop me, and her misty blue eyes lock with mine. "I don't know what part you and I play in what you're going through at the moment, but I can't watch you do this to yourself, Simon. And no one else should have to either. You're better than this. I know you're in pain, but I also know you're strong enough to pull through it. You're strong enough to come out on the other side and be happy again. I believe in you, Simon. I always have."

I try and fight off a bout of dizziness from either the lingering alcohol, or more likely the information overload I just experienced. I attempt a deep breath, but the nagging pain in my chest makes it near impossible. And even though the last thing I want to do is put my weakness on display for this woman, I can't stop the tears as they start falling. Realizing once again what a colossal fuck up I truly am, I lean my head back and close my eyes. Maybe I'll wake up soon. Maybe it's all a dream and I can just go back to the darkness. Please God let that be the case, because if I actually just heard Sydney say she believes in me, I know there's no amount of alcohol in the world that can erase those precious words from my head.

I pull myself off the sofa because I can't be near her anymore. I have to have some space before I explode.

"Okay, so if you're here to talk me off the ledge, so to speak," I wish the sarcasm in my voice was a more worthy opponent for the ache in my chest. "That's all fine and good, but I will confirm that one of the reasons I'm currently on said ledge is because of what happened between us, Sydney. And since I'll probably never get you back, because I'm self-admittedly the largest arsehole on the planet, how did you plan to talk me off the ledge, exactly?"

I put my hands on my hips and continue my pacing. No matter what she thinks, I'm permanently broken. I don't deserve her, and I try to keep repeating those words in my head, but it's still spinning from what she confessed a few moments ago. And because she's here, finally close to me again, my hands are shaking now with the need to touch her.

"The truth is...." She stands and moves close enough for me to hear her soft voice. "I'd gladly take you back, Simon. I wouldn't even have to think twice about it, but you don't need me. You need to do this on your own. I'm here for you and I always will be, but let's face it. Two shallow, self-absorbed people don't make a right. The bottom line is you're still punishing yourself for something that happened years ago, and you have to quit punishing yourself because it's not going to bring her back. Nothing's going to bring her back, and it's time you start accepting that and move on."

I stop my pacing, shocked by her words. Sydney looks away from me briefly, seeming upset with herself for what she just said, but soon enough, those fiercely determined eyes are back on me.

"I didn't know Melissa, personally, but I'm certain she loved you. And I'm certain she would never want to see you like this. As for me..." Sydney moves a little closer and my hands shake a little harder. "I don't want to see you like this either. You and I both may have a little growing up to do, but I still care about you Simon, and so do a lot of other people. I think the most important thing for you to focus on right now is to start taking some responsibility in those relationships. Start living again. I promise you won't be disappointed."

And with gentle hands, my final wall is torn down.

The look in Sydney's eyes tells me everything she's not saying. She loves me. I can see it. She loves me, and she believes in me. And even though I may feel like I don't deserve her, she's still here, still trying to save me, and I don't have the strength to fight anymore.

I'm in front of my goddess in only a couple of strides, and the shock barely registers before I take her in my arms. I pull her close and press my face so hard into her neck that I hear her gasp, but she wastes no time in putting her arms around me. Her fingers move to the back of my hair, and I sigh with relief before I completely let go.

"I'm so sorry, Sydney," I whisper through my sobs. "God, I'm so sorry. So fucking sorry."

I apologize so many times I lose track, as Sydney holds me and tries to soothe me. "Shhhh. It's okay. It's going to be okay," she tells me, but I keep apologizing just so she'll continue to soothe me, just so she'll keep those gentle hands in my hair and that sweet voice in my ear.

I have no idea how long we stay that way, but too soon Sydney pulls away and takes both of my hands in hers. "You're going to be fine," she tells me once more, and for the first time since I lost Melissa, I start to believe it.

But all I can do is nod at my sweet goddess, as what feels like a century's worth of tears continue to trickle down my face.

Sydney and I spent the remaining hours before tonight's show locked in my suite. We talked. We reminisced. We even laughed a little. And the entire time, we were touching in some way – holding hands, our arms around each other, my head in her lap or her head in mine.

It will go down as some of the best few hours of my life, and as I sit in my dressing room now preparing for tonight, I allow myself a few silent moments to commit it all to memory.

We talked about anything and everything, including an in depth discussion on the best and worst ice cream flavors, which had me falling in love with her all over again. She also told me about her family and her friends back home, and I shared some of the better stories that the guys and I have had over the years, which is mainly what kept us laughing. I even talked about Melissa for the first time in a long time, and it felt really good.

"Will you tell me about Melissa?" Sydney asked, throwing me off guard.

I pulled her closer to me on the sofa, like a safety blanket, and she gave me a small encouraging smile.

"What do you want to know?"

"Just tell me about her. What was she like?"

Oddly enough, no one ever asks me that. They normally want to know about us as a couple or the details of the accident, but Sydney wanted to know about Melissa and for some reason, I wanted to tell her.

So, I took a deep breath and started talking.

"She was beautiful," I told her, remembering Melissa's sweet face. "But she was also extremely patient and kind. She loved children. She was a primary school teacher, and she was wonderful at it." Sydney pulled away and repositioned us so her arm was behind me on the sofa, and her fingers were in my hair. Instantly soothed, I was able to continue. "She was very close to her family. Her two older brothers were insanely protective, and I had a hell of a time convincing them to let me take her on our first date. But when Melissa wanted something, Melissa got it. Thankfully, she wanted me.

"It wasn't love at first sight for us," I admitted. "We met through a mutual friend, and our first date was a disaster. After that, we decided we'd be better off as friends, and that's the way things remained for several months. She even went out on a couple of dates with Ollie, if you can believe that."

"No way!" Sydney gasped and I smiled.

"Ollie wasn't her type, but he's a riot, and Melissa loved to laugh. Obviously, things didn't work for the two of them, but they remained great friends. Ollie asked her to come on tour with us one summer while she was out of school. She and I ended up spending a lot of time together, and I'm not sure how or when, but I fell in love with her."

And then it was time to move toward the difficult parts.

Instinctively, I squeeze the locket in my palm for comfort as I remember how painful it was to discuss that night with her, but I wanted to get it out. And I wanted Sydney to hear it.

"You don't have to tell me," she said, but one look into her sweet, blue eyes and I found all the strength I needed.

"Melissa went out with some friends one night," I started, and Sydney curled up next to me on the sofa, her arms around my waist, and it felt so good I could have died right there. "And I didn't want her to go, but she hated disappointing people. Just as I had expected, they all ended up drinking too much and couldn't drive home. She called me in the middle of the night, and I was angry. I had a rehearsal early the next day, and she knew that. I remember thinking she was being so selfish, which looking back is absurd. If there was one thing Melissa was not, it was selfish."

I could feel Sydney's wet tears on my bare chest, so I rubbed my hand down her hair to soothe her, and she cuddled in even closer, waiting for me to continue.

"She knew I was mad, and she must have apologized a thousand times to me once I picked her up. I was all but wrapped around that woman's finger, so her sad, puppy dog looks usually worked like a charm, but not that night. I was tired and angry and driving even more recklessly than she probably would have been. Melissa and I were in the middle of an argument about my driving and before I knew what was happening, a pick-up truck swerved over into our lane, and hit us head on. We flipped a few times, and Melissa had forgotten her seat belt. She was thrown from the car."

Sydney buried her wet face in my neck and held me close, as I tried to relive one of the most painful memories of my life.

"She was in a coma for two weeks. I sat with her every day while she was in the hospital. I talked to her. I told her how much I loved her. I begged her to come back to me, but she never opened her eyes again. The guilt was overwhelming, of course. She was dead and I barely got a scratch. I killed her, Sydney. And worst of all, the last words I spoke to her were in anger. Her parents and friends hated me. Still do. I don't speak to any of them anymore, and I'm not sure what I'd say if I ever had the chance. I tried talking to her parents. I tried telling them how sorry I was and that even though the guy who hit us was arrested and charged with drunk driving, I would still take full responsibility for what happened. But it wasn't enough. She was gone, and that's all they knew or cared about. Even if I ever find a way to forgive myself, they will never forgive me. Never."

Sydney sat up and pulled my chin toward her so she could see my eyes. "That's their problem. Not yours. They have to deal with things in their own way, Simon. Don't let them keep you from moving on. You can move on without their forgiveness."

"I know," I assured her. "But it's still a hard thing to accept. They were all such a large part of my life. Melissa and her family were always there for me. I needed them after Melissa died, but they could barely look at me."

Sydney pulled away completely until she was kneeling beside me on the sofa, her face serious. "Simon, you have to know that they still love you. They're just angry," she told me. "And Melissa loved you, no matter what happened between the two of you that night.

One argument does not erase months or years of love between two people. If the accident never would have happened, you would have kissed and made up the next day, probably even that night. She loved you, and she knew you loved her. I know she did."

This woman's faith in me is remarkable, I remember thinking at the time, and I wanted to hug her close, kiss her, get on my fucking knees and worship her, anything to show her how much I appreciated that moment and what she was doing for me. But more than anything, I didn't want to push her away. I didn't want to scare her off, so I kept my distance and continued on.

"Honestly, it's not her love that I've questioned over the years. It's just been the guilt – the guilt over what happened, how things happened and the lack of forgiveness from her friends and family. It's been hard to live with, and I think in some ways I was acting out to try and prove to them how sorry I was for what I did. I wanted them to see how much I was hurting, but it didn't work, and after a while that wasn't my excuse anymore. I needed the darkness. I was more comfortable there. And once I got too deep, I couldn't find my way back."

"But you will find your way," Sydney told me with an encouraging smile. "I truly believe that. Don't you?"

"I'm starting to."

"Good," she said with an adorable little clap. "And you have so many people willing to help and support you, Simon. Don't try to do this alone."

I smiled, but her words didn't reassure me because I knew in that moment that unfortunately, she was right. This whole thing is bigger than Sydney and me, and although I hate the thought of not having her in my life, I realized then I was going to have to find my own way.

I'm no good for Sydney as I am now, but maybe I can be someday. And as I sit backstage now, still gripping the locket tightly in my palm, that's the hope I've chosen to hold on to.

After a few minutes more, I take a deep breath and put the locket away. I'm picking up my guitar to make sure it's tuned when Ollie pokes his head in the door.

"Ready, Si?"

"I think so."

"She's here," he tells me, and I look up at him.

"I know."

"I got her front row, to the left."

"Thanks, mate."

Ollie goes to walk away, and I stop him. "Ollie, wait."

He turns back to me, brow raised, waiting for me to say something.

"Thanks for...thanks for everything. And it's important to me that you know I'd do the same thing for you."

Ollie smiles and nods. "I know, brother. Now, if you can put your vagina back in your pants and get your arse on stage, we'd greatly appreciate it."

I toss my guitar pick at him, hating it's not something a little more lethal. Ollie dodges it with a laugh, and heads toward the stage.

I take another deep breath, wrap my guitar around my neck and try and prepare myself for what I'm about to do.

I fucking hate goodbyes.

CHAPTER 43 - SYDNEY

I'm shaking like a leaf as I sit and wait for the show to start.

The fans are all screaming around me, but I don't share the same excitement I see on their faces.

I know in my heart this is probably the last time I'll see Simon Young in the flesh, and just the thought of that makes my chest feel so heavy I can barely breathe.

I sit back in my seat and replay again everything that happened this afternoon. I thought there was no way I would ever get through to Simon. I thought I would never be strong enough to say what I wanted to say, but I just kept thinking about what Liz told me – to believe in myself and trust my feelings. It was nothing short of a miracle, but somehow, I was able to get through to him. And I was so high from finally pulling him off the ledge that the pain of my broken heart is just now sinking in.

Oh God. Even though losing him feels like it may be the death of me, I have to let him go. Liz told me to trust in my feelings for him, but I also need to trust in my feelings about us. I know I may regret this decision for the rest of my days, but for now, we'll go our separate ways. If it's meant to be, we'll find each other again when the time is right.

"Hello, Memphis!"

A booming voice comes over the speakers, and music is soon to follow. I get to my feet, and when the crowd starts to die down, the announcer gets back to the mic.

348

"In just a moment, I'm going to bring out the men you've all been waiting for, but first, let them hear how excited you are to see them!"

The crowd goes wild again, but I stand perfectly still in my front row spot, realizing I'm about to relive my teenage fantasy for most likely the last time. My legs start shaking so badly, it's all I can do to stay on my feet.

"All right, everyone. Please join me in welcoming your favorite group of guys and mine, The London Boys!"

As the guys take the stage, the roar of the crowd is nearly deafening. I want to cover my ears, but I don't want to seem like an old lady.

Simon zeroes in on me almost immediately after he walks on to the stage. I smile then look away, not wanting to get too lost in those deep brown eyes. Instead, I watch as James takes his seat behind the drums, Ollie straps on his bass and Rob moves on the other side of Ollie with his guitar. Simon puts his guitar in a stand, then takes a seat at the piano.

I'm happy to see the instruments on stage, and the fans seem to appreciate it too. The guys start off with a few of their own songs, and I love how the lack of smoke and lights showcases the true talent that each one of them possesses. This is exactly what I had pictured for them, and I'm glad Jasper obviously felt the same.

At a break between one of the songs, Simon grabs his guitar, moves to a stool at the side of the stage, and speaks into the mic.

"I hope you guys don't mind, but there's something I have to do tonight." The troubled look on his face stuns everyone silent, including me. "It's not going to be easy, and frankly, I'm tired of having to say goodbye, but it's an unfortunate fact of life, I'm afraid."

The crowd remains eerily quiet as Simon lets out a nervous laugh. I close my eyes, having no idea where he's going with this, but I'm certain I'm not going to like it.

"I've loved two women in my life," he says, and my eyes pop open to meet his. "I'm sorry to say that I somehow managed to lose them both, and even though nothing pains me more, all that's left to do is say goodbye and hope that someday, somewhere, both of those amazing creatures will find it in their hearts to forgive me."

Simon stares at me a moment longer, then he lowers his head as his fingers start moving across the strings.

I immediately recognize the cover, as Joshua Radin is one of my favorites, and I feel my heart rip open as Simon starts to sing. The song *Cross That Line* is definitely a goodbye, but it's a hopeful goodbye, and the lyrics, along with the soft, whispery sound of Simon's voice leave me breathless.

Simon's eyes meet mine again, as the tears start rolling down my cheeks. I try to look away, but he's positively captivating, even with pain clearly etched across his beautiful face. I couldn't look away from Simon Young right now if my life depended on it, which may just be the case.

His voice breaks in various places, and I can sense this strange concentration while he sings to me, but my heart is breaking little by little with every word, making it hard to focus on much of anything.

By the time Simon is finished, my heart and I are spent. I watch him hang his head and sit for a moment after the song is over. The break in eye contact is a relief.

I wipe at my eyes as the crowd cheers on, and eventually, Simon rises from his stool and makes his way over to me. He reaches a hand out when he's in front of me on stage, and with a depressing hint of déjà vu, I slowly walk toward him. When I offer my hand, he squeezes it in his and leans down to place a lingering kiss on my knuckles. He tilts his head and studies me a moment, then walks back to place his guitar in the stand.

I move back to my seat, ignoring the gasps and swoons from the people around me. I look back up at the stage and watch Simon push a hand into his pocket, and I see the sigh in his shoulders before he turns back to the crowd. But then he suddenly shifts his attention back to me, and the look on his face is completely unexpected.

I glance around, wondering if that intense gaze is possibly meant for someone else, but it's not. It's locked on me, looking for...what the hell *is* he looking for?

He grabs at his chest as he stares at me, and I wonder what I could have done wrong. Is he upset about me crying again? He certainly doesn't look upset. He looks...he looks...

CHAPTER 44 - SIMON

Holy shit, could this be possible?

When I turned to put the guitar back in its stand, the need for some kind of comfort had me automatically reaching down into my pocket. The moment my fingers touched the locket, the memory of my favorite fan from long ago came crashing into me, almost as if she was trying to tell me something.

I turned quickly back to the crowd and zeroed in on Sydney. And now, as I watch her surprised and vaguely familiar face, I have to wonder.

Could it be *her*?

I've always felt there was something strangely familiar about those eyes. Plus, Sydney *is* a fan. She's from Georgia. And if I take her age into account...

As I sift through the images of that concert ten years ago, I remember brown hair and adorably chubby – not the blonde, blue-eyed goddess standing before me now. On the surface, it doesn't seem possible, but it's been ten years. People change. *And those eyes.* How could I ever forget those eyes?

I grab at my chest again trying to slow my racing heart. I squeeze the locket, hoping for a clearer memory – a more vivid picture of that little girl from all of those years ago – but every image seems all wrong.

Except those stunning blue eyes.

Sydney's eyes.

James starts to speak again, but I can't peel my eyes or my thoughts away from Sydney. And even though her hand is currently covering her beautiful smile, and her blue eyes are clouded with unshed tears, it all seems so clear to me now that I'm amazed I didn't see it before. I can see that little girl unmistakably in her features, especially those damn eyes.

Fuck me, it's her.

In the flesh.

My favorite fan.

Sydney's the one. She's the owner of the locket. She's my beacon in the darkness.

My goddess is...my savior.

CHAPTER 45 - SYDNEY

I put a hand over my mouth when I realize he does in fact look happy, *very* happy. He's obviously content with what's happened tonight, at ease with his goodbye, and I smile without thinking because his happiness truly does mean more to me than my own. But that doesn't make this hurt any less.

James is saying something to the crowd, but I barely make out a few words before shooting out of my seat and heading for the door. I run as fast as I can to the nearest exit, and when I finally make it outside, I start gasping for air on the sidewalk.

"Are you okay?" some stranger asks me, but I wave him away.

I look up to try and find a cab, but my eyes are so blurry with tears, I can't make out a thing. I fall to my knees on the pavement, barely feeling the rocks cut into my skin through my jeans. It should hurt, and it probably will tomorrow, but right now, the pain in my chest is overriding everything else.

"I'll get you a cab."

This voice is British and somewhat familiar, and I allow him to pull me up and hold me as I start to sob uncontrollably.

At some point I'm placed in a car, and I immediately curl up in the back seat, as whoever was holding me tells the driver the name of my hotel.

"Give me a moment," I beg, when we finally arrive at the hotel.

I reach for my purse to pay for the ride, but the driver raises his hand to stop me.

"It's taken care of, miss," he informs me. "And take all the time you need."

I have no idea who could or would have paid for the cab, but I'm so very grateful. Still trying to catch my breath, I lean my head back and close my eyes until I compose myself just enough to make my way inside.

I go to open the car door, but the driver is already there to open it for me. "Have a good night, miss."

I wish I could smile, but I can't. I hope he understands.

I wipe at my eyes and make my way into the lobby. I walk as fast as my legs will take me to the elevator – which isn't very fast at all – eager to be alone in the dark. Thankfully, the lobby and elevator are empty. What a relief.

I finally make it to my room, unlock the door and fall onto my bed. I don't even bother to remove my shoes. I start crying again as soon as my head hits the mattress and I have to wonder if I'll ever stop.

The next thing I know, I'm startled awake by a knock on the door. I open my eyes and look around, feeling totally disoriented. It takes me a moment to figure out where I am.

By the time everything starts coming back to me, there's another knock on my door. Must be Ollie. I'm sure he saw me run out of the concert, and he's probably worried.

Even though I have zero desire to speak to him right now, or anyone else for that matter, I make my way off the bed and toward the door. I think for a moment what I must look like, but I just don't have the energy to do anything about it.

There's no peephole to look through, so I stop at the door wondering if I should open it without first finding out for sure who it is. But before I get a chance to speak, I hear a voice from the other side of the door.

"Sydney? Are you in there?"

My tired eyes go wide with shock, and my hand moves to my mouth to quiet my gasp. What is *he* doing here? He said goodbye to me. It's over. He has his closure. What more does he want from me?

"Sydney, please," Simon's voice pleads, and tears pop back into my eyes, so used to being there at this point, they come easily and uninvited. "Sydney, please let me in. Greg told me he made sure you got back here safe, and I had to beg Ollie for your room number. I just...please talk to me."

I take a deep breath, knowing it's pointless to try and resist him. I wipe under my eyes and pull my hair up on top of my head. I use the hairband from around my wrist to put it in a messy bun, then I kick off my shoes and make a few sweeps down my shirt to smooth it out. Unfortunately, that's as good as it's going to get.

I grab the handle and open the door slowly. I try to stay strong, but the minute my eyes meet his, I lose it. Simon rushes in the room and takes me in his arms.

"I saw you leave, and I've been so worried about you," he whispers into my hair, as I inhale his calming scent. "It took every ounce of strength I had to finish that damn concert, and now I come and find you like this? This is ripping me apart, Sydney. I don't want to say goodbye to you. I can't..."

Simon trails off, and I know I should say something, but I can't seem to stop crying long enough to get anything out.

"I realized something tonight...something extraordinary," he starts, and I feel his chest move with his uneven breaths. "I'm in love with you, Sydney. I have been for...a while now, and if you love me too, even the smallest bit, please just say it. We can make this work. Just say the words, and I'll hold you like this for the rest of our lives."

And that perfect speech makes me cry even harder.

I ball his shirt up in my fists as I sob, wishing I could hold onto him forever, just like he suggested. The thought alone is enough to make me happy for a long, long time, but I know it can't work between us. At least, not right now.

It takes a moment to pull myself together, but I keep my arms around him and his shirt clutched tightly in my hands. I stare into his beautiful brown eyes and try and find peace with what I'm about to say. I know it's the right thing to do, even if my heart is screaming at me to reconsider.

"It can't work, Simon." Simon shakes his head, about to interrupt, but I cut him off. "I won't lie and tell you I don't love you, but that's not what's important right now. What's important is that you heal and find the strength you need to move on. And I have some things to work through as well. I worry if we stay together like this, we may never find our way, and I don't want that to happen. We both deserve better. Don't you think?"

Simon brushes two fingers down my cheek, and I shiver in response. "All I can think about is how much I *need* you, how much I've always needed you. Why don't you feel the same way?"

"I do," I assure him, confused about some of what he's saying to me, but afraid to ask because... "I do need you, but I'm not sure that's healthy. I don't want to rely on you for my happiness, for my change. And I don't want you to rely on me for that either. We'll get through this alone, and maybe in the end, we can find each other again."

Simon rests his forehead on mine. "I don't want to let you go, my angel. Please stay with me."

Angel? No. But he's my angel. I hope he knows that.

"Simon..." I sigh deeply, trying once again to stop the flood of tears pouring down my cheeks. "Simon, I can't."

We stand with our heads together, and our lips only inches apart. Simon's obviously trying to find a way to make this work between us, but I'm sticking by this decision. It's what's best for him. It's what's best for both of us. I just know it.

With a heartbreaking sigh, Simon pulls his face away from mine. "Then do me one favor?" he whispers in the dark. "Let me make love to you tonight? One more time, Sydney? Please?"

I pull away from him, not really surprised by his request, and even less surprised by how willing I am to fulfill it.

Simon places both hands on either side of my face. "I realize I'm a complete arse for asking this of you, but I need to wake up with you in my arms just once more. Please."

"I'm yours," I say, easily giving up the fight.

His face is anguished as he continues to caress my cheeks with gentle strokes. "If only that were true."

I reach up, pull his hands from my face and place his arms around my waist. I stand on my toes and wrap my arms around his neck. My fingers start moving through the back of his hair, and Simon closes his pretty brown eyes and groans softly.

I lean up and place a soft kiss on the side of his mouth. "For tonight..." I place another kiss on the other side. "I'm all yours, Simon."

I focus on his eyes as I place a third kiss on his pouty lips, and Simon has me beneath him on the bed in a matter of seconds. From there, we both take our time kissing, touching, relishing this moment.

Simon removes my blouse, handling each button with care, and I slowly lift his shirt over his sides, gliding my hands over his soft skin along the way. But when I start to feel the sweet, sizzling sensations caused by his bare skin against mine, I know he feels it too because neither of us can seem to remove the remaining clothing fast enough. And by the time Simon pushes gently inside of me, I feel like I may ignite under his fiery touch.

"I love you, Sydney," Simon whispers against my neck. "And I will always love you. Only you. From this day on."

I weep silently, swept up in the intensity of the moment. It's so overwhelming, but I can't think of any other place I'd rather be right now, or ever.

Neither of us speak another word after that. And as Simon and I reach our climaxes together, I hold him close to me, and I'm hopeful for a moment that maybe things may work out for us someday. Because there's no way I could ever share with anyone what I shared with Simon tonight. I know in my heart that there's no way it will ever be any better than this. I will never love anyone like I love him. For me, no one will ever compare. And I don't want them to.

Simon and I make love twice more throughout the night, until neither of us can keep our eyes open any longer. We eventually drift off to sleep, completely entwined with each other, and I can't remember a time when I ever felt happier or more content than I do when I'm in his arms.

The next thing I know, I wake up to sunlight shining through the window. I smile, as I reach beside me, eager to have my hands on Simon once again, but he's not there.

I sit up in the bed, and look around, but I know he's gone. A quick scan of the floor and I see his clothes are no longer there. He's left. We said our goodbyes.

It's over.

The tears start immediately, as I pull the covers up to my chin and lie back down on the bed. I wish I could say it's over for me, but it's not. Not even close.

I stay in the bed a moment, letting the tears fall, before finally deciding the best thing for me to do is to get out of here. I have plenty of time for tears, but for now, I just need to go. It's time to go home. It's time to get back to reality.

CHAPTER 46 - SIMON

I never knew my father. He left my mother when he found out she was pregnant, and I spent a large part of my life paying for that act of cowardice. When my mum finally figured out that treating me like shit wouldn't bring him back, she packed up and left one night while I slept. I was twelve years old.

A few years ago, I lost my fiancé in a tragic car accident, and I was driving the car. No matter how you look at it, I had a part in taking her life, and I'm not sure I'll ever recover.

And I didn't just lose *her* in that accident. I lost a family. I lost friends. And because of the debilitating guilt I've insisted on carrying with me since the accident, I've been through dozens of other tragedies, losses and disappointments over the years.

But leaving Sydney this morning definitely ranks up there as one of the hardest things I've ever had to do.

I woke up this morning before the sun, and I stared at her for over an hour as she slept. I listened to that adorable snore of hers, wishing there was a way I could wake up to her beautiful face every morning – the same sweet face I remember from all of those years ago, and now I have to let her go.

Her smile, her eyes, they've been my religion for the past ten years, and I thought if I ever had the chance to meet her she would most certainly disappoint. I knew there was no way she could live up to the image I'd created of her in my mind. In fact, part of me hoped I would never meet her. I would never want anything to tarnish the memory of that night.

But of course she turns out to be wonderful, or better than wonderful, really. She's exquisite. She's my guardian angel, and she may not know that yet, but she will. I'm going to tell her. I don't know how or when, but I have to tell her what she's done for me – how's she's helped me, influenced me, without even knowing it.

I'll never be willing to let her go completely, but I feel like maybe Sydney's right. Maybe I do need some space to try and figure out how to live my life again.

It's going to be hard as hell, but I'm going to do it. I'm going to get better. I'm going to do it for me, but I'm also going to do it for Sydney. And maybe one day she'll come back to me. Maybe one day I'll deserve her.

"So, dare I ask how it went last night?"

Ollie plops down in the seat across from me on the bus, and I glance over at him then back out the window. The landscape screams by us as we make our way to the next show and I sigh.

I tried to talk the guys into flying, but they insisted we take the bus for this last leg. Even though we all somewhat kissed and made up in our meeting this morning, I'll be glad when this tour is over. I need a holiday. I need some time to clear my head and figure out my next move.

"That bad, huh?" Ollie asks when I don't answer, and I smile.

I haven't told anyone about the connection I made last night between Sydney and the locket. I'm not sure anyone would believe me if I told them. It still seems so surreal, even though I've never been more certain of anything in my life.

"We said our goodbyes," I tell him, still staring out the window, gripping the locket tightly in my left hand. "It's over, but I'm glad I got a chance to see her one more time. I guess I have you to thank for that."

It's almost painful to show gratitude to Ollie, and it's not because I don't mean it. It's because it inflates an already swollen ego to the point of imminent combustion.

"You're bloody right you do." He reacts to my appreciation just as predicted. "And don't you forget it."

"I'm certain you won't allow that to happen."

Ollie leans over the table with a smug smile and punches my left shoulder. "It's good to have you back, Si."

I nod thoughtfully as I look back out the window. "It's good to be back."

I know I'm far from better, but I'm on my way. At the end of the day, Sydney and my music are all I have left, and I love both too much to let them go.

I'm still not sure if staying with the guys is the best course for me, but I'm shelving that conversation for a later date. I need them too much right now.

I turn back to Ollie to find him grinning at me like a fool. "Did you need something else, or have you developed some kind of crush on me recently?"

Ollie only grins wider. "Fucking awesome to have you back, mate."

He takes a bite out of an apple and heads over to the sofas with the rest of the guys. I sit at the table a while longer, and before I know it, I'm lost in my thoughts once again. Soon enough, I'm dragged back out, but not by Ollie's antics this time.

"Can we talk, Si?"

James's face isn't angry, which is a relief and quite a change from the norm when chatting with me.

"Yeah, James. What's up?" I adjust in my seat, sitting up a little straighter.

James sits down with a long sigh. This can't be good.

"Simon, I want to tell you that...well, I wanted to say that I'm really...I'm sorry for the way I've treated you the past couple of years." I smile as I watch James squirm, and he gives me the one finger salute. "You're going to make this hard for me, aren't you?"

"Oh yes," I admit. "I'm going to enjoy this immensely."

James and I both have a laugh, before he starts again. "I'm serious, Si. I've been such a bastard, but I was just so angry with you. I hated you for giving up on yourself, for giving up on us."

"It's understandable," I sigh. "It was a selfish move on my part. No need to explain."

"Yeah, but I'm your friend." His sincerity is disarming. "We've all been like brothers over the years, and I should have been the bigger person in this. I should have stood by you. I'm sorry I let you down. I truly am."

I study James a moment, until I can't take the awkwardness any longer.

"Is this the part where we kiss and make-up?"

"Fuck you, Simon."

James smiles and I laugh as I raise my hands in surrender. "Ollie already asked, mate. But I've always thought you were sexier. Maybe we can get Rob to join in, yeah? I like his pretty lips."

"Any time, Si." Rob pipes up from behind me, but I can barely hear him over the roar of laughter coming from Ollie's big mouth.

"That's it." James stands and lunges for me, and I manage to get the locket back in my pocket before he pulls me onto the floor of the bus. We wrestle around a little, as Ollie and Rob stand around us and cheer us on. Both are betting on James, which is a smart bet. He has me pinned in under ten seconds.

I shamelessly concede, still feeling a little weak from my lack of sleep last night, and honestly, everything I've put my body and mind through over the past few years.

"Why don't you get some rest." James leans down to help me up from the floor. "It'll be a few hours before we arrive in Richmond."

I nod, and dust myself off. "Wake me if you guys stop for food, all right?"

"Will do," James tells me. "But Si?"

"Yeah?" I turn back to face him, only to find him on the verge of a smile.

"You might want to lock your door, just in case one of us starts feeling frisky later."

I smirk and walk back toward the bedroom. "In that case, I'll leave the door open, Loverboy."

I turn to blow a kiss to them, and close the door, just barely dodging a shoe coming full speed in my direction.

I laugh and plop down on the bed, feeling lighter than I have in a long time. I put one arm behind my head, and reach into my pocket with my other hand. I hold onto the locket as I close my eyes, hoping my dreams are of a sassy blond goddess who stole my heart.

CHAPTER 47 - SYDNEY

It's been six months since I last saw Simon, and although I haven't fully recovered from that last night we spent together, I've come to accept the fact that the empty feeling is here to stay. It's a part of me now, constantly aching, waiting, and hoping that maybe someday we'll find our way back to each other.

It may be foolish, but I'm not ready to give up quite yet. And I've heard from Lacey that Simon really is trying this time. Ollie told her he's been seeing a therapist regularly, and he's even writing again. It may be a long time down the road, but maybe someday we can circle back around. Until I see that he's married to someone else, or moved on in some way, I refuse to give up on him. I refuse to give up on us.

"Good morning!"

Lacey seems peppier than usual this morning, which peeks my curiosity. Since we moved in together a couple of months ago – I thought it was about time I start paying some bills and stop mooching off my friends – she's been skulking around, worrying about her finals coming up.

Therefore, I have to believe this peppiness could only mean one thing. She's up to something.

"Morning." I sit my coffee on the kitchen table and glance up at her. "What has you in such a good mood?"

"Funny you should ask," she replies, as she stirs her coffee. "I happen to have insider information that this ridiculously sexy new band is doing a small show downtown next weekend."

"Huh," is my only response, as I stare blankly at my friend.

"It's their first official show as the newly designed *London*, and word has it they're the hottest ticket in town. It seems a certain piano player in the group has started writing again, and they've been steadily climbing the charts." Lacey glances over at me out of the side of her eye. "But of course you already knew all of that, right?"

"Of course," I admit unapologetically, although I honestly didn't know about the concert, so the shock is still clear on my face.

"Well this particular show is invite only. They're still testing the waters in certain markets with their new sound." Lacey brings her coffee over to the table and sits next to me. "I just thought I'd mention it, in case you wanted to come along. I know you used to be a fan and all."

She smirks at me and takes a sip from her cup. I roll my eyes. "Okay, enough with the sarcasm, my friend. I've got it."

"Got what?" she asks, looking deceivingly innocent, which warrants a love punch on the arm from me.

We both giggle, but it does nothing to settle my nerves after this bomb Lacey just dropped on me.

"You know I can't go," I tell her, and she gives me a somber nod.

"I know. I just thought maybe you'd think about it."

"Not enough time has passed. I'm not ready. Not yet."

Lacey nods again, but this time with a thoughtful look on her face. "Ready for what, exactly?"

The innocent question takes me by surprise, and when I think about it for a moment, the answer that comes to me has me feeling ashamed.

"I want him to come to me," I pathetically confess to Lacey. "I want to make sure he's ready, and selfishly, I want him to need me like I know I need him. Is that awful?"

Lacey's shaking her head before I even stop speaking. "No, it's not awful. It's honest. There's nothing wrong with that."

"I wanted to give him some space, but now I'm afraid the distance between us has been growing over the past few months to the point where he may not want me back."

"Don't say that," Lacey tells me. "Simon had a lot of things to work through. Six months isn't that long in the grand scheme of things."

"It feels like a lifetime."

"I know," she sighs. "But he's still single. At least we know that."

"Yes, but the fact is he hasn't come back, Lace. And maybe you're right. Maybe he's not ready." I shudder. "Or maybe he doesn't want me anymore."

"Enough, Sydney," Lacey snaps, and then takes a deep breath. "I'm sorry. I didn't mean to be short with you, but we both know he loves you. You can't possibly doubt his feelings for you."

"You're right. I don't doubt him," I acknowledge. "Does Ollie ever say anything?"

I've always told Lacey I don't want to know – I don't want second hand information, but I feel like I'm starting to go crazy. I miss him so much. I can barely concentrate on anything anymore. I'm getting desperate.

"Not really." Lacey gives me a sad smile. "Simon used to ask him about you, after the concert in Memphis, but I don't think he's asked in a while. Ollie would tell me if he did. He's a worse gossip than you."

"That's what I thought," I sulk.

"I really wish you would come, but I'll stick by whatever decision you make because you're my best friend, and also because I'm just awesome like that."

"You are seriously awesome," I agree. "And thanks for telling me about the concert. You'll have to say hi to Ollie for me. I miss him."

Lacey stands and places her cup in the sink. "You could say hi to him yourself," she suggests, and I give her a look. "Okay, fine. I'll do it."

"Thanks, Lace."

Lacey moves to leave, but then turns back to me. "Will you just think about going, Sydney? For me, if nothing else? I'd really like you to go."

"I'll think about it," I say, but we both know that's a lie.

Lacey heads to her room, leaving me in the kitchen with nothing but my thoughts and a cup of lukewarm coffee. My heart flutters with anticipation at the thought of seeing Simon again, but I can't do it. I don't have the guts.

"Hey, Sydney?" Lacey walks back toward me in the kitchen. "I almost forgot. This came for you in the mail yesterday."

Lacey hands me a small package, and I look for a return address. It's a post office box in Los Angeles that I don't recognize.

"Maybe something you ordered online?" Lacey suggests, and although that would normally be a good guess, I haven't ordered anything in a while.

"I don't think so."

I shake the package, but unfortunately, that doesn't give anything away.

Lacey puts her hands on her hips. "Are you going to open it or what?"

I move to open it, but something stops me – a feeling or a warning of some kind, but all I know is that I don't want to open it. At least not right now.

I toss the small box on the table. "I'll open it later."

"Fine." Lacey gives me a disapproving look, then heads toward the door. "I'll be on campus until late tonight, so I'll see you in the morning?"

"I'll be here."

She blows me a kiss before leaving, and I spend the next half hour drinking a second cup of coffee and studying the small package sitting on my kitchen table. In the end, I'm no closer to finding out what's inside, but I have a feeling it's not good.

When I make it home from work on Friday, Lacey calls to me from her room. "Sydney! Come here for a second!"

I toss my purse on the small table by the door and head her way. "What's up?" I ask as I'm walking into her bedroom. I finally find her in her bathroom, getting ready for tonight.

"What do you think about this dress?" she asks me, as she spins back and forth in the mirror. "Too much?"

"Or too little." I smile at the strapless, black number that barely covers her assets. "I know lately we've kind of had some *Freaky Friday* stuff happening in the wardrobe department, but this tops the charts. Who *are* you?"

"Oh no." Lacey pouts. "You think it's awful?"

"Of course not," I tell her with a wave of my hand. The girl ditched those pearls a few months ago and hasn't looked back. Good riddance, I say. "You look worthy of the coveted *Sydney Seal of Sexiness Approval*. Ollie's going to flip when he sees you."

Lacey's frown turns upside down. "You think? It's been months since I've seen him. I really wanted to look nice."

"Mission accomplished."

Lacey leans in to hug me. "I wish you would go."

"I know, and part of me wants to," I admit, as Lacey goes back to her primping. "But I just wouldn't feel right. I know you'll have a great time with Ollie though, and remember to tell him I said hi."

Lacey smiles at me in the mirror. "I will. I love you, Sydney."

"I love you too."

I'm about to walk out when Lacey turns and stops me. "Hey, I've been meaning to ask. Are you ever going to open that package on the table? It's been a week."

"I'm in no hurry. Why?"

"It's from Simon," Lacey states bluntly. "But I know you already know that."

"I figured as much. How did you know?"

"Ollie told me," she shrugs. "I don't know what's in it, but Ollie said Simon asked him to find out from me if you've opened it."

What? Simon asking about me in any way has my heart pounding in my chest.

"When did this happen?"

"I talked to Ollie last night," Lacey tells me. "He wanted to give me the information I'd need for the show. He told me then."

"And what did you tell him?" I'm trying to keep my voice level, but it's taking an incredible amount of effort.

"I told him the truth — that it was still sitting on the kitchen table unopened."

My curiosity is peeked now more than ever, as I try and think about what could possibly be so important that Simon had to ask about it.

"So, are you going to open it?" Lacey asks, and I bite my lower lip as I study my friend.

"I'm scared. I'm not sure I can handle another goodbye from him."

Lacey grabs her purse and jacket on her way to the front door, but before she opens it, she turns back to me.

"Just open it, Sydney. I'll have my phone on, if you need me."

Lacey smiles as she walks out the door, and I move to the kitchen and glance at the innocent little package still sitting on the table in the same spot it has been for the past week. It's about the size of a box of checks from the bank or a small box of chocolates, but I doubt either guess is correct.

I sit down at the table and continue to stare at the package until I feel my eyes start to cross. I should just open it. Like a bandage, I should just rip and get it over with. But the idea that there's another farewell inside is crippling. I'm positive I can't make it through that again.

And then, as I sit and watch the little box, waiting for it to give me some kind of sign — some kind of clue that will help make my decision — I realize something. Even if this box does contain another goodbye, it can't be any worse than the two I've already suffered through with Simon. Perhaps there's something here that will provide me with the closure I've been so desperately searching for all of these months. Or better yet, why does this package have to be a bad thing? Maybe there's hope inside this tiny box, and I could use some of that right about now.

I pick up the package for the first time since I received it and hold it in my hands. *Band aid*, I think to myself as I rip the brown paper off the outside, revealing an ordinary white gift box – so far, nothing too scary. But when I open the white box, inside I find a beautifully ornate, silver jewelry case with a rose engraved on the top. I pull it out with delicate fingers, admiring the beautiful craftsmanship.

I'm about to open the case and see what's inside, when I notice a red envelope at the bottom of the gift box. I place the jewelry case on the table and decide to read the card first.

Tears are already in my eyes before I even have the envelope open. The beautiful gift, and the thought of reading his words...I start to hear his voice in my head, and I miss him so much I can barely breathe.

I open the card, and pull it out slowly. With the card finally in my hands, I wipe at my eyes before I start to read.

To the goddess, Sydney,

Several years ago, at a show in Atlanta, I was searching through an impossible sea of excited fans, and I noticed this blue-eyed beauty standing on the front row looking utterly lost. Those fierce blue eyes were in stark contrast to the quiet shyness she wore on her face, and when she looked up at me...for a split second I saw myself through those soulful eyes and I liked what I saw.

With just one look, that young girl brought this cocky seventeen year old to his knees, so needless to say, I had to meet her. I had to hold her hand in mine. I had to thank her in some way for that look – a look that said she believed in me, that she believed in my music. It meant more to me than any one mediocre serenade could ever express, but it was the best I had to offer at the time.

After the song was over, I reluctantly sent that beauty back to her seat, and when we finished our set, I secretly stole one last look at her from behind the stage. I'll never forget the look on her face. It's a memory that has stuck with me over the years and believe it or not, it has pulled me out of some of the darkest places a soul could ever know.

I came back out onto the stage that night after the concert was over and the crowds were long gone, and I took a quiet moment to relive that memory with my blue-eyed angel. Even then, I knew that moment with her was significant, possibly life-changing, and I wanted to give it the attention I knew it deserved.

Just as I was about to leave, I noticed something shining on the floor below. I jumped off the stage and bent down to grab a silver locket that I recognized immediately. I knew it belonged to my sweet angel, and although I could see from the photo inside it was most likely special to her, I was so happy to have something tangible to remember her by that I selfishly shoved the locket in the pocket of my jeans and left the city of Atlanta behind me.

But what I didn't know then and never expected, was that the locket would serve as my talisman. It's been with me every minute of every day since I found it, and over the years, when the darkness and the emptiness threatened to consume me, I would hold the locket tight and somehow it would bring me back. It would keep the demons at bay. It would keep me safe.

But now, ten years later, I've finally discovered something that works a million times better than my precious locket. I found love – a pure and natural, once in a lifetime kind of love. And miraculously enough, I found it in the arms of that beautiful, blue-eyed angel that I met all of those years ago. As fate would have it, it was her love that helped bring me permanently out of the darkness. It was her love that saved me.

So I'm sending the locket to you now, hoping it finds its way back to its rightful owner, hoping it finally finds its way home. And as for my angel, know that her memory is with me always, keeping me warm, keeping me safe. Because even though she's no longer in my life, she will forever be my lady, and my heart will always belong to her.

All of my love,

Simon

I read the letter several more times until I finally have the courage to open the box he sent to me. As promised, inside is my Grammy's locket. The locket that I thought I would never see again, and now I know it's been with the man of my dreams for the past decade, lighting his way, keeping him safe.

I love you too, Grammy. Thank you for protecting him for me.

And as hard as it is to believe, it seems I've been with him as well. He remembers me. He remembers that night, and not only that, but he tells me that night meant almost as much to him as it did to me.

I shake my head, sending tears flying out of my eyes. Is this possible? Could I have found the love of my life at thirteen years old? I most certainly thought so then. What if I was right?

Without another thought, I toss the locket around my neck and run to my bedroom. I'm in and out of the shower in less than five minutes, and then I quickly dry my hair and decide to leave it down to save time. I put a little make-up on, just enough to be presentable, before moving to my closet to find something to wear. Within a few seconds of scanning my wardrobe, my eyes zero in on a new black, peasant-style dress I haven't had a chance to wear yet. I throw it on, and take a quick look in the mirror. The sleeves and the dress are loose and flowy, but it still hugs my body in all the right places. And the short length and off-the-shoulder style add the ideal amount of sex appeal. This will definitely work.

I text Lacey to let her know my plans, then I pull on some socks and my red, knee-high Docs. I take one more glance in the mirror and I instantly fall in love with the person staring back at me. If my friends could see me now, they would flip, but this is the person I've wanted to be for years. I've just been too afraid to let her show. It took a certain teenage fantasy come to life to make me realize I shouldn't be ashamed. This Sydney is perfect. This is the new Sydney. This is Simon's Sydney, and I have to go get him back, because Simon's Sydney knows that she's nothing without him.

CHAPTER 48 - SIMON

We've barely finished the last song when the chanting starts.

It's the end of the night, and we've yet to play our latest hit. Everyone knows it's coming. In the last couple of shows we've saved it for the encore, and that's the plan for tonight as well. My fingers are already itching to play it.

I close my eyes and smile to myself, enjoying the roar coming from the crowd.

"Sydney's Song! Sydney's Song! Sydney's Song!" they chant, and I love every fucking minute of hearing her name shouted among the crowd.

The venue is smaller than we would normally play, but it seems the crowd here is as lively as ever. They've been incredible all night, and they're ending on a good note.

I turn my head back to the guys, and I notice Ollie has a huge grin on his face.

"What's up?" I ask into his ear when he approaches me, but he only continues to smile.

Rob and James join us, and we take a couple of bows. Then we each move to a different part of the stage to wave and blow some kisses.

"We've got five minutes, tops," James tells us, as we make our way backstage.

We all nod and head to our private dressing rooms. To my surprise, Ollie follows me into mine.

"What's going on with you?" I ask him. "And what's with all the bloody grinning?"

"We're doing the new song for the encore," he says, but it's a statement, not a question.

"Last I heard. Why?" I have to wonder what the hell he's playing at.

"I just like it. That's all."

Ollie's nonchalance isn't fooling me. He's the worst liar on the planet, but before I can question him further, he turns and walks out.

That was odd. Perhaps he's excited for Lacey to hear it live? I saw her on the front row, hoping I would see Sydney appear next to her at some point. I watched that spot on and off all night, but Sydney never showed.

I sigh and try and block the heartache out for the time being. *One more song. Just get through this last song.*

With a glance in the mirror, I see I'm drenched in sweat, so I decide to do a quick change. I pull on a dry t-shirt and run my fingers through my hair a bit. Just as I'm about to open the door, there's a knock.

"Let's go," James says from the other side.

I open the door and follow the guys back to the side of the stage. The crowd is booming, and my adrenaline starts pumping. James puts his fist out, and we each layer ours on top of the other.

"One more song." James repeats my thoughts from earlier. "Let's do this."

We slowly make our way onto the dark stage, and the crowd starts to recognize us as we begin to settle at our instruments. Pretty soon, the lights come up, and the crowd roars.

They start asking for Sydney's song again, and I have to smile.

"I think we have an idea of what you guys want to hear, but if you could just shout a *bit* louder..." Ollie cups his ear with his hand and turns sideways, egging the crowd on and it works.

But just when I think they can't get any louder, I adjust the mic a bit closer to me, and the sound nearly blows me off stage. Damn, I love the fans.

I look over at Ollie and Rob, and they're smiling like idiots. I wonder what the hell has everyone so cheerful? Probably the fact that we have the first hit song we've had in over a decade. I think James would leave his wife and marry me, if I ask him.

But the truth is I can't take full credit for our newly found success. I may have written the song, and I'll have to admit, I'm happy to be writing again. It feels good, and I didn't realize how much I had missed it – or how much it means to me – until I officially got that first song out. But I wouldn't have started writing again without the inspiration of a certain, beautiful goddess.

I love her. And I will always love her. I wrote this song for her, and there are many more songs to come. She'll always be my favorite muse.

I take a seat on the stool at the mic and adjust myself around my guitar. What I wouldn't give to see that smile again. I was hoping my last ditch attempt at getting her back with the locket may have worked, but perhaps I've waited too long. I should have contacted her sooner, and I should have done it face to face, rather than taking the cowardly route on paper. Maybe it's too late either way.

I've been searching for her face all night in the crowd, knowing it was a long shot, but I had hope. Now, we're about to sing the final song, and there's still no Sydney. I look over to where Lacey's sitting once more, but the vacant seat next to her – reserved for my goddess – is still empty. Lacey sees me glance over, and gives me a sad smile. I shake off the heartache once again.

"Thank you guys for coming out tonight," I tell the crowd and wait a moment for the shouting to die down. "As you know, this song is very special to me, and I'm glad you all seem to feel the same." I pause and swipe my hand through my damp hair. "Atlanta, you've been fantastic. We love you and can't wait to see you again soon."

I close my eyes, blocking out the applause as I strum the first chord. I play the entire song like I always do – eyes closed, thinking of Sydney.

I think about the first time I saw her at the bar in Miami. I think about the first time I held her in my arms, the first time I woke up with her next to me. I think about the way her fingers felt in my hair, how small her hand was in mine when I held it, the way her lips felt like velvet when she kissed me. I think about the way she looked at me with my favorite blue eyes – like I was the only thing that mattered. I think about how she makes me feel content, how she makes me feel safe, even when she's not around.

The memory of her will always be there, keeping me grounded, helping me move forward. I may not have her now, but I did have her, and those few moments with Sydney would be worth a lifetime of heartache. So whatever life throws at me from now on, I'll endure it. I'll endure it because I have to keep going to keep the memory of us alive. That memory is certainly worth preserving.

The crowd roars when we finish the song but I keep my eyes closed, locked on a vision of Sydney the night I kissed her on the observation deck. I was done for that night. That night I knew. I may not have wanted to admit it to myself or anyone else, but the instant my lips touched hers that night, I was finished. I knew there would never be anything that felt that right or tasted that sweet.

And then, when I realized who she really was, fate took hold. Not that I needed any convincing, but it was final after that. I knew I would love her forever.

An image of a young, innocent Sydney flashes across my mind right as I start to open my eyes. I instinctively reach into my pocket for the locket and smile. That's going to take some getting used to.

With my eyes open, I take in the still screaming crowd. Everyone is on their feet, and I wave and leisurely scan the audience until my eyes land on what I'm sure is a figment of my imagination. I blink a few times, wondering when the mirage will disappear.

Oh, please God. Please let it be her.

I pull my guitar off and lower it slowly to the ground. My eyes never leave her face – not for one second.

I hate that she's covering that beautiful mouth with her hands. *Let me see your smile.* Her smile always makes everything better.

The crowd is louder than ever, but it's easy to block them out. It's easy to block anything out, when I'm staring into Sydney's eyes. She's even more beautiful than I remember, and I may lose my mind if I don't confirm soon whether or not she's real, or if this is going to turn into another wonderful but disappointing dream.

I stand from my stool, and start moving to the left. I keep my eyes locked on hers, convinced she'll disappear any minute. It can't be her. Life is not this good to me.

I notice Lacey give Sydney a push toward the stairs to the side of the stage, but she doesn't move. Her eyes go wide with worry and her hesitancy makes me stop midstride toward those same stairs.

Does she not want me? Then why is she here? Perhaps to support her friend? *Fuck*. I knew it was too good to be true.

I sigh and give her a small smile. If nothing else, I got to see those bright, blue eyes again, but I don't think I can stay here and look at her any longer, not if I can't hold her in my arms. I can't have things half way with her. With Sydney, it's all or nothing.

I turn to Ollie, who shrugs in confusion. I want nothing more than to have that woman back in my arms, but I won't pressure her. I'll continue to try and be the best version of myself I can be, and hopefully she'll come back to me someday. But it doesn't look like today's the day, which is what I try and convey to Ollie with my eyes before I leave the stage.

Oddly enough, Ollie shakes his head at me and smiles. At the same time, the volume of the crowd increases by about a million percent. I turn my head back toward my goddess, but she's not there. I look to Lacey and see her pointing an excited finger at the left stairs, just as the rest of the crowd is now doing.

By the time my eyes find the stairs, Sydney is nearly at the top and the crowd is so loud I can barely hear myself think. I see our security guard, Greg, smiling at me out of the corner of my eye, but I don't respond. I can barely move.

I notice Sydney's face is cautious as she steps onto the stage, but I can't seem to get past the fact that my goddess is here – her lips mere feet from mine, those gentle fingers so close I can already feel them running through my hair, calming me, claiming me.

Two steps and I could inhale her lovely scent. Two more steps after that, and I could touch that beautiful face. A final step and my mouth could be on hers.

Five steps. That's all I need. Five. Fucking. Steps.

I take the first one, and that one comes so easily, I move for the second. Just as I thought, that intoxicating scent rushes into me, as invigorating and addictive as ever.

One more step, and I see Sydney's crying, but there's a smile in her eyes. Her hand is back over that delectable mouth, and I think to myself I just need two more steps and I'll be able to remove that hand personally.

One.

Two.

As soon as I remove her hand, Sydney tries to speak. "Simon, I'm so sorr–"

But that's all I'm willing to hear.

I wrap my arms around her waist and cover her mouth again, but not with a hand this time. I can feel her smile against my lips, and I smile back. Sydney curls her arms around my neck, and her fingers immediately move to the back of my hair, right where they belong.

I pull her close after we kiss and drop my forehead to hers. Now the need to kiss her isn't nearly as important as the need to hold her, the need to reconnect to the feeling of having her in my arms again. The next thing I know, my face is in my favorite spot – nestled into her neck, covered by that luscious blond hair.

"Ladies and gentleman, in case any of you were wondering...I'd like you to meet Sydney."

I hear Ollie talking and the clapping and chaos coming from the crowd, but it's all a distant noise. I won't allow any of my senses to drift too far from my goddess at the moment.

"I think these two may need some alone time," Ollie laughs. "So that means we better go. What a night! Thank you, Atlanta. You've been amazing!"

I never look back at the crowd. I know it's rude not to take bows with the guys or say goodbyes, but I'm hoping the fans will forgive me just this once.

As the guys are finishing up, I pull away from Sydney and grab her hand, and without a word, I lead her back stage to my dressing room. The minute I close the door, she's back in my arms. I didn't even have to ask.

"I've missed you," she whispers in my ear. "God, I've missed you so much, Simon."

I still can't speak, so I just nod against her neck and pull her closer as tears start streaming out of my eyes and soaking her skin. Thankfully, Sydney doesn't seem to mind. She only holds me tighter, and sobs right along with me.

We stand in my dressing room holding each other, for I have no idea how long. And who cares? I'd be happy in this room, with this woman, for the rest of my life.

Sydney is the first to pull away. You can bet it wasn't going to be me.

"Thanks for my locket." She removes one arm from around my neck to wipe her eyes, then she lifts the locket over her head. "But I want you to keep it. You have no idea how much it meant to me that you've held onto it for all of these years. I love the idea of you having this on you at all times."

"But I don't need it anymore. I don't want it."

She better not be thinking of leaving me again. Hell no.

Sydney removes her other arm from around my neck with a smile, then wipes my cheeks gently with her fingers. A contented sigh escapes me, but I keep my arms locked around her waist, daring her with my eyes to try and get away.

"I'm not going anywhere, Simon," she tells me, and I feel the tension exit my body in a rush. "But we can't be together every minute."

"Who the fuck says?"

Sydney laughs, and it's wonderful to hear.

"Well, we can try." She wraps one arm back around my neck, her fingers back in my hair. "But just in case, you can have the locket back. That way, I'll always be with you – just like I have been for the past ten years it seems."

"Sydney, I appreciate the gesture, but I don't give a shit about that locket. Once I had a taste of the real thing, that locket served no purpose to me anymore. You're my talisman now." My voice automatically softens as her eyes do the same. "You're all I'll ever need, and don't think I can't find a way to spend every damn second next to you. I'm never letting you out of my sight again. Understand? I'm even following you to the loo. You will have no peace, from now on."

Christ. Sydney's laugh is gorgeous. I've missed every single thing about her. Every damn thing.

She uses one hand to slip the locket back around her neck. "You cannot watch me pee, Simon." Her smile is drawing me to those lips. "But every other second, I'm yours."

I'm yours. My most favorite words.

I smile at her, and she smiles widely back at me. As I study her lips, so ready to kiss her again I think I may burst, I realize I have to know for sure. I have to hear her say it.

I run a couple of fingers down the length of her silky hair and feel my eyebrows knit together, as I try and build the courage to ask the hard question.

"Simon?"

I switch my focus from Sydney's mouth to her bewildered gaze. "Are you..." *Fuck.* I'm so afraid of the answer. Even with her standing here in my arms. I'm still so unsure.

"What is it Simon?" Sydney asks me, and I notice her voice is edgy now, nervous.

I need to get this out before we both go into cardiac arrest.

I take a deep breath, and try to focus on her eyes – those beautiful and absolutely stunning, even when they're tense, eyes.

"Sydney, I have to know...I want to hear you say..." I pause again and my sweet goddess starts running her fingers through my hair, trying to soothe me. It works. "I want to hear you say that it's for good this time. You can't leave again. I won't let you. I need to hear you say you want to be with me, Sydney. From today until forever."

I expect her to flinch at my use of the word "forever", but she does no such thing. Instead, she gives me a wide smile as her eyes start filling once more with tears.

"Simon..." She whispers my name, then brings a soft hand to my cheek. "It would be one thing if I ever really left you, but I didn't. You've always had a piece of me." Sydney gestures to the locket and gives me a meaningful smile. "You've crossed my mind at least once day since that concert when I was thirteen, and our time together on the ship made it officially impossible for me to ever get you out of my head or my heart. I think I was born to love you, Simon. I've loved you nearly half my life, and I'm positive I'll love you for the rest of it. You're a dream come true for me in so many ways, and the fact that you're standing here asking me if I want you forever is laughable. I want you for longer than forever. I just hope you're ready for me because I'm not going anywhere."

I stare at her smiling face, trying to collect myself after that speech. This woman owns me. And I fucking love it.

"Did I sum it up for you, or were you looking for a little more reassurance?" Sydney gives me a smirk that makes me want to rip this sexy as hell dress off her unbelievable body and have my way with her.

I wink, trying to one up her sexiness, which is a tough act to follow, but when I see Sydney's eyes move to my mouth – when I see her suck in her lower lip and bite down, nearly finishing me off – I have a feeling I may have come close.

"Goddess..." I tug at her chin, causing her to release that bottom lip with a pop. "That speech was exactly what I needed to hear."

"Good," she says, sweetly. "I meant every word."

"But if I'm being completely honest..." I lay another sexy smile on her for good measure. "You had me at Doc Martens."

Sydney glances down at her feet and then back up at me, with an adorable little giggle. "These old things?" she teases. "I heard you had a thing for girls in boots."

"I have a thing for *you* in those boots," I admit, unabashedly. "And I'm thinking I may like to see you in nothing but those boots in the very near future."

"I think that can be arranged," Sydney answers back, and gives me a look that leaves me breathless.

I lean down and press my lips against hers, and I can taste forever in this kiss. And it's the most incredible flavor imaginable.

EPILOGUE - SYDNEY

Seven months later...April the twenty-sixth, to be exact...

I don't think it will come as a huge shock to find out I absolutely adore weddings.

It's a combination of all of my favorite things – romance, flowers, good-looking men, pretty dresses and loads of attention, all wrapped up in one beautiful, chiffon and lace covered day. What's not to love?

I started dreaming about my wedding day at a very young age, and as traditional as I can be at times, I've never wanted a white wedding, especially after all of those times visiting my Grammy in the hospital when she was sick. White is boring. Sterile. Cold.

No. I dreamed about champagne and buttercream, pale pinks and light greens. I dreamed about getting married outside in springtime, with everything in bloom around us, and I could have my pick of fresh flowers to choose from. And even though I am self-admittedly a total princess, I always wanted a small wedding with just a few friends and family. Nothing too flashy.

Except my dress, of course.

And now, as I look down through the window at the beautiful scene below, I have to smile. The rustic wood-carved benches are set in rows with burlap tied wildflowers accenting each end. The handmade gazebo is decorated to match, with the same flowers and wistful vines interwoven through the gables. And all of the smiling faces are waiting for the bride and groom to make their appearance so they can finally make their love official.

This wedding is everything I could ever want and more.

"Are we ready?"

I turn to find my bestie, Liz, smiling behind me. "I'm as ready as I'll ever be."

"Well then, let's go."

Liz and I walk down the hall and take the stairs into the living room. My friend Sam's mother, Ms. Harper, is there fanning herself with a magazine.

"All this running around has me hotter than a Dixie Hat Band!"

Liz and I both smile. "You look beautiful, Ms. Harper," I tell her, admiring her pale blue dress and matching shoes. "I'm not used to seeing you so fancy."

"Well, you know I'd do anything for my girls," she smiles and kisses my cheek. "Even it means wearing pantyhose for the first time in twenty years."

Liz and I follow her into the kitchen, where the guys are seated at the table. I notice briefly that Rose seems rather cozy sitting next to Ethan's friend, Vick, but I quickly look away. Rose would die if I brought any attention to the coziness, and today's not Rose's day for attention. The attention belongs to the bride and groom, exactly as it should be.

And speaking of the groom...

"Get outta here right now!" I hear Ms. Harper say from the kitchen doorway. "You know it's bad luck to see the bride before the wedding!"

I look to the open doorway with a huge smile on my face. The man is a stunner, that's for sure. His tailored, Ralph Lauren suit fits him like a glove. The light brown color nearly matches his hair perfectly and makes his light eyes shine...or maybe that's more about how happy he is to marry the woman of his dreams.

It's official. Samantha Harper is one lucky girl.

"Sam's still upstairs, Ms. Harper," I say with a smile. "Stop worrying."

"Well, he still shouldn't be in here," she tells Ethan, hands on her hips, but a smile teases her face.

"Everyone abandoned me outside for your air conditioner." Ethan leans down and kisses Ms. Harper's cheek and her smile breaks free. "I promise to run if she comes down. I've waited this long to see her in a wedding dress. I can wait a few more minutes."

"*This long*?" Mrs. Harper huffs.

"I would have married her the first day I met her. You know that."

With a tear in her eye, Ms. Harper puts a gentle hand on her soon-to-be son-in-law's cheek. "And she would have said yes." Ethan smiles sweetly, as Ms. Harper composes herself. "Now, let's dry it up. I promised Lamont I'd fix him a snack before we get going."

"That's what I'm talkin' about." Lamont rubs his palms together, excitedly, and we all laugh.

Ms. Harper moves to her favorite spot – in front of her stove – and the rest of the group continues the happy conversation at the table.

I move to *my* favorite spot – Simon's lap – and snuggle close. "You look magnificent in that dress, goddess." He brushes the bodice of my bridesmaid's dress as he nuzzles my neck. "I love you in blue."

"You don't look so bad yourself, Mr. Young."

Simon's not much for dressing up. This is only the second time I've seen in him in a suit since we've been together. The first time was when he surprised me with a trip to Paris for my birthday.

The night before my birthday he took me to my first opera, which I loved. Then we had dinner in the city, dessert at this quaint little cafe on Champs-Elysées and at exactly midnight, on the Pont Alexandre III, he proposed.

What can I say? My man's a hopeless romantic.

Simon pulls my lips to his and gives me a sweet kiss. "You know, I'm very happy for your friends, but I'm counting down the days until I get to make you mine forever."

Sigh.

"Well, you don't have to wait much longer. The wedding is only a few months away," I remind him.

"Seems like an eternity."

"Don't be silly." I laugh. "We don't even need a wedding, really."

Simon eyes me curiously. "Are you saying you'd give up the chance to wear a ball gown and a tiara?"

He knows me too well.

"Fine," I smile. "I am pretty excited about being a bride. But what I meant was that I'm yours, wedding or not."

Simon's smile is dazzling as he caresses my cheek. "Bloody right you're mine."

"Forever."

"Forever it is."

Simon leans down for another kiss, and we don't break apart until we start hearing shouts and jabs from the offended bystanders.

"Get a room!" someone calls, and I feel Simon's smile against my lips.

"I think I'll go check on Sam." I give him a final kiss and a wink before signaling the other girls to come with me.

"Hurry her up, will ya?" Ms. Harper demands. "The ceremony is supposed to start in fifteen minutes, and the party can't start without the bride."

"Yes ma'am," all of us girls say, nearly in unison.

Ms. Harper winks and turns back to her cooking as we head upstairs.

"I hope she's okay," Rose says, as we take the stairs to Sam's childhood bedroom. "She's been so nervous the past couple of weeks."

"She'll be fine," Liz says. "All brides get nervous. It's not a big deal."

I knock on the door and we hear a quiet "Come in" from the other side.

Sam looks beautiful standing next to the window, looking down at the crowd below. Her dress is nothing I'd choose – a floor-length, strapless, lace number that hugs her fantastic body – but the casual elegance is perfect for Sam. Tears spring to my eyes when she turns to us, and I run to hug her.

"Oh Sydney," she scolds me. "Stop that or we'll all be a mess."

I lift my head and laugh through my tears. "I'm just so happy for you. And of course I love weddings."

"Well you get to have your own soon, pretty girl." Sam wipes my tears from under my eyes and gives me a kiss on the cheek.

"Are you okay, Sam?" Rose is such a worrier.

"I'm fine," Sam claims, but I notice for the first time she definitely looks a little tense. "I just...."

Sam sits gently down onto the bench in front of her bed and takes a deep breath. We all gather a little closer to her, waiting for her to continue, but she never does.

"It's only natural to be nervous on your wedding day," Liz offers. "Once you see Ethan standing there waiting for you, everything will be fine."

Sam nods, as she studies her sandaled-feet, but she doesn't seem convinced.

"What's wrong, Sam?" Rose asks. "You know you can tell us anything."

"I know." Sam takes another deep breath and looks up at us with obvious concern in her eyes. "I guess I'm still a little uneasy about moving us permanently into Ethan's life."

"And why in the world would you be worried about that?" I question with a shrug. The other girls narrow their eyes at me, but I thought mine was an appropriate question.

"I'm nervous," Sam sighs. "Ethan's life is nothing like we're used to. I love Ethan Grant with everything that I am, and Jake loves Ethan to death too, which is wonderful. But this past year has been kind of insane. As a mother, I think about Jake's safety and well-being before my own. This has been, and will continue to be a huge adjustment for both of us. I'm a little nervous about it. That's all."

"Sam, you know you couldn't leave Ethan now, even if you had to," Rose tells her with a smile. "And Jake would hate you if you tried."

"You're right," Sam laughs. "On both counts."

"I agree," Liz interjects. "Ethan would do anything for you, Sam. And I think he's proved that more than once."

"You're both right," Sam admits. "Honestly, sometimes...no, make that most of the time, Ethan seems too good to be true – like a dream. I keep waiting to wake up."

Well, that's an easy enough problem to solve.

"Sydney!" Sam rubs her upper arm where I pinched her.

"Looks like you're awake."

Sam's shock turns to a smile, as I hike up my dress so I can kneel in front of her.

"I know what you mean about the dream stuff," I tell her. "But if I've learned anything over the past couple of years it's that sometimes dreams really do come true. And it *is* possible to have everything you ever wanted, but never thought you deserved. It's also possible – and perfectly acceptable – to be happier than you ever could have imagined being."

"And surprisingly enough, it seems everyone is capable of change," Liz interrupts me. "Have I mentioned how proud I am of you lately?"

"Oh hush up." I wave her off with a smile, as I take Sam's hands in mine. "This isn't about me. It's about Sam and *her* happiness. This is your wedding day, Sam. And you're marrying Ethan freaking Grant. So, I suggest you woman up, and accept the fact that that Holy Grail of a man is crazy in love with you, and always will be. Or else I'll make sure you're punished with no Cherry Garcia for at least the next couple of months."

We all laugh, and the next thing I know, it's one big group hug as we crowd around the beautiful bride.

"I'm ready," Sam says after we all dry our tears and fix our make-up. "I'm ready to get married to the man of my dreams."

Liz walks downstairs first to make sure Ethan at least has cleared out. "It's just Jake and Ms. Harper," she calls up to us. "You guys can come on down."

It's tough to hold back the tears as we watch Jake prepare to walk his mom down the aisle. You can't fake the kind of pride and pure joy on that child's face.

Lamont comes in and walks Ms. Harper to her seat as the music starts, and I'm making my way toward the altar shortly after. Simon gives me a wink when I pass him in the crowd, and I can't stop smiling.

Liz is next down the aisle, followed by Rose, Sam's maid of honor. I watch the groom's face, as all educated wedding patrons should do, when Sam and Jake start making their way toward us.

And that's the moment I lose it.

There's no mistaking the way Ethan Grant feels about his wife-to-be as he watches her walk gracefully in his direction. His hands seem impatient at his sides, as if he can't wait to hold her, and you can see in his eyes that for him, *she's* the Holy Grail. She's the grand prize, and he considers himself the luckiest man in the world. I couldn't be happier for the two of them.

Sam leans down to give Jake a hug and a kiss, and then her hands are quickly in Ethan's. Seems she couldn't wait to get her hands on him either. They both seem to relax with the contact.

The minister quickly goes through all the formalities, before the bride and groom say their vows.

"Samantha," Ethan starts, "sometimes it feels like I've loved you forever, and I know it's because I could never imagine loving anyone the way I love you. The first night I met you, I knew you were meant for me. I knew I would spend the rest of my life trying to win your heart, if that's what it took. That night, your desires and your happiness became my own." Ethan pauses, and Sam reaches up to wipe a stray tear from his cheek. "You and Jake are my entire life. Your smiles are the reason I wake up every morning, and all I want to do every day from now on is make you both as happy as I possibly can because you gave me more than I could ever ask for when you agreed to be my wife. You are my heart, Samantha Harper, and I will love you forever and always."

Now there's not a dry eye in the place.

Rose passes Sam a tissue, but Ethan quickly takes it from her. He handles Sam with loving care as he gently wipes her tear-soaked cheeks, and the love between these two is a solid, physical thing now, pulsing in the air around us.

"Ethan," Sam starts, once she finally collects herself. "I still have a hard time believing you're mine, and not because I used to have posters of you on my wall when I was a teenager." Ethan and Sam both laugh, along with the rest of us. "I have a hard time believing you're mine because I don't know how I could be worthy of a man as extraordinary as you. You are the most talented, ambitious person I know. You spoil me daily with your affection and devotion, and you dote on my son as if he was your own. You are my dream come true, and I promise to never take your love for granted. Today and always, my heart is yours."

The minister finally makes it official, and Ethan and Sam kiss each other with enough passion to set the woods around us on fire.

After the processional, the wedding party and a few close friends and family all meet back in Ms. Harper's kitchen, while the rest of the guests move to the tent to eat, drink and be merry.

"I'm so happy for you two!" I reach in and hug Sam and Ethan at the same time, since it doesn't look like they have any plans to let each other go for the rest of the night.

"I'm not sure I've encountered anything more meant to be." Liz is up next for hugs and kisses, and then Rose tries to gather herself enough to say something, but we all end up laughing at the wasted effort.

Ethan lets go of Sam long enough for her and Rose to share a tender moment reserved only for besties, and I feel my eyes fill back up with tears as I watch.

Just as I'm wiping at my cheeks for the hundredth time today, warm arms wrap around my waist from behind and pull me close. "I know they're for a good reason, but I hate seeing those tears on your beautiful face, my love."

I turn in my man's arms and he lets me go so he can pat my cheeks dry with gentle fingers. "Happy tears are acceptable," I tell him, as I wrap my arms around his neck. "What if I cry at our wedding?"

Simon moves his arms back around my waist and smiles. "I guess happy tears are okay, as long as I can see your smile."

I flash my pearly whites, so he'll be satisfied. "How could I not smile when I marry you?"

"And I look forward to keeping that smile on your face for the rest of our lives." He leans in and nuzzles my neck as he whispers, "You make me so happy, Sydney. I thank God every day I found you."

Oh, my sweet Simon.

I reach up and bury my face in his neck and the tears start to fall once again.

"Those better be happy," he says with a chuckle.

"They're the happiest tears ever cried." I raise my head, and quickly pull Simon's lips to mine. "Now, let's make our way outside, so you can sing and dance with me all night, and then I can take you home and we can practice this whole keeping-a-smile-on-my-face-for-the-rest-of-my-life thing."

"Mmmm...How about we skip the singing and dancing?"

"I'd love to," I admit, "but you and the boys are the ones that agreed to play a few songs when Sam asked."

"Yeah, I know." He smiles and I give him one more kiss...just because I can. "I guess I'll have to wait until later, but I may get handsy in the car on the way to the hotel."

Okay, maybe a few more kisses.

"Holy shit, mate!" Simon and I break to smile at Ollie, who has Lacey tucked into his side. "Do you think you guys can keep your lips off each other long enough for us to sing a song or two?"

"You're one to talk," Simon laughs, then out of nowhere, Ms. Harper is smacking Ollie on the shoulder with the magazine she was fanning herself with earlier.

"Don't you use that language in this house, Oliver Sutton," she scolds. "And never around my grandson. You hear me?"

Ollie looks down at his Nikes as he rubs his shoulder. "Yes, Ms. Harper."

"Good." Ms. Harper pats his back lovingly. "Now, you still better save me a dance tonight."

Ollie looks up with a smirk. "Anything for your sexy bum."

"Oliver! I won't tell you again."

We're all laughing hysterically at this point, including Ms. Harper. Ollie gives Lacey a kiss and a wink, then offers Ms. Harper his elbow to escort her out.

"Sing my song for me tonight?" I ask Simon as we follow everyone out to the tents.

"Of course." Simon smiles. "Shall I bring you on stage with me?"

"No." I smile back. "This is Sam and Ethan's night. I just love hearing you sing it live."

"Anything for my goddess."

"You're too good to me."

Simon leans in and gives me a soft kiss on my neck. "There's no such thing, love. You'll see."

"For the rest of our lives?"

"That's my plan."

"Well then, Simon Young, I'm *all yours*."

The End

SYDNEY'S SONG

There go my walls.
Now I stand bare before you.
Exposed, I cannot hide
All the pain that's left inside.

Please don't go.
Here with you I feel sheltered.
I see a man I recognize
When I look into your eyes.

Run your fingers through my hair.
Whisper love songs in my ear.
Then please pull me close,
And I'll stay warm inside your heart.

In your arms I feel whole,
Alive and worshipped.
The future's there in every kiss,
Contented sighs and soothing bliss.

Feel me, touch me, taste my lips.
Consumed I'll be with your eclipse.
And then forever, you can
Hold me close inside your heart.

Promise me I'll always be
Safe inside your heart.

ACKNOWLEDGEMENTS

When I began this journey, I thought I would be lucky to publish one book. Now I'm on my third, with several more on the horizon, and that would not be possible without a ton of encouragement and support from some pretty incredible people.

To the readers: Thank you for taking a chance on me and my stories. I've been to a couple of signing events recently, and having the opportunity to meet some of you has been such a blessing. You humble me daily, and I couldn't possibly appreciate you more.

To my sweet husband: Even though I know you get frustrated at times by the lack of clean laundry and warm meals, you remain in my corner no matter what. I would never be able to do any of this without you by my side, so thank you for everything, H. Love you.

To all of my dear friends and family: Thank you for keeping me grounded and reminding me what's important. I don't know what I would do without you there, kicking me in the behind and refusing to let me give up on my dreams. I hope you know how much I love and adore you.

To my soul sister, Kristi: I will continue to remind you for the rest of our days that you are the better half of this friendship. My life is simply not complete without you in it, and I'm counting down the days until I get to hug you again...*nice and tight*.

To the brilliant, Kara at Kara's Kreative: I have no idea how you manage to outdo yourself with each cover design, but you do. You are THE most talented person I know, and I am so proud to call you my friend. Love you, woman.

To my lovely cover model, Sarah: You truly are beautiful inside and out, and I am honored to have you on this cover. Just don't forget us little people when you become big and famous, okay?

To Maya: I loved every minute of every hour you spent telling me about your cruise experience, and not only because I'm always up for a good fangirl story. Basically, I just love spending time with you any chance I get. Marry me?

To the best Beta Readers and Editors on the planet: Thank you ladies for once again dealing with my numerous plot holes and slight addiction to commas. I pray that one day I'm able to pay you with more than compliments and coffee mugs but until then, know that all drinkware is given with massive amounts of gratitude and love.

To my blogging friends, Tabby at Insightful Minds Reviews and Alison at Ali's Books: Thank you for taking a chance on me in the very beginning and offering advice and guidance when I needed it the most. You ladies can consider me a forever fan.

To Tabitha and Gia at Amazeballs Book Addicts: A huge thank you for sharing your vast knowledge with me, for keeping me organized, for hosting the blog tour for "Sometimes You Know" and for just being, well...*amazeballs*.

And to all of the bloggers who helped with the tour: Thank you for everything you do. You guys work hard to promote us authors, expecting nothing in return, and I promise to never take that for granted.

To Fallon at Snow Editing: Words cannot express how much I appreciate your formatting help and the insanely quick turnaround. Thank you for making me look and feel like a rockstar.

To the beautiful Heidi McLaughlin: It's official. I will never be able to act cool around you. You're just too awesome.

And last, but certainly not least, to all of my fangirl soul sisters out there: You are my kindred spirits, the moist to my towelette and I love you more than the number of pens in Dana's purse. Always and forever.

ABOUT THE AUTHOR

Melinda Harris is a part-time author and a fulltime fangirl. She currently resides in the great state of Georgia with her family, and when she's not writing, she likes to spend rainy nights with her nose in a good book and sunny days on a playground chasing her son. And most anytime – rain or shine – she can be found engaging in her favorite pastime, which of course is eating ice cream...lots and lots of ice cream.

To learn more, please visit Melinda's website:
www.melindaharrisauthor.com

Or, you can find her on the following social media sites:
www.goodreads.com/MelHarris
www.facebook.com/melindaharrisauthor
www.twitter.com/MelHarrisAuthor